CONTROLLED CHAOS

MCCULLOUGH MOUNTAIN 6

LYDIA MICHAELS

BAILEY BROWN PUBLISHING

Lydia Michaels

Romance
CONTROLLED CHAOS {McCullough Mountain 6}
Copyright © 2019 Lydia Michaels

DEDICATION

This book is dedicated to those whose lives have been touched by Autism.

And to Taviana.
They said you couldn't speak, but they were wrong.
Swing away, sweet baby.
Swing away.

McCullough Mountain
Publication Order

Find more McCulloughs in Jasper Falls!

CHAPTER 1

"*Y*ou just march right on over there and say... *Hi. My name's Becca. I'm celebrating the end of a very long and boring marriage to a man who only fucked me on anniversaries and birthdays, always with his socks on—in the missionary position—until he decided to seduce our neighbor, the succubus slut from hell, better known as Beelzebub's Whore. I think you might possibly be the most beautiful man I've ever laid eyes on and I want to offer you one night of wild, swinging from the chandeliers, no strings attached, smurf sex.*"

Becca Stevens' lips parted as her insane best friend, Nikki, said all that without taking a single breath. Shaking her head she swallowed and asked, "Is that all?"

Nikki's lips drew at her tiny swizzle straw. "Mmmm! You should also require he make you come—*at least* three times."

"I can't say that!"

Nikki sighed and placed her empty cocktail aside, leveling Becca with an uncompromising stare. "Honey, it's been a decade. A *decade* of sad, unfulfilling, plan your grocery list while he ruts for a grand total of two minute, unceremonious sex. You *need* to come."

Becca rolled her eyes. "I can't say *any of that*, let alone the part about *coming*! And what the heck's smurf sex?"

The waitress passed and Nikki flagged her over. "We'll take another round, please." She spun back to Becca. "Smurf sex is when you fuck until you're blue in the face."

"Oh."

Becca wouldn't know anything about that. If she calculated all the minutes she'd ever spent having sex, she'd probably only reach a grand total of two hundred. No, she was exaggerating. It would probably add up to an hour. Pathetic.

It had been ten years. Ten years of awful, unfulfilling, sometimes painful, sex. The realization of how bad her sex life had been came the afternoon she returned home and thought someone was being murdered in her house.

Cries built as she'd crept up the stairs to her bedroom, carrying a cast iron bookend. It was the only weapon she could find. Having never been prone to violence, she wasn't sure what she planned to do with the heavy bookend. The capacity to bludgeon someone really wasn't in her gentle nature. But someone was definitely being attacked—or so she'd thought.

Six months later and she still couldn't get rid of the image of her husband, Kevin, drilling into Loretta like he was trying to strike oil. The disgusting sight was permanently seared into her mind's eye. In ten years, he'd never once touched her like that. Not once.

Kevin appeared in her life at the end of her senior year, right after she and her mother moved to the area. First, he'd been nothing more than her shy friend. Over time he asked her out and eventually they wound up making out in the back of her cramped Beetle convertible.

After graduation he proposed. The proposal was unexpected, but she'd said yes all the same. There was a laundry list of unsound reasons why she agreed to be his wife. All of her friends were a thousand miles away in Florida. She was lonely. She had yet to make many new friends in Pittsburgh. And, believe it or not, Kevin was nice. Now, years later and much wiser, she understood he wasn't so nice after all.

When they were kids, Kevin was still in the ugly duckling stage of life. His confidence was nil and he'd seemed surprised a girl like Becca would notice him. Not that she was anything spectacular. To her thinking, she'd always been about average.

Always the quiet type, mostly because life hadn't presented her with many exciting opportunities, Becca learned to value the small things. That made marriage very easy for Kevin—until life got complicated.

She was sick of it, sick of being the good girl, the go-to girl, the quiet, don't make any waves and take one for the team girl. That was why she'd chosen Nikki to be her wingman tonight.

The divorce papers were signed that afternoon, sealing away a decade of her life she'd never get back. Nikki was well informed about what had happened. The more Becca confessed about her marriage, the more her friend became utterly appalled. Becca now understood how truly pathetic her marriage had actually been.

As Kevin approached his thirties, he started to change. Maybe he was suffering some sort of early mid-life crisis. He'd joined a gym, bought a new car they couldn't afford, and started fussing with his hair a lot. The whole thing puzzled Becca until one day she looked at her husband and saw someone she barely recognized.

His body trimmed down and his hair magically turned a shade darker than it had naturally been. His attitude swanked of confidence he'd never displayed before. Such flagrant boasting grated on her daily. It was around that time that he'd started acting "neighborly" with Loretta.

It hurt at first. In the beginning Becca had blamed herself for his cheating, knowing she'd traded her extravagant side for jaded sensibility several years ago. But no matter how low key her life had become, nothing justified his infidelity.

Kevin was the one who needed to prove something. Not once had he come to her stating he was unsatisfied with their personal relationship.

Their lackluster marriage was an oversight, sure, but there wasn't always time to primp and prep the way a waiting mistress could—certainly not in Becca's world. But she held no pity for herself and accepted even less from others.

While some might view her life as encumbered, she was happy to carry the responsibilities piled on her. Perhaps if her husband had lent a hand when family life turned challenging she would've been more invested in their sex life. Her lack of carnal enthusiasm was greatly *his* doing.

Nikki whacked her in the arm. "He's leaving!"

Becca glanced longingly at Mr. Beautiful. It wasn't like she was going to make the offer Nikki suggested. He was beautiful, though.

His hair was the perfect shade of blond, clipped neatly in a way that showed off the slight waves. The dark blue, tailored suit he wore matched the sharpest blue eyes she'd ever seen. No ring, but there was no way a guy that pretty was single. Either that or he was gay.

"You need to go talk to him before he gets away!"

Becca let out a disheartened breath. It was a fun fantasy, but that's all it would ever be. "No. He's not my type—" Her chair tipped and she was abruptly dumped onto her feet, luckily catching herself—none too gracefully—on the table before she landed on her ass. *"Nikki!"*

Her friend glared at her. "Why am I here?"

"Because you're supposed to be my friend." She attempted to reseat herself only to have the seat snatched away.

Scowling, and making quite a scene, Nikki snapped, "No. I'm here to make sure you close out the last ten years of your life with a physical bang and I'm not leaving until that's been accomplished. Thoroughly. You, my friend, are banging that guy tonight."

"Will you knock it off?" Becca hissed, her face heating to an uncomfortable burn.

"Not a chance. *Look at him, Becs!* He's gorgeous. Can't you imagine your legs wrapped all around those strong shoulders and stroking against that fine, wavy blond hair? No! Of course you can't, because you've spent the last decade screwing Kevin and his pintsize penis doing a sad impression of a baby toe. Now, I refuse—*refuse*—to let you go on living, never knowing what a full body, true, scream your lungs out, orgasm feels like. And that's the guy who's gonna give it to you."

Her face had to be bright red. Her chest heaved as she caught her breath. Licking her dry lips she whispered, "Will you please stop? People are staring at us." She didn't need the whole world knowing she'd never had a real orgasm.

Nikki reached for her purse. "How much will it take?"

"What?"

"How much?" She slapped her checkbook on the table and uncapped a pen with her teeth.

"You're going to pay me to have sex with someone?"

"No, I'm going to pay you to make a proposition. One line, only a few words, to that man over there, and I'll cut you a check, whether he takes you up on it or not. Give me a number."

She wasn't doing this.

"You know what? Forget it. I know exactly what I'll do." Her hand moved quickly as she scribbled. She tore the note away and handed it to Becca. "My gift, from me to you. I'm buying you a divorce."

Becca's jaw dropped. Nikki was loaded and Becca definitely was not, but there was no way she was letting her friend reimburse her the cost of her divorce. "No, Nikki—"

"Take the check."

"No!"

"Take the check."

"No!"

"Becca, take the damn check or so help me God, I won't be your friend anymore."

"What are you, twelve?"

"Take. The. Check."

"I'm not taking the stupid check. Now tear it up or I will."

"I'll tear it up if you go proposition him." A devious smile curled the side of her unreasonable friend's mouth.

Becca's teeth clamped tight and she growled, "I hate you."

Nikki laughed. "Go on. Before he escapes. And I'll be watching, so you better offer him exactly what I said."

Becca shook her head, but grabbed her purse, hissing, "I am not saying smurf sex." Turning, she stomped over to the other end of the bar. Once she spotted the man in question her steps staggered. Turning back to Nikki, she cowered as her friend shot her a threatening glare.

Right. To the guy.

Heart fluttering in her chest like a ballistic hummingbird, her lungs drew in a long ragged breath. He was perfect. Everything about him was a masterpiece. Sluggishly, she baby stepped in his direction. Her hand casually ran over her shoulder length blonde hair and she tugged at the bottom of her shirt, trying to show the slight amount of cleavage she had to offer.

Licking her lips she jaggedly took the last step in front of his table and froze.

His head slowly turned as he sensed her presence—the moron standing across from him, gawking. Blue eyes traveled over her questioningly and she cleared her throat.

He smiled a bit nervously. "Hello."

Oh. She needed to shut her eyes for a second. That voice was so thick and smooth she nearly hummed. *Crap. Was she humming?* Her lips firmed, cutting off any accidental sounds of nervous pleasure.

Forcing her eyes to meet his gaze, she squared her shoulders. *Deep breath.* "Hello. My name's Becca. I'm here celebrating my divorce." Why did she sound like a cyborg? "I noticed you sitting here and I was wondering if you might be interested in a night of..." She could do this. "...no strings attached sex. With me. Becca. And no strings. All night. Sex. Anything you want. The smurf kind even." *Oh, my God, stop talking.* "Me. Becca."

Those blue eyes glanced suspiciously around as though he were the target of a practical joke. "Is this a joke? Where's the camera?"

"No cameras."

His teeth flashed, as the corner of his mouth hooked upward in a devilish grin. Oh, boy. He was really, really pretty. "So then *not* anything I want."

His grin was contagious, but confusion cut her smile short. "Excuse me?"

He shifted and draped his elbow over the back of a stool. His smirk turned cocky and she shot Nikki a nervous glance. Her friend nodded rapidly and waved her on. *Dear God, she was starting to sweat.*

"So in all this no strings attached, wild, anything I want sex, no cameras are allowed? I wouldn't be able to take your picture?"

What? "Of course not! Why would you want to?"

He shrugged. "Souvenir."

"Oh." Was he serious? She couldn't tell. "Would my clothes be on?"

He chuckled quietly and she still wasn't certain if he was teasing. "If that was a condition, I suppose I could work with that."

She chewed the side of her lip. Now it seemed like the joke was definitely on her. "Okay."

His head tipped to the side. "Really?"

"Um. Yeah."

"And you said your name was Becca?"

"Yes. Becca."

He held out his hand. "Pleasure to meet you, Becca. I'm Braydon."

Braydon—such a great name—slowly reached for her wrist and lifted her limp arm, placing her palm softly against his. His fingers gave a light squeeze as he asked, "Do you live close?"

Holy Hannah, was he actually agreeing to this insanity? Did single adults really behave this way? "Uhhh..." Passing out was a definite possibility. Her belly flipped with anxious bravadoes and a touch of fear. What if he was a serial killer? What if he was the next Jeffery Dahmer? Was she insane? She could *not* do this! Her feet shifted back a step but his fingers remained closed over hers. "Actually—"

"Because my apartment's right around the corner if you'd rather go there."

Her mouth snapped shut.

"Is that your friend over there?" he asked. "She looks like she's leaving."

Her head twisted and Nikki was indeed paying the check and grabbing her purse, a satisfied smirk on her face. She ambled over to the man's table and extended her hand. "Hi. I'm Nikki."

Braydon finally released Becca and shook Nikki's hand. "I'm Braydon."

"Nice to meet you, Braydon. I just wanted to let you know my brother's a cop and my husband's an investigator. Becca here is my best friend and I love her very much. I also collect samurai swords and know how to use them. I work in real estate, so I know lots of abandoned properties that would be great for getting rid of a body in a pinch. I think you and Becca are going to have buckets of fun tonight, but I'm gonna need your ID until she's safely returned to me."

Braydon's expression was blank. It probably matched Becca's. Nikki had the biggest heart in the world. She was a tiny thing and had no problem showing the world that little things could pack a lot of excitement. Sort of like an atomic bomb, one measly spec of nothing, cut it open and—*Boom!*—there was crap everywhere. Nikki packed a bit more punch than that.

Braydon's cobalt eyes roamed over Nikki's small frame and his mouth twitched as he chuckled. "You're serious?"

Nikki tipped her head in agreement and held out her palm. "As an enema. Hand it over, sweet cheeks, and your wish is Becca's command."

"Nikki!"

She ignored her. Leaning forward, her friend stage whispered to Braydon, "Did she mention she took years of yoga? Those legs can bend in ways you've never seen."

Braydon reached in his pocket and placed his driver's license on the table. A small squeak escaped Becca's throat as she stared in shock as Nikki pocketed his ID.

"Awesomesauce. You kids have fun now. Call me in the morning, Becs." And with that she skipped off, tapping over her pocket holding Braydon's identity.

Becca slowly pivoted and glanced at Braydon. "She was my ride."

He grinned. "I like her."

Becca laughed, sort of hollow-like. "She eats guys like you for breakfast."

He stood and slipped his arm around her waist, startling her as he drew her body close to his. "I don't scare easily." Oh, he was warm and much taller than Kevin. Pressing his mouth to her hair, he whispered, "But it's a good thing I have you to keep me safe until morning."

God, he smelled so good her body shivered. Or was that a quiver of fear? Perhaps the kind someone suffers before they enter the secret lair of a mass murderer.

"Shall we go?"

Holy crap on a stick she was really going to do this. Blinking dumbly, a stab of something like her resurrected courage gave her a swift kick in the ass. Heck yeah, she was going to do this—after she found a pillow to scream into, of course.

Closing her eyes, she breathed and issued a fast mental pep talk. She deserved this after everything she'd been through over the years. This was her reward, her due, and her duty to women everywhere.

When she looked into his eyes again, the fanfare and trumpets playing in her head dwindled to a sound resembling a deflating balloon. How was she ever going to go through with this?

∼

BRAYDON TURNED the key and his apartment door clicked open. Placing his hand on Becca's back, he escorted her inside. "Can I get you something to drink? Wine? Beer? Whiskey?"

She stood awkwardly, shifting as if she wasn't sure what to do—accept or bolt. Her slight fidgeting told him she was nervous enough for the both of them. It wasn't like beautiful women frequently propositioned him.

Pale blonde hair caught the light. A narrow headband held the flaxen strands away from her face. Give her a pair of patent leather Mary Janes and she'd be a grown up Alice in Wonderland. Nothing about her fit a woman familiar with propositioning strange men in a bar. Yet here she was.

"I'll just have some water if you don't mind."

Braydon went to the fridge and removed a bottle. Taking down a glass from the stainless wall rack, he tried to ease some of the awkwardness. "So…how long were you married?"

"Too long." A nervous laugh hiccupped past her lips and she blushed. "Um, a little over ten years."

Passing her the water, she tipped it back, taking steady sips until the glass was empty. "Your place is nice. Clean."

"Thanks."

The condo was nice, but not home. It wasn't what he wanted long-term. Being an architect, he hoped to one day build his own house. There was plenty of property back home in Center County to build on, but he worked out of Pittsburgh, which complicated things. Settling down was, luckily, a long way off. Still, he'd been saving for that moment since he started working.

When he was younger, he imagined himself married right out of college. He'd even found a woman he thought was the perfect girl. Only problem…she up and married his brother. That was something that left a man a bit jaded and stuck in neutral.

His attention returned to his guest. "Can I take your coat?"

Becca shifted and slowly drew her arms out of the sleeves. After folding the thin wool jacket twice, she passed it to him. Carrying the coat to the wall, he hung it next to his. Not quite sure what was going to happen here, he played it casual, but certainly hoped she'd be removing more than her coat.

"So…"

"So…" she echoed.

He sat on the couch and waved a hand for her to follow. Perching on the edge of the farthest cushion, she sat like she had a dowel up her ass. "You can relax. I'm not going to attack you."

"Oh, I know that."

"Do you?"

"Well, no, not really. But you seem polite."

Chuckling, he said, "My mum would be glad to hear that." He eased back, trying to make her a bit more comfortable. "Do you usually proposition strangers at bars?"

She snorted. "No." It was a completely unladylike sound, but he found it charming.

"Yet you propositioned me. Why?"

Drawing in a deep breath, she explained, "It's a long story. You met Nikki. She made me do it."

"Why?"

Her expression tightened as if she were hosting some sort of mental debate. "Do you ever think *this is my life* and then—*pow!*—*you* realize everything you based your existence on was a crappy lie?"

"Yes."

Her surprise was evident as his response caused her gaze to jerk to his. "Really?"

"Yup, but I want to hear your story first. Did your husband cheat on you?"

"You could say that. I caught him having sex with our neighbor in our bed. Apparently she wasn't the first."

Luckily, no one had ever truly cheated on him. Well, not really. "How long were you together?"

"Since high school."

That was a long time. "Have you ever been with anyone else?"

"No. It's always been him. And according to Nikki, our love life was a joke."

"Why? I mean, aside from the other women."

Her lips pursed. "If you were married—*Oh, God*—you aren't, right?"

He laughed. "No. Never been married."

"Oh, well, if you were, how often would you…you know…?"

"Fuck my wife?"

Her eyes widened.

He chuckled. "Sorry. I figured, under the circumstances, we could talk plainly. How often would my spouse and I make love?"

"On average."

He considered this for a minute. "Probably four to five times a week. If we had children I'm sure that would change slightly, but I'd at least want to…make love to her a couple times a week."

"A *week*?"

"Yeah. How often did you and your husband make love?"

Her pale cheeks turned deep pink as she looked away. "Not that often."

"A couple times a month?"

"Try a year."

His brows shot up, pulling his face tight. "Was your husband gay?"

"What? No!"

He laughed, astounded. "I'm sorry, it's just…have you seen you? You're a ten."

"A ten?"

He didn't want to come off like a creep, but the minute she'd introduced herself he'd, of course, perused her assets. Her high, full breasts looked to be a large B or small C. Her hips swelled at all the right places and her legs went on for days. Plus, she had the whole innocent Alice thing going for her. Give her an aproned dress and a sign that said "Eat Me" and he was going to Wonderland.

"Trust me, you're very attractive."

Her sensuous little mouth twitched into a nervous smile. "Thank you. You're very handsome."

Braydon grinned. "So…do you want to tell me what smurf sex is?"

"Ohmygod…" Her face fell into her palms. "I'm going to kill Nikki."

"Why?"

"Because this is all her fault. I didn't even know what smurf sex was until an hour ago."

Though he didn't know much about her, she was highly entertaining. Such capriciousness usually faded in women her age. He laughed. "I still don't know."

"It's when you…" She waved her hand in repetitious circles.

"Fuck?"

She made a sound of distaste and scrunched her nose.

"Make love?"

"Yes. Until you're blue in the face."

His head tipped back and laughter bellowed from his chest. "So you just spent the last decade having religious sex and now you're going for smurf?"

Her brow crinkled. "We didn't have religious sex."

"Sure you did. Got *nun* in the morning and *nun* at night."

Her mouth opened and she looked offended, but the truth was the truth. "Well, it wasn't always like that. In the end it turned into hallway sex."

"What's hallway sex?"

"We'd only pass each other in the hall and I'd say *screw you*." Her eyes twinkled, her disposition no longer showing offense.

Now he was really laughing. "Well, I hope you at least had good courtroom sex and screwed the shit out of him during the divorce."

Her mouth tightened in a little smirk and the slightest chirp of laughter slipped out. Her fingers covered her lips as the chirps turned to giggles and then a snort snuck out.

"You have a great laugh."

She sobered and lowered her gaze to the floor. "I shouldn't be laughing about my marriage ending."

"It's okay to laugh about it, Becca."

Her returning smile was shy at first, then beautiful, like a flower coming into bloom. "It was terrible," she softly confessed. "Sometimes I wasn't even sure if he was awake or if he'd fallen asleep on me. Do you have any idea what it's like to be almost thirty and not know what certain things feel like?"

His amusement faded. "What do you mean?"

Apparently startled by her own words, her expression paled. "Nothing. Never mind."

"No. Tell me."

Her head lowered and she flicked a speck of lint off her jeans. "It was always the same, nothing fancy, and never with the lights on."

Looking at her, seeing her delicate profile and the feminine way she held herself, it was actually quite tragic this beautiful creature had been so neglected. "Did he at least make sure you...?" He censored his language, gathering she wasn't used to crass words.

The corners of her mouth pulled tight in a sad smile, and she slowly shook her head.

Jesus. Who the hell was her husband and what was wrong with him? He considered their situation. Although *she* was the one to put the offer on the table, once he discovered how timid she was, he assumed they wouldn't go through with it. But now...

It was an absolute tragedy that this woman didn't know what good sex was. "Did you really intend to sleep with me?"

Her head snapped up and she gawked at him. Somehow, after all this, he'd managed to embarrass her. Her voice quavered. "Oh, you don't have to. I can go if—"

"I don't want you to go." Her timidity was incredibly sexy. He was honestly growing more intrigued with every word she said.

Her breasts pressed against her shirt as her breathing picked up. "R—really?"

He tipped his head. Come on. She couldn't be that naïve. She had to know she was appealing as hell. She acted like he was doing her a favor, when in reality, he couldn't think of a more attractive woman. "How would you like to do this?"

She glanced around his apartment. "Should we go to your room?"

"Depends. What are you in the mood for?"

"I beg your pardon?"

"What are you hoping to gain here, Becca? Is there something specific you always wanted to try? Maybe a fantasy you had?" Figuring this was a one-time opportunity, he went for broke.

Her little pink tongue darted out and traced over her full lower lip. "Um… I used to fantasize that Kevin—I mean—I used to think it would be fun if a guy sort of came up and was so…full of passion he'd take me like his life depended on it."

He must have done something really good to earn this sort of karma. "Do you want me to take you like my life depends on it?" He hoped she said yes, as that would be no fucking problem at all.

Her face flushed and she lifted a shoulder. "It's sort of all fake if we plan it. I don't think it would be the same."

"Why don't we kiss and see where things go?"

The narrow column of her throat moved as she swallowed. In a hushed voice, she said, "Okay."

Braydon moved to the center of the couch. The energy of the room intensified and seemed to snap between them, turning electric and making the little hairs on his arm rise. Inflamed curiosity folded into raw desire as he breathed in her soft scent. Not wanting to startle her, he hoped she'd meet him halfway. "Come here."

Licking her lips again, she scooted close and he turned into her. Her eyes focused anywhere but on him. His fingers lifted her golden hair over her shoulder as he touched his lips to her neck, breathing in her delicate fragrance. At first, she flinched, but as his lips brushed her rapidly fluttering pulse, her posture slowly eased. "Mmm. You smell nice."

His tongue slowly flicked her ear and nibbled the tiny lobe between his lips. Sliding his fingers to her other ear, he tugged on the tiny pearl stud, massaging slowly until she shivered.

"Is this okay?"

"Oh yes." Her voice was breathless.

His palm caressed her arm, reached for her knee and gently squeezed. "Why don't you lie back and get comfortable?"

It was almost impossible to stifle his chuckle as she gingerly scooted lower on the sofa. Not much, but it was enough. Dragging his mouth over the fine contour of her jaw, he traced over the corner of her mouth. As her lips parted his lust was provoked beyond his patience. "I *really* want to kiss you, Becca."

Her chest lifted with each breath. "You do?" Long lashes hid her eyes.

His lips pressed to the crest of her cheek, dragging out the anticipation. "Mm-hm. I want to do other stuff to you too, but right now, all I can think about is kissing you like you've probably never been kissed before."

Soft breath puffed over his mouth and he could scent the fruity traces of whatever she'd been drinking at the bar. His fingers coasted up her arm, around her neck, and through her flaxen hair. His palm cupped the back of her head as his mouth slowly slanted over hers.

A moan escaped as his tongue coaxed its way past her lips. Her mouth was soft and sweet. Kissing her slowly, he drew out her passionate side. His other hand cupped her jaw, his thumb massaging gently over the fine arch of her cheek. As her shoulders melted into the couch, she sighed, rocking his body with a responsive throb.

The first timid caress of her tongue went right to his cock. He twisted his bulk and deepened the kiss. Her lips were perfect little slices of heaven, plump and succulent. It seemed she possessed some unfamiliar quality, a perfect blend of innocent curiosity that made her angelic. Nibbling her lower lip with his teeth, he chuckled against her mouth, his thoughts slipping into whispered words. "You're an angel."

Her delicate hands hesitantly relaxed on his shoulders. Rising to his knees, he deepened the kiss, urging her lower on the sofa. Her fingers flexed into his shoulders and her breasts dragged softly against his chest.

Easing back, he glanced at her through hooded eyes. Her hair was a spiral of gilded waves fanning out beneath her, her swollen lips a shade darker from kissing. The most peculiar colored eyes gazed up at him. They were Elizabeth Taylor eyes, such a fascinating shade of blue they could be mistaken for violet.

His mouth lowered and captured her lips. Long legs shifted as he settled over her. Every kiss brought his body to life. Learning each other's touch with slow caresses, he dragged his hips seductively over hers and those violet eyes turned luminous.

Who was this woman? "You have incredible eyes."

"Thank you."

Her fingers flexed against his arms as soft keening noises traveled from her lips to his. Easing back, he slowly undid the buttons of her shirt, pausing for only a brief moment to allow any objections. Her flushed face tipped as she watched each button come undone. Spreading the shirt wide, his eyes feasted on two perfect breasts framed in soft white lace.

Trailing his fingers over the scalloped edging, she arched in response, the violet of her eyes deepening with arousal. Soft fawn colored lashes lowered as he peeled the lace cups away and lowered, catching one tiny pink nipple in his mouth.

"Oh, God," she gasped, sounding almost panicky.

Pinching the tight bud gently between his lips, he traced his tongue over the hard tip and released her. "This okay?"

"Mm-hmm." She didn't sound too sure.

"Becca, look at me." He waited until her lashes lifted. "Are you okay with this?"

She nodded tightly.

"Tell me what you want. If it's too much we'll slow down."

"I liked what you were doing."

Cupping her breast in his palm, his thumb dragged slowly over the turgid tip. Maybe she was nervous and simply not used to experiencing such things. "You have very beautiful breasts."

Her blush traveled from her cheeks, darkening her nipples a shade. "Thank you."

"Can I see the rest of you?"

She licked her lips in what he was coming to recognize as something she did whenever she debated internally. "Do you have…protection?"

He nodded slowly, his body tightening another degree at what her question implied.

"Then yes."

Easing back, his fingers went to the snap of her jeans. He dragged the zipper down slowly, her breath quickening with each whispered tick. Matching white lace panties peeked out of the V of her pants.

Sliding off the couch, he turned her so her legs were draped over the edge. Plain black pumps covered her petite feet. Removing her left shoe, he lifted her foot and placed a kiss on the delicate arch. Her toes twitched and he wondered if she was ticklish. The image of tickling laughter from her turned him on even more.

Removing the other shoe he kissed her other arch. Slowly sliding her jeans down her long legs, her posture twisted, leaving her slightly flushed and disheveled as he peeled the sleeves of her shirt from her arms.

Displayed in only a bra and panties, he took his time regarding her. She was absolutely perfect. He let out a slow breath, feeling a bit outmatched. He wanted to make it really good for her, but her beauty left him staggered.

Placing a kiss on her knee, his lips travelled leisurely up her thigh. His fingers traced the lace edging of her panties and down they came beneath a gentle tug. Brushing his knuckles over the fine patch of golden curls, he met her gaze.

Watchful eyes studied him as he slowly nudged her thighs apart. Pink, dewy folds opened and he was mesmerized. Taking his time, he kissed down the crease of her thigh, and licked over the tiny pearl nestled at the peak of her sex.

Her body jolted and he glanced up at her, but gave her no chance of escape as he pressed his tongue deep. Her mouth moved over a tangle of whispered words he couldn't make out. With soft, penetrating strokes of his tongue, he tasted her. Her head fell back and she moaned as sweet heat met his tongue.

His palms glided up her inner thighs, his thumbs parting her folds as he drove her closer to climax. Her cries increased in volume and rhythm. Sinking the first finger deep, her knees drew up and she keened. Twisting his wrist, he withdrew and entered her again. Her arms lifted, elevating her breasts as she gripped the cushion of the couch behind her wild hair.

His lips teased her clit as his fingers fed into her slit. Slicked and primed, he inserted another finger and pressed deep, brushing soft tissue hidden inside.

Her eyes flashed open. His lips held her tiny jewel tight as he watched her. Burying his fingers deep, he tickled a bit more and she shattered. Lips parted, body quivering near violently with each intense tremble, she cried out and he drank her pleasure.

Quiet, gasped breaths filled the room as he leaned back. Licking his lips, he gazed at her, lowering his weight to his heels. "I want to fuck you, angel."

Her eyes flared as his crude language penetrated. He was so damn turned on he'd forgotten she shied away from curse words. There was that little tongue again. She deliberated for only a few seconds and then whispered, "Yes."

Standing, he lifted her like a feather, her languid weight drifting easily into his arms. She modestly attempted to cover her figure, but he caught her hand and shook his head slowly. "Don't hide. You're beautiful."

Deep pink crept from her breasts to her cheekbones as her hand dropped delicately to her hip. Lowering her feet to the floor of his bedroom, he went to the dresser and removed a condom, placing it on the nightstand. Turning to face her, he slowly peeled off his shirt, and reminded himself to take it slow.

"Oh, boy..." she rasped and he almost laughed. The lights were definitely staying on.

With deliberate slowness he undid the clasp of his belt. Toeing off his shoes and socks he slid the pants to the floor.

"Ohmygod." Her mouth opened, as she seemed to take a step back, but never actually moved. That, indeed was the most flattering reaction he could ever recall earning.

Her attentive appraisal sang to him, bringing a quick rhythm to his heart and heating his blood. Those violet eyes crawled over every bit of exposed flesh like a caress.

"Tell me what you want," he whispered, voice husky under the weight of his arousal.

"I...I'm not sure." She glanced at his large bed, hesitated, and slowly took a step closer.

Her fingers stroked the duvet and she glanced over her shoulder at him. She was stunning. The long line of her back tapered to her succulent ass. Her hips flared with feminine flawlessness. Artists couldn't paint a more perfect picture.

Her body tensed when he stepped behind her, slowly dragging his fingers down her bare arm and grazing his rigid front against her delicate back. "Whatever you want, angel, it's yours. Just tell me what you like."

Slowly pivoting, she wreathed her arms around his neck and gradually leaned in to kiss him. His fingers squeezed her hips lightly, nudging her toward the bed.

"Lie back," he said, as his mouth brushed over hers.

She lowered and scooted onto the bed as he gingerly crawled over her. His cock rested at her hip as his hands learned her curves. Her body stretched and writhed beneath him as he plucked and licked at her breasts. He made quick work of removing the bra still twisted around her ribs and tossed it to the floor.

"Braydon, please..."

Reaching for the condom, he slowly slid it over his length. "May I?"

"Yes," she breathed, opening her thighs for him. His motions had turned a bit more desperate since they'd reached the bed, but he intended to give her everything she needed, his own need fueled by hers.

Lining up his cock with her sex he slowly slid in. Heat wrapped around his length like a hot glove. His spine tingled as his eyes rolled back in ecstasy.

"Oh God," she breathed.

He withdrew a few inches and slowly thrust deeper. Crying out, her fingers tightened over his back, nails pressing deliciously into his skin.

His hand coasted over her soft thighs, curling around her delicate knees as he lifted and plunged deep. His pelvis kissed hers and he held the position for a long, delicious moment. Not wanting to rush, he focused on pleasing her. As her nails scraped over his shoulders he filled her again and again. "Tell me what you want," he whispered, pressing his lips to the soft curve of her throat.

"Faster."

He increased his speed.

"Harder."

Each thrust became firmer, stabbing deep into her core, rapidly filling her with each penetrating advance. Her voice grew high in pitch as she cried out with each plunge. Her body tightened and pulsed around him as he gave her everything she begged for.

Driving deep, he rotated his hips and her composure dissolved, her body rocking with uncontainable trembles. Her sobs filled the air, driving his control to the brink. He fought back his release, but it was impossible with her body clamping down so lusciously. His seed left him in a rush and he nearly collapsed with the force of it.

Pressing his brow into her shoulder, he breathed hard. Her arms fell to her sides as she caught her breath. After a while she sighed and said, "I've never experienced anything like that before in my entire life."

"Are you pleased?"

She laughed a bit nervously, but it was a charming sound. "Pleased isn't the right word. I'm shocked."

Pressing his smile to her neck, he chuckled. "I'll be right back. I'm going to clean up."

He withdrew and his cock twitched, already missing her heat. Her body was a sanctuary. Standing, he went to the bathroom and shut the door. Unsure how he'd tempted the gods of karma, he was certain he'd done something great.

He tossed the condom and washed up, wanting to get back to her as soon as possible. Exiting the bathroom, he asked, "Do you need any—" He frowned. "Becca?"

The door in the living room clicked. Hustling out of the bedroom, finding no evidence of her presence, he frowned.

She was gone.

CHAPTER 2

*N*ikki's door fell open with a startling crash. Becca grabbed the frame, still needing to brace her weight so her wobbly knees didn't collapse.

"Becca? What are you doing here? I thought you were hanging out with GQ boy."

Becca pushed her aside and shut the door, throwing her disheveled body against the heavy wood. After catching her breath, she paced and collapsed into the chair in the hall. "I was, but I left."

Nikki shuffled closer, two hairy wookie slippers coming into view. "Did he do something wrong? I'll get my nine iron."

"No. He was incredible. I mean…*really* incredible."

Nikki clapped. "Well, that's fantastic! But why are you here?"

"I don't know. We'd just…you know, and then I panicked. I left before I even had my pants buttoned." Her face heated as she hissed, "I can't find my underwear."

Nikki laughed. "Well, pull yourself together and go back there."

"I can't go back there now! He's probably furious."

"So you had the best sex of your life with a gorgeous man and you're never going to see him again? He must've literally fucked your brains out."

Leveling her best friend with a hard stare, she confessed, "I got scared. If this is what sex is supposed to be like…I feel like I've been drinking juice all my life while the rest of the world sipped champagne." She growled. "I want to kill Kevin! For the past year I've been beating myself up, thinking I was inadequate. He's the one that sucks!"

Nikki chuckled and squatted next to her. "Yeah, Becs, Kevin sucks, but why is tonight a bad thing? Look at what you learned. Sex is fun. You should celebrate your new single status. Get out there. Live a little."

"You know I can't do that."

"Why?"

Her heart was still racing at a rate that made her insides rattle. "I didn't expect it to be so...*intense*."

"Mmm...that good, huh? Well, maybe Mr. GQ isn't *the guy* for you, but there're lots of guys. Go hog wild. Don't look at this time of your life as a moment for mourning your tragic marriage. Look at it as an experience in newfound freedom, filled with *shebang-igans, tom-fuckery*, and absolute *dick-bauchery*. You go get yourself some ass!"

She frowned at her friend. Nikki didn't get it. Becca couldn't do casual sex. She just couldn't. There was a fine line between having fun and being irresponsible, and she needed to keep her head.

Terrible guilt swamped her for sneaking out without thanking Braydon, but she'd been so embarrassed at her inexperience she wanted to cry. If she'd lost it in his apartment, she would've been completely humiliated.

Her life had many facets she wasn't comfortable letting others intrude on. Her priorities had always been meticulously kept at the top of her list of concerns in life, the lesser desires buried at the bottom, including fun, dating, personal pampering, and, of course, sex. Dating wasn't something she ever planned on doing again. It simply didn't fit in her world.

Nikki sighed. "Do you want to stay here?"

"No. I should go home. I need to get stuff together for work on Monday. The clients for the Apricot deal are showing up and we're finally meeting with the architectural firm."

"Okay. I'll see you at the office. Try not to beat yourself up too much. Single Becca lives without regrets."

Ha. That was a lie.

That night she lay in bed replaying the evening in her mind. Her body still held his scent. Her breasts were tender from his handling and other parts of her were swollen from the deliciously rough way he took her.

She never knew it could be like that. A little knowledge could be a terrifying, but curious thing. Why had Kevin never touched her that way?

Braydon said she was a ten. Playing back his words, she smiled. A ten. Refusing to go down a path of more self-doubt, she focused on all the wonderful things Braydon said and the way he made her feel, committing his words to memory for a future lonely day—or several.

A marriage based on lies was not a dependable source of information. The painful knowledge of how false her entire foundation had been, never eased. Perhaps someday she'd get over the lost years of her twenties, but today wasn't that day.

~

BRAYDON ENTERED the bar and scanned the patrons. She wasn't there.

"Back again?"

He turned as the waitress addressed him. "Yeah. I was hoping to find someone here."

"Got a description?" She perched her tray on her apron swaddled hip.

"Blonde, deep blue-violet eyes, ivory skin."

"Sounds lovely. Sorry, I haven't seen her."

"Figures."

"Can I get you a drink?"

He ordered a beer and took a seat at the bar. Their chance encounter had awakened a curiosity in him he hadn't expected. He held no false illusions about their one night stand, but it smarted knowing she'd fled maybe five seconds after climax. Was she not satisfied?

He should have gotten her last name. Her friend had his damn ID and he didn't have more than a vague description.

He had nothing of hers aside from the panties she'd left stuffed in the cushion of his couch. Was he being a creep, trying to find her when all she'd promised was one night? Maybe, but something drew him back to her, provoked him to find her again. He wished he'd had her number or something.

The longer he waited in the bar the more disgusted he became with himself. It was as though the entire experience were an erotic dream. He refused to accept that she just bailed without even a goodnight. Despite his earlier self-doubts, he believed she hadn't faked that sort of unveiled pleasure.

They had a connection and it scared her. Probably because her marriage just ended.

Tossing some money on the bar, he grabbed his coat and decided to chalk the incident up to sheer luck, which had obviously run out with her. But no matter how he tried, he couldn't get her out of his head.

The drive back to his quiet apartment was made in comparable silence. Though he'd moved from the country to the city, home was a much noisier place. There was always something going on at home. The city was busy, but it wasn't the same sort of noise he'd grown up around.

Everything in the city tended to blend into white noise. The cloak of professionalism he wore also veiled a bit of the day-to-day drama. Truth be told, he missed the chaos, missed his family, missed being able to let loose and kick back. He really needed a trip home before this hankering for company got the better of him.

As he entered his apartment, tossing his keys onto the glass table by the door, he sighed. His imported furniture and state of the art sound system brought little comfort. No matter what he filled his place with, he couldn't seem to convert the apartment into a home. It was a dwelling, a shelter, but not the warm and welcoming abode he as an architect should be capable of creating. Something was definitely missing.

Knowing he'd likely never run into little Ms. Perfect again, he refused to admit it wasn't something but some*one.* He'd traveled that long road for too long and couldn't get hung up on searching for his other half, especially when the woman he was fixated on clearly wasn't meant to be in his life long term. If there were someone out there for him, surely he'd know and not have to go searching a city the size of Pittsburgh trying to chase her down.

Taking a deep breath, he decided to let go of the fantasy and let kismet take the wheel. If he had another half, she would come to him naturally. But letting go was easier said than done. He never expected to be alone at this stage of his life. Nor did he expect to be the last of all his siblings to find his happily ever after.

When he went to bed that night her scent still clung to his pillows. Every time he shut his eyes, visions of her flaxen hair filled his mind. Why was he so fixated on her? It was more than loneliness. He was fine with his single status before meeting her. There was something specific about Becca, something he couldn't put his finger on, but he really wished he'd had more time to get to know her.

One thing was certain, if he ever saw her again he'd ring her neck for toying with him. Women *never* had this effect on him. Of course, the first to really grab his interest took off without even providing her full name. Definitely not meant to be.

~

MONDAY MORNING BECCA rushed into her office, depositing her files and coffee on her desk and quickly revisited her presentation for the meeting that morning.

"How was the rest of your weekend?"

Becca's gaze bounced from the computer screen as Nikki lounged in the doorway. Her sharp pantsuit and slicked back hair hid a goodly amount of her wild side. "It was fine. Quiet."

"Will you have to see Kevin tonight?"

Becca sighed. There were the unannounced moments that Kevin popped in to pick up more crap he "forgot", but that wasn't the case this time. These transitional encounters would be the norm until he demanded a change to their agreement. She needed to get past the reoccurring trepidation. "Yes, but I'm getting used to it. He'll only be there for a minute or two."

Nikki nodded her understanding. "You ready for your meeting?"

"As ready as I'll ever be."

"Good. Mr. Dillard's assistant just arrived. The rest of them should be here shortly."

"Thanks for the heads up."

Nikki left and Becca saved her work to a thumb drive. The anxiety was already building at the thought of seeing Kevin that night, so she submerged herself in work and focused on preparing her presentation.

At two minutes to nine, she gathered her materials and headed to the conference room. Mr. Dillard and his assistant, Mike, were already seated. She set her items on the table and smiled.

Extending her hand, she said, "It's a pleasure to have you back, Mr. Dillard. I think you'll be happy with the company presenting today. Their architects are all fresh minds with diverse backgrounds in commercial branding."

Mr. Dillard shook her hand. "I'm sure you won't disappoint, Becca."

They settled into their seats and she slipped the thumb drive into her laptop. Making sure everything was lined up with the overhead, she set her presentation to the first slide. Eyeing the clock, she stifled her nerves, hoping that the architect reps would be there soon. "Can I get you more coffee before we begin?"

"No, thank you. We have everything we need. Should we wait?"

Her toes twitched in her shoes under the table. *Come on.* Finally the door opened. A slender woman with a cocoa complexion stepped in and Becca breathed a sigh of relief.

The woman, dressed in a slate gray power suit, extended her hand. "Sorry we're late. I'm Miranda Robinson. Mr. McCullough will be with us in a moment."

Hands were shaken and Becca again offered refreshments. When the door opened again, every nerve in her body tensed as *Braydon* stepped into the conference room. *Oh my God!*

Forcing her mouth shut, she formed a poor excuse for a smile. Braydon stilled only for the briefest second, and extended his hand to her. "Braydon McCullough."

"Becca… Stevens," she greeted tightly, ignoring the jangling of nerves racing up her arm as he gently shook her hand. Her body shivered with too many reminders of how he had touched her so intimately.

His casual grin appeared sincere, but there was no missing the shrewd set of his eyes. He was angry with her.

Turning away from his scrutiny, she quickly said, "Mr. McCullough, this is Mr. Dillard, CEO of Apricot Inc. and his assistant, Mike."

The men shook hands and Becca returned to her chair. Everyone took their seats and stared at her expectantly.

"Shall we get started, Becca?" Mr. Dillard prompted.

"Oh. Right." Kick-starting her delayed brain, she turned to the overhead screen. "Apricot Inc. has been a trusted brand among the…" As she dove into her presentation, her mind working on autopilot, she tried to fight back the sense that Braydon's eyes were not on the screen, but on her. Extremely self-conscious of every word's pronunciation and every twitch of her body, she hoped to God her scripted spiel was making sense. This was a big deal for their company.

Somehow, she reached the end of her pitch without screwing up too badly—she hoped. "So you see, it is with complete faith that our company recommends Bradford Architectural Corp. to set the new trend in the market and create a renaissance, a rebirth, of the great company that is, and will continue to be, Apricot Inc."

Miranda appeared pleased. Mr. Dillard also looked happy. She didn't dare glance at Braydon.

"I'm intrigued," Mr. Dillard said. "Why don't you show us what you prepared?"

She'd maneuvered her posture so Braydon was at her back. When his chair squeaked she tensed. His tall form came into view as he carried a small thumb drive to the front of the conference room. "May I?"

Her breath caught as he reached over and closed out her program. Removing her drive, he slipped his USB into the port and punched in a few keys. His familiar scent swirled around her like an opiate. Shutting her eyes, growing dizzy with memories of his body filling hers, his hands touching and caressing her flesh, his mouth—

"Bradford would like to take Apricot to a new dimension..." Braydon's deep voice took command of the room.

Becca's eyes flashed open as he dominated the meeting with his presence. Easily the most beautiful man she'd ever seen, only now he was dressed in another sharp suit that did wonderful things to his broad chest, strong shoulders, and piercing blue eyes. This one wasn't the same deep blue he'd warn the other night, but she liked him in gray as well.

As he presented, various things became apparent. When necessary, Braydon possessed quite the commanding attitude. This made her recollection of their tender yet deliciously forceful encounter seem all the more intimate.

Commercial architecture was a lucrative profession. He presented with a polished ease she didn't think she'd quite mastered in her career. They were in two different leagues. She was simple functionality and he was sophisticated luxury. The memory of their one night together replayed with resounding mortification.

It was only a ten minute presentation, but it lasted entirely too long for Becca's poor, palpitating heart. By the time Braydon concluded his show of designs for Apricot's headquarters and chain of future franchises, she felt drunk. Drunk with very wet panties and very hot cheeks.

Braydon returned to his seat and her lashes lowered as her head swirled. Even from two feet away, her body reacted as if he was on top of her.

Miranda took over. "So, gentlemen, as you can see, we've taken your mom and pop appeal and turned it into something superior, without losing that mom and pop impression. Every franchise will boast the same conveniences and treasured amenities as the original Apricot Inc. Neighborhoods everywhere will gain a sense of familiar homecoming whenever they cross Apricot's threshold, no matter what state they're in."

Mr. Dillard nodded, a satisfied curve to his mouth. "I like it. Mike, what do you think?"

"I have a few notes on schematics, but other than that I think it's great."

"Wonderful," Miranda said. "Braydon will forward the paperwork to Mrs. Stevens, and we can carry on from there once you initial any changes in the deal. I don't see any reason why this project can't begin immediately."

Everyone stood and pulled out their phones, marking various dates for future meetings. Keeping her eyes on Mr. Dillard and Miranda only, Becca entered a few dates and stepped back as everyone gathered their belongings and exited the room.

Once she politely said her goodbyes and thank yous, she gave them her back and compiled her notes into a folder. When the room silenced and the door finally clicked shut, she let out a depleted sigh and pressed her palms into the table, her shoulders collapsing and head hanging low. How she ever survived that was a miracle.

"This was unexpected."

Her spine stiffened and twisted so fast she nearly lost her balance. Braydon leaned against the inside of the door, blue eyes trained on her, strong arms crossed over his chest. A master of insipid tameness, she skeptically kept her distance. Such consistent friendliness didn't exist, certainly not after the way she'd abandoned him with no explanation after what they'd done together.

Breathing was impossible. Her skin turned sticky under her blouse. His impenetrable calmness had to be an act. What guy wouldn't be pissed? Forcing herself to stand straight, she lifted her chin. "I'm sorry about the other night, but in light of the circumstances it was probably best I left."

"You think so?" he asked, voice expressionless, leaving her clueless as to whether or not he agreed.

"I do." She swallowed breathlessly.

Oh God. His shoulders shifted as he pressed away from the door and slowly approached her, his motions purposeful yet languid like a large jungle cat. His arms dropped to his side and he didn't stop until he was directly in front of her, forcing her head to tilt back so she could keep her eyes on his.

"I disagree," he whispered, voice low and gravelly. His larger form crowded her until she dropped into a conference chair, but that didn't make him back off. His strong hands pressed into the arms of the chair, long fingers coiling around the metal as he leaned close.

Their mouths were only centimeters apart. His breath was a warm caress over her lips as he spoke.

"I think this is the universe's way of telling us our association's far from over. We're going to be seeing a lot of each other over the next few months, angel. This is a big deal for both of us and neither of us can afford the distraction of sexual tension, which I know you feel too. I propose we call it what it is and work as professionals when our jobs require it, but maintain a…friendly…relationship after hours. You were running the other day, but it looks like I caught you, Becca. I think we should finish fucking out all this chemistry so we can get the job done right."

She swallowed and rasped, "I don't know what you're talking about."

He chuckled. "Yes, you do. I'll put one hundred bucks on the table that your panties are soaked right now. By the way, you left your other ones in my couch."

Her chest lifted as she drew in rapid breaths. How could he know that? "I'm afraid you're wrong, but I won't take your money—"

Her lie was cut off as his mouth crashed down on hers. Her head pressed against the back of the leather chair as he bullied his way past her lips and stole her kiss.

The punishing force of his tongue gentled, and she melted as he licked at her lips, pulling them between his and nibbling softly. Every kiss she'd ever experienced paled in comparison to this man's kisses. His mouth was meant for kissing.

Braydon pulled away slowly and studied her through hooded eyes. "Now, what were you saying?"

She needed to give the deal to someone else. She'd just tell Nikki what happened and her friend would surely understand.

Turning away, she quietly confessed. "I know we're attracted to each other, but doing business together is only another reason we can't carry on like this."

"Why? No one has to know."

"But they will know. Nikki's my boss, Braydon. And I have other responsibilities I need to consider. Having a torrid affair is so far from the top of my priority list I can't even begin to make you understand. I think it'd be best if we just forget the past and started fresh, two associates, nothing more."

She mentally patted herself on the back. That little speech came out better than she expected. There was no arguing with such logical, well-expressed reasons.

His eyes narrowed. "No."

Or maybe there was. She scoffed. "No? Um, you can't make me sleep with you again. That's against the law."

"You'll come to me willingly. I guarantee it. It's only a matter of time before the sexual tension gets to you. Don't pretend to be cold with me, angel. I know how hot your blood runs."

The tension was already getting to her, but that didn't mean she should give in. There were other things to consider. Things Braydon knew nothing about and never would. Her personal life was private and she needed to have her wits in order to function without drowning in the difficult moments.

There was no doubt he could torture her with meaningful looks, innuendos, and other sex strategies she was clueless about. There was no time for that. She'd offered him one night and that's what he got, even if it was cut short by her Houdini act. Her life couldn't afford the distraction, nor allot the time and energy needed for what he proposed.

"I see that mind of yours working, angel. Give in. It'll feel so good."

His arrogance was intended to soften, but it only hardened her resolve. "I can't. I'm sorry. My life isn't set up for what you're suggesting. I don't have the time or the energy to give you what you want."

"I want to please you. Make the time."

Yeah right. Her experience with men taught her they had ulterior motives in everything. "I'm sorry, Braydon. The answer's no. Please don't make this harder than it already is."

"Why *no*?"

"Because—"

The door opened and Braydon quickly stood. Becca's gaze jerked to the entrance. Nikki stood, clearly aware she'd walked in on something unexpected. "I'm sorry, I thought you were finished." Her brow shot up. "GQ?"

"Nikki, could you give us a minute, please?" Becca spoke quickly and Nikki smirked mischievously.

"Sure. Take all the time you need. I'll move our meeting to the other conference room. Don't mess up the table, kids." She turned with a wicked grin and sashayed out of the room.

"Your boss is the samurai sword lady?"

"Yeah. I told you that." Great. She'd never hear the end of this now. It was difficult enough convincing Braydon they couldn't continue their affair. Convincing Nikki would be plain impossible.

He paced to the other end of the table. "Let me take you out for dinner tonight."

"No."

"Why?"

"I can't. I have plans." It was true and the easiest excuse.

His expression hardened. "With another man?"

Two actually. "My ex-husband's coming by."

"Do you see him often?"

"A few times a week. It's complicated and inevitable."

"Why?"

She sighed. He was trespassing on some very personal territory. Explaining herself would only involve him more in her personal life, where he wasn't welcome. "You don't have to worry about the whys of it, Braydon. You just need to understand that the other night can never be repeated. And it won't."

Objection flashed in his eyes, determination to prove her wrong evident on his strong features, but thankfully he didn't argue. He gathered his belongings and simply said, "Tomorrow I'll be here with the negotiated terms of agreement. We'll discuss more of this then."

When he left she dropped her head back and groaned. There'd be no surviving another face off with Braydon McCullough. While she had very valid reasons not to let him into her life, her body wanted him there in a way she'd never experienced before.

Bracing herself for the oncoming hours of the day, she gathered her items, and returned to the sanctuary of her office.

～

BECCA CHANGED from work clothing into cotton pants and a T-shirt. The rattle of the garage door echoed at quarter to six as Kevin arrived. Steeling herself for the unpredictable hours to come, she noted his premature return.

A sharp shrill filtered through the walls before she made it to the garage. Her mind prepared a list of approaches as her feet swiftly carried her across the kitchen floor.

The sound of Hunter's high-pitched squeals doubled in volume, piercing her ears, as she opened the door. Becca drew in a deep breath and called loudly over the ruckus. "Welcome home, Hunter. I missed you."

Her son ignored her welcome and paced to Kevin's car, repeatedly opening and slamming the door. "No, no, no, no, no."

Becca tensed. Kevin's ill-concealed impatience spoke of his utter hopelessness. Leaving the shade of the garage, she approached the driveway. "Hit the locks," she muttered to her ex as she passed him.

When she reached Kevin's car, she plainly said, "Oh no. We don't slam doors. That's how we hurt ourselves. Why don't you come inside and have some juice, bud? You can tell me all about your exciting weekend with Daddy."

With quick reflexes, she caught her eight year old's wrists as he pivoted and shoved her. Rotating his back to her belly, she struggled to force his arms low. Crossing one arm over his chest, locking down the other flailing arm, she dodged his thrashing attempts to lash out in a show of desperate defiance.

Controlling his outbursts had become a bit more challenging with his recent growth spurt. He'd always been strong, but since sprouting up another six inches and packing on a goodly amount of weight, it wasn't as easy as it had once been to detain Hunter when his tantrums struck.

His head swung wildly from side to side as he carried on. His frustration mounted, segmenting his words into nonsensical sounds. Becca pinned her arm around his chest, holding his limbs down in an attempt to subdue the thrashing.

Sharp pain exploded in her jaw as his head jerked back and she winced, blinking back the burn of sting-induced tears. "Hunter," she said sternly. "You hurt Mommy. Take a deep breath."

His shoulders heaved as he muttered sounds, waging an internal battle. Becca's arms remained around him, holding his back tightly to her front and his temper slowly waned. Resting her chin on his soft brown hair, she carefully transferred both his wrists to one hand, and used her other arm to apply pressure to his shoulders. "That's it. Deep breaths."

Her grip remained secure, the impersonal pressure of her hold settling him. It took well over five minutes before she could let him go. When she finally did, she braced for another attitude shift.

This was difficult for all of them. Kevin's absence from the house hadn't disturbed Hunter so much in the beginning, but once they'd started custody visits, many of Hunter's older habits returned with a vengeance.

Hunter, like many children on the autism spectrum, needed a dependable routine. Becca talked with his team at school and they helped her create charts that adapted to their new family schedule. On Friday, Hunter had been fine. However, returning home, even after three days with his father, seemed to be too unsettling for her son to handle gracefully.

"Are you ready to come inside?"

"Mmm," he mumbled, affirming he was ready.

She took his wrist and slowly led him through the garage. They weren't quite out of the woods yet.

The tendons in Hunter's small hands and fingers flexed as he widened his fingers and rotated his wrists like talons. His head bopped as he repeated quietly, "Come inside. Come inside. Come inside." Echolalia was a tendency of Hunter's whenever he came out of a tantrum.

Shooting Kevin a glare regarding his usual lack of assistance in a crisis, helped dispel some of her frustration. Thankfully, Kevin's need to escape prevented him from lingering.

"I'm gonna take off," he said as Becca released Hunter's arm as he entered the house.

Pulling the door only partially closed she asked, "Has he been like this all weekend?"

Kevin's expression showed offense. "No, Rebecca, just today when I mentioned returning home." His fingers forked through his hair. "I thought we were past this shit."

That was the thing with autism. It never ended. It had taken her years to come to terms with her son's limitations, but it wasn't all work. There were days Hunter blew her away with his abilities to do what ordinary people could not. She had, over time, embraced her son's world, submerged herself in helpful literature, and met frequently with the people involved in his progress. Kevin had done no such thing.

Being a parent of a child living with autism was tiring in ways most families couldn't comprehend. But what utterly exhausted her was trying, for eight years, to teach her husband that their son was different, not broken.

She retrieved Hunter's bags and sighed. "How did you handle it?"

With uninformed arrogance, Kevin said, "Rebecca, don't assume to tell me how to parent my own son."

"We need to remain consistent. It's what the—"

"I know how to handle him!" he snapped, then huffed. "I have to go. I'll pick him up Wednesday from school."

She nodded and entered the house. The sound of Kevin's car pulling away dragged a lot of her tension with it. She found Hunter in his room pacing, a Koosh ball flapping in his hand as he marched from corner to corner.

She placed his belongings on the floor by the bed and sat. "Did you have a nice weekend at your father's?"

"Daddy's house is blue." He paced to the other corner. "Wild Blue Yonder," he said, matching the house to the exact crayon color.

"That's a nice shade of blue. Would you like to help me put your things away?"

"Mmm."

She unzipped his bag and refolded his shirts. At least Kevin washed them. "Can you find your shirt shelf?"

Hunter wandered to the closet, where the doors had been removed, and tapped the label with a picture of a shirt. "Good. Put these shirts there please."

He carried the shirts over to the shelf and shoved them into place.

"Pants next."

They repeated the process until all of his belongings were put away. Hunter was being vocal, but his words were still pitched in a way that told her he was far from relaxed.

They had dinner and that was another battle. Tomorrow would be better, because Hunter would be waking up in his usual bed and following his customary routine.

It was anybody's guess how long the trial period of split custody would last. If Hunter didn't eventually adjust to their separation, she'd have to speak to the courts about altering the agreement, due to their circumstances and Hunter's needs.

If it came to that, Becca feared she'd burn out. Being a parent was hard work and could overwhelm anyone. But being a single parent of a growing boy with autism was daunting. Her skills would be tested to the max as she weathered the days alone.

Kevin had never been the greatest helpmate, but he at least was there for the moments she needed to do the shopping or just take five minutes to regroup. Not to mention the moments she was physically drained and needed his strength to situate their son. Hunter possessed an inexhaustible energy and could be quite stubborn at times.

Kevin loved their child, but part of her suspected it would be easier for him to simply offer monetary support and visit occasionally. It was only the remainder of his tattered conscience that seemed to keep him from making such a request, that or misplaced pride. His version of pride would never mirror hers in terms of their son. For some reason their son's limitations had always fed his personal insecurities, where she tended to appraise Hunter's progress with delicate discrimination.

She wanted what was best for Hunter, but she also didn't want Kevin in her house. The hollow joys of marriage were not worth the unbearable tension and betrayal. The day she relinquished her ideals of a united family she suffered crushing sorrow, not for herself or her husband, but because family should have been the one thing she provided for Hunter, and theirs was broken.

All of these reasons were why she couldn't take on one more thing in her life. She was tapped out.

That night she battled with Hunter to brush his teeth, a tactile torture he hated, but tolerated, due to positive reinforcement and a detailed token economy developed with his team. Her reflection showed a bruise forming on her chin where he'd head butted her earlier.

It wasn't easy staying small as Hunter grew. Bruises were a commonplace occurrence. On the calm and content days he was a gentle-hearted boy, but when his frustration toppled his ability to communicate, the storm brewing within, often erupted and devastated his temperate nature.

Her body ached as she stripped off her sweats and slid on a nightshirt. Another blotch of purple marked her arm. Before she went to bed, she quietly walked through the house and adjusted Hunter's charts for the morning. Their life was orchestrated by routine.

After she transferred every illustrated label to its proper place, she slowly took the stairs. Her mind briefly conjured Braydon, but she lacked the energy to consider what their association might become.

Her body was tired and her concentration shot. Closing her eyes, she settled into her pillows and quickly fell into a dreamless rest.

CHAPTER 3

$\mathcal{N}$ikki burst into Becca's office like a storm capable of blowing the shutters clear off a house. "I brought éclairs!"

Shoving the box of chocolate goodness on Becca's desk she collapsed into a chair, draping one leg over the arm of the seat. Becca raised an eyebrow and asked, "Whatever would possess my dear carb-terrified friend to enter a bakery this early in the week? She certainly wouldn't be making an attempt to butter me up with chocolate bribery."

The thin cardboard lid snapped down on her exploring fingers. Nikki gave a shameless grin. "Those pastries will cost one confession, please."

Pulling back her fingers and licking away a smudge of chocolate, Becca sighed. "There's nothing to confess."

"Bullshit. I saw you two yesterday. He looked ready to take you right on the conference table."

More to the point… "Did you know he worked for Bradford?"

"No. I swear. He must be fairly new, because I thought I knew everyone on their staff."

Becca had done some nosing around that morning. Turned out, Braydon was 'newer', but not the brand spanking kind. He'd been with the Bradford firm for almost three years according to their company bio page. This was likely one of the biggest deals he'd ever acquired. That bit of information gave her strength.

If this deal was important to him, he had something to lose.

Becca could use that to make sure he didn't cross a line. Returning Nikki's impatient stare, she asked, "Are you really going to come in here parading donuts and not let me have one?"

Her friend huffed and fell back in the chair, nudging the box forward. "No. Eat them before I do."

Becca stole an éclair and moaned as the sugary scrumptiousness filled her mouth. The flaky pastry was still warm and the custard was just right.

"So what happens now? You two will be seeing each other a lot if the deal goes through."

"The deal's going through."

"Does he want more?"

"Doesn't matter what he wants. What matters is that I do my job and take care of my responsibilities in this world. Braydon McCullough isn't one of them."

Nikki studied her for a moment. "Is this about Kevin or Hunter?"

"This is about me. My life needs to be as simplistic as possible. I need to protect myself from events I can't abide. Yes, Hunter needs me, but I need him too. I need him to be happy. The divorce was hard on all of us. I'm not sure the custody agreement's going to last. Hunter isn't dealing with all the shifts well and that may mean, eventually, I have him all the time. I'm not complaining, only being realistic. What man wants to get involved with all that?"

"There are plenty of men out there with autistic children, Becca."

She pursed her lips. "Nikki, please don't pressure me on this. Yes, there are some great men out there, but they want great women with ordinary lives. Hunter's own father couldn't handle the way our life is. I can't expect an outsider to step up to the plate. The divorce rate of families touched by autism is eighty percent. Who willingly takes bets with the odds piled against them? I won't take that risk with my son. I won't put him through more than he's already been through. It's too risky."

Nikki's face was serious. She reached across the desk and pressed her hand into Becca's. "Okay, sweetie. I understand." She stood and went to the door, her fingers brushing over the picture of Hunter hanging on the wall. "He's getting so big, Becs."

Indomitable pride filled her heart. "I know."

Nikki smiled despondently. "Why don't we go to the park this weekend, the three of us?"

"Hunter would love that."

"Then it's a date."

After Nikki left, the fax came through with the negotiations between Apricot and Bradford. Their firm was scouting various locations for the new franchises to develop.

By noon, she was starving and figured she'd pack up early for lunch. She had a showing downtown at one. As she lifted her purse out of her bottom drawer there was a knock at her door. "Come in."

She stood and stilled.

Braydon smiled over a large box reeking of takeout. "I wasn't sure what you liked, so I brought eggrolls, pizza, fries, and salad."

Her jaw dropped. He'd brought her lunch?

"I also have the updated contracts for you to look over," he said, stepping into the room and placing the box on her desk. His gaze snagged on the leftover box of éclairs, his long fingers flipping up the lid and noting the last of the bunch. "I'll remember you have a sweet tooth next time."

There wouldn't be a next time. Dropping her purse back in the drawer, she asked, "May I see the contract?"

Sliding into a chair with smooth agility he removed the document from his breast pocket. Tossing it on her desk, he snatched up the last éclair. His mouth closed over the soft pastry, full, kiss-provoking lips wreaking havoc on her senses.

Shaking off the effect he was having on her, she swept up the paperwork and paged through.

"Can I interest you in an eggroll?"

Bracing herself, she glanced at him over the pages. "No, thank you. I have a lunch date in an hour."

His gaze zeroed in on her. "With a man?"

"As a matter of fact, yes."

"Would this be a business lunch, or a personal one?"

Crap. *New Becca's strong. Don't back down.* "I don't see how that concerns you."

"It concerns me, because I want to see you naked again and don't like the idea of other men doing the same."

Her jaw unhinged. She was outmaneuvered. "Braydon—"

His head rolled back as he shut his eyes and moaned almost sexually, throwing her off. "I love when you say my name. Do it again."

She snapped her mouth shut and pursed her lips. "Please—"

"Mmm, that's it. Beg me, angel. Your wish is my command."

Her brow scrunched. "Come on!"

"Oh, yeah, angel, make me come."

That's it. She smacked the papers down on her desk. "Will you stop that!"

His mouth kicked up and he peeked through one eye at her. "I'm just trying to be friendly."

"You're trying to make me uncomfortable."

"Is it working?"

Exasperated, she huffed. "Yes. Now, knock it off."

"Will you eat an eggroll?"

It wasn't funny, but his sarcasm disrupted her irritation. Crossing her arms, she said, "I don't like eggrolls."

"Pizza?"

"Fine."

He unwrapped a warm slice already on a paper plate, the grease seeping through the thin cardboard. Sighing and giving him a look that should convey how unimpressed she was with his tactics, she bit into the slice.

"Have mercy. I love watching your mouth work."

Dropping her chin and tossing the plate on her desk, she scowled. "That lasted all of two seconds."

"Well, that's not what any man wants to hear. Go on. Finish eating. I'll behave."

"Will you?"

"I suppose. But it won't be easy. I should be rewarded for my efforts."

"I'll be sure to pass along my praise to your boss."

"Oh, I wouldn't do that. We just broke up."

Her mouth paused mid-bite. "You dated your boss?"

He shrugged and dug through the box of takeout. "Dated isn't the right term. We...satisfied each other for a time."

The sudden jealousy snaking through her was completely inappropriate and uncalled for. "Like...she was your booty call?"

He unwrapped another eggroll. "More like I was hers."

"What's the difference?" What kind of man sleeps with the boss? One, it was unethical. Two, the woman was about twenty years older than Braydon—weren't men supposed to be superficial about that sort of thing? And three, the idea of Braydon with that beautiful, dark skinned, willowy CEO made Becca really covetous and insecure about her own shortcomings. Not characteristically territorial, her bitterness was unsettling.

"The difference is, she called the shots."

Becca frowned. "You mean you only came over when she suggested it?"

"No. More along the lines of I only came when she permitted it."

"*What?*" She hadn't meant to rudely blurt her shock, but… *What?*

This was the same man that had dominated her body the other night, owned the boardroom the other morning. She simply couldn't imagine him acting subservient in any way, even to an impressive woman like Miranda.

Braydon shrugged. "We had a different sort of relationship, but it worked…for a while. When it no longer suited both our needs, it ended. We're still friends."

Her mind went over everything she knew about Braydon. He wasn't a softy. He definitely had an intimidating presence, nothing short of capable. As a matter of fact, he had a distinct air of authority about him, something a man didn't acquire, but was born with. Imagining him being bossed around by a woman like Miranda Robinson simply didn't make sense.

"To each his own, I guess." And if he was the sort of guy who only entertained a relationship "when it suited", all the more reason to steer clear of him.

Braydon paused and cocked his head to the side. "Really? I didn't expect judgment from a woman who had sex as infrequently as cicadas over the past decade."

Her mouth snapped shut. The humiliating truth of his words stung even if he was only teasing. She resented his knowledge regarding her personal past. "That's not nice. And for your information, I had sex more than once every seven years and I'd appreciate it if you'd butt out of my personal business."

He chuckled and went back to eating. "You know," he said, almost contemplatively. "I have no problem with taking control. The dynamic Miranda and I shared was unique. I liked pleasing her and she enjoyed asserting herself. You shouldn't knock it until you've tried it."

Tried what? Bossing him around or allowing him to take control? Both were unlikely. She already had enough people to decide for and whenever people tried to tell her how to live her life she tended to get uppity. With no time for dating she had even less time to contemplate fetish dynamics. All she'd hoped for in life was a typical marriage and family. Captain Kinky over there was again proving way out of her league.

She really didn't need to think about this. "I don't think so."

"Could be fun."

Unwelcome memories of their encounter flooded her mind. He was probably right, it could be fun, but she couldn't allow things to go that far—no matter how much her body wanted it. Shifting her weight, her legs crossed in an attempt to relieve some of the unexpected tension building inside of her. Flutters of excitement teased her lower belly as pressure built.

She needed to focus. Finished with her pizza, she dropped the crust on the plate and wiped her mouth with a napkin, making sure there wasn't any grease on her chin.

When she looked at Braydon, his easy manner evaporated. "What the hell happened to your face?"

"What?" Her hand fluttered to her jaw.

"Did somebody hit you?" He stood and rounded her desk, not giving her a chance to brace for his nearness.

Crap. She must have accidentally wiped away her concealer. Quickly reaching for her purse, she said, "It's nothing. I bumped—"

Her words cut off as he gently cupped her jaw and turned her face. His eyes were hard as he scowled at the bruise. "How did this happen?"

"I told you. I bumped—"

"You said you had to see your ex yesterday. Did that son of a bitch do this to your face?"

Fury radiated from him, completely contradicting the gentle way he held her chin as he examined her.

"No. Kevin would never hit me. It's nothing. Really. Just drop it."

Braydon's gaze roamed over her body. His strong hand picked up her wrist and turned her arm. "What are these marks from?"

Feeling cornered, she snatched her arm back. "Look, I appreciate your concern, but I assure you it's misplaced." She grabbed her purse and stood, hating how exposed he made her feel. "I have an appointment. Thanks for lunch. I'll send the paperwork over to Mr. Dillard's assistant when I get back. You should have it by Thursday at the latest."

He didn't look pleased, but that wasn't her problem. Taking the long way to the door so she didn't have to get close to him again, she fled her office. She held her breath as she raced to the elevators and didn't exhale until she was safely tucked inside and rushing toward the ground.

~

THAT AFTERNOON, as Becca drove to Hunter's school, she couldn't stop thinking about the things Braydon had said. She recalled the way he asked if he could touch her, the way he announced his desire to please her. The entire experience took on a different feel, now that she knew his past with Miranda.

Having to make enough decisions for everyone in her little world, she definitely didn't want anything to do with a guy that needed a woman to decide for him. But still…something didn't add up. No matter how she tried, she couldn't imagine Braydon being ordered around. Asking was one thing. Manners were always nice. But thinking of him behaving subserviently in any manner was absurd. Maybe that was why he and his boss had broken up.

Once buzzed in to the aftercare room she spotted Hunter at the computer, a set of cushioned headphones covering his ears.

"Hi, Becca," Natalie, the after school aide, greeted. Natalie was also an aide in the resource room, so she was great for Hunter. The woman was familiar with her son's needs and often sat in on their IEP meetings.

"Hi, Natalie. How was he today?"

"Good. A little off in the morning, but he was fine by snack time. He actually did so well sorting today he earned an extra ten minutes on the bike."

A proud smile crept to her face. Those slight victories were worth their weight in gold.

Hunter had various preferred activities. Above all, he loved music, especially The Rolling Stones. But he also enjoyed other activities like riding the bikes in the resource room at his school, piecing together model trains, and, his most recent affinity, playing the piano.

The bike was a special treat because it was a one-on-one activity. The teachers shadowed him as he took the large bike with training wheels around a circle of cones. Every time she observed him maintaining his balance it delighted her, seeing him beam with unspoken excitement. It was amazing to witness his progress considering his visual perception issues.

Strolling to the computer she placed a hand on his right shoulder. He turned and offered a wide smile. "Mom! Work's over?"

She removed the headphones so he'd realize he was shouting. "Work's over. Did you have a nice day?"

"I rode the bike! Work's over now. Natalie, work's over now!"

Natalie smiled. "Yup. Time to go home, bud."

"*If you start me up I never stop*," Hunter said and laughed loudly. Becca chuckled at his form of a joke. He frequently quoted lines in his best Mick Jagger impersonation.

She laughed and patted his shoulder. "You ready, bud?"

"*You make a grown man cry*, Mom." He laughed again. The return of his pleasant mood filled her with calm and relieved some of her worry.

Natalie came to their side with Hunter's belongings. A few minutes later Becca was buckling him into his seat in the van. They drove home, The Stones CD playing along as Hunter hummed to the beat.

Part of the reason Hunter loved The Stones was because Becca did, but he also liked the fact that he and Mick were both born on June 26. Hunter emulated the musician from his dance moves—which were sometimes amusing—to his preference of instruments. Her son was—in her mind—a genius when it came to the piano, never needing a single sheet of notes, but he also enjoyed the tambourine, the harmonica, and the guitar, just like Jagger. The other instruments were difficult for him, but for some reason the piano seemed to be an extension of his soul.

When they settled in for dinner, Hunter was still chatty. She'd take that over his silence any day. Carrying over a plate of bacon, she slipped into her chair. Breakfast for dinner was one of Hunter's favorites and since Kevin left, she'd started preparing it once a week.

Her son's motor skills had come a long way. His occupational therapist was great. Though his motions were broad and his tidiness was not that of a typical eight-year-old boy's, he was now capable of feeding himself with a fork and that made Becca's life a bit more manageable.

Nibbling her eggs, she laughed as Hunter folded and wedged half a pancake into his mouth. "Fork, please," she reminded.

"Sorry," he mumbled lynd chewed.

"Chew first, then talk."

Forcing his lips closed as he chewed with exaggerated bites and laughed heartily. He opened his mouth a minute later. "Gone."

"Good. I have a surprise for you."

"What?" Hunter lunged forward and rocked back.

"Aunt Nikki's taking us to the park this weekend."

Hunter clapped and rolled his head over his shoulders happily. "Tomorrow?"

"No. Saturday."

"Today's Tuesday."

"Correct."

Hunter looked at the clock on the wall. "How many hours, Mom?"

"That's you're department, bud."

Glancing back at the clock, he contorted his fingers as his eyes flinched. "Seventy-seven hours until Saturday."

She didn't know how he managed to do such fast math, but it had always been a gift. Without needing to check, she said, "That's right."

"The Rolling Stones played in Hyde Park on July sixth two thousand thirteen."

"Is that right?"

"Mmm."

After dinner she cleaned up the dishes. "Bring your plate over." When he didn't acknowledge her words, she approached him and placed a hand on his right shoulder, prompting him again. "Can you bring your plate over for me?"

Hunter stood. His shoulders rotated as he jerkily walked his plate to the sink. Once he dropped it in the basin, he went to his Velcro chart and moved the picture of a place setting to the finished column.

"What's next, bud?"

He hummed as he counted down each row of the chart. "Bath!"

Bath time was always an experience. Becca was usually given her own shower by the time it was through. "Why don't you go listen to two songs on your iPod and then we'll take your bath?"

Hunter happily obeyed, snatching up his iPod and carrying it to the living room. That would keep him in a tranquil mood, but Becca was certain it wouldn't last.

Five minutes later, she was finished the dishes and filling the tub. She went to find Hunter. "Ready, bud?"

He appeared to see her, but made no move to acknowledge her presence. Becca placed her hand on his shoulder. "It's bath time."

He jerked away and rocked to his music. "Hunter, if you want to go to the park this weekend we need to have a good week. It's bath night. You can listen to your music when you're done."

He still didn't relinquish the music. Sighing, she removed the device from his hands and gently pulled out his earbuds.

"No!"

Becca stepped back. "Hey. Don't hit me."

He threw his back into the couch, his legs kicking out in protest like a pinwheel.

"Hunter, you need to take a bath."

He shouted a moan as he kicked again, knocking his shoe off in the process.

"There you go. Now take off the other one."

He twisted and grabbed the pillow, jamming it into his belly as he rolled, pressing his face into the couch to scream. Becca went to turn off the water. It was going to be one of those nights.

Hunter's screams carried through the house, regardless of how he shoved his face into the leather of the couch. She stood back as he carried on. His hands curled and twisted. He grabbed at his clothing and pulled. When his hand punched the side of his head she intervened.

"Hunter, do *not* hit."

Face flushing with frustration, he growled and screeched into the furniture. Becca walked away, ignoring his outburst. She only intervened when Hunter was hurting himself, others, or damaging property, but it wasn't always easy to pretend indifference to his tantrums.

Tough love was an unfortunate part of maternal solicitude. Every struggle beat at her heart.

She laid out his pajamas and turned down his bed. Five minutes later Hunter was motionless on the couch, breathing hard, but quietly staring out the window, the side of his face now pressed into the cushion.

"Are you ready now?"

He didn't show any signs of hearing her, but that didn't necessarily mean he'd missed what she'd said. Sometimes Hunter had so much going on in his mind, words were a nuisance.

"If you want to listen to another song before bed, you need to come into the bathroom now."

He grimaced and stomped to the bathroom. Becca followed and turned on the faucet, filling the tub the rest of the way. "Take off your clothes."

He peeled off his clothes, yanking hard as the collar twisted around his neck. Becca waited until he was undressed. Patience was a virtue, rewarded by his developing independence. "Get into the tub."

Grudgingly, he took her arm and stepped into the water, but refused to sit.

"We need to finish in ten minutes or no more music tonight."

He screamed and Becca's hands rushed to her ears as she winced. When the blood-curdling outburst abruptly stopped she calmly asked, "Why are you screaming?"

He stomped his foot, kicking water onto the tile. Breathing hard through his teeth he panted, each breath accompanied by a bleating cry. The intoxicating hum was all part of his progression toward something he found insufferable.

The water wasn't too hot or too cold. It was simply a process for him to lower his body into the tub. "It's slimy."

"I know, but you're dirty and need to get washed." She patiently waited for him to give up fighting the inevitable.

"Five minutes," she announced looking at her watch.

He dropped to the water. *Go time.* Becca grabbed the loofa and squirted a hefty amount of body wash on it. Boys were messy and her son was no different.

She scrubbed his back, arms, neck, chest, and feet. Picking up his hand, which he now held stiffly, she closed his fingers over the spongy ball. "Do your belly, Hunter."

Hand over hand, she guided his motions as he washed the rest of his body. He was getting older, and it was imperative he master the task of bathing himself independently. It would be so much easier to simply do everything for him, but that wouldn't help Hunter's development. Independence was vital.

Scooping up the plastic pitcher, she rinsed his shoulders. He screeched when she wet his hair. "Eyes! Eyes! Eyes!"

She quickly placed the hand towel she always kept at the ready into his twitching fingers. "Almost done."

He wiped his brow and calmed.

"Find the shampoo."

Hunter handed her the bottle. He had some tactile issues with slippery substances, which was one of the reasons bath time was always so challenging.

"Open your hand."

Begrudgingly, he held out his palm. She squirted shampoo in the center and he flung it off and squealed. She gripped his wrist and added some more. "Put it in your hair, Hunter. We're almost finished. I wonder what song you're going to listen to when you're done."

She guided his hand to his hair and rubbed shampoo over his head until a lather formed. "Head back," she said as she proceeded to rinse out his hair.

Once he was out of the tub and somewhat dry, she followed him to his room to help him dress. "You did great, bud."

He immediately went to his dresser where she'd placed his iPod. Without saying a word, he plugged in his earbuds and lay down on his bed.

Wiped, Becca grabbed the comb and quietly brushed his hair. The only reason he tolerated the gentle touch was because he'd likely exhausted himself bathing. She savored the moments she could get close to him, as they didn't come often. By the end of the song he'd calmed.

By the time he was asleep she was dead on her feet. She'd made her rounds, returning all the task charts to their morning positions, cleaning up the pillows on the floor of the living room, and shutting off the lights. As she checked the locks at the front door she paused, a strange thought occurring.

She'd always done this. Since Kevin left she'd assumed a heap of additional responsibilities would be thrust on her shoulders, but the truth was, she'd been doing this on her own since Hunter was young.

It was hard, recalling how utterly inept Kevin was, and not letting her frustration get the better of her. Their marriage was over, and as tired as she was, part of her was glad it ended. It was better to depend on herself than to constantly wind up disappointed in the person intended to help her, not to mention the waste of energy, waiting and hoping for that aid. If only he'd shown more interest in helping her, being present in their day-to-day family life, their marriage might have survived and her family could have been whole.

~

OVER THE FOLLOWING two weeks Braydon seemed to take the hint that she wasn't interested and left her alone. It wasn't until one Friday morning that he leapt right back into the forefront of her memory. There was an envelope on her desk with Nikki's scribble on the front.

. . .

DIDN'T KNOW what you wanted to do with this...

BECCA PEELED the envelope open and found Braydon's ID. Jeez, even his driver's license picture was pretty. *So not fair!*

She stashed the envelope in her purse to deal with later, which was where it stayed for another week. Sure, she thought of him, but with every manifestation in her mind, she banished his memory to the back of her head—over and over again.

The following Wednesday while doing bills, she found the envelope. Frustrated that this man's presence was still haunting her, she copied his address onto a fresh envelope, sealed it, and shoved it in with the rest of her bills.

Feeling vindicated and free of the temptation he caused once and for all, she submerged herself in typical routines hoping to reinstate some much-needed balance to her life. She spent the following days organizing the house, purging things she no longer used, and boxing up the items Kevin left behind, which was quite irritating. How difficult was it to *move out?*

Becca was running the vacuum while Hunter pounded away on the upright to the tune of *She's a Rainbow*. She hadn't heard the knock at the door and was completely unprepared when she heard a deep, muffled voice call her name.

"Becca?"

Frowning, she shut off the vacuum and rushed to the hall, coming up short when she saw Braydon's face pressed against the glass, yellow roses at his hip.

What the heck was he doing there? She undid the locks and yanked the door open.

He smiled. "Hey."

Her brain wasn't working nor were her eyes blinking. So taken off guard, when she finally spoke her voice rushed out in a waspish tone she never used before. "What the heck are you doing here?"

He grinned, his invariable pleasantness grating on her. "I brought you flowers."

"How do you know where I live?"

"Your address was on the envelope you used to mail my ID."

She shook her head. Who popped over to someone's house without ever being invited? The ID was meant to break their personal connection. "I was returning it to you, not inviting you over!"

His smile faded, but not as much as it should have. "What are you listening to? Is that The Stones?"

She quickly shoved him out the door with a forward motion and shut it behind them. "You can't come by like this, Braydon."

He took a deep breath. "I'm sorry. I just…missed you."

Frustrated, she folded her arms over her chest. "You don't even know me!"

"I want to."

She'd gone from being thoroughly ignored by a husband of ten years to being stalked by a gorgeous, stage-five clinger that couldn't take a hint. "You have to leave." The piano abruptly cut off. "Now."

"Is someone here with you?"

"Braydon, I'm not kidding. This is my home. I take my privacy very seriously. It's completely unprofessional for you to burst in here and start asking questions."

His brow knit and guilt for her harsh tone tickled her conscience. Unexpected guests had a way of hijacking her son's contented mood and she really didn't want this unplanned visit to ruin an otherwise peaceful Saturday. She also didn't have the time to explain all of that to Braydon. She didn't want to be nasty, but mean seemed the only thing that got through to him. Everything wasn't a joking matter.

Hurting others was never easy for her, and when rejection showed in his crestfallen eyes, she instinctively wanted to apologize. He dropped the flowers on the steps of the porch. "You should probably put them in water."

When he turned away she winced, an apology for being so crass on her lips.

The door opened. "Mom? I'm hungry."

She shut her eyes, as her solitude was irrevocably disturbed. There was no way Hunter would miss Braydon's presence. It had nothing to do with who her son was as a person and everything to do with protecting him. Despite their history, she didn't know Braydon well enough to gage how he'd respond to her son.

Braydon turned, as the reason for her reluctance was laid bare. "You have a son?"

She never considered dating, because she never wanted Hunter to get attached to someone that wouldn't stick around. There were simply too many jerks out there and her son was extremely sensitive, whether others realized it or not. It was an easy sacrifice to make if it protected him.

She twisted and faced Hunter. "Why don't you have a banana, buddy? And when I come inside in *two minutes*, I'll make lunch."

Hunter rubbed his ear on his shoulder and worked his jaw as he studied Braydon from the corner of his eye. His wrist twisted as his fingers tightened. He was stimming—self-stimulating—which usually meant he was experiencing anxiety, fear, or anger, but it could also be his way of blocking out the distractions over-whelming him. Most likely he was anxious since a man he'd never seen before was standing on their porch.

Panicking that Braydon might ask something hurtful, her entire being tensed in preparation. If he crossed a line, she wasn't sure she'd be able to hold it together. It wouldn't be the first time a stranger pointed and rudely asked what was wrong with her son. Constant persecution and memories of Hunter's feelings getting hurt threw her into Momma Bear mode.

"Hunter, go wait for me in the kitchen. I'll be there in two minutes."

"One twenty."

"Yes."

The door closed and she faced Braydon. His brow was drawn with confusion. "I didn't know you had children. I saw a picture in your office, but I just assumed it was a nephew or relative."

"Hunter's my only child."

"How old is he?"

Very aware of the time ticking by, she quickly answered, "He's eight and I need to go be his mother right now."

He took a step forward. "Can we go out sometime? Does your ex take him on the weekends or something?"

A humorless laugh slipped out, because, of course, he only wanted that part of her, not the part including her child. It was foolish of her to have led him to believe one was separate from the other.

That was exactly what she'd tried explaining to Nikki about men not wanting to date a woman with a situation as complicated as hers. "That's not going to work either, Braydon. On the days I'm by myself I'm usually so whipped I can barely hold my head up straight. I need that time to recuperate. I think you should find someone else. I'm sorry." She needed to go inside. No matter how logical her words were, her heart grew heavy with sorrow and longing that there wasn't more she could offer. She really did like him, but her time was already pledged to her son.

Regretfully, she hung her head and said, "I have to go."

Scooping up the flowers, she shut the door behind her, pressing her back into the glass. No one had brought her flowers...ever. It was a shame she couldn't be happier about them.

CHAPTER 4

*B*raydon sipped his beer and stared at the bottles along the mirrored wall in front of him. Becca had a son. A son who obviously had special needs. Funny, there was no way he could have known that, but he kept beating himself up as though he should have.

Recalling every encounter, he made sure he hadn't been a moron and somehow missed the moment she mentioned having a child. Nope. She hadn't mentioned it.

Of course, that was probably because she'd never intended to see him again, and when their paths crossed she'd done nothing but make it perfectly clear how disinterested she was in pursuing a relationship. Her inexplicable reluctance to date suddenly made sense.

Problem was, Bray had done nothing but fantasize about the perfect woman who'd been in his bed and left all too soon. Realizing now her life was far from perfect, he also acknowledged he knew nothing about special needs kids.

His sister in law, Sammy, sometimes taught students that needed a little extra attention and Bray could recall a kid from grade school that had seizures, but that was the extent of his knowledge on the subject. His ignorance made him feel like even more of a jerk.

How could he be so incredibly naïve in this day and age? Reaching in his pocket, he pulled out his phone and connected to the bar's Wi-Fi. Opening up the Internet, he searched, *Special Needs*

Children, which entered him into an overwhelming world of blurbs and articles on everything from peanut allergies to cerebral palsy. How was he supposed to know what each condition looked like?

He typed in, *What does special needs look like?* And came across images of everything from kids in wheelchairs to kids that looked just like his nieces and nephews.

"Shit." This was getting him nowhere.

Tossing a twenty on the counter, he finished his beer and left. When he got back to his apartment he called his oldest brother. "Hey, Colin."

"Hey, Bray. You coming home this weekend? It's been a while."

Braydon collapsed on his couch. "I've been busy with a new deal our firm's handling. Probably won't be home for a while still. How're the kids?"

"Kids are good. Sammy's still not ready to try for another one yet. I'm okay with that. You'll never guess who is expecting though."

Family news was always a welcome distraction. "Who? Mallory can't be pregnant again."

"Not Mallory."

"Ash?"

"Nope, Ashlynn's not either."

He thought for a minute. "Do not say Kate." His eldest sister already had five kids. She should be done. "Oh my God, Shei-devil?"

"Wrong again." That was a little disappointing since Sheilagh and Alec had been trying, but their situation was complicated.

"Who then?"

Colin laughed. "Luke."

"Wait, what?" Luke was his older brother. He was married, sort of, but his spouse's name was Tristan. "How is that possible?"

"They've been talking about it for a while. I hooked them up with a few agencies that help place abandoned babies. It's sort of a spur of the moment situation that only crops up so often. But they should be getting approved any day now."

"That's nuts! Are they ready to have a baby?"

"Tristan definitely is. Luke's more worried about being physically prepared. He's putting an addition on the back of the barn and Mom and Dad's garage is full of all sorts of crap they've been buying. I think he'll be fine once he feels in control." Colin laughed. "Like any parent has control. It should be fun to watch."

"How likely is it they'll get a call?"

"Don't know. Guess it depends when their son or daughter's born and how soon the agency approves their application."

Braydon whistled, loving Colin's positive attitude. "It's like baby roulette."

"I'm happy for them. I think they'll be great fathers."

"Speaking of kids, is Sammy around?"

"Yeah. You wanna talk to her?"

"If you don't mind. I have a question for her about…a friend's kid. Since she's a teacher and all…"

"Sure. Hold on. *Samantha! Bray's on the phone!*"

Bray chuckled. "Hey, Col."

"Yeah?"

"Remember when you used to be the quiet one?"

Colin laughed. "A lot's changed. Here she is."

Braydon waited as Colin handed over the phone and Sammy gave him instructions on making sure Lula, their eldest, brushed her teeth properly.

"Hey, Bray."

"Hey, beautiful. I got a question for you."

"Shoot. You just saved my butt from bath time with the hooligans. I'll tell you whatever you want."

"I met this woman."

"Ooooooh."

He rolled his eyes. "Settle yourself. Anyway, she has a son."

"Really? Interesting."

"He's… Why is that interesting?"

"Oh, come on, Bray. We all know how you cling to perfection. It's fun when life throws curveballs—especially to you."

"Well, God definitely pegged me in the head with one today."

"It's a kid, Braydon, not a nuke."

"I know, but her situation's a little different."

"Different how?"

"God, I don't want to say this wrong. I think her son's…special?"

"Special like you like him a lot or special like he has an IEP?"

"What would a kid be doing with a bomb?"

"Not an IED, you ass. An *IEP.* An Individualized Education Program."

"Oh, he probably has one of those. He looks somewhere between eight and ten."

"What disability is he living with?"

"That's why I'm calling. I don't know."

"Did you ask?"

"I can't ask that!"

"Why not? If you're interested in this woman and this is her son, she's aware he's different. If you like her, you better get comfortable with his dissimilarities, Bray. If it makes you uncomfortable, back out now. Single moms don't have time for games. Single moms of children with special needs have less."

He frowned. He wasn't an asshole. "I'm not a jerk, Sammy."

"I know you're not, but I also remember what it was to be your girlfriend. You can be very self-involved and you weren't always there when I needed you."

Ouch. "I was a kid, Sam. I'm thirty years old now."

"And I hope you've grown up, especially if you're thinking about dating a woman with a child. Take away the unique technicalities for a minute. Kids are loving little beings and they get attached. You need to go into this fully aware of what you're agreeing to."

He sighed. This was getting way more complicated than he anticipated. "I haven't done anything yet." Not really. "But I like her. A lot. I just need to understand her situation better."

"Well, what's her son like?"

"He looks normal."

Sam huffed. "Keep away from that term. No kid is one hundred percent normal. Lula won't stop eating her boogers, and one of Finn's boys pooped in the lake this summer and proceeded to use the turd as a battleship."

Bray laughed. "You mean a battle*shit*."

"Whatever. My point is, no parent likes that term, especially when their kid doesn't fit society's definition. Describe what you saw and maybe I can help."

"Well, I only saw him for a minute. At first I didn't notice anything out of the ordinary, but then he started, like, twitching."

"Like tics or stimming?"

"Uh, I don't really know what you're talking about."

"A tic could be Tourette's, you know, when people have outbursts with curses, but verbal tics are less common than physical tics. They're sort of like tiny flinches."

"What's the other thing you said?"

"Stimming. That's different. Stimming's a behavior that calms or is intended to calm. It's triggered. A lot of children with autism stim, but it usually fades as they get older and learn more self-control."

"What's it look like?"

"Depends. We all stim. It can be as simple as twirling hair or biting nails. It's just a form of self-comforting. When autistic people do it, it can be anything from flapping their arms to punching themselves."

"Punching themselves?"

Sammy sighed. "Yeah. It's a complicated neurological disorder and no case is alike. Did your girlfriend's son flap?"

"Not really. He sort of twitched and moved his jaw. His head rotated like he was cracking his neck and his hands contorted. I don't think he liked me."

Sammy laughed. "Sorry. No. If this boy's autistic or is on that continuum, he hasn't formed an opinion about you yet. He's still trying to digest what you are and why you're in his environment. A major reason they react differently to the world is because their perception's completely dissimilar from ours. Their processing's out of synch. While we see a man standing in front of us, a child with autism sees the buttons on his shirt glistening in the sun. He could be distracted by the scent of his cologne or the sound of the wind in the trees. Every new situation's overwhelming. Plop a stranger in the midst of an otherwise ordinary day and their brains go on overload."

He was on overload. Everything Sammy explained was probably why Becca was so pissed he'd swung by unannounced. Shit. "How do I know if her son's autistic?"

"The laziness stops now if you intend to continue with this woman, Braydon. Go to a computer and type in autism. You'll figure it out."

"Why are you being nasty?"

Sam huffed. "I'm not. I just don't want to see you hurt this woman or her child."

He deflated. In a low voice he asked, "Was I really that terrible of a boyfriend?"

She sighed. "No, you weren't. But you always seemed to be the last to know what was actually going on with *me.* What are their names?"

"Her name's Becca and I think her son's name is Hunter or it could be Buddy."

"Okay, well let me put it to you this way. If you date her, it can't be *The Braydon Show*. It's probably never *The Becca Show*. Her life is that child. Every minute of her day's tuned to *his* channel. So you either have to be willing to sit through a lot of uncomfortable episodes or go back to the premium channels you're used to."

"Okay."

"You can't go running off for boat rides and expect them just to pack a lunch and join you without a—"

"I get it, Sam. You can stop pointing out all my flaws now."

She was silent for a second. "You know I love you."

"I know. I love you too. I just…I'm tired of not being good enough."

"You *are* good enough, Braydon. You just have to commit to always putting your best side forward and don't give up when things don't go as *perfectly* as you expected. Get rid of your unrealistic expectations and you might actually fall in messy love. Trust me. It's way better than fake picture-perfect love."

"Thanks. I'm gonna go look online." Haunting insecurities from his past had him hesitating. "Do you think I should forget about her?"

"If you can't handle it, then yeah, that's probably best. But my money's on you, Braydon. There isn't much you can't handle. Put all that optimistic charm to use and you may actually be just what this woman needs."

"I'll let you know what happens. Thanks for talking to me."

"Anytime. And when are you coming home? We miss you."

"Maybe sometime next month. I miss you guys too. Tell everyone I said hi."

When Bray got off the phone he went to his office and powered up his laptop. An hour later he was totally overwhelmed. Concerning autism, finite answers didn't seem to exist.

He wound up perusing YouTube and watching documentaries. Then he came across home videos of families living with autism. Shock wasn't an adequate term for what he was feeling.

What looked like a normal temper tantrum, the kind that earned him and his brothers a swift kick in the ass as kids, became so much more. The longer he watched, the more he identified the internal struggle each child worked through.

Some kids got so frustrated their faces flushed beet red, their little bodies tensed, and their parents had to restrain them. He couldn't imagine Becca dealing with such combative behavior. Then he recalled the bruises on her and everything started to make sense.

By the time he went to bed he was exhausted. Reading about

autism was taxing. Watching parents cope with situations was draining. Imagining sweet little Becca dealing with some of the things he'd witnessed online on a regular basis was impossible. How did she have the strength left to work a fulltime job or have a social life?

That was when the light bulb finally exploded. *This* was why she refused to date him. It had nothing to do with her ex or her divorce. It had to do with her plate being full. Hell, her plate was overflowing. And he'd pushed her buttons like an insensitive jerk. Sammy was right, he was set to *The Braydon Show* and it was time to change the program.

~

THE WEEK PASSED QUICKLY. Bray's nights were spent at home in front of his computer. He'd conducted so much research he deserved some sort of honorary degree. He'd also done a lot of soul searching. Samantha was right. He was a shitty boyfriend. He didn't know if he had what it took to date someone like Becca, yet he wanted to.

A very small but real voice whispered in his head, *is she worth it?* Was she? This wouldn't be like dating other women. Dating a mother meant making sacrifices he wasn't used to. It also meant there wouldn't be time for childish games. Oddly, that appealed to him. He was done wasting time with momentary companions. It was time for the real deal and Becca was as real as it got.

However, Becca's situation was perhaps too real. To be honest, parts of her situation were out of his comfort zone. He wasn't afraid of her son, of course. No. He was afraid of coming to find out he wasn't man enough to handle what she seemed to manage on her own.

There were definitely some shaky confidence issues lingering from his past. Weariness set in as he rubbed his brow. Was she worth it?

Yes. No matter how insignificant their night together may have been to her, it meant something to him. Beyond the sex, were the similarities in their fields that intrigued him. Seeing her at work validated the self-conscious strength he'd suspected the first night he met her. Their interactions in the office spoke of a chemistry not easily ignored. They connected on a level that was new to him. He didn't want it to be over. She was enchanting and surely worth his effort. He couldn't promise his future, but he wanted to explore the possibility of a woman like Becca being a part of it.

The only thing to do was talk to her. Figuring there had to be some sort of custody arrangement with her husband, he emailed her on Thursday.

I'D LIKE to get together to talk. Just talk. Please let me know when you have time.
~Braydon

THE REPLY CAME through that afternoon.

BRAYDON,
I don't understand what it's going to take. I thought I made it perfectly clear my life does not allow time for dating. Please stop.
~Becca

SO THAT APPROACH wasn't going to work. Neither would another surprise attack. It was a shame her feistiness only provoked him. For as timid as she was that night at his apartment, there was an underlying assertiveness to her, very visible in her job, which turned him on. Why he became so focused on this woman was a mystery, but he couldn't shake the sense that he needed to spend more time with her.

True, at first he'd thought she was perfect. However, that old adage about judging books by their covers was finally sinking in. So what if she had a child that needed some extra attention? Her homelife didn't detract from her beauty, it added to his respect for her. And the more he understood autism the less it intimidated him. Before, he wasn't prepared for surprises. Now he was banking on them.

Friday afternoon he took a cab to her building. Yes, she hated surprise visits, but this was her work and he'd brought some papers for her regarding the deal with Apricot. He could have faxed them, but—

"Mr. McCullough."

The hair on the back of his neck prickled. Slowly turning, he came face to face with the crazy sword lady. Great. He ignored the urge to cup his balls protectively. "Hello, Nikki."

"We didn't expect you here today. Is there something I can help you with?"

"I need to drop some papers off to Becca."

Nikki eyed him appraisingly. The girl was a tiny thing, but she somehow managed to provoke the intimidating awareness one might achieve while aiming a switchblade at the boys downstairs. "I can deliver the papers to her."

He cleared his throat. "No, I'd like to speak to Becca."

"And if I say she's busy?"

"I'll wait."

Nikki arched a narrow brow. He imagined her in a Viking helmet commanding an army of crazy bastards and shook it off. "I could kill you, you know."

"I know."

"Don't give me a reason. I just got a new shovel and I want to keep it clean and shiny for a while."

She was completely insane. How she was the boss of this set up was beyond him. "I promise if I hurt her I'll bring my own shovel and dig the hole myself."

She nodded. "She has a meeting in twenty minutes. If you want to catch her, you better head in now."

"Thanks."

He followed the hall to Becca's office. When he knocked lightly on the door she called out an invitation. The moment he stepped inside she visually tensed.

"Jeez. Stalk much?"

"I needed to drop off these papers and I wanted to give you this."

He placed the papers on her desk and dropped a puzzle piece on top. While researching autism he'd quickly figured out the puzzle piece was a symbol for awareness. It represented how different each case was. It also symbolized each child being a part of the puzzle the world was trying to solve. But mostly, it was intended to show her he understood.

Her eyes followed the small puzzle piece and she swallowed. She didn't look at him.

"I understand why you've been blowing me off. I just want to talk, Becca. Let me take you out, treat you, whenever you have some time for yourself. No pressure. You're worth waiting for."

Her shoulders lifted and he had no idea if she was pissed, upset, moved, or thought the whole display was a cheesy attempt to get back in her pants. It wasn't about her pants. It was originally, and if he were being honest with himself, he craved getting her back in his bed, but he was really interested in the woman behind the mask.

He placed a business card on her desk. "There's my number. I can be patient."

He was disappointed she let him leave without saying a word, but he didn't want to intrude too long. Maybe he truly wasn't meant to be with her. Maybe God figured he'd be in way over his head if he forced her hand and this was His way of protecting her.

He'd given her his best effort, made it perfectly clear her home-life and any obstacles with her son weren't enough to deter him. If that wasn't enough for her to give him a chance, then maybe it was time to— His phone buzzed.

WHERE WE MET. 7:00. No promises.

A GRIN slowly took shape as he read her words. Finally, some headway. His chest lifted as relief set in. The doors to the elevator closed silently. Pocketing his phone, he smiled at the small victory and threw his fist into the air. *"Yes!"* He traveled to the ground floor doing a touch down dance the entire way. As the doors parted, his professional façade fell seamlessly back into place.

The rest of the day passed in a blur of work he sincerely hoped he did well, because all he could think about was seeing Becca again, just the two of them.

Braydon waited inside the bar, at the same table where they'd first met, and sipped his beer. At seven o'clock on the dot, Becca wandered in, her posture protective and hesitant.

His body reacted to her presence immediately. His stomach tightened with excitement as his vision widened at the stunning image she created. Slowly, she approached, and he sensed her nervousness. Her soft fragrance sank into him, filled his senses, infiltrated his brain, and twisted his body like a crank. He was literally in knots over this woman.

"Hi," she whispered, her gaze darting to the floor.

He stood and pulled out a chair for her. "Hi. Thanks for meeting me."

She lowered into the seat and looked around. She obviously needed a drink.

"Can I get you something from the bar?"

"Um, a glass of white wine would be nice."

"Be right back." He went to the bar and returned a minute later with her glass of wine. Waiting for a waitress meant possible interruptions later and he wanted Becca all to himself. This might be his only shot at convincing her he wasn't the enemy.

Her delicate hand took the glass, holding the stem between her petite fingers as she sipped. Her nails were short and clipped neatly. No polish. Odd, but that little detail did things to him. His mind pictured them tracing over his skin, but at the same time he attributed this telltale trait as a testament to her competence as a hands-on mother.

The glass clicked down on the ceramic surface and she patted her palm lightly over the lip of the table. She was still nervous.

"I asked you to meet with me, because I realized some things I didn't originally know."

Her eyes closed as she breathed out a soft breath. "You don't need to explain yourself to me. This is why I tried to keep my distance."

"Becca, I still want to know you. Very much so."

Her lavender eyes flashed up at him, surprise clear on her face. "But I have a child."

He nodded. "I know."

Her mouth tightened. "Having a child's a full time job, Braydon. Having a child like Hunter is like having two jobs. Being a single parent makes three. Add that to my actual job at the agency and I have four. I can't take on another job right now. Dating is work. I just…" Repressed sorrow transformed her face. "I have nothing left for that."

Weariness showed in purple shadows beneath her lashes. Her soft blond hair didn't have the same bounce it did when he'd first met her. Her shoulders hunched slightly and he wanted to pull her close and hold her. When she said she had nothing left, he realized the luxuries she went without were mostly the ones meant to pamper her. "You're tired."

She met his gaze, her chin jutting out slightly with patient endurance. "I'm exhausted. Tired's just my baseline."

"I have no intention of being another job, Becca."

"Everything's a job."

"How often does Kevin take him?"

"Every other weekend and overnight on Wednesdays, but that may change."

"Because Hunter doesn't deal well with shifts in his routine?" Her gaze flicked to him and he smothered a grin. He'd caught her attention. "I did some research. I wanted to better understand your situation. I'm far from an expert, but I sort of get it now."

She shook her head. "No one gets it completely. You can't get it in a visit or from reading an article. Unless you've lived it, you'll never know what it is to be responsible for a child with autistic."

"I believe you."

"All the victories we cherish in life, Hunter will likely never experience, because they aren't triumphs to him. His view of the world's so different from yours or mine or anyone else's. He'll celebrate his own personal joys, because autism's personal. But all the other stuff, making new friends, getting promoted, falling in love ... those things will never matter to him."

"How do you know that?" he asked. "From what I've read there are lots of kids like Hunter that grow up to live independently."

"Because each case is unique and I know my son. He can't be measured on levels. Autism's a spectrum. I don't know the future, but I know my son. He can't tolerate being touched. His shoulder is basically the only place I get to hold him. I know some day he may develop the independence to live on his own, but I'll always worry he'll inadvertently burn down the house—even when he's fifty. And when I'm gone, who's going to worry then?

"Most children his age are riding bikes and playing with friends. Hunter doesn't have friends, because he doesn't understand our way of socializing. He's not interested in socializing. It isn't a choice. He simply doesn't possess the skills. No matter where I take him and what we go through together, he's getting an experience that's nothing like mine. He'll never see our world as we do and all I can do is celebrate the small moments I get a glimpse through a window into his world."

"And what about you, Becca? Do you care about falling in love?"

"I've been in love. The fall nearly killed me. I can't suffer that again."

"Love isn't supposed to hurt."

"Yet it has the ability to beat us down more than any other emotion."

Braydon swallowed. She was really sharing quite a bit. He'd

hoped she would, but pairing her confession with the look of longing and defeated hope in her eyes, was a lot to take in. "Hunter sounds like an amazing kid."

"He is." Her smile was sweet, telling of engrained affection. "Hunter can do things we can't. He can tell you any part of a train, play the piano, not the greatest concertos, but The Rolling Stones without instruction." Her eyes glazed with moisture and her lips trembled as the next words seemed to require some effort. "But he can't hug his mother."

His chest constricted with blighted happiness. Placing his fingers over hers, sensing she could use the physical contact, he squeezed. This incredible woman had gone through life with a son incapable of showing her physical affection and a husband who neglected to provide almost all contact.

His family was so affectionate it was stifling. He had six siblings and every single one of them hugged him every time he returned home. He couldn't imagine not having that easy physical affection he'd always taken for granted. His skin would starve to death.

"I can't imagine what it's like for you, Becca."

She nodded. "That's my life. I've adapted to it. I don't expect others to be so accommodating. They don't have to be. I know he's different, but he isn't my burden. He's my gift. I love him with every ounce of my being. Which is why I won't let just anyone into our life."

"Life's a long time, Becca. Do you plan on going at it alone? That's a lot for one woman."

"Well, I may be one woman, but I've done a hell of a better job than the man intended to be my match."

"Sometimes we choose wrong for ourselves." A familiar concept to him. "I don't need to meet your ex-husband to know he didn't appreciate the good thing he lost."

Her lashes lowered. "No. He didn't appreciate us." She sighed and sat back. "But the thing is, he got the real me. He didn't get me on my way to a meeting or out for drinks with friends. He got the everyday me. She's not fancy. She's not tidy. And she's not interested in stroking some grown man's ego, because she's too busy trying to raise a man, against most odds. And anyone who isn't with her, is only in her way."

There was such quiet strength to this woman it boggled his mind. "*I* want to be with her."

Glancing away, she shook her head slowly. "You don't know what you're saying."

"Explain it to me then."

Her fingers brushed over his cuff link and his chest swelled at the slight contact. Her eyes combed over his tailored suit. "You're a very well dressed man, Braydon. I've seen your home. It's impeccably kept. You even have tiny glass jars for each one of your spices all stacked in a row. My life's messy. My house is hardly ever clean. That's my reality. Glass breaks."

"It's only glass. I'm sturdier than that."

"When Hunter has a meltdown, I take the brunt and it rips me apart. I don't get to lose it at home, though sometimes I want to. He needs Mom to be Mom under all circumstances, come rain or come shine."

"It's understandable that you need an outlet, Becca. And yes, my apartment's immaculate. It's just me and I'm hardly there. I'm an architect, not a neat freak. I grew up in a house of nine. *Nine*, Becca, and not a single one of them is normal. Our home was complete chaos most of the time. Nothing was ever where it belonged, people were always coming and going, and there was never a single peaceful room in the house."

She smiled as if this bit of information amused her. He'd made the mistake of judging her before really knowing the real her and he didn't want her to make the same mistake. The professional he was in the city was very different from the guy he was at home.

"And you know what? I miss the pandemonium. It's lonely as hell here. That's probably why I never hang out at my place. I need the noise. I crave the chaos. You think a messy house and some shouting's going to scare me off? Not a chance. I was bred from a clan of Irish psychos—well, not psychos, but they're all a bit nuts— in a harmless way, of course."

She shifted and her lips firmed like they did whenever she was silently debating with herself. "It's more than shouting."

"I watched videos online. I saw how difficult it can be. I promise not to run scared. Let me in, Becca. Show me how it works. Teach me. And for once, accept the help being offered to you."

Her face tightened and she drew in a deep breath. "Why are you doing this?" she whispered. "There're so many other women out there. Easier women with easier lives."

"I want *you*."

A tear slid past her lashes and fell to disappear somewhere on her lap. "I'm nothing special."

Those quiet words ripped at his heart. "You're everything special. At first, yes, it was all superficial, but now…after everything I've learned about you…I think you're extraordinary. I want it all, Becca. The sexy woman, the tireless mother devoted to her child beyond all else. I want *you*, just as you are, jagged edges and all."

"I think you're running toward false illusions."

"I'm an architect. My job's to envision ideals and build them. Let's build something great together. We have a connection, Becca."

A shallow laugh slipped past her lips. "I can't devote my life to ideals. I exist amongst tangible realities."

"You have to dare to dream."

"I've learned to dread dreaming. I'm better off being content with the simpler gifts in life. Wishing only gets me hurt." Someone needed to shatter the oppressive emptiness filling her.

His hand closed over hers and he gave a small squeeze. "Then let me show you some of the simpler gifts. Don't be afraid to let yourself feel what we share."

She reached in her purse and he thought she was pulling out a tissue. Disappointment and the extreme sense of failure flooded him when she placed a ten on the table. Slipping her hand from his, she stood and he did the same, panicked she was leaving and not ready to let her go. "Becca—"

"My car's out front. You can either drive with me back to my house or follow me there."

"What?"

"If you *really* mean it, Braydon, everything you just said, then you're welcome to come home with me. Hunter won't be back until Monday evening."

His pulse doubled. She was letting him in?

"There's one condition though," she quickly added.

"What?"

She swallowed then faced him, her eyes serious. "If it becomes too much and you can't take it, you tell me. Right away. I don't have time for games. And neither does Hunter."

He stepped close, catching his hands on her hips. His lips pressed to hers—a small gasp of surprise slipping past—and he whispered, "I can take it, but I also promise, I'll always be upfront with you about my feelings."

She twisted out of his hold. "And one more thing."

"You said one condition," he teased.

"I changed my mind. That happens a lot. Get used to it."

He loved when she got fresh with him. "What's the other condition?"

Her face flushed and she seemed to struggle forming the words. "I'm not trying to sound presumptuous or scare you, but…"

Now he was intrigued. "Tell me."

She met his gaze. "No *I love you's.* I can't take it and I have no interest in hearing anything you don't mean. Those words are big and they mean something to me. They mean commitment, longevity, and unconditional acceptance. They aren't to be thrown around."

Braydon had never said he loved another woman aside from those in his family. It shouldn't be a problem. "Agreed."

Her smile was cautious, but eventually it formed. "Shall we?"

He took her hand. "Yes."

CHAPTER 5

*B*ecca turned the key in the lock of her front door as Braydon's luxury sedan pulled in behind her van. Her heart beat erratically in her chest, her disbelieving mind still reeling at the fact that she was brazen enough to invite him. A big part of her assumed he'd get cold feet and bolt.

He'd clearly done his homework. Never expecting to date after her divorce, Braydon was ahead of the game. Somewhere deep in a hidden corner of her mind she'd categorized the difficult steps of dating as a single mom and found it so improbable she never thought on the subject again. Yet, the unformed plan was there. It would start slow, maybe a few dates to see if there was a connection. From there, she'd explain that her child was autistic and watch for any telltale signs of discomfort that meant the man couldn't handle that.

If said man didn't run for the hills, she'd give him the book that got her through the first five years of Hunter's life. If he didn't read it, he didn't have what it would take. If he did, they'd discuss his theories and concerns. She'd share her strategies and theories and once they'd deliberated enough and she felt the man had a grasp of what to expect and an understanding of how she might parent in a pinch, she'd let him meet her son. If that went well, they'd breach the more intimate areas of dating.

Problem was, that was all a fantasy, and a draining one at that. Nothing about her plan was remotely sexy like new relationships probably should be.

She assumed it would never happen so she must have tucked that plan away with the ones labeled, *plan to tour Europe, plan to bring roses to your child's recital, or plan for rambunctious sleepovers with a rowdy houseful of your son's friends.* She had lots of plans that would likely never come to fruition. So she was utterly unprepared for this one to take shape. Adding to her unpreparedness was the fact that they'd already slept together, which landed them in uncharted territory.

Braydon followed her inside the house. Self-consciously, she scanned the mess. Balls were everywhere. The sink was full of dishes from breakfast. Hunter's shoes spilled out of a basket in the hall. The wall had chipped plaster from where there had been an episode last year. Labels and PECS—a common picture exchange communication system—were everywhere.

Her breathing picked up as she worried this was a mistake. "I'm sorry for the mess."

Braydon removed his jacket and hung it on the hooks on the wall. Approaching slowly, he took hers from her shoulders, surprising her and sending shivers down her arms. Kevin never did things like that.

He grinned. "Don't apologize. Does the mess bother you?"

She laughed nervously. "I'm used to it."

"Would you feel better if I helped you tidy up?"

What? Who was this man? "That's okay." How mortifying. The condition of her house was a result of her busy schedule. She wasn't a typically sloppy person. Maybe it bothered him. "Unless it bothers you."

"It doesn't, but you seem self-conscious. I promise I don't mind either way. If you'd like me to help you put away a few things so you can relax, I will. If you just want to ignore it, that's fine too."

Oh, my God. His acceptance managed to expose her in some intangible way. It was comforting that he genuinely didn't seem to care, but on the other hand it embarrassed her. She couldn't leave the house like this.

"Why don't you watch some TV for a bit? I need to change out of my work clothes anyway. Give me a second to do that and at least put a few things together, then we can talk about ordering dinner or something and I'll be less distracted."

He studied her for a moment. "Okay."

She led him to the living room and quickly fixed the pillows tossed all over the floor. Grabbing the remote from the basket on the mantle, she turned and handed it to him. "You sit. Twenty minutes tops. The code for the premium channels is 0626."

"No worries, angel. Go do what you need to do."

"Right."

She rushed up the steps and quickly stripped. When she pulled open her drawer of house clothes she frowned. Nothing she owned was cute. *Darn it!*

Settling on a pair of black yoga pants and a fitted plain white T-shirt, she changed and headed to the bathroom. She smelled fine, but threw on some extra deodorant anyway. After she brushed her teeth, she pulled up her hair and scowled at her reflection. Crap. Not good.

Reaching into her shirt, she hoisted up her breasts and tightened the straps of her bra. That was better. Adding a dab of perfume to her pulse points she looked at her watch. Crap.

Running through the second floor, she scooped up dirty clothes, shoes, toys, and anything else in her path. Stuffing the clothes in the bathroom hamper, she shoved them down and shut the lid. Whisking the shower curtain closed, she grabbed a wipe from the cabinet and quickly scrubbed away all the toothpaste marks in the sink.

She was sweating and grateful she'd added extra deodorant by the time she headed downstairs. Music was playing. It was *Stand* by R.E.M. and it was loud. Her steps slowed as she reached the landing.

All the balls were back in their baskets. The shoes were tidied. She whipped around the corner and looked at the empty couch. Where was Braydon?

R.E.M.'s bouncy sound pumped from the television as she hastily searched for him. When she reached the kitchen she skidded to a stop, her jaw nearly hitting the floor.

Braydon stacked dishes on a towel draped over the counter as he bopped his head to the beat. The counters sparkled and miscellaneous things had been piled on the table.

The song stopped and he shut off the water, dishes done. When he turned and saw her he stilled, a guilty smirk on his face. "I swear it wasn't because it was bothering me. I just wanted you to myself and figured I could have you there sooner if everything was done."

Her chest lifted as she breathed. She'd never wanted to run at a person so much in her life. She wanted to throw herself at him, tackle him to the floor, and maul him with kisses, until they were rolling through the kitchen, naked…and other stuff.

"Are you mad?" he asked.

The music coming from the television started up again. She immediately recognized the song as *No Rain,* by Blind Melon and had visions of a little girl dressed as a bumblebee dancing around. It was one of those strange, upbeat, one hit wonders she'd loved from her youth, but forgotten about. It made her smile. No, he made her smile.

Braydon slowly stepped closer and took her hand. Holding her by the fingers, he tugged until her chest bumped his. "You have a lovely smile, Becca."

Blinking up at him, she searched for words. He sucked in his lower lip and smirked, his shoulders dipped slowly from side to side and he started to dance. The hand at her hip nudged her to move with him.

She laughed, unnerved by his nearness. She hadn't danced with anyone in ages. As the guitar beat picked up his teeth flashed in a brilliant grin. Lifting her fingers high over her head, he pushed her hip, twirling her across the floor. As she spun, she giggled—then of course snorted. He pulled her close and cupped his palm with hers and they danced, right there in the kitchen, like it was the most ordinary thing in the world.

When the song ended Braydon didn't let her go. Their steps slowed as the raspy vocals of 4 Non Blonds sang *What's Up?* Braydon's cheek pressed to her ear as he hummed with the chorus.

Her eyes focused on the slowly revolving objects of her kitchen and she had a moment of certainty. He was really there. Why did she fear letting the happiness sink in? His presence slowly penetrated the guard she'd tried so hard to build around her heart.

The lyrics of the song filled her mind. She connected with them, all of them, crying in bed to get out all the things in her head, wanting to scream from the top of her lungs, continuously trying to get up that great big hill of hope… It was all her and—maybe, just maybe—he understood.

Stepping back, he met her eyes. His fingers trailed from her ear to her lips and his lashes lowered. As he pulled close she caught her breath, but nothing prepared her for the way his lips pressed gently against hers.

The chorus kicked up as the lead singer bellowed. Becca's arms wreathed around his neck and she was scooped off her feet. He carried her up the steps, never taking his lips from hers.

She had no idea how he managed, but he found her room and lowered her to the bed, his body blanketing hers. The kiss deepened and she ran her fingers through his wavy gold curls, arching into him. She denied wanting him for so long, but now the truth was upon them and she surrendered to all the feelings this man provoked inside of her—as scary as that was.

He didn't rush things. He kissed her for days. It was the most enjoyable kiss she'd ever been given. Lost in every draw of breath, every swipe of his talented tongue, her body became so relaxed she couldn't conjure a single thought beyond wanting him.

Her fingers plucked at the buttons of his shirt, her hands tugging at his tie. Braydon sat up and loosened the knot, yanking it over his head and tossing it away so he could kiss her some more.

The touch of his warm palm to her belly startled her, but as he slowly dragged his hand upward her body came alive. Arching into his touch, his palm curled around her breast, his thumb dragging over the tight tip pressing into the lace.

She reached down and hauled up her shirt, breaking the kiss for only a second as she tossed the shirt away. Braydon yanked down the cups of her bra and when his mouth fastened to her needy flesh she cried out.

His tongue curled around her nipple as his lips held her flesh in place. Becca's ponytail had come loose, strands of hair stroking her shoulders, as she moaned and writhed over the covers. Her hands yanked at the last button of his shirt, and once she had it spread wide she became a woman on a mission.

Her legs twisted around his hips, flipping him onto his back and straddling him. He laughed and she grinned, recalling his penchant for letting women take control. Although the idea didn't originally appeal, it was fun to try.

Slowly lowering her mouth to his beautiful chest, she licked his nipple. There had been so much she fantasized about over the passing weeks, no matter how much she tried not to. Never had she imagined actually getting the chance to make those fantasies a reality.

Her hands mapped his body, traced every bulge of muscle, as her hips slowly rocked. Braydon rested his hands at her thighs, flexing his body beneath hers. She reached behind her back and unclasped her bra, sliding it from her arms and throwing it across the room.

Perhaps the greatest turn on was the empathetic earnestness he'd surprised her with tonight. His sweetness and consideration softened her inhibitions in ways she never expected.

His head lifted and he captured her nipple in his mouth. She trembled and moaned as he suckled her flesh, her fingers sliding through his wavy hair. His hand glided to the apex of her thighs and he massaged through her pants. Oh God. She was drenched and going to come at any second. Shades of their first night together.

He groaned as he pulled her other nipple into his mouth, those devious fingers rubbing in exactly the right spot. Her knees tightened around him. "Oh God!"

"That's it, angel. Let me give you what you need. Let me make you feel good."

His thumb concentrated on a sensitive nerve and her body splintered into a million pieces. He sucked her nipple hard as she came right in her panties. When her eyes opened he was watching her, hooded eyes, dark with lust, intent on her every reaction.

Her desire turned wild. "I want you."

"Tell me how you want it," he whispered, voice gravelly and deep.

"How do you—"

"No. I want to know what you like. Tell me. Let me please you, sweet Becca."

Yes, this must be what it was like for him and Miranda. It was amazing to see a man as commanding as Braydon McCullough flip a switch like that. And all the more fascinating, was that his desire to please didn't diminish his appeal in the least.

She bit her lip. No one ever asked what she wanted. She and Kevin had survived the dullest sex life of all time. She didn't know any fancy moves or neat tricks, but she surely wasn't wasting such an opportunity.

She slid off of him. She could try being the boss, though she wasn't sure she'd want the position long-term. Deep down, she knew the greater appeal was to have a kind and assertive man, something Braydon definitely was. "Take off your pants."

As Braydon removed his slacks she slid out of hers. Crap. "I don't have a condom."

"In my wallet."

She shyly scooped up his pants and handed them to him. He removed his wallet and pried loose the condom. Handing it to her, he said, "Put it on me."

She'd never done that either. Carefully, she tore the foil and climbed back on top of him. Her fingers tingled as she lined the circle up with the top of his erection. He lifted his hips upward and she slowly slid the latex over him.

Meeting his gaze, she flashed an accomplished smile. "I never did that before."

"We can do lots of things you never tried before."

What a foreign concept. She'd become so used to simply riding the waves in the wake of her life she'd stopped thinking about her personal desires. "I want you inside of me. Like this."

Braydon reached for her hands, curling his fingers around hers, as she shifted and lifted her body over his. He released her hands and caught her by the hips. "Put me inside of you."

Reaching between their bodies, her fingers coiled around his thick length and guided him to her folds. Lowering herself carefully, she trembled as her body stretched and he filled her. Her eyes rolled back in pleasure once she seated herself. Braydon groaned and his fingers flexed, digging into her hips.

Her mind short-circuited for a few seconds as her shoulders shook, rolling into a full body shiver. Having him inside of her was incredible. She wanted to simply savor him there for a moment before she started to move.

Her hands shifted to his shoulders as she leaned over him. Her hips lifted and slid down with excruciating slowness.

"Does it feel good, angel?"

Her eyes flashed open. "Mmmm. It feels incredible."

His hands slowly slid lower, cupping her rear. Blood rushed to her face. No one ever held her so intimately. "Rub your clit on me, Becca, each time you come down, drag yourself over my body."

She lifted and as she pulled back she felt incredible friction at the top of her sex. "Oh, my God."

His hands squeezed her behind. "That's it. Do it again."

She did and each time a jolt of pleasure shot to her core. Her eyes fell shut, but she continued to peek through her lashes. Braydon's half-mast gaze was trained on her. It was unnerving, but the more she got used to it, it empowered her.

"Do you always give the woman control?" she whispered as she slowly rode him.

His lashes lifted and the side of his mouth quirked. "I never used to, but then I learned how sexy it can be, watching a woman take what she wants. I want you to challenge me, Becca. Use me for everything your body needs. I won't break."

Her fingers dragged over his shoulders. "I'm not really sure I know how to do that."

"It's simple. If you want me to eat your pussy, you say, *Braydon, I need your mouth on me now.*"

Her eyes widened as she drew in a deep breath through her nose. She couldn't possibly say anything like that. Images of Braydon's soft blond hair between her legs filled her mind. She was on sensory overload.

"Would you like me to make you come, angel?"

She stilled. "What?"

"Would you like me to make you come? I could, in a matter of seconds. Or we could let it build slowly and when you say the word, I'll bring you to the sweetest release you've ever experienced in your life."

Being that she'd only ever had orgasms with him, she didn't find his statement hard to believe. Even at her own hand she was never quite able to reach that point of surrender when the mind disconnected from the body long enough to taste total bliss.

His hand left her ass and traveled up her forearm and around her bicep. His palm smoothed over her skin chasing decadent chills over her flesh. Oh, to be touched, she loved it. Fingers traced up the column of her throat and tucked a strand of hair behind her ear. Like a cat, she pressed into his caress.

"Tell me what you need," he whispered.

"I want…to be held. Tight."

His hand slipped to the back of her neck and pulled her down until her mouth met his. He rolled her to her back, wrapped his arms under her waist, and thrust into her. Somehow he withdrew almost completely without ever breaking the press of his hard stomach to hers.

His right arm banded around her middle, lifting her with each stroke, while his other hand caressed her thigh. He dragged his touch up her side, over the inside of her arm, petting back down to her breast. No one had ever been so close to her.

His mouth kissed her jaw and he nudged her chin with his nose. She tilted, allowing him access to her throat, where his breath beat against her pulse. His arms slid beneath her, lifting her, and traveled up between her shoulder blades. Then he was hugging her, holding her, satisfying her, and she never wanted to be let go.

"Jesus, Becca. Being inside you is incredible. I never want to leave."

"You feel incredible too. It's never been like this, never this good." He rotated his hips and touched on something amazing inside of her and she gasped.

"Do you like that?"

Breathing fast she said, "Oh, yes. That's—" He did it again and she moaned. "Braydon!" Again and again, he continued to rub himself deep at that same spot. Her cries carried and collided as the deep pressure built and suddenly shattered.

Her limbs quivered as her body tightened. Her heartbeat reverberated down to her toes. She could feel her pulse everywhere, including where her sex gripped him.

"Mmmm," Braydon moaned, pressing his face into her shoulder. "Did you like that?"

Words danced around in her mind, not a single one of them making sense. Her eyes remained closed as she came back down to earth. His mouth found hers and placed sweet kisses there.

"What about you?" she finally asked, between staggered breaths.

"Not until I'm sure you're satisfied, angel."

"Oh… I think I passed satisfied an hour ago. Please, Braydon…"

He met her gaze and pulled back only to thrust into her hard. By the second thrust he was coming, his cock pulsing deep inside of her. His face was a work of art. His jaw locked, every tendon in his neck taut as his lashes lowered.

His forehead lowered to rest over her breast as he panted. Eventually, he mumbled, "I'm not getting up until you give me your word you won't move a muscle. I want you here when I get back."

She couldn't move if she tried. "I live here."

"Still. I'm not done with you."

She turned his face and kissed his beautiful mouth. "I promise, I'm not going anywhere."

When he slid out of her, she was bereft. She gaped as he sauntered into her bathroom. His body was lean and muscled, an amazing display of male exquisiteness.

He returned a few minutes later and her face heated as he unabashedly gave her a full view of his front. Wow. His abs glistened under a sheen of perspiration. A tiny dewdrop traveled slowly down the deep-set slope of his hip. Dark golden curls nestled around his arousal, which hung heavy between his strong thighs. She'd never seen a man built so well. As much as she was enjoying the show, her hand twitched to cover her own body in the face of such perfection.

He lifted her and she wasn't sure what he was doing until he drew back the covers and climbed in beside her. The moment he pulled her body close to his and covered her with his thigh, she sighed. She loved being held and Braydon apparently had no issue holding her.

CHAPTER 6

*B*raydon awoke to the scent of bacon. Turning in bed, he found the rumpled covers short one beautiful Becca. As his ears adjusted to his surroundings, he picked up traces of her voice, harmonically carrying up the stairs. Well, not harmonically, but she *was* singing.

His body stretched as he brushed the shadow of his jaw with his palm. She was making him breakfast. Didn't that just spell awesome? However, rolling into her softness and greeting the morning with sex would have been nice too, but he was a man of many appetites and knowing she was cooking for him touched him on a personal level.

Jumping out of bed, he went to her bathroom and washed up. He didn't have anything other than the clothes he came in, so he found his wrinkled slacks and slipped into them.

As he snuck downstairs her hummed words became clearer. She was singing the song they'd danced to last night, but no music played in the background.

Creeping into the kitchen, he took a moment to simply watch her bare legs sway and her undulating hips move, as she stood in front of the stove, the rest of her luscious body concealed by a long T-shirt.

He stepped close and wrapped his arms around her from behind and she screamed. Loud. He chuckled and placed a kiss at the side of her neck. "Good morning, angel."

"You scared me." She wiggled in his arms, but didn't try to

escape. "Breakfast will be done in a few minutes. There's coffee on the counter."

He sighed contently, needing a little Becca before he had his coffee. "Did you sleep well?"

"I slept like a rock."

His gaze went to the clock. It was just before eight. Once again he noticed the many labels and signs tacked to the walls. Stepping back, he approached a chart and looked at the pictures. Each laminated image was attached with a strip of Velcro.

"That's for Hunter. It's part of his plan."

"Did you make all these?" He detached a picture of hands being washed.

"They're PECS. It's a picture exchange system. They're pretty universal."

"How does it work?"

Becca removed the last strip of bacon and placed it on a paper towel. "Well, in the beginning he'd just have to touch the image of what he wanted." She carried over a board with a sort of menu on it. There were images of fruit, cereal, beverages, sandwiches, and so on.

The board was divided into quadrants. She pulled off a picture of milk and juice. "I'd give him options and ask him if he wanted milk or juice." As she did this, she took his hand and touched it to each picture as she said what it was. "He'd choose. As he got older he'd have to hand the card to me. The more he learned the more I'd require of him. If he wanted the milk, he'd have to hand it to me and make the *mmm* sound. Eventually, he learned to say the word."

"They should do that with all kids. It seems like a great way to teach speech."

"You have no idea what it's like to have a non-vocal child. It's frustrating for everyone, but mostly for the child. Communication's so important and I'm very lucky Hunter speaks now. Sometimes he struggles to find his words," she said quietly as if to herself.

"Do you ever wonder if they just have too much going on, too many words to choose from?"

She smiled, but the expression seemed sad. "Their entire existence is sensory overload. Sometimes they need the sensory, but sometimes it hurts. Many children with autism don't develop speech until after age three, but that doesn't necessarily affect their intelligence. Sometimes the world just isn't concrete enough for them. Albert Einstein didn't talk until after he was three. He was dyslexic, but nowadays he'd definitely be considered on the spectrum." She grinned. "He was a pretty smart guy."

Braydon eyes softened as he turned to her. "Yeah. He did all right."

They sat at the table and made up their plates of pancakes and bacon. He contemplated the bruises he'd seen on her. Hunter was a child, but Becca was small. His eyes caught on the broken chair tucked in the corner and the cracked tile on the wall. "Did it cause a lot of trouble for you when I stopped by a few weeks ago?"

Her eyes moved as though she were thinking. "Actually, no. He isn't used to surprise visitors, but you weren't here long enough to throw off his entire day. We had a snack and then I gave him some down time to stim."

He didn't want to use the wrong words and offend her. "That's self-stimulating, right?"

She nodded as she took a bite. "Yeah. It's important he not get carried away. I try to limit it at the breakfast table and when he should be focused on a task. It takes constant prompting and redirecting, but sometimes he needs to let off steam. I usually give him at least an hour to get it all out. He'll pace and flap and jump and when he's done he seems more centered."

"Why do they do it?"

She shrugged. "Why do people fidget? I mean, sometimes he can't help it, but if I ever want to see him integrated into society on some level, he has to make an effort to control it."

"For the sake of others?"

"Unfortunately, yes. People judge what they don't understand and there's still a lot of ignorance out there regarding autism. Hunter does a lot of flicking by his eyes. That's because his visual sensory's a mess. Light overwhelms him. Where we see a florescent light, he sees the steady stream of strobes coming from the bulb. It's distracting and annoying to him, sort of like what Chinese water torture would be to us."

"Does he wear glasses?"

She shook her head. "His vision seems to be fine, though it's very difficult to get an accurate reading with Hunter. It isn't a vision problem with his eyes. It's a perception issue with his brain. All his sensory endings fire off so rapidly you'll see him flinch his eyes shut over and over again. He can't help it. There's no way to shut it off."

After reading a lot about various children, his curiosity became centered on Becca's. "Is there medicine that helps?"

She groaned. "The drugs out there are endless. The problem is, pharmaceutical companies want to make money. What worked great in the nineties might be generically available now, so they aren't promoting it and doctors are suggesting the next hot thing, which may be crap. No drug comes without side effects. I've read so much on medication. Mostly, Hunter's taken things for anxiety, but I have to be very careful with his dosage. He's only eight. But as far as his sensory issues... No, there really isn't much out there that's worked for him."

"That surprises me, with the numbers what they are."

She sipped her coffee. "Yeah. Maybe someone will invent something someday that actually helps." She laughed. "Whoever it is will probably be on the spectrum. We wouldn't have half the advancement we do today if it wasn't for abstract thinkers. Look at NASA. I bet those scientists are loaded with Asperger's tendencies. People see them for the innovators they are and suddenly their social awkwardness becomes excusable."

He loved her way of thinking and she was probably right. He'd read about savants and professors, artists, authors, and even Pulitzer Prize winners all touched with ASD. "Maybe someday people will recognize the advantages as much as the challenges."

Such passion showed in her eyes as she smiled. "For some reason, our society puts too much emphasis on socialization and behavior. They're more concerned with a kid distracting others by flapping and shouting than they are with the actual functions of the brain. I guarantee you, if they found a way to quiet autism the research would decline, sadly. It's incredibly frustrating, as a mother, to have a son who can do things most 'intelligent' people can't, yet get castigated for not always walking in a straight line or sitting quietly."

"Do people make fun of him?" he asked quietly.

Her expression was pained but accepting. "We're taught to be compassionate. It's expected in this day and age. But parents don't always teach their children early enough. People stare. I ignore the looks and try not to hear the comments, but sometimes it's hard. At this point, Hunter isn't really bothered by other's opinions, but over time that'll change. Eventually he'll know he's different and he won't be able to choose to be the same like most adolescents. He has feelings just like every boy. Maybe sheltering him isn't the right thing to do, but it protects him. We do go out, but probably not as often as we should."

"He sounds like a sweet kid."

Pride sparked in her eyes. "He is. I cry a lot, but I also laugh. You have to when this is your reality."

They'd finished eating and Becca looked tired from talking. "What would you like to do today?"

She seemed startled by the question. "I don't know. I assumed you'd have things to do."

"I do. I have a beautiful woman to entertain. I don't think anyone's done anything for her in quite some time, so it's really important that I get started on that."

Her cheeks flushed and she lowered her lashes. "You don't have to—"

He took her hand. "I want to. Tell me something you'd like to do. Something you haven't done in a long time."

It wasn't a complicated question, but she seemed to really struggle with the answer. "I miss...all of it." Her shoulders slumped. "There's so much I miss. I miss grabbing a cup of coffee or a bite to eat simply because someone invites me along. I miss peace and quiet, moving at a slow pace, having a chance to breathe it all in. I miss...my health."

Jesus. It became imperative to improve her outlook, which, strangely, excited him and made him fondly recall the simple things life often got in the way of. "Let's get dressed and go out. We'll take a quiet walk, maybe see a movie, and when that's done, we'll grab a bite to eat."

Her expression became contemplative. "It's so strange not having him here. I have this constant paranoia I'm forgetting something."

"Maybe this is good. Everyone needs a break from their day to day life now and then."

"It probably is, but it doesn't feel that way. I know our custody arrangement's wearing on Hunter, all this switching back and forth. I just wish he could tell me if it's unpleasant or excruciating. I can't seem to shut off the worry, even when I know he's with his dad."

The amount of stress she coped with on a minute-to-minute basis was immeasurable. Her love for her child was apparent, her worry beyond that of a typical parent's concerns. A walk wasn't the solution, but it was a start.

"Come on. Let's get dressed. I need to stop by my place to grab clothes and then we'll go have a relaxing day together."

Becca showered and he cleaned up from breakfast, lost in thought about what she'd shared. When they reached his place he bathed and quickly threw on jeans and a T-shirt. "What's O'Malley's pub?" she asked, reading his shirt.

"My family's bar back home."

"Where's home?"

"Center County. About three hours east of here."

"Do you miss it or do you prefer the city?"

Her curiosity triggered a sense of happiness inside of him. He liked talking to her about the personal stuff most conversations grazed over. It was…intimate. "I miss my family. I'd like to someday be able to run my own company, bid out jobs and travel site to site, but I need to get a bit more experience under my belt first. Relocating's a definite possibility though."

"Oh." Disappointment flashed in her eyes, but she quickly covered it. "This Apricot deal should help your portfolio."

"Definitely. I'm the frontrunner on the project. If all goes well, I may be able to break away from Bradford Corp in a year or two." Being away from his relatives was torture.

"Will you go back to Center County?"

He shrugged, not wanting to add another check in the complication column of their relationship. He wasn't in a rush, but returning home was definitely in the plan. "I guess it all depends on where I am at that point. Hard to say."

They drove to the park and Becca's expression turned serene the moment they set foot on the path. "This is nice."

It was. Fleecy clouds coated the autumn sky, giving the changing trees a picturesque backdrop. "Do you ever bring Hunter here?"

"Sometimes, but only when I have someone else with me. He runs and I can't always do it by myself. Most days we play in the yard because it's safe and contained. I never get to stroll like this. It's funny, I almost forgot all the pretty sounds of nature. I'm usually too distracted to pay attention."

He slid his hand into hers and interlaced their fingers. They walked in silence, pointing out various hidden glimpses of wildlife among the clustered trees. Squirrels chased one another over fallen leaves. Birds chirped and pecked in the saplings. It was a lovely day, but none of the beautiful sights topped Becca's expression.

"So you like The Stones?"

"I *love* The Stones."

"They're all right," he teased.

She swatted his arm. "All right? Aside from The Beatles they're one of the most influential bands in music history and it just so happens my son was born on Mick Jagger's birthday."

"No kidding?"

"It's true. Got him out in the last few minutes."

He laughed. "That's a dedicated fan."

"That I am."

"Do you like being a mom?"

She took a moment to answer. "Yes. I think I'm good at it. Some people say it's a thankless job, but I think it's one of the most rewarding jobs there is."

"When did you know Hunter was different?"

"I had my instincts. A mother's very attuned to her child's development. But I wasn't certain we were dealing with something big until he was over a year. Hunter didn't make eye contact the way other babies his age did. I had his hearing tested, because he wouldn't always look when I called his name. His hearing was fine."

"My nephew, Lachlan, wears a hearing aid—something about when he was in the womb with his twin, Declan. I remember my brother getting scared when they went through all the tests."

She nodded with understanding. "Having your child tested is always scary. But when you know something isn't right, you have to be courageous. The hardest thing was the cuddling. Hunter's never responded to physical contact the way other children usually do. When I touch him, it's either for therapeutic pressure or because he needs direction. My son doesn't need to be held." Her lashes flickered and her mouth tightened. "That's hard, because sometimes a mother really needs to just hold her child."

He stilled on the trail and faced her. Those violet blue eyes blinked in question. He didn't want to explain his motive, only wanted to give her something she'd been missing.

Reaching for her shoulders, he pulled her into the shelter of his body and wrapped his arms around her frame, hugging her tight. She stiffened, then sighed and melted into his hold. McCulloughs were great huggers and his angel was starved for contact. It was a win-win, because even platonic contact with Becca was special.

They stood there for a long time, simply hugging, his arms holding her tight. When they finally started walking again, he kept his fingers entwined with hers. He was an affectionate person and her need for contact suited him well.

"Does he get upset when someone touches him?"

She took a deep breath and seemed to collect herself. "It depends. Pressure helps calm him, so there are varying ways he'll tolerate touch. When he has a meltdown, I sometimes have to put him on his beanbag chair and lay on top of him with another beanbag. He favors that sort of deep pressure. Cloth swings help too. But he hates soft touches. It's too much for his skin to tolerate. A lot of his learning requires hand over hand direction." She gripped his forearm. "I'll hold him here, use my fingers to turn his chin, and sometimes place a hand on his shoulder to let him know I'm waiting."

The more she opened up the more he became interested. There was nothing simplistic about this woman, yet simplicity seemed to be the goal she strived for in everyday life. With every detail she shared, it became imperative he not complicate her life. It would, indeed, be strange to go into a relationship trying to avoid the sought after excitement most people craved, but the slow, compatible pace they'd adopted surprisingly suited him more than he'd expected.

~

AFTER THEIR MORNING at the park, they visited the Cineplex. "What kind of movies do you like?" he asked.

"Something easy. Nothing violent or too intense."

They settled on a chick flick, which Braydon actually enjoyed for the most part. The movie itself was cheesy as hell, but the scent of her hair, the nervous way she squirmed each time their fingers brushed together over the popcorn, the way her features became animated as she watched the screen, that was truly entertaining.

After they left the theater he suffered that strange confusion one gets when exiting a matinée and realizing it's still fairly early in the day. "Are you hungry?"

They visited a small café with outdoor seating. "I never go to places like this anymore," she said after the waiter took their order.

"How come?"

She shrugged. "It gets old, the people giving us the stink eye, because we're disturbing their meal. I try to limit our outings to places that are more accepting of kids like Hunter. It isn't about *my* sensitivities. It's about trying to find safe and supportive settings for my son."

"Tell me about a time it was hard for you."

She sighed, her head tipping back in thought. "A few years ago I was grocery shopping. Hunter was around four, an age kids still have tantrums. Well, he'd had a big one and a crowd gathered." Her mouth tightened. "I could hear them, you know? Commenting about my parenting skills, saying my kid needed a spanking. He began hitting himself and a man said something about me needing to control my child. I sort of lost it."

"What did you do?"

She stifled a laugh. "I think I said something along the lines of *when you're done staring at my son, maybe we can work on* your *social skills!* Then I called him a jackass and gave him a lecture on autism. He abandoned his shopping cart and left the store."

"Wow."

"Not my proudest moment." She smiled sadly. "You love your child more than anyone else in this world ever will. When kids are bullied or made fun of, it hurts the parent in a way I can't describe. I just want to protect him because he's not capable of defending himself, but he's capable of crying tears as real as any other child. He's very smart and his hearing's just fine. Sometimes people are just cruel."

It was becoming quite clear that autism wasn't something Becca coped with. It was her life. It was difficult to imagine something powerful enough to completely alter a person's existence. That was autism. He had nieces and nephews. He knew parenting was a selfless job, but this was somehow different. His siblings shared themselves with their children. Becca, on the other hand, surrendered herself to be exactly what her child needed.

He was learning so much, but worried his curiosity might be irritating her. "Do you get tired of the questions?"

She tilted her head. "What do you mean?"

"I mean, when people ask—like I'm doing—does their ignorance become annoying?"

"I was uninformed once too. When Hunter was born he was just like every other baby, but special because he was mine. I was like every other mom. I breathed in his hair and dreamed of everything he'd someday become. Then I realized how different our lives were and I had to be the one asking questions for a while. The thing is, no child's alike. I don't mind the questions when they're asked respectfully. It's the assumptions I hate."

Even though he had yet to spend time with Hunter, a protective wave ran through him. Hunter was an extension of Becca and he had the urge to protect him as much as her. "What do people assume?"

"That every child with autism will someday be Rain Man. Hunter's gifted in some ways, but he's not a savant. His ability to play the piano is more of a compulsion. He's good at math, but doesn't necessarily relish it. His IQ's actually right in the middle. But worse than the assumptions of giftedness are the misinformed comments rude people make. It's never easy to hear someone snidely refer to your son with a label that's become nothing more than a derogatory slur."

He never used words like that, but he'd certainly heard them spoken, always in a vulgar manner, toward anyone slightly differ-ent. Perhaps this was one of the reasons Becca censored foul language altogether, because she was never sure when such terms would be carelessly thrown out. He hoped no one ever said anything like that in his presence. Discussing Hunter was delicate, so he steered the subject in an easier direction for a while. "Tell me something about you, now."

That quick, her expression changed, excitement mingled with curiosity illuminating her eyes. "What do you want to know?"

"What's your favorite song?"

"Oh, that's a tough one. I love music, that's probably where Hunter gets it from. However, I can't sing or play an instrument to save my life."

He chuckled. "I heard a little of that singing this morning."

She blushed and one of those cute snorting giggles slipped out. "So you know."

"And you can't pick a Rolling Stones' song."

"Why?"

He shrugged with feigned regret. "It's the rules."

"Your rules stink."

He shook his head. "Rules are rules."

"I don't know if I have a favorite song."

"Fine. What's your favorite food?"

"Sweets. I love chocolate, especially pastries and cakes. What's your favorite food and song?"

He thought for a minute. "I basically love anything my mum

cooks." He paused as her face lit with an adorable smile as though she had a secret. "What?"

"You call your mom *mum?*"

His skin heated. "Yeah. I'm sort of a momma's boy. She spoils me rotten and I let her."

"So what does your *mum* cook?" Her mouth pinched with a teasing smile.

"Doesn't matter. It's all good. Nothin' like Mum's home cooking."

"And your favorite song?"

"I'm a big fan of Coldplay so probably something by them."

"I like Coldplay."

"We still need to figure out your favorite song."

"I'll let you know when it comes to me."

As it turned out, he and Becca had a lot in common. They enjoyed the same actors, liked a lot of the same music, both desired to see the world despite their lack of time for travel, and agreed there was something particularly nice about quiet rainy days.

After lunch Becca seemed tired. "Do you want to come to my place?" Braydon offered.

"Sure. But I have to call Kevin and check on Hunter."

When they reached his place, she went to his office to call her ex. He was curious about their relationship, but tried to give her privacy. When she emerged from the back room she looked flustered.

Unsure if he should form a stance on the ex, he tried not to let the other man's presence in Becca's life annoy him. The guy did him a favor, not appreciating the woman he had. Unfortunately, that also hurt the woman Bray now cared very much about, which made him dislike the guy on principle. "Everything all right?"

She sighed and sat on the couch. "Yeah. Kevin said he's fine, but I could tell by Hunter's voice he's having a rough day. It's really hard not being in control."

He put his arm around her shoulders and pulled her close. "Anything I can do to help you relax?"

She laughed. "Believe it or not, this has been one of the most relaxing days I've had in years."

It was amazing how much her words flattered him. He hadn't done anything extraordinary, but perhaps that was what made spending time with her so special. Becca was complicated, but also appreciated the simple pleasures in life. She was easy to spoil in a manner of speaking and he was really becoming addicted to indulging her. "Well, why don't you let me make it a little better? Lie back."

He eased her back on the couch so she was taking up the length of it. His fingers unsnapped her jeans and he watched her as he slowly lowered the zipper, her mouth quirking with a sweet smile.

Carefully, he removed her sneakers and socks and proceeded to massage her dainty little toes. She hummed happily as he worked the arches of her feet and even kicked him playfully when he pretended her shoes smelled.

"I'm only teasing. Your feet smell like roses." He rolled his eyes and fanned his nose.

"Jerk." She laughed.

Catching her foot, he proceeded to massage her—and tickle her —and massage her some more. Working up her legs, he pulled away her pants and panties. Her thighs touched, showing the soft patch of blond curls at the apex. Braydon ran his hands from her ankles to her knees, kneading gently. "Open for me, angel."

Her face flushed as she allowed him to gently pry apart her legs. Soft ivory skin greeted him. Carefully, he lifted her ankle and draped it over the back of the couch, exposing her. Beautiful.

Her slit parted by the slightest degrees, giving him a view of her glistening pink folds. He leaned over and softly kissed the inside of her thigh. Her skin was so smooth beneath his lips and she smelled incredible.

Placing her other foot on the floor, he eased closer to paradise. His gaze caught her watching him and he grinned. She seemed suspended in a moment of surreal anticipation. He wanted to take that feeling to unmatched ecstasy.

Flattening his tongue, he slowly licked her sex. She sighed and stretched, softly whispering his name. His mouth placed soft kisses over her folds as his fingers slowly parted her. She was beautiful everywhere, but especially here.

"I want to make you feel good, angel. Just relax." He kissed the tiny bud peeking past her folds.

"You are," she whispered breathlessly. "Whatever you're doing feels incredible."

His spine tingled at her approval. Maybe he should be concerned with how much her praise affected him, but he rarely got complaints about his desire to please. There was something so powerful about driving a woman mad with his mouth. It wasn't about being subservient, but being a generous lover. But something about pleasing *this* woman trumped all other experiences.

Twisting his wrist, he slowly slid his longest finger deep inside of her. She moaned, and he wanted to push her limits. "Do you like my fingers inside of you, angel?"

"Yes," she panted as he slowly withdrew and drove the finger back in. She was very wet.

Extending his tongue, he gave her clit a few swipes. "And do you like my tongue on you?"

"Oh, God…"

"Tell me."

"Yes!" Her head was tipped back, hiding her expression, but her hands were gripping the cushions.

"Fast or slow?"

"I…I don't know."

"Yes, you do. Tell me. Don't be afraid to ask for what you want."

She deliberated for a few seconds. "Fast."

His motions immediately picked up speed. His finger plunged in and out of her as his mouth latched onto her swollen clit. She cried out and he slid another finger inside of her slick channel.

She was sexy as hell. Her voice was sweet and breathless and nothing sounded better than his name on her lips. Reaching deep, he found her G-spot and tickled the sensitive tissue. Her cries blurred into one long moan after another as her cream coated his knuckles and she came.

Gradually, he withdrew, kissing and licking away her climax. He wanted to fuck her, but waited to see what she needed. As she caught her breath, he watched the deep flush of her cheeks dissipate.

Her eyes slowly opened. "Wow."

"More?"

"I think I need some time to recuperate. I'm not used to all this." Her gaze traveled over him. "I want to do it to you."

His heart beat with palpitating excitement.

Her eyes turned heavy, her smile a seductive smirk. "I want to make you feel like you make me feel."

His body hardened. "How do you want me?"

"Take off your clothes."

Breath filled his lungs as anticipation pumped through his veins. He rose from the couch and faced her. Crossing his arms at his waist, he stripped off his shirt. Toeing off his shoes, he kicked them aside. His fingers undid the snap of his jeans. Never once did he take his eyes off of her. God, he wanted her. So much so it was dizzying.

His hands pressed his jeans and briefs to the floor and he stepped out. Rising to his full height, he met her stare. Her lips parted as she breathed. "No man should be that pretty."

He grinned. "And no woman should either." He folded his hands at the base of his back and asked again, "How do you want me?"

She smiled. "Every way possible." Her body slithered off the couch and onto the floor. Rising on her knees, she looked up at him. "I haven't done this in a really, really long time."

His hand coasted over her hair and he stared into those spectacular eyes. She slowly reached for him. The press of her fingers curling around his flesh was enough to rock his knees. He breathed through the anticipation and when her mouth touched him he drew in a hissing breath.

She took him slowly, carefully. His eyes rolled shut as he savored every sensation. Her hand stroked the length she couldn't fit in her mouth. When she pressed her lips to the base of his cock he lifted to his toes. "Becca…"

She pulled away and blinked up at him. "I like hearing you too. Tell me how to do it, Braydon. You tell me what you want."

"Take me deep again." She did and he groaned in pleasure. "That's it, angel. Tighten your lips. Nice and slow. God, your mouth's incredible."

She proceeded to suck him, her hand stroking with every motion. When she drew back to catch her breath, her lips were swollen and pink.

"Rub my cock on your lips."

Her mouth parted and she gripped him, stroking slowly, dragging the tip over her lips and leaving them glossy. Fuck. She licked up the underside of his shaft and his entire body shivered. He forced back his climax as she slowly took him deep again.

His force of will battled with his natural reflex to hold off as long as humanly possible. He treasured the build, savored the strength it took to be in control.

She increased her speed and it became almost impossible to hold back. "Becca, I need to come."

She eased back. Her eyes were glazed with lust. "Do you have a condom?"

He nodded. "In the bedroom."

She reached out a hand and he instinctively caught her fingers, helping her stand. Once in the bedroom, she stripped off her shirt. "I want you inside of me, Braydon. So deep I feel you for days."

His mouth crashed to hers, delivering a dizzying kiss. "How do you want it?"

"From behind. Hard."

He opened the drawer and removed a condom. Handing it to her, she tore the foil and slipped it over him. Catching the back of her neck, his lips smashed against hers again. She kissed him fiercely and he loved this feisty side of her. When he ripped his mouth away they were both breathing raggedly. "Get on your hands and knees."

She climbed onto the bed and his eyes flared at the sight of her perfect ass. He dragged her hips back until she was kneeling on the edge of the mattress. "You're sure you want it hard?"

"Yes. Please. I need it."

And those were the magic words. Braydon stepped close to the bed, his thighs brushing the backs of hers. He lined himself up with her opening and drove in, burying himself to the hilt.

She lunged forward and cried out. "Yes!"

Gripping her hips, he pulled her back and slammed into her. Again and again, his body rocked into hers, shaking the bedsprings, knocking the frame into the wall. The slap of flesh on flesh was only a compliment to their needy cries.

Her body fit his perfectly and he never wanted to leave her heat. He ground his hips into her and her sighs pitched higher. Lunging back, he drilled into her and her muscles locked, her cries mounted, and then he witnessed utter serenity as she surrendered to sweet release.

He slowed and folded his body over hers, holding her tight. Their bodies a sultry kiss of flesh.

His lips played between her shoulders. She was boneless. Brushing his hand down her spine, he rose and thrust into her one last time. His body strained as he finished. Head tipped back, he moaned, "Becca."

It took a long time for him to withdrawal from the sanctuary of her body. All he wanted to do was remain inside of her and curl up under the covers. Unfortunately, that wasn't possible with the condom. Reluctantly, he removed his body from hers and quickly went to tidy up.

After cleaning up he grinned at the soft pile of Becca on his bed.

She looked good there. He scooped her up and tucked her under the covers. Once he crawled in beside her and pulled her close, she turned to face him.

Her palm rested on his chest as she smiled drowsily at him. "You're amazing. Thank you for making me see that."

He wasn't amazing. She was. He kissed her nose. "Sleep over tonight."

"Okay." Her quick agreement told of how far they'd come.

She snuggled into him and he sighed. They had Sunday left and then he'd have to give her space again. He understood how limited her personal time was and could be accommodating. But that didn't mean he wasn't already dreading their goodbye.

BECCA WOKE in the middle of the night, the silence of her surroundings jolting her into alertness. Recalling she was at Braydon's, and Hunter was safe with Kevin, she calmed, but couldn't go back to sleep.

Her mind rolled over the things she needed to do in the oncoming week, breaking off onto random tangents. She lay awake so long the early morning dawn filtered through the curtains, catching on Braydon's strong features.

She didn't require much sleep. Maybe that wasn't true. She loved sleep, but her body, over the course of eight years, had become conditioned to only tolerate it in small doses and she never slept as soundly as she once had. It was as if her mind would never again fully shut off. Sort of like Hunter's, always working, always analyzing.

When Hunter was younger, he'd sometimes go two weeks straight without sleeping more than twenty minutes at a time. Those nights were excruciating. She insisted Kevin install child safety locks on all the doors, but they only worked for a short time. Eventually they upgraded all the doors with hotel grade latch locks bolted high enough that Hunter couldn't reach them.

It only took one incident of her son escaping and running into oncoming traffic to realize how important those locks were. Her life ran on fear, but fear could sometimes become debilitating. Terror was different. The day Hunter ran into traffic her body snapped into motion so fast, she'd never suffered such panic in her life. It was jolting and powerful and utterly horrifying. Thank God

Hunter now had a general understanding of boundaries, but most days she still locked the doors.

"You awake?"

She turned and found Braydon watching her. "I couldn't sleep."

His hand traced over her belly and found her breast. She was still adjusting to being touched in such a way, but she liked it. She liked it very, very much.

"Tell me about your family," she said, wanting to redirect her thoughts from worrying subjects.

He drew in a breath and kissed her shoulder. "What do you want to know?"

"You said you have, like, ten brothers and sisters, right?"

He laughed. "No. There are nine of us. I have six siblings. I make seven. My parents make nine total."

"That's a lot. Are you the oldest?"

"No. I'm one of the younger ones. Sheilagh's the baby. She's in her late twenties now. Then comes my brother Kelly. Then me. After me are my brothers, Luke and Finn. They're twins. Colin's the oldest brother and then there's my sister Kate."

Recalling what he'd told her about his nephew with the hearing aid, she surmised, "Twins must run in your family."

"Finn's a twin and has twins, but that's it. I have eleven nieces and nephews and may be getting another one real soon."

"Wow. Do they all live close?"

"They all live on the same property."

She frowned imagining some sort of compound. "What?"

"My family owns a lot of acreage. It's a mountain—literally. Luke's place is right behind my parents', but the rest of them are pretty spread out. We all own a part of the mountain."

This made her smile. It sounded like something from a sweet sitcom. "McCullough Mountain."

"Yeah," he agreed softly, his hand still massaging her breast, the sensations both comforting and arousing. No one ever touched her with such a sense of possession. She loved it.

"What about your family?"

She sighed. "My mom passed away when Hunter was eight months old. She never realized he was different. Sometimes I wished she did and sometimes I'm glad she saw him just as a grandmother should see their first grandbaby. Perfect. I never knew my father. He died in a mining accident two weeks before I was born. I was premature and my mother believed his death pushed her into early labor."

"You don't have any siblings?"

"No. The closest I have to sisters are Nikki and Carla."

"Carla?"

"Nikki's sister."

His brow arched. "She's a little scary, that one."

She laughed. "Yeah, she can be intimidating, but she's one of the biggest hearted people I know. So long as you don't get on her bad side. And if you think she's crazy, you should meet Carla."

He grinned. "Tell me something that makes you happy."

She thought for a minute. "I love Christmas. I love carols and seeing the stores decorated. We don't do a lot for Christmas anymore. I miss it."

"How come?"

"It's time consuming. I put up a little tree every year and usually do holiday crafts with Hunter, but it's nothing like I used to do."

"Then that's not really a happy thing."

"It's a happy memory."

"Give me another one. What's your happiest memory?"

"Boy, I don't know. What's yours?"

He thought for a moment. "Last year my brother Luke was in a coma. Seeing him wake up was pretty incredible. I don't think anything ever made me as happy as seeing his eyes finally open."

Her heart dropped into her toes. It would be horrifying to see someone she loved in such an unpredictable state. "What happened to him?"

He shook his head. "Another time. I don't like talking about it. I only think about the recovery and the moment we knew he was coming back to us. Tell me one of your happiest memories."

It took longer than it probably should've to come up with something. When a memory occurred to her she smiled, knowing it was definitely one of the greatest days of her life. "I got one. I'll never forget the first time Hunter called me Mom. He was six. I was sitting on the floor, doing a puzzle with him and he smacked my hand and said, *'Go, Mom.'* I started to cry. I waited so long to hear him talk. I never thought words like that would ever come. I'll never forget that day."

"That's a beautiful story."

"There are lots of them. The first time he sat through a meal instead of running around the table, the day we finally gave up diapers. I guess every parent goes through milestones like this, but when you're unsure if you'll ever reach them, crossing the finish seems a bit more meaningful."

"Tell me a happy moment from before you were married."

"That's a little harder."

"Why?"

"I forget who I was. The way I used to think, it's a foreign concept to me now. I was an ordinary kid, I guess. I got excited over ordinary things. But now, the things that excite me most are the little things, because, in a quiet sort of way, my life's pretty extraordinary."

"Will you ever have more kids?"

Her mind shut down. Too many memories of fights and ragged tears.

"Sorry. Too personal?"

Lowering her gaze she shook her head. "I don't know the answer. Hunter's incredible, even if he challenges me. I'd do it all over again, because he's my son and I can't live without him. But I don't know if I have the strength for another child. Even a neurotypical child needs a ton of attention. I'm lucky if I have time to brush my hair on an average day. It isn't fair to take on more than I can handle. Not to me, not to Hunter, and not to any child."

He kissed her nose, but made no comment. She was too afraid to ask if he wanted children. The idea that they might want different things in the long run was very unwelcome and she shouldn't be thinking in terms of longevity with Braydon.

"Tell me what you fear?"

Simple questions sometimes carried the hardest answers. "Death," she whispered. "I have to live forever. Who will take care of him when I'm gone? Even his father can't do what I do. Dying, and leaving my son alone in a world that isn't ready for him is the greatest fear I've ever known."

He nudged her chin, tipping her face back in his direction. Those deep blue eyes studied her. "Can I meet him?"

Breath stilled in her lungs. "Do you want to?"

"I'd love too."

Her heart swelled, but she still harbored reservations. "Maybe someday soon." It was too great of a promise to make a definite commitment, but part of her really wanted him to meet her son, to see how incredible he was.

They lazed in bed until late afternoon. Braydon was a big fan of napping and that suited her just fine. They ordered takeout and when Braydon returned with the food he also picked up a box of fudge for her. She was coming to realize that Braydon enjoyed doting on women. Such behavior couldn't be specific to her. It had to be a part of his nature.

After dinner they made love on the floor of the dining room. It had started out as innocent fudge eating, but things quickly turned dirty. The next thing she knew, Braydon was on top of her, feeding her chocolate, and her breasts were smeared with sugary kisses.

Afterward they shared a shower, which was another escapade in the sex department that was new to her. She couldn't recall ever laughing so much. Braydon made her happy and, in a way, that worried her.

While he said all the right words, it was easy to pretend compassion and acceptance. Living up to such claims would be more challenging, especially when those virtues would be an ongoing requirement. Fear that he wouldn't be able to manage her reality had her shying away from the idea of submerging him in her everyday world. If Braydon couldn't tolerate the actuality of her day-to-day life, she'd have to let him go. She was her son's future and they were a package deal.

As she gathered the last of her things, Braydon waited by the door with her coat. "I don't want you to go," he said, helping her on with her jacket and pulling her hair from the collar. His lips pressed a kiss to her neck, sending chills skating over her skin.

"I don't want to go either, but I need to get ready for work and I still need to grab a few things from the store for the week."

"Can we do lunch tomorrow?"

Were they moving too fast? "Let me see how my morning goes. Email me and I'll let you know."

He kissed her goodbye and walked her to a cab. "I could drive you home."

She wished he'd mentioned that earlier, but now the idea of going through another goodbye was too painful. He'd given her the perfect weekend. It was sad to see it end, but she'd cherish the memory of it always.

"That's okay. This is easier."

He pressed his lips to hers and he whispered, "I'll miss you."

Her heart fluttered unbelievably fast. They were crossing into dangerous territory. She pulled away, afraid she might blurt something completely emotional and inappropriate. "I'll talk to you soon."

Nodding, he took a step back and she slid inside the taxi. Turning back to him, she called, "Braydon?"

"Yeah."

"Thank you. You gave me another happy memory to hold on to."

He smiled. "There'll be more. I'm not done with you yet, angel."

Yet. Her smile trembled. "Bye."

CHAPTER 7

It was utterly ridiculous how much Braydon looked forward to seeing Becca the following day. When noon approached and she still hadn't emailed, he began to worry. At twelve-fifteen he sent her a brief *"Everything okay?"* email.

By one he'd ventured out to find his own lunch, debating popping in on her with something chocolaty, but refraining. What if she had a change of heart?

When he returned to his office the stirrings of a headache started. Frustrated at his empty inbox, he checked his phone. It buzzed the second he fished it out of his pocket, but his relief was short-lived. The screen read *Devil.*

"What's up, Shei-Devil?"

His little sister chuckled. "That's Shei-Devereux to all of you, now. What's happening in The Burgh?"

Bray sat back in his chair and sighed. "Nothing much. I was just waiting for a call and thought you were it. What's new with you?"

"I'm painting and I got bored."

"Painting what?"

"Our living room. Alec has some obsession with a funeral home's color palette and I can't take it anymore."

"Oh, boy. What color are you painting that poor man's house?"

"*Our* house. And it's chartreuse."

Braydon laughed quietly. Chartreuse was a trendy green with some of his clients. It sometimes worked well with dark, cherry finishes, but it would definitely be an adjustment for Alec. "Does he know that's the color you picked?"

She scoffed. "He doesn't care as long as I'm happy. Besides, it's keeping me out of his hair. He's been so damn busy now that he's head of the philosophy department."

"Shouldn't you be busy with your own classes?"

"You'd think, but I finished my syllabuses last week. I'm going out of my freaking mind."

"They really should give you more classes."

"I know." She sighed. "I'll be graduating in less than a year and going for my Masters. Let's hope that's a bit more time consuming."

"What if you're pregnant by then?" She got quiet. "Sheilagh?"

"Yeah?"

Worry tightened his brow. "You okay?"

There was a slight sniffle she covered with a cough. "It didn't take."

Shit. Alec was older than his sister and he'd already had a vasectomy when they'd met. The reversal, from what he understood, was no easy procedure, but Alec wanted to give her babies. "I thought the odds were something like ninety percent."

"That's if it's reversed within the first few years. Once ten years pass, it drops to thirty percent. Alec had his boys tied off almost twenty years ago."

"I'm sorry, Sheilagh. Are you sure it's totally out of the question?"

She made a noncommittal sound. "I'm not God, but I need to accept that it probably isn't happening if it hasn't happened by now, or else I'll drive myself crazy and drive my husband away."

"That's not true. Alec adores all of your personalities. But seriously, are you okay?" She'd been through a lot of ups and downs with clinical depression. It wasn't always easy to tell what his sister had going on in that big brain of hers.

"I'm gonna have to be. I mean, I'm happy. I don't need a baby. Lord knows what kind of mother I'd be with this gene pool."

"You'd be a great mother, Shei."

She was quiet for a moment. "Thanks, Bray. That means a lot." She sighed then groaned. "Maybe I'll be weird cat lady, married to the professor, anti-social by choice, and profoundly intelligent in a mysterious way."

"So you're buying a cat? You have all that other junk going for you already."

"Shut up." She grumbled and it sounded like she was plopping into a chair. "I want to go home, but I'm afraid all the babies will make me nuts. Did you hear Luke and Tristan are trying to adopt?"

"Yeah. That's an option for you guys too."

"No."

"Why *no?*"

"I don't know how to explain it. I'm a McCullough woman. I'm made to breed. I'm okay with not having a child if it wasn't meant to be—sort of—but what kills me is that I'll never know what it feels like to create life. Do you have any idea how cool it would be to have the ability to grow a human and I can't because…" She growled. "Never mind. I sound like an asshole."

"No, you don't. You sound like a woman who's being denied something God gave you and you're upset. It's understandable, Shei."

"Blah. I'm done whining. What's going on with you?"

He grinned. "I met someone."

"Yeah? Who? When? Give me all the dirty details."

"Well, we met about a month ago, but it took me a while to pin her down. I think I finally got through to her though."

"What's her name?"

"Becca."

"Becca. Becca McCullough. That has a nice ring to it."

"Whoa…slow down. No one's getting married."

She snorted. "Who are you kidding? You've been looking for the perfect bride since you hit puberty."

"It's complicated."

"Why?"

"She just got divorced."

"Ahhhh. Any kids? Ooh! When do we get to meet her? You should bring her home and Alec and I can come that same weekend."

"Sheilagh, calm yourself. You're making me dizzy. We're just starting out. Besides, it isn't that easy for her to get away. She has a son."

"Aww, we'd both have stepsons!"

"Jesus! Will you chill? No one's getting married! And it isn't like Wes really counts as your step-child."

"Does too. I remind him every day to call me Mom."

He chuckled. Wes was only a year younger than Sheilagh. "He must love that."

"The question is, do you love her?"

"I—" The intercom buzzed. "Hold on, Shei." He clicked the phone on his desk. "Yes, Natalie?"

"Mr. McCullough, there's a package here for you. It was messaged over from the firm handling the Apricot account."

He grinned. "Who's the sender?"

"A Ms. Becca Stevens."

"I'll be right out. Shei, I gotta run."

"She sent you a package? Dirty. I wonder what it is?"

He rolled his eyes. It was probably the finalized contracts. "Goodbye, Devil."

"It's *Devereux!*"

"Love you." He ended the call. Taking a deep breath, he disguised his grin and entered the reception area.

All the secretaries were chattering and quieted the moment he appeared. He cleared his throat and Natalie handed him a small box wrapped with a pale blue bow. His cheeks flushed as he took it. "Is there anything else?"

His secretary smirked as though trying not to laugh. "No, sir."

Returning to his office, he shut the door and heard the group of receptionists burst into a fit of giggles. Nothing like being discreet. Ripping open the package he unwrapped the tissue and stilled. It was one of those PECS things Becca had all over her house. On it was a smiling face with one word written underneath.

Happy.

His heart sped up as he tried to grasp what she was telling him. She was happy. That gave him a sense of accomplishment he couldn't fathom. Unearthing the tissue, he checked for anything else in the box. On the bottom was a note.

Sorry I couldn't do lunch. Swamped. I had a lovely weekend and wanted to say thank you again. Xo Becca

He hadn't realized how much he'd doubted himself until her package came, delivering sweet relief and confidence. He picked up his phone and buzzed Natalie.

"Yes, Mr. McCullough?"

"Natalie, call down to Fritz's and order a fresh tray of double fudge brownies. Have them sent to Ms. Stevens's office with a note that reads…" What could he say? "Ditto."

"Yes, Mr. McCullough."

Five seconds after hanging up he heard the receptionists let out a communal "Aww."

He picked the phone back up and buzzed his secretary again. "Yes, Mr. McCullough?"

"And get back to work."

The following hour passed with the distracting images of Becca moaning over fresh brownies. He'd barely accomplished anything productive aside from fantasizing.

Around closing, Miranda strolled into his office and quietly shut the door. "Want to have dinner tonight?"

As he met her gaze he recognized the suggestive set to her eyes and realized she was offering more than a meal. "No thanks. I have some stuff I need to get done."

She sauntered to one of the chairs across from his desk and sat down, crossing one long leg delicately over the other. "I'd like to see you. What night do you have free?"

This was unexpected. He and Miranda had called it quits a couple months ago. There had been one night they'd spent together after the official break up, but he'd assumed that would be it. Things were different now. He was with Becca.

"You should know I've sort of started seeing someone, Miranda."

Her narrow brow lifted. "Have you? Who is she?"

With he and Miranda's intimate past he could probably trust her not to overreact if she discovered the woman he was dating was also a client. Yet, she was still his boss and something told him to protect Becca's privacy. Miranda might not use the same ethical scale for others as she did for herself.

"No one you know."

"Doesn't sound too serious. How about Wednesday night? I'll wear that black slip you like."

"Sorry, Miranda. I can't."

She pretended to be unaffected, but Bray knew she didn't like being told no, especially from a man she saw as her subordinate.

Leaning forward, she reached into the tiny box Becca had sent and pulled out the picture. Frowning, her eyes drifted to him questioningly. He remained silent and she tipped the box, skimming the note. "Becca? That wouldn't happen to be the same Rebecca handling the Apricot account, would it?"

Easing back in his chair, he steepled his fingers, refusing to buckle under her scrutiny or show any signs of intimidation. As far as ethics went, Miranda had been the one to initiate their affair and she shouldn't throw stones at glass houses. "Why are you so curious, Miranda? We ended our relationship months ago."

Her full lips pulled into a smile that didn't quite reach her eyes. "That must be quite different from what you're used to, Bray. She's quiet as a church mouse. I can't imagine she gives you what you need."

He refused to let her put Becca in a negative light. "She gives me something I never had. You wouldn't understand."

"Try me."

"Let's just say it's different with her."

She laughed. "You like this woman."

"Yes."

"Hmm." She stood. "Well, you have my number. Call me when you realize you want a real woman in your bed again."

His eyes narrowed as she sauntered out of his office. Miranda may have confidence in spades compared to his angel, but suddenly that wasn't so appealing. Not that he thought of Becca as insecure. On the contrary, she was incredibly capable. The appeal was in the quiet, graceful way she applied herself to everything she did.

Becca was gentle and feminine with soft doe eyes and delicate features. Miranda was a python, a vixen, but not someone you toyed with unless prepared to handle her bite. Hopefully she just had an itch and some other guy would come along to scratch it, because he really didn't want to deal with her tampering in his new relationship.

～

"Sylvia!" Nikki waltzed into Becca's office, her voice pitched in true sing-song, the style of Sylvia and Mickey's *Love is Strange*, circa 1956.

Becca looked up from her monitor and rolled her eyes. "Yes, Nikki?"

"How do you call your lover boy?" her crazy boss sang.

Becca snorted. "I don't have a lover boy."

She sashayed into the office, bumping the door closed with her hip. "These brownies beg to differ."

That got Becca's full attention. "Brownies?"

Nikki nodded.

Grinning, Becca dropped her voice deep and said, *"Come'ere, lover boy!"*

Nikki skipped over and dropped the box on her desk. Becca could smell the chocolate fumes through the package, which had been tampered with. She eyed the label emblazoned on the lid. "Fritz's?" Impressive.

"I know, right? You must have really done something good to deserve these."

Becca's face heated. "I see you took the liberty of opening them for me. Thank you."

"You're quite welcome. He also sent a note." The tiny envelope dropped to her desk as she pulled a plump brownie from the box. Dear God, the flaky crispiness to fudgy goo ratio was perfect. Licking away a bit of still warm batter, she scooped up the card—also opened.

Ditto.

She couldn't help it. Her heart went into a round of summersaults.

"What's he dittoing?" Nikki asked as she swiped her own brownie from the box.

"Nothing. I let him know I had a nice weekend and that he made me happy."

"Imagine that," Nikki said over a mouth full of chocolate. "Becca Stevens is happy again."

Her lips pursed, but she couldn't hide her cheerfulness. Holding up a fudge smudged finger and thumb, she confessed, "A little."

Nikki laughed. "Oh, please! You're using every bit of composure you have right now not to scream like a fourth grade girl."

The door crashed opened. "Who's a fourth grade girl?"

Becca's smile bloomed at the sight of Nikki's sister, Carla. "Carla, what are you doing here?"

Carla, who managed the bookkeeping for the firm and mostly worked from home, tromped into the office and plopped in the chair next to her sister. "Turning in the quarterly reports. Why else would I drag my ass outside the house and put on a bra. You know I hate people."

Becca giggled. Carla was her own unique person. She came off grumpy and a bit abrasive, but there was a huge loving heart in there somewhere. "Have a brownie. They're from Fritz's." She slid the box across the desk and Carla lit up.

"Oooh, see, Nikki, this is how one shows proper appreciation for my pleasant services."

"I'll remember that next time Alice does payroll. Sweets are cheaper than currency."

"Shut up," Carla mumbled, as she shoveled a brownie in her mouth and hummed in ecstasy. "Who sent these?"

"Becca's boyfriend."

"Nikki!" She turned to Carla. "I don't have a boyfriend."

"You got *something* if he's sending you treats from Fritz's. Wait… did you have the sex?"

Becca's chest filled with a warm, buttery goodness—not from the brownies. Oh yeah, she'd had the sex. "Maybe."

Carla clapped like an excited chimp. "When? Ohmygod! I can totally see it now. You're all glowie and you have that stupid haze in your eyes girls get after having orgasms. Oh, you had *good* sex. Clearly it wasn't with Kevin—"

"Ew," Nikki chimed in.

"—so spill. I want all the filthy details."

It was impossible to keep all the emotions inside, so Becca spent the next twenty minutes ignoring her work load and gorging herself on the most delicious brownies in Pittsburgh while informing Carla and Nikki all about her weekend.

"…and then we just napped. Napped! Can you believe I found a guy who likes sleep as much as I do?"

"So all the things you've been deprived of—sex, orgasms, sleep, fun—are now coming back into your life. This is outstanding news!" Carla declared.

"I made her talk to him." Nikki grinned smugly, demanding her due.

Becca smiled. "Yes, and I finally forgive you."

"So are you going to introduce him to Hunter?" Carla asked, sobering the mood of the room.

All the warmth in her chest solidified as tension set in. "I don't know. I want them to meet. I think Braydon would be really patient with him. I mean, he's the most patient person I've ever met. I didn't know men like that existed in real life. But I'm…"

"Afraid?" Nikki and Carla asked at the same time.

"Yeah." Becca slid the empty box off her desk and into the trash, hiding all evidence before her sugar coma set in. "I always had these imagined rules for situations like this that I never thought I'd actually have to use."

"Rules are meant to be broken," Nikki sang happily.

"Not where Hunter's concerned," Becca reminded seriously. "I don't want to introduce him to someone who may not be around in a few weeks."

"Did you tell GQ that?"

"Well, no. I don't want to sound presumptuous."

"Yeah, but you have extenuating circumstances. Hunter's a great kid. He deserves to be surrounded by great people—like Nikki and myself. This guy should know greatness is expected of him."

"Carla, I can't tell him he can only meet my son if he promises to stick around. No one can make a commitment like that."

"Well, then he doesn't get to meet Hunter. It depends on what you want more, Becs, him to meet your son or him not to get that involved."

"I don't know what I want yet." That was the truth. It had only been a couple of weeks since she met Braydon, and only one weekend since changing her opinion of him.

"Well, you'll figure it out. Eventually, it'll start getting annoying only being able to see him when Kevin has Hunter—"

"Blah. Kevin. I hate that little testicle," Carla interrupted.

Nikki continued, "—I mean, think how much it'll suck only being able to see him every two weeks and maybe every Wednesday."

"I know. It's so weird, but I already started missing him before I even said goodbye last night. We were supposed to have lunch today."

"Why didn't you?"

"I had to finish up the paperwork from last month's deal."

"Well, at least you get to see him at work," Carla said. "Oh, you guys could have all kinds of secret rendezvous! It'll be like a naughty liaison! Promise you'll fax me a copy of his ass cheeks when you do it on the copier."

"Just wipe down the conference table when you're done," Nikki grumbled.

"I am not having sex at work!" Becca hissed.

"Why the hell not? I do all the time," Carla said.

"You work from home," Becca said dryly.

Carla shrugged.

Nikki turned and gaped at her sister. "Clearly I'm paying you for nothing. And who the hell are you having sex with?"

Blinking with innocence, Carla said, "People."

Nikki frowned. "What people?"

"Electrical people and the men of my fantasies."

Becca snorted and Nikki rolled her eyes. "You need help."

Carla perked up. "Help would be great. Why don't you hire some decent looking men and send them to my office?"

Shaking her head, Nikki stood. "Your office should be in the building with everyone else's."

"No, that won't work. You know I don't play well with others."

The girls eventually staggered out of the office on a sugar high. Becca didn't get another chance to think about the matter of Braydon and Hunter until she was falling into bed that night, too exhausted to make any real, big girl decisions.

THE FOLLOWING day she rushed into work after a trying morning with Hunter and didn't seem to catch her breath until she was cracking open her email.

GOOD MORNING, *angel. Lunch today?*
Ps: You never called last night.
~Bray

GRINNING—DEAR God, she *was* turning into a fourth grader—she punched out a reply.

GOOD MORNING. *I have a meeting at 12:30, so it will have to be a late lunch. How's 2:00? Someplace close to my office, if you don't mind. I have another meeting at 3:00.*
PS: You never asked me to call.
~Your Angel

. . .

HIS REPLY DIDN'T COME for over an hour, during which time Becca displayed some humiliating dependency issues she wasn't aware she possessed, A.K.A. obsessively checking her inbox and pouting when she found it empty. When his reply finally showed, she squeaked with a mortifyingly girly voice she also didn't realize she possessed.

SORRY, Angel, no can do. My afternoon's booked solid. I suppose drinks after work are out. When will I see you again? It's almost embarrassing to miss someone this much.

PS: Of course I told you to call. Did you not hear my subliminal pleas yesterday? I was using Jedi pathways to get your attention.

~Bray

BECCA LAUGHED. He was a dork, just like her, and that was unbelievably refreshing. Her skin tingled as she reread the line about him missing her.

MY HEAD MUST HAVE BEEN TOO fuzzy with chocolate residue to pick up your subliminal signals. I miss you too. (A lot...insert corny smiley face here) I promise I'll call you tonight, because, yes, drinks are out. Sorry. Told you my life was complicated.

~Your Angel

I DON'T MIND COMPLICATED. Just trying to figure my way into the mix. Did you enjoy your brownies?

~Bray

SILLY BOY, I made love to those brownies. It was dirty, sinful, and I was utterly useless afterwards.

~Your chocolate lovin' Angel

HIS REPLY WAS QUICK.

. . .

ANNNNND...NOW I'm hard. I want you.

BECCA FELL BACK in her chair and sighed. How the hell was this happening to her? Things like this didn't happen in her life. Men like Braydon McCullough didn't want her. There had to be something wrong with him she wasn't seeing. He was just too...perfect.

That evening, she didn't have the house shut down until well after nine. Hunter didn't have the best day and it was bath night. She could barely keep her eyes open as she dialed Braydon.

"Hello," he answered and she was reminded of just how delicious his voice was. She was also reminded that most adults had plenty of stamina after—she glanced at the clock—nine-thirty-two. Good grief she was a waif.

"Hey."

"You sound tired. You okay?"

"Tired is an understatement. I'm not even sure if I'm still breathing."

"Bad night?" He sounded so upbeat and energetic. She envied that and couldn't recall the last time she'd outwardly displayed that sort of oomph.

"Normal night. I'm just tired." She sighed, taking vicarious pleasure in his mood.

"Does Hunter like pizza?"

Before she answered she paused, alarm bells going off in her head. She couldn't deal with another pop in, but maybe that wasn't what he was hinting at. Exhaustion was likely making her presumptuous. Still, she answered cautiously, "Yes."

"Well, I was thinking, maybe—if it would help—one night I could come by with a pizza, meet Hunter, and save you some time in the kitchen."

It still shocked her that a single man would push so hard to find a way into her chaotic life. The sincerity seemed impossible, yet he sounded so genuine. She laughed quietly, her face sinking deeper into the pillow. "Where did you come from?"

"Center County."

She hummed happily and mumbled, "Must be a magical place."

"I'm serious."

"I know you are. That's what's so incredible about you. How

would you like to come over tomorrow night after work? Hunter goes to his father's on Wednesdays."

"Can I sleep over?"

"Yes." Her lips tightened with a smile.

"Mmm, then yes. Should I bring the pizza?"

"Yes, please."

"Perfect." Becca was thinking the same thing, only applying the word to him. "Can I pick up anything else? A bottle of wine? Brownies?"

"No more brownies for at least a week. I have no self-control and my pants still don't fit right since the other day."

"I think you eating brownies could be incredibly sexy. Maybe just one."

She groaned and giggled. "You're killing me, Smalls."

"Okay, fine. One pizza, a bottle of wine, and one teeny, tiny brownie."

"Fine."

"I'll let you get some sleep. Sweet dreams, angel."

"Sweet dreams, Braydon."

THE FOLLOWING afternoon Braydon rushed out of work and headed to the liquor store. He'd ordered the pizza from a place near Becca's and planned to pick it up after he swung by Fritz's for her brownie. As he climbed back into his car, his cell rang.

"Hello?"

"What's up, little brother?"

"Well, if it isn't the future father of the year," Braydon said, recognizing Luke's voice.

"Yeah, right. That title will definitely go to my significant other."

"Oh, stop. Congrats by the way. Colin told me you guys are going on a waiting list."

Luke sighed. "Yup, that's what we're best at—waiting. Waiting for Congress, waiting for children. We're getting pretty good at it. Right now we're waiting for the approval so we can wait on the list, but hey…" He could sense his brother's nervous happiness. "We may actually get a son or daughter. There aren't words for how incredible that is."

"You'll get there—on all counts. I have faith. So what's up?"

"Nothin'. Just driving home from work and I realized I hadn't talked to you in a while. Tristan's got the flu so I'm driving stag. Figured I'd give you a call."

"That sucks. Stomach or other?"

"Other. He had a fever this morning and chills—the whole nine yards. He's pretty much quarantined."

"Maybe he's pregnant," Braydon joked.

"Ha. Ha."

Bray smirked at his brother's newfound ability to get his stones broken. The truth was, since last year his brother was a totally new person. He'd softened more than Bray ever thought possible, and of all his siblings, Luke seemed to check on each McCullough the most. It was as though he were making up for lost time.

"Please, I can't get near him the way Mum's doting over him. Thank the Lord she's there, though, because otherwise I'd never be able to feed him."

Braydon laughed. It was nice hearing his brother regard their family with such open affection. It was a refreshing side to Luke they were all still adjusting to.

"She's sort of why I was calling."

Bray's brow tightened with concern. "Mum? Why? Is something wrong?"

"No, nothing's wrong. I just realized next year's their fortieth wedding anniversary. I thought we should plan something special."

His expression lightened and he laughed. "Aww, look at you embracing your sexuality and branching into party planning."

"Blow me. I want everyone to be there. I think we should have a big bash, make it really special. They deserve it."

If anyone deserved it, his parents did. "I'm down. Just tell me when and where."

"Well, when Tristan feels better we'll work out the logistics. Right now we're just giving everyone the heads up. Kate mentioned something about having them renew their vows."

"That would be cool. It's a shame Gramps won't be here to see it."

"Yeah, but it'll be nice for them to make vows with witnesses this time. Italian Mary's already volunteered to make Mum something pretty to wear."

"It's gonna be awesome, Luke. She'll love it. Let me know what you need and I'm there. I gotta run, though. I just pulled up at my next stop."

"All right, bro. Talk to you soon. Love ya."

His chest warmed. There really was no way to describe what it felt like to hear those words from a brother he almost lost. "Love you too, Luke."

He tucked away his phone and headed in to pick up the pizza. He couldn't wait to see Becca, even if that made him frighteningly whipped. She'd been all he'd thought about since Sunday.

When he arrived at Becca's her minivan was in the garage. He grabbed the wine, brownie, and pie and rang the bell. The locks disengaged with multiple snicks and he sucked in a deep breath when he saw her.

She was a vision. Her hair was tied up in a simple ponytail. Her face was scrubbed clean of makeup. A vintage Stones shirt boasting a red, white and blue tongue clung to her curves over a pair of worn cotton pants. His gut tightened. This was dangerous territory, but he chose to ignore all the warning signals he usually heeded, the kind that told him he was assuming too much and moving too fast.

She smiled. "Hi."

"Hi." He leaned over the pizza box and kissed her. He hadn't meant for it to be more than a peck, but she surprised him by jerking him close and turning it into more. The pizza and wine left his hands and landed on some piece of furniture he hadn't noticed as her arms wreathed around him, tugging his shoulders down to her height, and the door slammed.

"I missed you," she whispered against his lips.

Backing her to the wall, he kissed her fully, dragging his hips against her warm thighs as he lifted her. "Mmm, I missed you too."

Her fingers tugged at his tie, loosening it. His jacket was ripped from his shoulders. Barging in and stripping her wasn't part of the plan, but it definitely worked.

Lifting the hem of her shirt, he skimmed it clean off her body. His arms wrapped around her nipped waist and lifted her off the ground. Her legs curled over his hips as his mouth trailed kisses to her bra.

She was incredible. Never in his life had he anticipated a welcome like this. He'd intended on feeding her and seeing if she needed any help around the house. A patch kit sat in his trunk for that hole in the wall, but he didn't want to freak her out by offering to fix things. Now, he couldn't think about anything other than pounding her into the wall.

Her voice hummed over his pulse as she dragged her mouth up

his throat. Apparently, the shyness was fading. "Take off your pants."

His body tightened another degree at her breathy request. Snaking his hand between their bodies, he undid his belt and fly, taking a few seconds to play with her. His cock grew rock hard. "You're wet."

"Only for you."

"Sweet Jesus, woman. Grab my wallet out of my back pocket."

She fished out his wallet and tossed it to the floor after locating the condom. Somehow she managed to tear it open and get it on him in a matter of seconds. He spun her to face the wall and yanked down her cotton pants, hoisting her hips back. When he filled her she cried out his name and he nearly came.

It was fast and it was rough, but that was exactly how they needed it in that moment. He didn't finish until he was certain she'd been satisfied. When it was over, they collapsed on the cold tile floor of the hall and sighed.

Taking a minute to catch his breath he brushed her hair out of her face and whispered, "I brought you a brownie. I'm going to feed it to you then cover your body in chocolate fingerprints and lick them off."

She panted. "It's ridiculous how juvenile you make me feel."

He chuckled. "You make me feel silly too. It's fun. I can't remember the last time a girl made me so nervous and excited."

She snorted. "Please. I'm a hot mess." Her gaze skittered away. "And I really need to dust under that hutch."

"Hot sexy mess." He leaned up and grabbed the pizza box, which was no longer steaming, but still warm. Tearing off two slices, he handed her one. Gracefully, she took her piece and nibbled as she nestled into the curve of his arm. When she shivered he pulled his suit jacket over her belly and kissed her forehead.

They never made it to the brownie or wine. After the pizza, they showered and climbed into bed. As much as Becca denied she was tired, the exhaustion in her eyes was evident. Braydon, however, found it difficult to sleep.

Venturing downstairs, he made a slow tour of her house, straightening things along the way, and quickly sweeping under the hutch in the hall. He didn't want to be intrusive, only help out any way he could.

Becca didn't have typical décor in her home. Rather, her house was a hallowed shelter designed for functionality and safety, as well as what he assumed was purposeful stimulation.

His mind dissected every difference he noted and tried to pinpoint the rationalization behind it. The color scheme of the house didn't seem to flow. One room was purely white, while the next was painted vibrantly, three of four walls done in bright primary colors and the fourth done in a black and white checkered pattern.

The furniture, including the beds, lacked any hard frames or edges. Pillows in various shapes and sizes were stashed in the corners of every room. There were also swings and bolster objects he didn't quite understand.

Cabinetry had been removed and replaced with open shelving. Closets and pantries with remaining doors sported locks. And labels were everywhere.

As he wandered through the house, Braydon came to realize how much Becca had eschewed her own identity for her son. If she had a personal style, it didn't show in her home like most women's.

Venturing back up the stairs, he peeked into Hunter's bedroom. The walls were a very dark shade of blue he typically wouldn't use in a design for a young child's room. The drapes were of the blackout sort and there was a white-noise maker mounted to the dresser. As he dragged his hand over the bedcovers he realized they were heavier than standard blankets. He assumed every element was designed to encourage rest, something Becca and her son both seemed to have difficulty finding.

Not wanting to linger too long where he wasn't invited, Braydon returned to bed and quietly curled around Becca's side.

"Were you snooping?" she whispered, startling him.

He shifted and brushed the hair from her eyes. "No, learning."

"What did you discover?"

"Nothing I didn't already know. You love your son very much. You've created quite the home for him, Becca."

She smiled softly, her cheek pressing into the soft cotton. "It took some time and adjustment, but thank you. Bet you never dated a woman with a swing in her living room."

He laughed. "Not that kind."

"It must not make any sense to you as an architect."

He frowned, hoping she didn't assume he was partial to sterile environments and artistically praised structures. "I can see the sense in a lot of it. Homes are designed for aesthetic purposes and functionality. You've accomplished both."

"I don't know if I'd call it aesthetically pleasing."

"But I imagine your son would."

"True. What did your childhood home look like?"

He smiled at the mention of home. Talk about the unsterile environment. The familiar ache of homesickness filled his chest. "I'll show you my childhood home sometime. It's beautiful. My dad built it after he eloped with my mum. It's a true log cabin with a big, open family-style kitchen we can all fit in and tons of bedrooms. We call it the big house."

"It sounds lovely."

"How about you? What was your childhood home like?"

"Small, plain. We had hideous carpet and the ugliest orange tile in the bathroom. I always swore my house would be fancy and sophisticated when I grew up." She laughed. "That wasn't in the cards."

"What's your version of fancy and sophisticated?"

She sighed then blushed. "It's stupid, really. I always dreamed of one room that was all monochromatic with one of those old fashioned fainting couches. Keep in mind I dreamed this up when I was a kid, but that's what I thought every sophisticated woman should have in her home. I also wanted one of those farm style doors that were always open and dainty white café curtains in every window, which of course would always be open so the fresh air could trickle in."

Becca didn't have windows that opened. They were all locked and secured with sensors, much like the doors.

She toyed with his hair and drowsiness set in. "Which sibling are you closest with?" she whispered.

He chuckled. "That's not a fair question to ask when I'm falling asleep. I don't have favorites."

"I asked who you were closest with, not your favorite."

Shutting his eyes, imagining all his brothers and sisters, he sighed. "I don't know. I talk to them all the time, but not living there anymore…I don't really feel that close to anyone lately."

"You miss them."

"You have no idea."

"You should go for a visit."

He opened his eyes and peeked at her. "Would you want to go with me?"

She considered his invitation for a long moment. "That depends."

"On?" Her free time was so limited he'd been struggling with sacrificing Becca time for family time, but if she could go with him…that was the best of both worlds.

"Well, it would have to be on a weekend that Kevin has Hunter and I'd have to drive separately in case I needed to return home for some reason."

"If you needed to get home I'd go with you."

"No, I wouldn't want to interrupt your time with your family."

"We could always go on a weekend you have Hunter. I wasn't kidding when I said I wanted to meet him." Intruding wasn't his motive, but he wanted her to know he was sincere.

Her face softened with the sweetest smile as she leaned close and kissed his nose. "You confuse me, Braydon. Tell me something rotten about yourself so I know you aren't as perfect as you seem."

Perfect? Laughter tickled his throat. "If you think I'm perfect, Becca, you're doomed for disappointment. I'm just an ordinary guy."

"Nope. I want something rotten. Give me a regret."

Drawing in a deep breath he sank back on the pillow. Her ceiling needed Spackle and a fresh coat of paint. "A regret? Okay. I regret not spending more time with my grandmother. She's sick now with dementia. Last time I was home she didn't know me at all."

"Oh, I'm sorry. Were you close?"

"Not really. Not as much as we could've been." His heart pinched with a sense of inconclusiveness that would never get resolved. "How about you? What do you regret?"

"My marriage." Her answer was quick.

"But your marriage gave you Hunter."

"I could never regret Hunter. My life would be incomplete without him. I just wish I didn't marry my ex. Hunter's the only part of our relationship I don't regret. But at the same time, I don't know if Kevin would've strayed had Hunter been a typical child. I didn't have a lot of time or energy to be a typical wife once I became a mother. I have no regrets in that department, because Hunter's worth every bit of my effort, but Kevin… I guess the real regret is that he never seemed to try with us, as though losing us meant nothing."

Not knowing the right words after such a confession, he simply stared at her, enjoying the way her eyes softened every time she mentioned her son and the gentle play of a smile at the corners of her mouth. "You're a good mum, Becca."

Her face transformed with a full grin. "Thank you. What's your mom like?"

He laughed. "Crazy. Awesome. We're gonna have a big party for her and my father's fortieth anniversary. Wanna come?"

"When is it?"

"Sometime next year."

She turned, her face tight with confusion. "Braydon...a year's a long time from now."

"I know. I also know how to tell time and do long division. What's your point?"

Her head shook against the pillow. "How do you know if we'll still be together?"

"Are you breaking up with me?"

"Are we in a relationship?"

"Yes."

"Well, I'm certainly not looking for an escape, but..."

Turning to his stomach, his weight pressed into his forearms as his shoulders lifted. "Becca, I'm not afraid of commitment. Nor am I afraid of your circumstances. Stop expecting me to bolt at the first glimpse of chaos. I was raised in chaos."

"You're right. I'm sorry. I'm just scared."

"What are you afraid of?" Truth be told, he was scared too. Every relationship prior to this one had failed. Sammy had been an eye-opener, because with her he'd thought it would be easy. Turns out if a woman appears easy, a guy really doesn't have a clue about her. All women were complicated as hell.

"It's frightening depending on others. I don't have good luck with that."

"Angel, if you needed me, I'd be there. I don't care if it's the middle of the night and you have a bug bite that needs scratching. If you call, I'll be there." The issue was garnering an invitation. She was still holding him at a distance. "I'm not going anywhere. I...like you."

Her cheeks turned a soft shade of pink. "I like you too."

Leaning close, he kissed her brow. "Stop worrying and get some sleep."

Twisting to his back, he adjusted the covers and tried to settle for the night. His mind wandered and his thoughts drifted.

In high school he'd dated a girl, Jenn, who was popular, but not very nice. Then there were some fun years in college when he didn't want to be tied down. When he met Samantha, something told him she belonged with his family. He was right, but she didn't belong with him.

Losing Sam to Colin was right, but difficult all the same. His ego took a hit on that one. In the end Sammy said it best. They were great as friends, but nothing more.

His mum teased him constantly about trying to be perfect. He never really tried. In his mind there was just a certain way things were meant to be.

He was almost asleep when her hand crept onto his belly, stirring him.

"Braydon?"

"Yes?"

"Would you like to come over this Saturday and meet my son?"

His chest filled with true excitement. Her offer told him she was finally starting to believe he was serious about her. "I'd love to."

CHAPTER 8

$\mathcal{S}$aturday morning Becca was a mess. Her hair was still wet from the shower, the house was an absolute disaster, and Hunter was worked up over the approaching storm clouds. She'd considered calling Braydon to cancel, but called Nikki instead, digging for reassurance and courage.

"No. You're not cancelling," Nikki announced. "Suck it up, Becca. Your life isn't perfect. He's well aware of that. It's time for him to get his feet wet and see if he sinks or swims. You can do this."

"I know, but I have this horrible knot of anxiety in my stomach."

"You'll be fine. Go to the bathroom and get over it."

"How can you say tha—" There was a knock at the door and she did a double take. "What time is it?"

"Eleven."

"Oh my God, he's early." She turned in circles like a dog searching for the best spot to lie. "Nikki, he's an hour early!"

"So answer the door, whacko."

Becca peeked out the window and frowned at the sight of a municipal truck. Glancing to the door, her confusion was slightly relieved. "Wait, it's not him. Hold on while I see what this man wants."

She unlocked the doors as Hunter shouted. Tucking the phone by her hip, she greeted the man in a mechanic-type shirt. "Can I help you?"

"Are you the owner of the house?"

"Yes."

"Here you go." He handed her a thick envelope. "We're notifying all residents in your neighborhood of possible interruptions to service. The county's redoing the sidewalks and we've marked certain days you'll be without water and sewer. There's also information there about the trees lining the curbs and the customary procedure for removal."

She blinked at the stranger, feeling like an idiot. Didn't he know she was expecting company? "What?"

He checked his clipboard and double-checked the address on the mailbox. "Looks like you won't have use of water sometime during the ninth through the fourteenth and that tree's going to have to be removed. We're recommending homeowners contact their insurance and schedule a line inspection. There's been a lot of root damage reported lately and if it goes untreated too long you could be looking at upwards of twenty grand in repairs."

This had to be a bad dream. She was having a hard time following with Hunter shouting in the background. "You want me to cut down my tree?"

"I believe you were notified about the tree several months ago." He flipped pages on his clipboard. "Yup. Says here they notified you back in September and again in December of last year."

"I got a letter *suggesting* trees may need to be removed due to new sidewalks. No one said I had to remove it."

"Well, the township can remove it, but you'll be billed."

Her brow lowered. "How much?"

"About two grand."

"Two thousand dollars? Are you out of your mind? I don't have that kind of money."

"I'm sorry, miss, but the roots are interfering with the township renovations. They notified residents nearly a year in advance to lessen the burden. There's a list of contractors in that packet I gave you. Maybe if you shop around you can get a lower estimate."

"But I like my tree."

"I'm sorry." He turned, and that apparently was all he had to say.

Backing into the house, she locked the door and debated throwing a tantrum much like her son was doing at that very moment, or perhaps falling into a puddle of tears. Her name squawked from the phone at her hip. She'd forgotten about Nikki.

Lifting the phone slowly, she said, "I have to cut down my tree."

"What?"

"I don't know. They're putting in new sidewalks and my tree's somehow in the way. I'm also not going to have water for a few days, but I have to look at the paperwork and figure out when exactly that is."

"Can they do that?"

"I guess so. This is a nightmare."

"We had a tree removed a few years ago. The guy did nice work and was pretty affordable. I can get his number for you."

"How much did it cost?"

Nikki hummed as she thought. "I think it came to a little under twenty-five hundred."

"*Dollars?* For a tree? That's obscene. If the township wants it moved they should have to pay for it!"

"Okay, calm down. Maybe call around and find out if there's a way to get out of paying for it."

"That's not the point! I like my tree."

"It's a tree, Becca."

She couldn't explain it, but that tree had been there since she bought the house. It was a good, sturdy, pretty tree. It didn't deserve to get cut down because it was in the way of some superficial project to make their neighborhood's already functional sidewalks better. "There's nothing wrong with the tree."

And how the hell was she going to come up with the money to remove it if she couldn't convince the township the tree should stay? Hunter released a high-pitched scream and she winced. "I gotta go, Nikki. There's a storm coming and Braydon's going to be here soon."

Her friend sighed. "Try and relax, Becs. A little mess and noise isn't going to change his opinion about you and if it does, you're better off without him."

That was the problem. She didn't want to be better off without him. At this point she really, really wanted to be with him. Reality had a funny way of always interfering in the things she wanted, however, so she was preparing for the worst.

When she hung up with Nikki, Hunter was marching around the den, stimming, and repetitively checking the windows. Storms upset Hunter and there was no way of predicting if this would be a passing shower or her son's personal terror torn from the heavens.

Checking the Doppler app on her phone, she grimaced as a large green mass moved over their area. The forecast predicted forty percent chances of thunderstorms over the next few hours. Time to get Hunter into a Zen place.

Glancing out the window, noting the lengthening shadows, she gauged the storm would start sometime in the next hour. Dark clouds rolled through the deep blue sky. Her goal was to distract Hunter with activities that masked outside disturbances and caused anxiety.

"Hey, bud, how about some music?"

She shouldn't have stayed on the phone so long. Parading through the den, Hunter yanked on his shirt and continuously flicked the right side of his face. Becca tucked the packet from the township away and tightened the laces of her shoes.

"I'm going to dance. Do you want to dance with me, Hunter?"

"Dance," he echoed as he marched in a circle, now jumping in place every few paces.

"Yes, dance." Opening the cabinet above the stereo, she shuffled through the CDs.

Locating the one she sought, she placed it in the player and nudged the beanbag to the side of the room. Dropping to her knees she invited him to join her. The music started and Hunter opened his mouth wide the moment he recognized the opening tune of *Paint it Black* by The Stones. "Let's drum."

Hunter wandered over, his head tipped with curiosity, as he made a sound of excitement, but quickly back stepped and continued to trek to the window.

Becca matched the fast drumbeat with her fingers banging the floor. Hunter shouted and returned, this time dropping roughly to the floor. He loved this song and some of his anxiety due to the oncoming storm was slightly distracted. He sang the song about wanting to paint the red door black and they hummed the chorus together.

Becca's palms stung from drumming and the backs of her arms pulsed with the oncoming ache of the fast pounding repetition. By the time the song was over, her heart rate elevated. *Sympathy for the Devil* was next.

Hunter shouted the first line, begging to introduce himself, just as Mick Jagger sang.

Twisting behind her, she reached in the music bin and grabbed a recycled water bottle filled with grains. She held the beat as Hunter belted out the quick lyrics.

His voice wasn't designed for singing, but he was easily Becca's favorite vocalist, because when Hunter sang she heard his words, words that had been absent for the first half of his life.

"Let's see your air guitar!"

Jumping up and down, rattling the items around the room, Hunter did his best Mick Jagger while Becca let out the "Hoo-hoos" of the backup singers. Glancing between the blinds covering the window, she spotted spatters of drizzle hitting the glass.

Distracting Hunter from a storm was an exercise in endurance. She'd started doing this a few years ago, and sometimes their impromptu concerts only lasted thirty minutes, but sometimes they went on for hours.

There was no way of predicting what time the storm would pass. Ideally, it would be best if Braydon came later, once the weather settled, but she didn't have time to call him now that the rain was underway. She barely had time to think up alternative solutions. Her mind was solely in the now and focused on preventing a meltdown.

Gimme Shelter was next. Already out of breath, she pushed to her feet and performed their *Gimme Shelter* dance. Luckily, this one was a bit slower in tempo. Her arms mimicked the swaying branches of a tall tree, stretching her tired muscles. "Dance with me, bud."

Hunter studied her out of the corner of his eye and let his arms wave. There was a flicker of lightening outside against the deep gray sky.

"Watch my arms. Let me see your arms blow in the wind."

Casually, she cranked up the volume, anticipating the pound of thunder that would likely follow the flash of lightning. When the thunder rumbled, she flinched, but smiled because Hunter barely noticed.

The song ended and she was panting from exertion. *Ruby Tuesday* started and she directed her son to the upright. "Will you play for me?"

Without hesitating, Hunter slid onto the piano bench and picked up the note. The piano added to the vibration of the thunder and music, masking the storm further.

"Be Jagger, Mom!"

Standing to his right, she nodded and belted out her best, *"Goooooooodbye, Ruby Tuesday!"*

Hunter sang as well. As his focus remained on the keys, she sidled over to the window and closed the blinds the remaining centimeters, blocking all views to the outside.

Her attention dragged between her son's performance and the door. Praying for another piano song, her stomach tightened when she thought she caught the swirl of headlights against the blinds. Thankfully, *Brown Sugar* was next and Hunter rolled right into the riff.

Backing toward the door, her head swirling with the overly loud music and throbbing a bit from jumping around, she almost laughed. Had she actually entertained the fantasy of Braydon walking in on some peaceful, quaint picture of homelife?

As she twisted the locks, her heart stuttered with a bolt of pride and possibly courage. *This* was her homelife and seeing her son smile through a storm as he pounded on the ivory keys with The Rolling Stones, *that* was her happiness.

She pulled the door wide and smiled, "Welcome to my life. Come in."

Braydon's face showed a fleeting trace of shock at her sweaty, disheveled appearance, but she didn't have time to worry. She had to get the door closed before Hunter took notice of the downpour outside of their sanctuary. As she tugged Braydon over the threshold, she peeked past the awning. Blue showed behind the clouds in the distance. Thank God.

Turning, after the last lock was engaged, she found Braydon beaming. "Wow," he said, tipping his head toward Hunter. "He can really play."

Pride pinched her heart. She smirked and nodded, having to raise her voice to be heard over the music. "He's wonderful. Just give me a few minutes and I'll introduce you."

Braydon hung back as she returned to the piano. Hunter played a few more songs and Becca sung backup, blushing each time her horrid voice cracked in front of Braydon. He was an outstanding audience, never once interrupting the show and wearing a steady expression of enjoyment on his face.

When it seemed the worst of the storm had passed, she lowered the volume of the stereo. "Hunter, I want you to meet someone." Her hand lightly touched her son's right shoulder. "Can you stand up, bud?"

Hunter stood and immediately walked to the window, peeking through the blinds. His eyes blinked as his mind made obvious observations. The ground and branches were shades darker from before, now hanging low with the weight of raindrops. The walks were sprinkled with soggy leaves and the color of the sky had transformed from steel blue to gray.

"Rain's gone, Mom. No rain!"

"Yes, the storm's over. See, that wasn't bad at all. Would you like to meet our friend, Braydon?"

Braydon remained at the entrance to the den, just within Hunter's peripheral. Hunter's fingers reached for his temple and twisted at the corner of his eye, telling Becca he'd spotted their visitor. He vocalized short, repetitive hums as he took in Braydon's presence and Becca waved Braydon into the room.

Taking slow steps and pausing about three feet away from Hunter, but only a few inches from Becca, he said, "It's nice to meet you, Hunter."

Hunter turned, still in an apparent good mood from their jam session and giggled. His fingers curled and tapped over his lips, as his attention seemed drawn to Braydon's shirt.

"Can you say hello to Braydon?"

"Hello." Taking a step back, Hunter's attention turned to the piano, where he tapped a key persistently.

"I heard you playing. You're very good," Braydon complimented, but Hunter paid him no mind.

"Can you say thank you to Braydon?"

"Thank you to Braydon." He laughed at his own jest and slid onto the piano bench.

"Would you like to show Braydon how you play?"

A stream of notes pelted from the piano in reply. It wasn't a song, but the melody was eloquent enough to raise Braydon's eyebrows. Becca grinned with pride. This wasn't so scary.

She turned off the stereo. Hunter's shifted his seating and segued into what was a stunning performance. Glancing back to Braydon, she saw his lips part in awe and there was a sudden tightening in her throat. It was nice, bringing someone into their world and sharing the beautiful secrets she and her son kept, especially when life calmed enough to notice such things.

"He's incredible," Braydon whispered.

"He's my Hunter," she whispered back.

"How long has he been playing like this?"

"About four years. I bought the piano from the church that closed two years ago and since then he's just blossomed."

The song concluded and Braydon clapped. "Well done, Hunter!"

Hunter bounced and started another ballad. Braydon's head tilted as he followed the notes. "I know this. What is it?"

"*As Tears Go By.*" Her eyes prickled. "If you don't exclude The Stones, *this—*" She patted her heart and smiled. "—is my favorite song."

The warmth of Braydon's fingers curled around hers. "It's beautiful."

Inviting Braydon into her home with Hunter had emotions surging through her from all angles. As the song finished, she wanted nothing more than to hug her son. He was perfectly imperfect and in that moment she gratefully accepted all of the challenges for these incredible gifts that they'd been given. Basically, she needed to get a grip.

Pressing her hands together, she suggested, "How about some lunch?"

"Lunch would be great," Braydon said as Hunter stood and bolted into the kitchen.

She laughed. "Shall we?"

Braydon followed her to the kitchen where Hunter bounced by the chart on the wall. "What would you like for lunch, bud?"

"Hot dog." His fingers plucked the hot dog picture from the chart and moved it to the square for lunch. He then chose apple juice for his beverage.

"Okay." She pointed to the task analysis on the wall. "Wash your hands."

As she followed Hunter to the sink and adjusted the water, Braydon kept in her shadow. "Can I help?"

"Um, no thank you, I think I have it. Are hot dogs okay with you?"

"Hot dogs are fine."

"Now dry them, bud."

Handing Hunter a towel, he dried his hands and chattered as he made his way to the table. Becca pulled out the hot dogs and plates as a pot of water heated on the stove. Hunter stood and went to the look at the clock on the wall. He ran to the window and tapped on the glass. The sky was hazy, but a softer shade of blue as the sun now fought to return.

"Where should you be, Hunter?" He returned to the table and rocked in his seat.

Becca counted out two hot dogs for Braydon and two more for her and Hunter. Once lunch was ready, Braydon helped her carry everything to the table. Before sitting, she gathered a Velcro board with a cut up picture of an iPod on it.

The second she sat the plate in front of Hunter he shoveled a cut piece of hot dog in his mouth. "Wait, please. We're not going to use our fingers today. Here's a fork."

Hunter whined, but took the fork.

"What's that?" Braydon asked, pointing to the Velcro board.

Speaking loud enough to include Hunter in the discussion, she said, "Hunter, can you tell Braydon why we use the iPod board?"

Hunter aimed his fork at the food and said, "I get music."

Becca explained, "If Hunter uses his fork instead of his fingers, he can have some music after lunch."

Her son struggled with the utensil, sneaking his fingers in to help pierce the meat with the tines. Showing a bit of frustration, he picked up the morsel and shoved it in his mouth. "Uh-uh. No fingers." She pulled a piece of the puzzle off the Velcro board with a scrape and Hunter groaned.

Lowering her voice, she explained, "He isn't always focused on what I'm doing, so hearing the sound of the Velcro snap helps him register the change. We're working on table manners."

As lunch carried on, there was little time for adult conversation. Braydon remained observant and asked questions when he didn't understand the reasoning behind a certain action, and she found his curiosity refreshing. Kevin never paid attention to such behavior modifications. After lunch Hunter was given his iPod and she and Braydon cleaned up the kitchen *together*—another thing she wasn't used to.

Her home was fairly open, so she kept a continuous eye on Hunter. He'd calmed since that morning and was playing in the den while she and Braydon shared a cup of coffee in the adjoining room. It seemed like the first time she'd caught her breath that day. She glanced at the clock—2:00—not bad.

"Sorry I didn't have time to fix myself up. I must look pretty scary."

His fingers gave a gentle tug to her sloppy hair. "You look pretty." Such acceptance had a way of heightening her nervousness.

"I had a hectic morning," she confessed.

"Hunter doesn't like storms?"

"No. I try to distract him, thus the concert you walked in on."

"He has amazing talent."

She nodded. "He does. I don't know where he gets it from."

"You can tell he really likes music."

"Music's probably our biggest motivator. He also likes trains, but music's more available." Her attention was pulled when Hunter started banging on the wall. "He does that sometimes," she explained, without apology.

Braydon made no show of annoyance. "So what's new with you?"

She sighed. "I have to cut down my tree." A snort of derisive laughter slipped past her lips. "Sorry. I don't really have much excitement in my life. You're probably used to more stimulating conversation."

"Not really. What's wrong with your tree?"

She unleashed her frustration on the napkin, twisting it into little pieces. "Absolutely nothing. The township came by and told me it has to be removed for the new sidewalks. They're doing something with the sewers too. The roots are corroding the lines or something. I don't know. They gave me a big packet that explains everything."

"Can I see what they gave you?"

Taken off guard, mostly because Kevin always let her handle things like this, she blinked. "Sure." After finding where she stuck the packet, she handed it to him.

Braydon paged through the information.

"Is there a way to get out of it?" she asked hopefully.

"According to this, I don't think so."

"Great. I heard it's around two grand to take down a tree that size. Maybe more."

"Nah, I can get you a better price."

She perked up. "Really? I don't want the tree to go, but if I have no choice I'd love to save as much money as I can. If I let the township remove it they'll bill me and their quote was way out of my budget."

"I know people. Why don't I make a call and see if I can get them out here this week."

"People?" She laughed. "Are you involved with the tree mafia or something?"

He chuckled. "No, they're professionals—most of the time."

Throat tight with gratitude, she whispered, "I'd really appreciate that."

Braydon made some calls, as Hunter required some of her time. They ordered takeout for dinner and then did a puzzle together.

After the bedtime routine that Braydon waited patiently throughout, the house was quiet and she collapsed on the couch, resenting her lack of energy. She didn't want him to go, but she also really wanted her bed.

"I have some wine in my trunk. Want me to bring it in?"

"You can if you want some. If I have wine I'll probably fall asleep."

"Do you want me to go?"

There it was, that grip of reality on her heart, tightening and twisting. She wanted nothing more than for him to stay, but it had been such a draining day she wasn't going to be much fun. "I don't want you to leave."

He turned, assessing her. "Sleepover?"

The debate in her head lasted only a second. Why not just invite him? "Would you want to?"

"Let me think. Yes." His answer was so fast it made her laugh. "I have a bag in my car."

"Look at you, Mr. Optimistic."

He kissed her cheek. "I missed you. I knew once I had you I wouldn't want to leave."

Her fingers pulled on one of his golden waves. "Haven't had me yet."

"Is that an invitation?"

"Maybe."

"I'll get my bag."

~

CLIMBING INTO BED, Braydon placed a condom on the nightstand and pulled Becca close. She'd showered, and her skin smelled of flowers and soft girlie soap. His lips pressed into her shoulder and she hummed pleasantly. "What are you in the mood for? And you better not say sleep," he teased.

She giggled and turned. "Thank you."

"For?"

"Today. You handled everything perfectly. Not many people do."

Her praise was a tremendous relief. He'd been a nervous wreck about meeting Hunter, because he really liked this woman and her son meant the world to her. He wanted Hunter to like him. "Thank you for letting me meet him. I like getting to know this side of you."

Leaning in, he kissed her lips softly, parting them with gentle nips. After seeing what an average day in the world of Becca was like, he found even greater empathy for her day-to-day trials and wanted to do something nice for her.

Kissing a trail along her belly, he drew down her panties. Her legs scissored slowly against each other as he nibbled her thigh. When his mouth found her center, he licked and kissed until she was moaning softly. His fingers parted her folds and she arched into his touch. He loved the sight of her there, so pretty, pink and delicate.

"You're so beautiful."

He teased her center and she opened like a flower. For some reason he didn't want to go fast. Taking it slow, he brought her to climax, her voice low and weighted with desire. He reached for the condom.

"That's my job," she whispered, her face flushed with a soft rosy glow.

He handed it to her and she carefully slid the latex on. Easing her back down, he crawled over her and looked in her eyes. For unknown reasons, he tried to summon visions of past lovers in that split second, but came up short. All he could see was Becca, an angel beneath him.

Pressing into her, his body rocked with need and something much more potent. Something was happening here, something he didn't think either of them was prepared to handle. They took their time, savoring each slow thrust, her hands holding him close while he was buried deep inside of her.

His eyes studied her through the shadows and he tried to catalogue the moment, wondering why it felt so different from all the other times. Then it occurred to him. This was making love in its finest form.

The sudden thought left him staggered. He'd never been in love and wasn't clear on how to recognize the sentiment. Signs of authenticity were unspecified to him, yet he wanted to define it then and there.

"Are you okay?"

Blinking down at her, he shook off the unfamiliar thoughts and emotions. "Yeah, sorry."

Jarred by the overwhelming sense of love, his release broke free and he shook with need. Kissing her deeply, she moaned and held him tight. Unforeseen fears pushed his passion. This was his woman. A territorial need barreled through him to claim her, all of her, and never let go.

"Wow," she whispered. "That was intense."

Relieved she experienced the intensity too, he nestled into her shoulder. The idea of pulling away from her was so repugnant he stayed there a while longer. He needed to get a hold of himself. Her one rule was no *I love yous.* And what if it really wasn't love?

AS THE BATHROOM DOOR CLOSED, Becca turned to her side and bit her knuckles. What just happened? She saw it, the moment Braydon's mind clicked. A second later, she felt it. Never in her life had she experienced such a poignant connection while making love.

Worry had her biting her lip. She was definitely falling for him. Oh, who was she kidding? She'd fallen. Her heart raced as she worried how this would change things.

Her mind clouded with rising misgivings. Depending on others was dangerous. If she became conditioned to expect Braydon's presence, she'd be left weaker for it when on her own again. No matter how she came to care for him, the fear of eventual failure never subsided.

The bathroom door clicked open and she shut her eyes, pretending she was asleep as his body curled around hers under the covers. What if she was imagining things and he didn't feel it? What if he was simply that nice of a guy and she was misinterpreting everything? She was so jaded and he was so idealistic. It wouldn't be difficult to garner the wrong impression from such a nice guy.

Her mind went in circles until she'd truly exhausted herself and fell asleep.

Morning came all too soon. Slipping out of bed, she tiptoed downstairs to start on breakfast. It wasn't long before she heard Hunter up and moving.

Placing her mug of coffee on the counter, she went to say good morning. As she worked through their morning routine of brushing and dressing, she thought she heard the shower running in the other bathroom. Her nervousness was back, and she wondered how Hunter would react to Braydon still in their home.

"Okay, bud, let's head downstairs for breakfast."

Leading Hunter down to the kitchen took several minutes.

They moved his chart and he marched around the house as she started the French toast.

"Truck! Mom, truck!"

"What?" Placing the last slice onto a plate, she turned to see what Hunter was shouting about.

"Truck. Truck in the yard."

Frowning, she went to the window. There certainly was a truck in their driveway. It was large and muddy and she had no idea what it was doing there. A horn beeped and she quickly directed Hunter to the den. "You can listen to three songs."

"I wanna go outside and see the truck," he argued.

The doorbell rang and she unraveled the earbuds from the iPod. "I don't know who those people are. Stay here."

"No!" He pushed off the sofa and Becca gave up on trying to get him to stay inside. She was still in her pajamas and without a bra.

Taking Hunter by his arm, she guided him to the door. "Okay, come with me." As she unlocked the door, holding Hunter tight, all words left her head.

"Hi. Are you Becca?"

There were two of them, two shockingly handsome—identical —men standing on her porch. Hunter darted for the yard and jerked her arm in its socket. Her grip remained tight as she pulled him back.

"Y-yes. Can I help you?"

"We heard you need a tree removed. Is it that one there?"

They had to be twins. "Um…" Hunter writhed to get outside. Pressing his arms to his chest she struggled to restrain him. "Yes. Who are you?"

"I'm Luke and this's Finn." The guy glanced at Braydon's car in the driveway. "Is Bray here?"

"Oh, you're the people Braydon called. I didn't expect you so soon." Hunter started to really jostle her around. "I'm sorry. Would you mind holding on for a second while I situate my son?" The men smiled as Hunter shouted about wanting to see the truck. "I'll go find Braydon."

Shutting the door and locking it, she turned Hunter just as his hand swung out and caught her on the cheek. Stinging tears rushed to her eyes. "Enough," she said sternly. "You hurt Mommy."

Issuing a scream that had her flinching away, she waited, never releasing her hold on his arms. Braydon came barreling down the stairs in a panic.

"Becca?"

Not having time to answer, she looked at Hunter. "Say sorry."

Hunter screamed again and Braydon took a halting step forward. When her grip slipped, Hunter shoved her. She dropped from where she squatted to the floor, taking her son as much onto her lap as possible. Her arms contained him in a tight basket hold and he started to shriek, attempting to smack her. She rocked back and forth trying to sooth him. "If you quiet down I'll take you outside to see the truck, but not until you calm down."

She couldn't see Braydon from where she was sitting, but she imagined he was terrified. Hunter screamed again, this time punching himself in the head.

"Hey! No hitting." Her son was fast and strong, making it difficult to keep hold of him. She only restrained him when there was a chance of injury, but he hated being touched and that made episodes like this all the more difficult. His legs kicked the floor hard and she twisted like a pretzel, wrapping her own limbs around his, while trying to protect herself as well.

Her strength waned the longer he fought. His arm slipped past her hold and punched into her leg as he screeched and suddenly a large fist closed over her son's smaller, flailing hand. "Hunter."

Glancing up at Braydon who kneeled beside them, her son froze. Braydon looked nervous, but his focus remained on her son. Using a soft voice, he said, "I saw her today..."

Hunter tensed, every muscle in his body flexing tight, but Braydon held onto his fist, not with force, but with definite control.

"Help me out, buddy. A glass of wine..."

"Hand," Hunter shouted.

Braydon glanced at her, his expression pleading for the next verse. Becca panted out the next lyric.

Hunter thrust his body forward on the floor then screeched out the next verse.

Braydon met her gaze and smiled, nodding. Together they whispered the chorus about not always getting what you want.

Hunter moaned and Becca released her hold. Braydon dropped further to the ground as her son stomped toward the piano but didn't settle. His body rocked as he hummed the chorus and shouted, "Get what'chya need!"

Becca caught her breath and as much as she should be admiring the sudden transformation in her son, she couldn't take her eyes off Braydon. He was watching her too, his eyes tense with concern. His hand lifted slowly, the back of his fingers grazing the sore part of her cheek Hunter had hit.

Her vision blurred at the awkward sense of exposure and she lowered her gaze.

"You okay?"

She nodded. If not for him, she'd still be restraining her son. "Your friends are here for the tree. I think that triggered him. He got excited about the truck."

"Oh, Becca." He looked away and slowly shook his head.

She didn't want him to feel guilty for helping her. "It's okay."

"I'm sorry. I should've given you a heads up they were coming first thing. I didn't expect them this early."

"You're doing me a favor, please don't apologize. Who do I make the check out to?"

"Don't worry about it."

She met his stare. "Are they just doing a quote today?"

"No, they'll take care of it."

"Well, how are they going to get paid?"

"You can try to pay them. They won't take it." He stood and held out a hand to help her off the floor. Hunter rocked and pounded a few notes on the piano each time he passed the keys.

Braydon stood and carefully helped her off the floor. "Come on, let me introduce you." He glanced back at Hunter. "Did he want to see the truck?"

"Yeah."

Braydon stepped close, but didn't touch. "Hunter, are you ready to see the truck?"

He stilled and flicked the side of his face. There was no eye contact and his motions were jerky, but that was typical behavior after a tantrum.

Becca stepped forward, snapping out of her trance. "Hunter, do you want to go outside and see the truck?"

His arms flapped. "I want to see the truck."

"Can you say sorry first?"

His personal struggle was evident as he paced. Falling back on his signs, he rubbed his chest and mumbled an apology. She accepted the sign for sorry and gently touched his shoulder before placing her hand on his arm. "Let's go see the truck."

After pulling on a jacket for the sake of the neighbors, they made it to the driveway. The men were inspecting the tree, and Braydon talked to them as Becca took Hunter to the truck. It was large and orange, and had a high reach on the top and a chipper attached to the back. Her son was utterly fascinated by its presence dominating their yard.

"Becca?"

She turned as Hunter inspected the handles on the side. Braydon waited a few steps away with the men. She smiled nervously, knowing the men probably weren't expecting such a demonstration that morning.

"These are my brothers, Finn and Luke. Guys, this's Becca and her son, Hunter."

Oh my God, they're his brothers!

One man held his hand out. "Pleasure to meet you, Becca. I'm Finn."

She shook his hand, her palms sweating, and glanced at Braydon. "Brothers?"

"Two of them."

Her grin quavered. "You're the twins."

Luke shook her hand as well. Recalling her disheveled appearance, she fidgeted. Lovely. This was his family's first impression of her.

"I didn't realize. You'll have to excuse my appearance. Can I get you some coffee or…" She wasn't prepared for this. Perhaps this was one of Braydon's faults—spontaneity.

"Why don't you get dressed, and I'll show Hunter the inside of the truck?"

Her mouth opened, ready to object. Overbearing didn't accurately describe her parenting. She was a jumble of protectiveness and reluctance for a reason. "I don't know if that's such a good—"

Before she could finish her objection Braydon stepped close and kissed her temple, whispering, "You can trust me, angel. I'll keep an eye on him. I promise."

Control wasn't surrendered easily. Glancing to his brothers, she nervously shook her head. "He runs—"

"So does Finn. Trust me, we can keep him safe for a few minutes. Go get dressed and we'll be fine."

They did look like a capable threesome. Feeling a little outnumbered and chastising herself for being her usual overbearing self, she grudgingly forced herself to bend a little. "O—okay."

With a sense of empty handedness, she returned to the house. When she made it to her bedroom, she glanced out the window. Braydon and his brothers surrounded Hunter, each one smiling as

Hunter pointed out various parts of the truck. Luke climbed into the driver seat and Braydon held Hunter's shoulder as the high reach extended. They grinned with her son as his excitement tumbled into laughter.

Her hand pressed into her chest as the pinching over her heart tightened. She was an emotional mess.

Quickly slipping on clean clothes and sneakers, she brushed her teeth and pulled up her hair. When she returned to the front yard the men were all cheering as Hunter yelled into a walkie talkie.

Becca came to Braydon's side. "Who's he talking to?"

Braydon chuckled. "My dad."

"All the way in Center County?"

He nodded then shouted. "Tell him we're gonna take down this tree, Hunter."

Hunter laughed and shouted into the hand held device, "We're gonna take down this tree!"

A scratchy voice came over the speaker, "Ten Four."

Luke gave Hunter a hand climbing out of the truck. Hunter immediately ran to her side and informed her he used the walkie talkie and was inside the truck. "He said Ten Four, Mom! Ten Four!"

"I heard! How about we go inside and have breakfast then you can watch Luke and Finn cut down the tree from the window?"

It seemed the tree was the perfect motivation. Luke and Finn followed them inside and Becca apologized for the mess. She served up the French toast as they talked. There was always a touch of insincerity whenever new people came into her home. There was no way of telling if the people that didn't outwardly comment on their situation were simply polite, or judging them in their heads or, rarest of all, not really bothered by the differences.

She jumped when Braydon approached her at the sink after breakfast.

"Skittish this morning?"

"You snuck up on me."

"I came to give you a kiss." His lips pressed into her neck. "Hunter's waiting at the window, so the guys are gonna get started."

"Shouldn't there be more help? Are two guys enough to remove a tree like that?"

A smile, full of cockiness, spread over his face. "We're McCulloughs, Becca. We're used to handling big things."

She smacked him with the towel. "Cocky."

"Exactly."

Of course he was right. Two McCulloughs were plenty to handle the tree. Hunter wasn't the only one fascinated by the removal. They all gawked as Luke and Finn climbed the limbs with saws and chopped it into nothing. The most exhilarating part came when the trunk went down.

A bit of sadness came with the new, open view in her front yard, but something about the day's events lightened the burden of having to say goodbye to the tree that had been there since she bought the house.

When they finished there was nothing but sawdust where the stump had been. Braydon's fingers curled around hers as he quietly asked, "How about we order some pizzas for dunch?"

"Dunch?"

"Dinner slash lunch. The guys have a long ride home. My treat."

She nodded. "Okay, but I'm buying." Pizza was the least she could offer. At dinner the men talked to Hunter about trucks and trees and she saw a new interest come to life in her son's eyes.

"You guys should hear Hunter play the piano. You think Kate's got talent? She's got nothing on Hunter."

Finn smiled. "Really? You like the piano, my man?"

Hunter nodded. "Rolling Stones."

"Oh, yeah?" Finn stood and carried his plate to the sink. "I've been told I got the moves like Jagger."

Hunter laughed. "I can play now?"

She nodded, enjoying this social moment. "Go ahead."

Typically her son didn't acknowledge outsiders, but he was really taken by these men. He wasn't the only one.

They traveled to the piano and Hunter settled onto the bench. The moment he touched the keys, his talent impressed the men. Hunter played a beautiful rendition of *Angie*.

He performed several songs, and when it was time for the guys to head home it was nearly eight o'clock. She'd offered them money, but they refused. They also invited her to come to what they all seemed to call McCullough Mountain and meet the others.

It was tempting, but intimidating. Again she worried if leaving the area while Kevin had Hunter was wise.

After putting Hunter to bed, she and Braydon finally delved into that bottle of wine. "What are you thinking about?"

Braydon turned. "I want you to come to Center County with me. I know you're worried about Hunter, but he'll be fine. We can bring him or if you'd rather come when he's with Kevin, we'll come home immediately if anything goes wrong. I don't want to drive separately."

Curiosity overruled caution, her answer slipping out with little thought. "Okay."

He seemed surprised at her agreement. Truth be told, so was she, but meeting his brothers intrigued her. She wanted to see if they were all that nice. "Really? Just like that?"

"Your brothers are really sweet. I'd like to meet the rest of them."

His shoulders lifted as he drew in a deep breath. "Just…"

She tipped her head in question as a glimpse of insecurity showed in his eyes. "Just what?"

"Promise you won't go falling in love with any of them."

She laughed. "What?" They were all nice looking, but no one would ever top Braydon.

"Last time I brought a girl home to meet my family, my brother ended up marrying her."

Her expression sobered. "Seriously?"

"Yeah. He was the last brother I was worried about poaching from me. If he'd never met Sammy he'd be a priest right now."

"He was going to be *a priest*?" Talk about scandal.

Braydon laughed at her shock, but there was a telling concern in his eyes he couldn't hide. He'd been hurt on some level by what had happened, no matter how much he accepted it now.

"Do you talk to them?"

"Of course. I could never ignore my family. I love them and, believe it or not, they make a lot of sense together. I just get nervous bringing anyone home. She was the last girl I introduced to the family."

That was huge. "When did this happen?"

"When I was still in college."

"Did you love her?"

His head twisted and he thought for a long moment. "No. Not the way a couple should love each other I think, but I didn't know that when I brought her home."

"Now I'm nervous," she confessed.

He grinned. "They're savages, really, and there's no way of predicting how they'll behave. But so long as I have your word…"

Pressing her lips to his cheek, she promised, "I swear I won't fall in love with anyone at the mountain. I've already got the best McCullough anyway."

"Or the pub. Kelly's another one I have to watch."

"Wait, aren't all your siblings married?"

"Yes, but flirting's an incurable affliction every McCullough suffers."

He was so cute. "When did you want to go?"

"It's up to you. I'd like to go sometime in the next few weeks."

She contemplated her schedule. It would be nice to go when Kevin had Hunter. She hadn't had any sort of vacation in years. "How about over Thanksgiving? Kevin will have Hunter and I was dreading spending the holiday alone, but this'll distract me."

"Perfect. I'll tell my mum to add an extra place setting."

"Oh." Her hopes crashed. "I promised Nikki and Carla I'd spend Thanksgiving with them since Nikki's husband's going to be away on business. Well, maybe they'll understand."

"You could always invite them."

She snorted. "I don't think that's a good idea. Carla's just as bad as her sister. They might break your mountain."

He laughed. "Trust me. We can handle them."

CHAPTER 9

"Giddy up!" Carla yelled as Braydon tucked the last of Becca's belongings into his trunk. "Now, how many brothers did you say you have?"

"They're all married, Carla. Calm yourself," Becca said, rolling her eyes.

"Yeah, but you have cousins, too, right, Braydon?"

"I have some single cousins."

Nikki beeped the horn and yelled out the window of her car, parked behind Braydon's Jetta. "Get in the car or I'm leaving without you."

Becca turned and gave Carla a hug. "Try not to distract Nikki while she's driving. Call me if you get lost. We'll be right ahead of you."

Braydon advised them to stay close, because once they made it to the mountain GPS was useless. Hunter had gone to Kevin's that morning and Becca had five whole days to relax and have fun. She was actually excited, even if she was incredibly nervous.

"They'll be fine," Braydon said tapping her knee.

She snorted. "Let's just hope they don't back into a tree. Carla's not the best co-pilot."

"What about Nikki?"

"She's consistently a maniac, so her typical blanket warning applies."

Once Becca was buckled up she turned into a ball of energy. "How far is it?"

"A little under three hours."

"Wanna play a game?"

He laughed. "You're hyper."

"I'm a free woman for the next five days. I haven't done this since…ever."

"What about before you were a mother?"

She shrugged. "I don't know. I was a kid."

"How about when you were first married?"

She snorted. "Kevin's no fun."

That really made him laugh. As they drove they chatted about the deal their companies were working on together. Now that the construction was underway, her part was nearly finished.

"Your boss makes me nervous," she admitted.

"Miranda? Why?"

"She's very pretty, and you two have a history."

"That's in the past."

"Yeah, but dating her was probably a lot different from dating me."

"It was, that's why we broke up. I prefer us."

Reaching into the console, he picked up his phone and powered it off, which was strange since it wasn't ringing. Maybe he didn't want to be disturbed while on the highway. His hand curled over hers and squeezed.

When they arrived in Center County it was mid-afternoon. Braydon turned onto a desolate street and her heart raced as they followed the incline of dusty road. "Is this the mountain?"

"Yup. In about two miles you'll see my parents' house on the right. Look for a cleared patch in the trees and a log cabin on a hill."

The fresh air was exhilarating. Deep patches of evergreens made up an impressive horizon. Deer nibbled at shrubs as they crept up the scenic path. They were deep in the woods, but every so often a house would come into view. "That's Sammy and Colin's house over there."

"Your ex?"

"Yeah, but I hardly think of her like that anymore. Over there's Finn and Mallory's home. You can't really see it through the trees, but if you take that bit of road you'll hit it."

"You guys all really live on the mountain?"

"Everyone but Sheilagh and Kelly. Kelly lives on the farm with Ashlynn."

"And Sheilagh?"

"She's in Princeton, but she'll be home for Thanksgiving with her husband Alec."

"The professor?" It was a lot to keep track of.

"Right."

When she spotted the log cabin she gasped. It was striking, perched at the top of a grassy knoll. Immediately she thought of things like stacked pancakes and Abraham Lincoln, plaid tablecloths and other Americana representations. "It looks like a centerfold in *Better Homes and Gardens*."

"One day I'm going to build something equally as breathtaking."

His dream was sweet, but with the admission came a sharp bite of anxiety. "You really aren't staying in Pittsburgh?"

He glanced at her. "If I had to I would, but I miss home. I always imagined building my wife her dream house right over there."

Her eyes blinked as her stomach rolled with disappointment. It was a beautiful patch of land behind a divide of tall pines. She could imagine Braydon building the perfect home there—when he found the perfect wife. Somehow, that vision didn't seem to include her, but then, she'd known that when they embarked on whatever this was.

They parked next to a large barn and Carla and Nikki pulled up beside them. As they climbed out and stretched their legs, the screen door on the porch snapped open and a striking redhead emerged.

"Mum! He's here!" The girl shrieked as she barreled down the porch steps, her pace not slowing until she propelled herself into Braydon's arms.

"Hey, Devil! Welcome home."

Becca realized this must be his youngest sister, Sheilagh. Sheilagh brushed her hands over Braydon's face and smiled. "Welcome home, Bray."

The screen door opened again and a woman in an aproned dress with work boots came out followed by a tall man dressed in flannel and denim. "Stop hogging him, Sheilagh, and let us all get a piece of him."

Braydon's head turned and a childlike smile lit his face. "Mum," he whispered, taking Becca's hand and pulling her to the front of the house. "Come let me introduce you."

Nerves jangled inside her as he towed her along to meet his family. Carla and Nikki introduced themselves to Sheilagh, who Becca had yet to garner an introduction to.

"Well, now, will you look at our boy, Frank? That's the look of a man in love."

"Hi, Mum," he hummed, as she pulled him into a tight hug. It was probably the most darling thing Becca had ever seen, the way Braydon's eyes closed in a moment of bliss as he rested his head on his mother's shoulder and simply breathed in her familiar form. Envy at such a precious moment had Becca smiling.

"I'm Frank."

She turned and shook the man's hand. "It's nice to meet you. I'm Becca. Your home is beautiful."

He nodded his appreciation and Braydon's mother finally released her son. "Now, who do we have here, love?"

"Mum, this is Becca, my girlfriend."

Becca held out her hand and nearly groped the woman as she ignored her outstretched palm and yanked her into a bear hug. "Welcome to our home, love." She gripped Becca's shoulders and pressed her back a step. "And what a lovely little lass you are! She's cute, isn't she, Frank? Well, introduce me to your other friends, Braydon." Turning to Becca, she announced, "Now, all my boys are married. I'm afraid you got the last one on the market, but I have strapping nephews. Are your friends married, dearie?"

Good grief the woman spoke fast. "Um, Carla's single. Nikki's married. Her husband's away on business until Saturday."

Braydon's mother clapped. "Perfect. Braydon, you'll have to call Ryan and introduce the two. Which one's Carla? Oh, they're both pretty."

"Maureen, give them a second to settle before you go trying to marry everyone off," Braydon's father said.

"Hush, Frank."

They met the others at the cars where Carla and Nikki were laughing with Sheilagh. "Bray, these girls are a hoot! We're gonna have so much fun this weekend."

"Take it easy, Devil."

"Hey, GQ, how come you never mentioned having a cool sister? She doesn't have a bit of that conservativeness you have going on," Nikki teased.

Maureen, Braydon's mother, frowned. "You better not have gone and turned conservative on us, Braydon. You're a McCullough. We don't do moderation well."

Braydon tugged Becca close. "Sheilagh, this is my girlfriend

Becca and I see you already met Nikki and Carla. Becca, this is my baby sister, Shei-Devil."

Like her mother, Sheilagh pulled her into a tight hug. "Welcome to our mountain."

Overwhelmed by such an enthusiastic welcome, Becca simply smiled. There were only three of them at the moment, but they each seemed packed to the gills with vitality. Well, everyone but Frank, that is. Braydon's father appeared the most refined.

Suddenly, Braydon's sister tensed. It was very subtle, but Becca picked up on it. Turning to see what caused the slight change in her demeanor, Becca recognized Luke coming out of the barn followed by another man. A second later, yet another man, this one wearing a tweed blazer, emerged from the big house and Sheilagh noticeably relaxed.

"Hey Becca," Luke greeted, giving her a gentle hug. "This is Tristan, my partner."

"It's nice to finally meet you, Becca," Tristan said, with a slight southern lilt to his speech.

The man wearing the blazer wrapped an arm around Sheilagh's shoulders. "Hello. I'm Alec, Sheilagh's husband."

Taken off guard by his British accent, Becca drew in a breath, hoping she could keep everyone's names straight. "Nice to meet you, Alec. I'm Becca and this is Carla and Nikki."

"Pleasure."

"Well, why don't you kids settle in and then we'll have dinner. I'm sure your brothers'll be wantin' you to join them at O'Malley's tonight, so I'm just making soup and dumplings. Tomorrow I'll be cooking up a feast, and I'm saving my strength."

Sheilagh leaned close. "You may want to take a room far away from Mum and Dad's. They're perverted and loud now that Dad's hearing's going."

Braydon stilled, his face contorting with a frown. "Ew." Shaking his head he glared at his sister. "Why would you put that image in my head, brat?"

She shrugged and took Alec by the hand. "Just trying to warn you. We're in Kate's old room at the *far* end of the hall."

Braydon carried their luggage to his childhood bedroom and Becca enjoyed the glimpses of his personality displayed there. It was very similar to his apartment in that it was decorated in cool gray colors and straight edged furniture. However, in this room there was a touch of earthiness she didn't find at his home in the city.

A large antlered skull was mounted to the wall and a fur blanket covered the bed. "Did you catch that?"

"Nah, it's hard to catch a deer. Shot it with an arrow though."

"What was he armed with?" she joked.

He grinned and placed their belongings at the foot of the bed. "That was my first kill."

She wasn't a fan of hunting, but something about imagining fancy Braydon out of his suit and geared up for the hunt did things to her. It was difficult picturing him in such a rough and wild setting, but she was slowly piecing it together.

The sound of the girls making their way up the stairs had them turning. "Where did they go? This place is huge." She heard Nikki wonder aloud.

"We're in here."

The girls dropped their luggage in the hall. "Where are we sleeping?"

"Carla, you can take my brother Kelly's room down the hall and Nikki, you can take Sheilagh's since she's in Kate's old room."

"Which one's Sheilagh's room?"

"It's the hideous pink one at the end. You can't miss it."

The girls disappeared and Braydon shut the door. When he gave Becca "the look" she giggled. "What do you want?"

"You know what I want." Stalking her with slow strides, he backed her to the bed.

"Your mother's making dinner."

"We have a few minutes. Let me do bad things to you."

Her mouth tightened in a smirk. "Maybe I want to do bad things to you."

That brought him up short. "Really? Like what?"

Her lips pressed to his and she hummed, loving the taste of his kiss. "Mmmm, I don't know. How much time do we have?"

"I'd say at least twenty minutes until the natives get restless."

"Oh, I can do a lot in twenty minutes," she purred.

"I have no doubt. Show me."

"Did you lock the door?"

"Of course."

Her fingers went to his belt and she quickly unclasped the latch and slid the leather free. Slipping down his zipper, she fed her hand into his pants and wrapped her fingers around hot, hard flesh. He groaned in pleasure as she slid to her knees. Since Braydon awakened this new sexual side of her, she'd acquired quite a taste for his body.

"Wow, what did I do to deserve this?"

"I've actually been fantasizing about doing this since last night when I was packing. It just so happens seeing you here tipped the cuteness scales in your favor, and I can't wait any longer."

His fingers brushed down her cheek, but something held his words back. There was something in his gaze that had her heart beating rapidly.

She loved him. She loved him and wanted to tell him, but this wasn't the right time.

Rather, she leaned forward and focused on the task at hand. Her lips closed over warm flesh and he went up on his toes, his fingers tunneling through her hair and pulling her close.

She never enjoyed doing this before Braydon came along. He made it pleasurable for both of them. Perhaps it was the gentle yet possessive way he handled her. Or perhaps it had more to do with how attractive she found his endless kindness and patience. Either way, she loved touching him like this.

Taking him deep in her mouth, he whispered her name. "Oh, sweet Becca…"

They didn't have much time before someone came looking for them, so she made quick work of bringing him to climax. His grip tightened in her hair as her mouth quickly worked over his flesh.

Sometimes Braydon seemed submissive in bed, always asking permission before he laid a hand on her, but other times his actions spoke of great control and hints of dominance. They were still learning each other and she liked discovering varying sides to his sexuality. He helped her find new sides of herself as well.

When she finished him, there was something languid in the air between them. This weekend would surely take their relationship deeper, but she wasn't sure how deep either of them was prepared to go.

~

"Frank!"

Sheilagh rolled her eyes as her mother yelled. "He's watching the game with Alec, Mum."

"I need to run to town. I'm out of flour for the dumplings. Any of you girls want to take a ride with me?"

Carla and Nikki, who were slicing carrots at the table, perked up. "Sure."

"Good." Her mother grabbed a set of keys off the hook. "Sheilagh, tell your father I'll be back in a few minutes. Don't let him touch the soup."

"You got it," she said as she finished up the carrots.

The moment they left Sheilagh breathed a sigh of relief. It was strange, since living alone with Alec she'd come to appreciate life's moments of stillness—which didn't exist in the big house. Carrying the carrots to the large pot on the stove, she dropped them in.

"Mum?" The side door opened and she tensed at the sound of Luke's voice. "Oh. Where's Mum?"

Still unable to meet her brother Luke's gaze head on, she busied herself with picking the chicken off the bone. "She ran into town to get flour for the dumplings."

"Oh. I, uh, needed to see if she has any chocolate chips. Tristan's attempting brownies."

It still gave her pause, hearing Luke mention Tristan with open affection. She rummaged through the pantry for chocolate chips. "Tristan bakes?"

"Yeah. It's his new passion, but he's not too good at it, so brace yourself."

She laughed, because it seemed polite. *Where the hell are the chocolate chips?* Her mind reached for sounds of Alec in the next room, drawing strength from his nearness.

She didn't know if she'd ever be comfortable in Luke's presence again. It had been a long time since their big fight, and a lot had changed. But, because she no longer lived on the mountain, she never truly felt they got the closure they deserved. Maybe she didn't deserve closure in his eyes.

It also had a lot to do with her being too afraid to face him. She loved Luke, but he had the ability to pulverize her on an emotional level and send her to a dark place she no longer wanted to visit.

"Here they are." She turned and came to an abrupt halt when she found her brother right behind her. "What are you doing?"

He looked at her for a long time without saying a word. Awkwardly, she glanced to the stove. The soup was fine, but she wished it wasn't so that she could get away. "Luke, I have to check on the soup. Here." She held out the chips, but he brushed them aside.

"I love you, Sheilagh. I don't want it to be weird between us anymore."

Her chest tightened and she desperately wished for Alec to come and rescue her. She didn't do situations like this well, especially on her own. "I love you too, dork. Now, let me check the soup."

"No. The soup's fine. I need to say this."

"Luke—"

"Just listen to me for a second." He drew in a long breath. "I was awful to you. I was wrong. You were a kid and I had so many problems. I hated everyone around me, but I hated myself most. The things I said to you, they weren't right and they weren't true. You're a good sister and when I see you with Finn and Bray and the others, I get so angry with myself, because I damaged that. I want my sister back."

The pain in her chest doubled as her throat constricted and her vision blurred. "I can't do this." She pushed past him, but he caught her arm, surprising her by forcing her into a firm hug.

His cheek pressed to the top of her head. "Yes, you can. I'm not going to fight with you anymore. I promise. I'm so sorry, Devil. For everything. I love you."

Too many emotions caused her will to collapse. A hiccupped sob escaped her throat and her arms tightened around the bulk of his body. How long she had waited to hear his apology. He might be the one asking for forgiveness, but to her thinking, that testified to him forgiving her as well. "I love you too, Luke."

Her face pressed into his shirt, where she could scent traces of Tristan's cologne. "I'm sorry, Luke. I'm sorry for everything. I'm sorry for what I did. I'm sorry for judging you. And most of all I'm sorry for not having the courage to face you when you needed your family most." She had so much regret from the summer before last when her brother was nearly killed and laid up in a hospital bed.

She'd been hysterical and distraught, wanting to go to him, but too afraid her presence wouldn't be wanted. Luke had been the one to call her during his recovery, but his apology was so out of the blue and he'd been on serious pain meds, she wasn't sure if he was sincere. Now she belie/ed him.

"Never again, baby girl. Never again."

She simply held on to him. He was so strong and they'd been

through so much. There were hundreds of moments they could have talked, but they both seemed hesitant. Perhaps they needed the extra time to heal. Or maybe they each needed the time to find themselves, find their perfect counterparts, and find peace, which they had.

Luke had Tristan and she had Alec. How had she ever questioned such things? It was difficult for her to comprehend her past feelings toward Tristan now that she understood true love and witnessed it every day with her husband.

"Sheilagh?" Sniffling, she peeked past her brother and found Alec, a look of cautious concern on her husband's face.

"Hey."

Luke stepped back and faced the wall, taking a moment to find his composure. Alec glanced at her brother and frowned. "Everything okay?"

She laughed, a bit watery. "Everything's great."

Luke turned and approached Alec. "I was just making a long overdue apology. I believe I owe you one as well." He held out his hand, which seemed to surprise her husband. "And a thank you."

"A thank you?"

Luke nodded and cleared his throat. "For being there for Sheilagh when she needed someone most. For loving her and making her happy. She deserves a good guy and she found one in you."

Alec grinned and shook her brother's hand. It might have been the first time they ever touched. "Thank you," Alec responded, clearly taken aback by Luke's words.

The side door opened again. "Maureen—" Tristan's steps cut short. "Hey. What's going on?" His expression turned guarded, as he took in their weepy eyes and the unusual grouping of her, Luke, and Alec, alone in the same room.

Luke grabbed the chips off the counter and handed them to Tristan, placing a kiss on his cheek. It was the first time Sheilagh saw her brother openly kiss his partner. "I did it," he whispered to Tristan.

Tristan glanced at Luke and smiled. It seemed this moment had been something they'd discussed in private. "Good."

There was so much affection in the look they shared, Sheilagh felt a bit like an intruder. Before she could think of something to say, Tristan pegged her with his familiar eyes. Holding out his arms, he said, "My turn, baby girl."

She glanced at Alec who nodded with a smile and she rushed to Tristan's arms. He lifted her off the ground and hugged her tight. God, she'd missed her friend.

His lips pressed to her hair and she snuggled into him. He had been such a part of her life, the distance between them over the past year had drained her more than words could express.

"I love you, baby girl."

"I love you too."

"Is dinner ready?—Oh." Braydon stilled as he came into the kitchen, clearly aware he was encroaching on a private moment. She beamed when she saw the way her brother clasped Becca's hand possessively. Something told her he wasn't letting this one out of his sight.

Wiping away her tears, Sheilagh apologized. "Sorry, we were just talking."

"Everything all right?" he asked nervously, pulling Becca into the room. "Where are Carla and Nikki?"

"They went with Mum into town to get some things."

Braydon's face dropped. "Shit."

~

"Hold on girls!" Maureen yelled as she whipped around the turn into traffic. "Now, see over there, that's the farmer's market my daughter-in-law owns. She and my son Kelly run it when they're not running the bar?"

"O'Malley's, right?" Carla asked, excited to tour the town.

"That's right. Have you been there?"

"No, but Braydon told us about it."

"Oh, 'tis a lovely pub. Would you like to stop in for a nip?"

Carla glanced at Nikki who shrugged. "Sure."

"All right then." Before they had a chance to brace themselves, Maureen yanked the wheel and made an abrupt U-turn.

Nikki laughed. "Oh, I think I like you, Mrs. McCullough."

"Call me Maureen, love. And I like you too. Like everyone. Unless you're on my shit list, that is. Perhaps my nephews will be there. Do you like Irishmen?"

"What's not to like?" Carla asked.

They pulled into the parking lot of O'Malley's. It looked like your average small town pub, stucco walls, simple green door, with a wooden sign on the exterior. This should be fun, Carla thought.

"Come along, girls." Maureen hopped out of the truck and removed her apron. The woman had endless energy.

"Do I look all right?" Nikki asked as she climbed down.

"What do you care? You're married."

"I'm not dead, though. There're Irishmen in there. McCullough Irishmen."

"Yeah, but from what I hear, all the good ones are taken."

"Not all of them, love," Maureen said with a grin as she slapped her lightly on the cheek. "Come along. Sheilagh's watching the soup and she'll only be able to fight off the men for so long. Once they realize she's got food they'll be up her arse like a bad thong. But she's a fighter, my devil."

Carla stilled. "Oh my God, I love this woman."

They followed her into the bar and Carla's eyes adjusted to the dim lighting. The second she noticed the man behind the bar she froze. Choirs sang and mystical doves seemed to release from somewhere in her mind. "Holy mother of man flesh. I think my ovaries just exploded. Tell me that one's single."

Maureen laughed. "'Fraid not, love. That there's my rogue. Kelly!"

The gorgeous bartender turned with a smile. Yup. When God said let there be sexy he definitely had this man in mind.

"Who let you out without supervision?" the bartender teased.

Maureen waved his words away and dragged them closer to the tattooed, blue-eyed devil at the bar. "I ran out of flour."

Kelly laughed. "We don't sell that here, Mum."

"'Tis a shame. I suppose I'll just have to buy a nip instead. Give us three shots of Tully, love."

"And who are your friends? Picking up hitchhikers again?" He turned and winked a sharp sapphire eye in their direction and Carla wiped her gaping jaw, doing a quick drool check.

"Holy shit, he should have a license to carry a face like that," Nikki whispered.

"I'm sorry," Carla said, leaning close, but keeping her eyes on Kelly. "My vagina's in some sort of spasm right now. I couldn't quite make out your words."

"Yeah," Nikki mumbled.

Carla nodded, thinking she hadn't blinked in about four minutes. "I could break him."

"I could break him better," Nikki said.

Carla frowned at her *married* sister. Shoving Nikki aside she climbed onto a stool. "Hi. I'm Carla, Becca's friend."

He slid three stout glasses across the bar. "Are you Becca?" he asked, tipping his chin toward Nikki.

"She's nobody. I'm Carla. Car-la. Try saying it."

He laughed nervously and eyed his mother. "Mum?"

"They're Braydon's friends, love. He's brought home a lassie and these two followed along to take in the sights. Seems this one likes the sight of you." She laughed and slung back her drink, leaving not a drop in the glass.

Carla did the same, enjoying the slow burn as it traveled down her throat. Letting out a whistle, she decided she liked these people, liked this place. Definitely liked the bartender.

"Are they coming here tonight?" Kelly asked as he refilled his mother's glass.

"Oh, I believe. They'll be staying until Sunday."

"And you say he brought a girl home? Has Colin met her yet?"

Maureen laughed, slapping her son's arm and slinging back another shot. "Don't you start, Kelly. Your brother's a married man. His days of stealing Braydon's girlfriends are over."

"Someone stole Braydon's girlfriend? Do tell," Nikki said, sliding her empty glass back to Kelly.

The next hour passed in a blur. Kelly was excellent at his job, especially when Carla imagined him doing it naked. He told them all about Colin, the once intended priest, stealing Braydon's girlfriend in college. He also told amusing tidbits about Finn and Luke and Sheilagh. It seemed with such a big family there was plenty of juicy gossip to keep a happy hour quite happy.

BECCA'S HEAD WAS SPINNING. Braydon hadn't been kidding when he said his family was big. He also wasn't exaggerating when he said he was used to chaos. She'd escaped for a brief moment to catch her breath and call Kevin.

Closing herself in what looked like an infrequently used sewing room, she dialed.

"Hello, Rebecca." His irritable tone told her he was flustered.

"Hey, is everything okay?"

"As good as can be expected."

Hunter's voice could be heard in the background and she hated not being able to see him in that moment. "Has he eaten?"

Kevin scoffed. "I know how to take care of my son, Rebecca. Give me a little credit."

She tried, but when it came to Hunter she was a control freak and for good reason. "He sounds agitated, did you—"

"He's perfectly fine," Kevin snapped. "Did you call to check in on him or me?"

"Well, both, I guess."

"Nothing you could do anyway, all the way out in the middle of nowhere with your new *friends*," he grumbled.

"Kevin…"

"Rebecca…" he mimicked. "Look, we're good here. Get back to your vacation."

She hadn't taken a vacation in years and it wasn't fair for him to make her feel guilty about getting out of town rather than sitting home alone over a holiday. "I just wanted to make sure you didn't need anything."

"Yeah, sure. As my *wife* is spending her Thanksgiving with a family she doesn't know and I'm here trying to figure out how long to defrost a turkey, yeah, I'd say we have it covered."

Her brow tensed. What did he expect? "Ex-wife."

"Whatever. Have fun." The line went dead.

His bad attitude should have made it easier to write off his comments, but this being her first holiday away from her son made that a little difficult. Desperately trying not to get overly upset, she didn't allow herself much time to think about past years' traditions. That life was over now, over because her husband never was on the same page as the rest of them, and it was time to close that book.

However, old habits die hard and when a woman committed a lifetime to a man, it wasn't always easy to discard the failed result. So many years fighting toward a happy marriage made it difficult to restructure her thinking and move in a new direction, no matter how much her rational brain decided forward was the way to go, her heart and long-term memory seemed to keep pulling her backward.

Perhaps every divorced person struggled with letting go. She wasn't necessarily mourning the loss of Kevin, but mourning her failed marriage. It certainly was a process. On top of that process was the difficult acceptance of who Kevin had become. He was not the man she'd married. Yet her heart couldn't seem to separate the two. Moments like this, moments when he was cold and short with her, brought that realization home.

When she returned to the kitchen the McCulloughs multiplied like *Gremlins*. Each one shouted over the other, and she was beginning to worry that Carla and Nikki weren't back yet.

Braydon's gaze connected with hers and his brow creased with concern. Sidling to her side, he whispered, "Everything okay?"

"Yeah, just Kevin being Kevin."

His gaze traveled over his relatives as he offered a knowing nod. But he didn't know. He would never know how much she still hurt over the fact that she'd married wrong. The fact that Hunter's father threw away their vows on some sleazy neighbor yet had the ability to make her feel like a criminal for walking away.

Refusing to dwell on her divorce while spending the weekend with her boyfriend's family, she shoved all worrying thoughts away and pasted on what she hoped was a convincing smile.

"When can we eat?" Finn shouted. He'd arrived shortly after they came down stairs and interrupted what seemed like a touching exchange between Sheilagh and Luke. "Mum's been gone for over an hour."

"Lord knows where your mother got off too. I'm going in," Frank said, taking the ladle from Kate.

Children were everywhere. Ashlynn, a tiny thing in overalls, nudged Frank out of the way with her hip. "You'll make a mess. Let me do it."

Mr. McCullough handed over the spoon and Ashlynn dished out soup. It was like a line at a soup kitchen the way these people rushed for food. Hadn't they been fed today? Soon as the kids came barreling in, she decided it was more like a litter of puppies racing for milk.

There were so many dark heads and bright blue eyes. Braydon seemed the only blond, and though Finn and Luke had lighter features, the rest were what she assumed was referred to as Black Irish. Even the children were beautiful. What a family of heartbreakers.

Braydon handed her a bowl and directed her to the long table. Everyone settled in and a hush fell over the crowd as they began to eat. Wow.

Becca brought the spoon to her mouth and froze as the flavor settled over her tongue. "Oh my gosh. This is delicious."

Braydon smiled, shutting his eyes. "Mum's cooking. Told you it was the best. This doesn't even have her dumplings."

The phone rang and no one moved. Mallory, Finn's wife, was

the first to acknowledge the ringing. "Frank, do you want me to get that?"

"I'll get it," he grumbled, stealing one more bite before rising. He plucked the phone off the wall and Becca smirked as she noted it was almost three decades old. "Hello? She's what? Sweet Jesus, Kelly, you know better."

"Is that Kelly? Tell him to bring home milk," Ashlynn shouted.

Frank sighed. "I'll come get her." He hung up the phone and grabbed his keys. "I have to go get your mother. She's snockered."

"She's supposed to babysit," Mallory said.

"I can watch the kids," Kate, the eldest sister volunteered.

"All of them?" Colin, Sammy, and Finn asked at once.

Kate glanced at the little ones piled around the table in the dining room like a litter of puppies nursing off a momma. "I suppose, but each one of you owe me babysitting next month."

Becca's eyes bulged. Kate had five kids. These people were pros in the child-rearing department.

"Deal," Finn said.

After dinner everyone dispersed to drive the children to Kate and Anthony's house. She gave Sheilagh a hand cleaning up the kitchen while Braydon disappeared somewhere with Alec.

"What do you think of the family, so far?" Sheilagh asked. "It's a sign of strength that you haven't run off screaming yet."

Becca grinned. "I think they're wonderful."

"Good, because I can tell Bray really likes you."

"Oh?" She pretended to pay close attention to the dish she was washing. How did someone have so many children without a dishwasher?

"Don't act like you don't see it," Sheilagh remarked, stacking the bowls back in the cabinet.

"I have nothing to compare it to. I only met him a couple months ago."

"Trust me. You're different."

"Well then I guess the question is what does the family think of me?"

Sheilagh snickered. "We won't know that until we see how you hold your whiskey."

Becca jumped as a pair of familiar hands snaked around her waist and pulled her close. "Don't let her scare you, angel."

Relaxing in Braydon's hold, she finished the last of the spoons. "Are you ready?"

"Yup. Sheilagh, you wanna drive together? Alec said he isn't drinking."

"What?" She stomped off into the other room.

"Is she mad her husband isn't going to drink?"

Braydon shrugged. "Probably, but it's for the best. When Alec drinks he starts spouting off lines from Hamlet in a cockney slur and no one knows what the bloody hell he's talking about. Come on. I'll get your coat."

They arrived at the bar the same time as Mallory and Finn. Becca had been worried about Carla and Nikki until she spotted them—dancing with two flannel-covered men on the dance floor.

"Oh, look, your friends made new friends," Sheilagh laughed.

Becca frowned. "Do you know them?"

Sheilagh squinted. "Nope. But I think that one works at the bank."

Becca frowned, trying to imagine the flannel covered man with a belt buckle the size of Texas as a bank teller.

"Braydon! Welcome home!" The man behind the bar yelled, causing Becca to do a double take. He was gorgeous, in a tattooed bad boy sort of way.

Braydon stepped up on the footrest and leaned over the bar to hug the man. "Thanks, Kel. This is Becca, my girlfriend."

That was the fourth or fifth time he'd introduced her as such. She wasn't complaining, but wondered why he felt the need to label her to his family. "Nice to meet you," Becca greeted, shaking his hand.

"Your friends are a little crazy," he said, tipping his chin toward the dance floor. "Especially the short one."

"Yeah, you better watch her," Becca warned. "She's on the prowl."

"She's a few years too late," Kelly said, waving his ring finger in the air, his thumb tapping his wedding band. "Happily married. She's a feisty little thing though."

"Did Dad pick up Mum?" Braydon asked.

Kelly rolled his eyes. "Yeah, and she's no help. Wait until Ashlynn hears how she encouraged your friends. Anyway, what are we drinking tonight?"

Braydon ordered himself a beer and her a glass of wine. The men pushed two tables together so everyone could fit. Once the drinks were flowing everyone wore a smile and started in on funny anecdotes.

"Finn, let's dance," Mallory said, rising from the table.

"Oh, I love your shoes," Becca complimented. Mallory was so pretty and full of life. There was something so romantic about the way her husband never took his eyes off her. Sheilagh and Alec followed the couple to the dance floor.

Samantha, Colin's wife, slid into Mallory's seat. "So your Bray's girlfriend. I didn't really get a chance to talk to you at the house with the kids running around. He told me about you though."

This was Braydon's ex. She wasn't sure how to process the fact that he'd discussed their relationship with the other woman. "What did he say?"

"He told me about your son. Hunter, right?"

All of her guards went flying up at the mention of her son. "That's right."

Oh God. This was the moment she'd been dreading. The moment when the truth came out about how Braydon really felt. She'd tolerated years of ignorant misconceptions from uninformed people regarding autism. It would crush her to find out Braydon might be putting on an act.

"I'm a teacher, so he had some questions."

No wonder he'd been so accepting and unshakable. He was directing all the awkward questions at his ex.

"Did I say something wrong?" Sammy asked, looking confused.

Becca shook her head. "No, I'm sorry. I'm just surprised he discussed Hunter with you. I didn't realize others knew I had a son."

"Well, we all love children. No one's judging the fact that you have one."

But she'd seen all their children. Each one appeared developmentally on target and socially well-adjusted. It wasn't the same. Even parents could harshly judge what they didn't understand. Glancing nervously at Sammy, her train of thought derailed.

What the heck was she doing? These people had been nothing but accepting since the moment she stepped foot on their property.

There was a fine line between protecting Hunter, and being the one to constantly reiterate that he was different. He was her son. Period. Her paranoia over others' acceptance was becoming more cumbersome than the actual reality. It wasn't right for her to be so hyper focused on Hunter's differences when no one else was making a big deal out of their situation. She needed to chill.

"Is he with his father for Thanksgiving?"

"Yes."

Sammy smiled sadly and surprised Becca by patting her hand. "That must be difficult for you, missing a holiday with him. Maybe one weekend you can bring him back so we can meet him."

Becca took in the other woman's kind eyes and soft smile. She seemed very sincere. "Hunter has difficulty with large crowds."

"Oh, well, of course we wouldn't want to overwhelm him. If he came for a visit you guys would be more than welcome to stay with Colin and me for the weekend. Colin has a way of keeping his relatives at bay when necessary. Of course, there're still our little guys, who can be a bit rambunctious, but I'm sure they'd have a blast with Hunter. You should think about it."

Samantha was really nice, she decided. They all were. It was baffling and incredibly refreshing at the same time.

Braydon returned from the bar and placed a fresh glass of wine in front of her. She desperately needed a sip. "Wanna dance? I picked the next song on the jukebox for you."

Glancing over the rim of her glass she beamed. "You did? What did you pick?"

"You'll see. Come on." He took her hand and pulled her to where the others had been dancing to a fast paced song.

"What's Finn doing?"

Bray shrugged as his brother did a strange impression of a bird. "He has his own special kind of dancing. We just nod and smile."

He took her hand and swung her close. "Are we slow dancing?"

"Maybe."

The song came to an end as a new one started. She recognized it right away as her personal favorite, *As Tears Go By.* "I love this song."

His voice was low, his eyes twinkling in the dim lighting. "I know. You said. It reminds me of you."

They moved in a slow circle, his hand holding hers tight as the rest of the world fell away. "What do you think they're singing about?" he asked, his voice low and close to her ear.

Her mouth pinched, guarding her secrets. "You'll laugh."

"No, I won't." His gaze met hers and held. "I promise."

Drawing in a deep breath, she rested her head on his shoulder and quietly confessed. "I think he's singing to me. The day that Hunter was diagnosed I went to the park and cried as I watched from my car while all the children played. This song was playing on the radio. It was the one time I let myself really face what I was up against. My son wasn't talking and the specialists warned he might never speak."

His hold shifted, putting enough space between them so he could meet her gaze again. "I didn't realize it was a sad song for you." His expression was weighted with regret. "I'm sorry."

"It's not sad, not anymore," she quickly reassured, not wanting to diminish his sweet gesture. "That was the first day of the rest of my life. Since then the song has taken on a different meaning."

"How so?"

"I think when they sing about the evening of the day it represents our unpredictable schedule and the nights we went without sleep because Hunter needed to be awake. The tears going by are his victories, like the first time he said my name or made eye contact with me and smiled—all the things I was told not to expect. Those moments didn't happen when expected, but they happened."

Relief softened his features and he pulled her close again, hugging her as they danced. She loved that Braydon was so affectionate, always holding and touching her and hugging her. She'd gone without such things for so long they still seemed to surprise her and take her breath away.

She pressed her cheek to his shoulder and quietly confessed, "I miss him."

"I know it's difficult being away from him, but I'm glad you're here with me."

"It's hard being apart for so long."

"Understandably." He kissed her cheek and they danced silently for a bit. "Becca?"

"Hmm?" she hummed, lulled into a state of contentment, safe in his arms.

"Don't get mad."

Safe feeling gone. Lifting her head, she met his gaze, trepidation causing her steps to falter. "What's wrong?"

"Well, I have to tell you something and you're not gonna like it."

She didn't want him to spoil their peaceful night. "Then don't tell me," she said childishly, as though that would solve anything.

"I have to." His brow puckered with regret. "I did something you told me not to."

She stepped back, releasing her hands from his hold. The music faded to white noise as her head filled with panic. If it was something she specifically told him not to do then it was something meaningful she didn't want to happen. "Tell me."

He offered a half-smile, but she could see whatever he was about to admit was serious. She waited, fearing they might all be driving home in Nikki's car that night.

Glancing down, he drew in a breath then met her expectant stare. "I've fallen in love with you."

Her breath held for an uncalculated length of time as she stopped moving. Her lungs began to burn and she sucked in a gulp of air, throwing the earth back into motion.

Shaking her head, certain she hadn't heard him right, she frowned. "What?"

"Don't get mad. I know I promised I wouldn't, because those words aren't little to you, but they aren't little to me either. They're big, too big to keep inside anymore. I love you."

Her vision wavered and her lip trembled. "You...love me?"

"Yes. I love everything about you. Being here with you only made me sure of everything I've been feeling. You're right for me and I want to be right for you."

Her heart beat erratically. "Oh, Braydon..."

"You don't have to say it—"

She cut off his words, lunging herself at him and sealing her mouth to his. Silly boy. How could he not realize she'd fallen head over heels for him? There was a sudden outpouring of applause and catcalls. Pulling back, she ducked her face into his shoulder, heat burning her face. "Everyone's looking at us."

"Well, let's give them something to really shout about." He dipped her back and kissed her deeply. The group of drunken McCulloughs went crazy, shouting and whistling like they were at a sports event.

When he dragged his lips away she was dizzy.

He grinned with cockiness, pressing his forehead to hers. "I played another song for you."

The Stones ended and Blind Melon took over singing *No Rain*. She laughed, remembering when they danced in her kitchen. "God, I love you too."

His grin froze, a million sentiments flashing in his eyes. The main one she recognized was relief. "You make me happier than I've been in a long time, Becca. Dance with me."

Taking her hand he spun her around the dance floor. The rest of the McCulloughs came out to join them, Finn led the pack with his unique dance moves and had them all cramping with laughter. It was likely the best night she'd had in...well, ever.

CHAPTER 10

They stumbled into the big house sometime after two. Becca giggled uncontrollably as her foot caught on the carpet and she did a not so graceful wild turkey dive into Braydon's room.

"Good night, lovebirds!" Sheilagh called from down the hall as her door slammed.

"Good night." Braydon shut and locked his bedroom door. "You're in trouble."

The bed covers fluffed as she collapsed onto the mattress. "I like trouble."

He shook his head. "You're a giggly mess. I'm shocked I haven't lost you to a fit of snorts."

On cue, air went up her nose in the most unladylike snuffle. "Oops." Her fingers covered her nose, but it was no use. Her laughter turned to unladylike snorts and she was inconsolable for some time as she had quite the one woman, drunken giggle fest.

Once the last giggle seemed drained from her lungs, she flopped to her back and hummed happily. "Tonight was fun."

Braydon removed his shoes and stripped off his clothes, yanking clothing off Becca at the same time. He'd been waiting hours to get her back to his room. Dropping to the bed, he stripped off her shirt and unclasped her bra, wasting no time getting one of her pert nipples into his mouth. She moaned and twisted beneath him.

"I want you so much I can't stand it," he whispered, plumbing her breasts and teasing the tips.

She stretched beneath him, extending her arms into the pillows and wrapping her legs around his hips. "I'm yours." Her eyes closed, a content, punch drunk grin curving her lips.

He paused. He didn't want to overestimate the meaning of her words seeing as she'd had a lot to drink, but he wanted there to be sincerity behind her muttered statement. Releasing her breast, he rose to study her face. "Are you?"

Her eyes slowly opened and she nodded. She was his. His lips crashed to hers as he kissed her with all his pent up passion and desire. Her tongue dueled with his as her fingers tunneled through his hair.

Need thrummed through his veins, demanding he claim what was his. Taking her hand, he pressed it to his cock. Her palm gripped his hard flesh and pulled at his length, sending chills up his spine. His fingers delved between her thighs and found her sex, wet and hot. She arched into his touch as he probed deep between her folds. "Tell me what you want."

She writhed, lost in the passionate moment. "I want you to take control. I don't want to decide."

Pressing two fingers deep, he stilled, holding her body on the precipice of pleasure. "You like when I'm in control?"

Head tipped back into the mattress, cheeks flushed, she nodded shyly. Drawing in a deep breath, scenting her arousal, his jaw twitched as his inner caveman growled. Withdrawing his fingers, he slowly lifted the digits to his mouth and tasted her.

"Turn on your stomach."

She obliged, scrambling to her hands and knees and giving him an outstanding view of her ass.

"Scoot forward so you can reach the headboard."

Hoisting her hips higher, he traced his fingers down her spine as he admired the view. His lips pressed into each rounded cheek, needing to taste more of her. Twisting, he dropped to his back and slid his shoulders between her knees.

Heaven.

Gripping her ass, he tugged her low, extended his neck, and made a long sweep with his tongue over her glistening sex. She shot up, but he held her close, sipping from her, nibbling at her soft skin as though it were succulent fruit. "Stay still," he commanded, pulling her sex down to his mouth. Peeking upward, he watched her breasts swaying as her body gyrated over him.

Her keening cries filled the room as he tormented her in the sweetest way possible, holding her to him as her pleasure climbed. Every encounter quickly unraveled into that moment, trumping all other experiences. Nothing compared to what he felt with this woman.

Her shyness disappeared as he awoke every carnal part of her being. Her taste covered his lips and he savored every drop as she came, crying out his name and trembling in his grip.

Braydon quickly pulled her down his body, cradling her narrow shoulders as he held her through the aftershocks of her climax and kissed her passionately. Adjusted their position, he slid her to her belly and climbed to his knees.

Lining up their bodies up, he admired her figure and entered her from behind in one fluid motion. She cried out as he filled her. His hand snaked beneath her body, cupping her breast as his chest lowered, pressing sensually to her back. He couldn't get close enough. Rising, he hitched her hips, raising her back flush against his front.

The angle didn't allow for speed, but it made up for it with depth. The intensity doubled as he held himself buried inside her heat and caressed his hand down her front, spreading his fingers wide across her abdomen. Her head tipped back to his shoulder, and he felt as though he were encroaching on her soul. Her arms looped around his neck as he caressed her chin and kissed her.

His fingers followed the long curve of her arm, tracing down from her raised elbow to her breast. "Do you feel that?" he whispered against her soft lips. "I've never felt anything like it. Your body fits mine perfectly."

"Oh, God..." She moaned and whimpered as he slowly rocked into her. She did some fancy move with her hips, taking him deeper.

His palms traced around her ribs and glided down to her trembling thighs. "You're so hot and tight." Her sex fluttered with every word he spoke. "Being inside of you is heaven."

She sighed as he teased the soft patch of hair above her sex.

"Fuck, angel, I don't ever want to leave you."

Her fingers locked in his hair, jerking his lips to hers. "Then don't."

He chuckled, his lips mashing to hers.

Her hands left his hair, teasing down his neck before reaching for her sex. Her delicate fingers stroked over his balls and toyed with her clit until he felt her break once more. Her body tightened around his length, as wet heat coated his cock and his own release tunneled out of him. They existed, in that moment, on some intrepid plane of bliss he'd never visited before.

It was the most unadulterated sexual moment of his life and it only took him half a second to destroy it. "Marry me, angel."

~

BECCA FROZE, her ears still ringing from the incredible, full body orgasm she'd just experienced. Her skin turned cold. "What…what did you just say?"

Silence.

"Braydon…" Needing to see his face, she crawled forward, disentangling her body from his. "Say something."

He remained quiet. She reached for the blankets, needing shelter after such a vulnerable show. His expression was blank. Her eyes traveled over his body and awareness as to why the sex was so incredible set in. "We didn't use protection."

He blinked, but made no comment.

Furious and feeling like she was speaking to a brick wall, she squirmed back and glared at him. "Braydon, say something. Now."

His Adam's apple shifted as he noticeably swallowed. "I don't know what to say."

Gripping her temples, she shook her head and snapped, "We forgot a condom."

"Are you upset?"

Upset? Yes, she was upset! How was he calm? Rather than respond, she did quick math in her head. She had her period about two weeks ago. That meant—oh God.

Breath filled her lungs, leveling her back into the headboard. *Calm down. Don't freak out.* He still wasn't talking, which only added to her frustration. Sliding her hands behind her head, she fisted her hair and exhaled slowly, hoping to expel some of her fear. It wasn't helping and neither was he.

Needing to take some form of action, she bolted off the bed. "I need to take a shower."

That seemed to jerk him back to reality. "Wait." He jumped off the bed and grabbed her hand, but she flung him away, unable to tolerate closeness at the moment. She paced with agitation. Her mind fragmented with hypotheticals and worst-case scenarios. He seemed unbothered by the implications of their actions. Didn't he understand?

"I can't wait, Braydon. You just came inside of me!"

"Becca, please calm down. Besides, what the hell is showering going to do?"

Her palms covered her face and she squeezed as regret growled out of her. "I don't know, but I can't have babies." She flung her hands down, resenting her absent wits that had been chased away by booze.

He frowned at her. "What are you talking about? You had Hunter."

"Exactly." She needed fresh air—or a shower—or a drink. Anything outside of that room would help at the moment. "Where are my pants?"

"Becca, stop for a minute. I'm sorry I forgot a condom, but I think you're overreacting. The chances—"

She turned on him. "That's what you're missing, Braydon. I can't afford to take chances. Do you know what my life would be like if I had another child? I can barely handle Hunter on my own."

He drew back and scowled. "Who the fuck said you'd be alone?"

"Don't curse at me."

His lips thinned. "Don't make me out to be an asshole. I'm not Kevin."

She found her shirt and snatched it off the floor. When she couldn't turn it right side out she huffed and thwacked the garment in the air. "You're right, you're not. You're some guy I met a couple months ago who has no idea about how difficult my life is." Why wasn't this shirt—

The room spun and he was suddenly in her face, gripping her shoulders. "That's enough. I love you, Becca. That means that I know you enough to care what your daily life entails, I wanna be there to help, and I respect you, God damn it. Stop acting like no one else can comprehend your job as a mother."

His harsh honesty left her shaken, her words readily jumping from her mouth to shield her heart. "They can't! If you could you'd understand why I can't have another child."

"You *can* have another child. The only thing stopping you is you!"

Her jaw trembled. "No, Braydon, the only thing stopping me is reality. How many hours will I sleep with an infant in addition to Hunter? Who's going to care for my baby while I'm working, which I'll be doing until I'm dead, because—news flash—autism is expensive! Hunter's medication costs me more than my car payment each month, not to mention his afterschool care and therapy sessions and all the equipment he needs. I couldn't even afford to have a tree cut down! And I have to consider the amount of attention my son needs. What will that cost his siblings? I can't emotionally afford another child and it's completely selfish of me to dream of one when I'm already stretched to my limits on a daily basis. You don't get it."

He dropped to the bed and stared at the floor. "But what if..."

"What? What if I had a neurotypical child? Some studies claim there's an eighteen percent chance of recurrence. It runs in families, Braydon. And even if I had the easiest, neurotypical baby in the world, babies require more effort than I can spare. You have no right to question me on this! And I have no right bringing another life into this world when I can barely manage my own."

"All right!" he shouted and she jerked back a step. "I said I was sorry. It was an accident." He glared at her, and she didn't like the hardness in his eyes.

She turned to find shoes.

"I can live with not having children."

Pivoting slowly she frowned at him. He wasn't her husband. This entire issue was premature; their relationship not nearly developed enough to withstand such pressure. "Why should you have to?"

"Because I want you and that's what you want."

God, she would ruin him. She couldn't stand the idea of depriving someone like Braydon of a family he obviously expected. "No, Braydon, none of this is what I want."

"Stop saying stuff like that. You're upset."

"I'm real." It hurt. The truth ripped into her like a hot poker cauterizing her dreams from actual reality. But it was her reality, not his. "You have this idea in your head about me that isn't right. I've been telling you from the beginning, my life's chaotic and I'm not some sweet little innocent."

"And I've listened to you, Becca. I've learned everything I can about autism. I read articles every day. What I can't find is the part of you *not* defined by autism. I'm trying to figure you out, but you won't let me in."

Her face lowered, as she could no longer look him in the eye. "There are no other parts. It's my life."

He shook his head. "You're wrong. You're in there. You've been neglecting yourself for so long, you can't recognize the woman I catch glimpses of, the woman I love."

They should have never said those words. "Why are you trying so hard?"

"Why are you waiting for us to fail?" His shoulders drew up tight. He shook his head. "I guess I thought trying was what people did when they cared. I've never experienced so much opposition in my life."

Her heart turned heavy. "Braydon—"

"Just stop. You know, I watch you with him. You'd move mountains if it meant making a minute of his life a little less difficult. Why is it so hard for you to believe someone would want to do the same for you? You're right, I don't know the first thing about being a parent or being a parent to a child with symptoms of autism. But you're wrong if you think you have the market cornered on love. The one thing my family taught me, is to do anything for those you love. I guess I thought we could move more mountains together."

With that, he stood, shoved on his jeans, and left through the connecting bathroom. The door to the neighboring bedroom closed and locked. Shutting her eyes, she fought the urge to burst into tears.

For several minutes she stood, trembling. Her body slowly moved to the bathroom, her mind someplace else. Becca showered, knowing that would do little to change their circumstances, but needed to anyway so that she could tell herself the wetness on her cheeks wasn't tears. As she dried off, she listened at the door to the other bedroom connected to the adjoining bathroom.

Silence.

She was having a hard time recalling exactly what she'd said because she was still quite intoxicated. Everything happened so fast, she'd panicked, spewing her deepest fears, the ones she never shared.

Shame knifed through her. How could she have said those things? Her personal opinion of herself in that moment was very low. Braydon never got angry, but she'd insulted him and he was definitely upset.

Maybe she should apologize in the morning. It wasn't his fault they were careless. They'd both had too much to drink and got carried away. The only person responsible for her body was her. Fear gave way to shame as she considered the degree she'd over-reacted.

Kevin was Hunter's father and he couldn't handle their life when he was the man intended for the job. How was she supposed to expect another man to handle what Hunter's actual father couldn't? Simply put, she was safest facing parenthood as a solitary job and she was at her limit with the responsibilities she already needed to handle.

She'd begged Kevin for more children. After years of his rejection, all his fears somehow became her own. It wasn't an easy realization that she and Kevin were somewhat alike. If her husband of ten years didn't think she should have more children, what did Braydon know? They'd only been together for two months.

The topic of pregnancy was an old wound that had never quite healed. It hurt every time she picked at it, and over time, she'd found it easier to simply accept she was better off only ever having one child.

Still, as she lay in bed alone and thought over the incredible family she was staying with, the love thrumming through the walls, the affection each sibling shared, she longed to be a tiny part of all that love. The McCulloughs were no typical family and the thought that she could be carrying the next McCullough gave her a reckless sense of happiness.

Sighing, her hand drifted from her stomach to the covers. She was an idiot. Braydon was such a nice guy and she'd hurt him. Maybe she was unlovable. Not that she couldn't be loved, but rather, she rejected love in order to continue swimming against the current—alone.

She was so desolate. And tired. Even when she was married to Kevin she'd been swimming alone. Dragging someone against the current with her was simply exhausting.

～

BRAYDON AWOKE in Colin's bed to the smell of poop. Scrunching his nose he turned and found his nephew, Liam, smiling at him as Colin changed his diaper on the bed beside his head.

"Jesus, Colin, did you have to do that five inches from my face?"

"You're in my room."

"That's no excuse."

"Hi, Unca Bray!"

"Hi, Liam. Shouldn't you be potty trained by now?"

"He doesn't like to poop on the potty."

Bray raised an eyebrow. "You'd rather sit in it?"

"I can't want that," Liam said.

"Can't want what, poop in your diaper?"

"I can't want that," his nephew repeated.

"Okay, buddy, you're all set. Go see what your mom's doing."

Liam toddled out of the room and Colin faced him after wiping his hands down with a wet nap. "So why are you in here?"

"Becca and I had a fight."

"I figured. The friend, Carla I think, said they might be leaving today."

He sat up. "What? No they're not."

"That's what she said when I talked to her."

"When did you see her?"

"She was having coffee on the porch. She doesn't seem like quite the morning person, so maybe she was just grumbling while the caffeine kicked in."

"Shit."

"What did you fight about?"

Scrubbing his hands over his face he groaned. "I don't even know. We were having a great time and then I blurted out something stupid without thinking. The next thing I know, we're having an argument about why she doesn't want children."

Colin's brows shot up. "How do you feel about that?"

"I don't know. Since when do you have to decide that when you're only dating someone?"

"Probably around the same time you realize you can't imagine your future without that someone."

He hated asking questions about the time his brother betrayed him, but his curiosity got the better of him. "Did you know that you wanted children when you and Samantha…"

"We're different. When Sammy and I…you know…I wasn't clear on anything I wanted. I thought I still wanted to join the priesthood, but then I couldn't do that either. I couldn't picture my life without her."

"But you decided to marry her after you found out about Lula."

"No, I decided to marry her the moment I watched her leave. I just didn't know how to go about fixing the mess that was suddenly my life. Tallulah was a bonus."

"Maybe we should go home and cool off. She was so pissed off last night. She wasn't listening to reason."

"Bray, no woman's ever rational when they're in love. There's a lot of emotion and things way above our heads going on in theirs. I can tell you one thing though, from experience."

"What's that?"

"Don't be the idiot I was. Don't let her leave."

"What if she wants to go and I can't stop her?"

"Make her want to stay." Colin stood and grabbed the wrapped up diaper off the dresser. "Good luck, man."

Braydon lay in bed a while after his brother left. The house sounded busy downstairs and he was reluctant to join the others without first talking to Becca.

He washed up in the bathroom and knocked on the door leading to his room. "Becca?"

"Come in."

He pressed into his room and stilled at the sight of her refolding the clothes in her suitcase. "What are you doing?"

Her shoulders lowered and she visibly deflated. "I don't know."

"Can we talk?"

She huffed. "Sure."

She wouldn't meet his eyes. He approached the bed and took the shirt she was folding out of her hands and placed it on the suitcase. "I'm sorry about last night. I should've remembered to use a condom and I had no right interrogating you about having children."

"I may have overreacted," she said quietly. "I have some unre-solved issues I need to work out. It wasn't your fault I got so upset."

"If you're thinking of leaving, please don't. I want you to stay."

She sighed and sat beside him on the bed. "Braydon, I think we want different things in life."

His eyes closed. What was it with this place? Every time he brought a girl home they broke up with him. He glanced to the exact place Samantha had been standing when she'd said almost those same words. "I don't want to break up."

"Neither do I, but what happens in a few years when you want to start a family and I can't give you one? I'm not even sure if I want to get married again. Marriage is hard and I'm tired."

"You're always tired." Her head jerked back. Shit, he attempted to retract his words, but it was too late. "Becca, I—"

"I'm *always tired* for good reason, Braydon. Look, I don't want to fight. I barely slept last night, I miss my son, and I don't have the answers you're looking for."

"I'm not looking for answers. I'm just looking for you."

Purple crests marked the delicate skin under her tired eyes. "You deserve more than I can offer."

"What about all the things you deserve, Becca?"

"That's... I'm okay with my simple life."

"No, you're not."

Her lashes flickered as she blinked back tears. "I can handle the way things were. I don't know if I can handle this."

"What about us? Can *we* handle this?"

"What happens when we return to Pittsburgh? We're moving so fast."

"Why do we have to predict everything, Becca? Has assuming the future ever solved anything for you?"

Her lips tightened and she frowned. "No."

"Then stop trying to guess what happens next. Let life take its course and, for once, enjoy the surprises it brings." That was good advice for him as well.

"I've never been good at that," she quietly admitted. "The last surprise I got was my husband screwing my neighbor. I didn't take that too well."

He pinched her chin and turned her face until her gaze met his. "You have to let go. We're only human, we can't control everything."

"I never wanted control."

"Then let others help you when they offer to take some of the weight off your shoulders. I don't offer things unless I intend to follow through. When I said I'd be there, I meant it."

She drew in a deep breath and, startlingly, he saw something shift in her entire disposition. Her face crumbled as she started to cry. "I'm so scared."

"Hey, it's okay." He pulled her into his arms and held her tight. "Talk to me."

Her head shook as she sniffled. "I don't know how to trust people. It's like I've lost all faith in mankind—including myself."

He didn't mean to chuckle, but she sounded so hopeless. "That's not true."

"Yes, it is. I've become so paranoid, I'm skeptical of everyone I meet. People can be so mean. I hate taking Hunter anywhere, because I can't trust others to be decent. They stare and talk without thinking. It's like they don't think he can hear or process their nasty comments, but he can. Hunter's more sensitive than half the people in this world put together. I just don't want to see him hurt, but maybe I'm hurting him by sheltering him too much."

"Mean people suck," he said, holding her close. "But not everyone's mean, Becca."

"There's a shortage of goodhearted people. That's what life's shown me. Then I come here and meet your family, and I have no point of comparison for such genuine acceptance. I've never seen anything like it and it terrifies me."

"Why?"

"I don't know. Your parents raised seven children. Their love is palpable, the way it's supposed to be. Why couldn't Kevin love us like that?"

Taking a slow breath, he drew back. He could talk about this. It was all part of Becca. But it was also a very difficult topic. "Becca, sometimes people grow apart. Don't be one of those people that waste their lives chasing after someone that doesn't appreciate them."

She sniffled. "All I ever wanted was a marriage and family."

"There's still time for that."

Her lashes lowered as her shoulders drooped. "I don't know why I can't let go. I'm aware my marriage is over, but something inside of me can't accept that I failed." Pressing her lips tight, she whispered, "I failed my son."

He took her fingers in his hand and squeezed. "No, Becca. Kevin failed."

"But Hunter paid the price. We decided to have a child and to me that decision came without conditions. Hunter deserves the family he was meant to have, but I can't give that to him. No matter who did what, somehow we both failed."

Unfortunately, he had no words to ease her pain. In time, she'd hopefully see she hadn't failed. She was an incredible mother and her ex's faults were not a reflection of her own. "There are a lot of assholes out there, Becca, but I swear I'm not one of them."

"I know you're not. You're probably one of the nicest guys I've ever met. Your family's incredible and has been nothing but kind to us since we arrived. I don't know where you people come from, but you're not normal."

At that, he did laugh. "No, we're certainly not. We've got more heart than common sense, but that's what makes us McCulloughs."

"It must have been nice growing up in such a small town with such a close knit family."

"Yes and no. Everything has a cost. Look at Luke. He spent years pretending to be someone he wasn't because he was afraid people wouldn't accept who he really was. And Sheilagh's the best actor of all of us. Only in the past two years did she actually find the courage to share her real feelings about things. And Mallory, my God that girl has put herself through hell and back."

She frowned. "Finn's wife?"

"Yeah."

"Why? She's seems so confident and funny."

"When she moved here she was about a hundred pounds heavier than she is now. She had zero confidence and was bullied about her appearance all of her life. The girl's her own worst critic."

"Mallory was fat?"

He grinned. "Some would say she still is. We don't, because we see her for the beauty she is. It doesn't matter what size she is. She's our sister and we adore her—all of her."

"You're really lucky, Braydon. Most people don't grow up with such an accepting family."

"Every single one of them would accept Hunter too. You saw Finn and Luke with him. We aren't judgmental when someone's different. The outside world probably looks at us like we're crazy, but anyone who knows us knows it's the best kind of crazy."

She laughed. "Yeah."

"Tell me you'll stay."

She sniffled and nodded. "I'll stay."

"And tell me you won't end our relationship because the future scares you."

She pursed her lips and looked away. "Sometimes I get freaked out."

"And when that happens we'll talk it out and find steady ground again. Together."

"Okay. Just be patient with me. I'm not used to nice people."

"Carla and Nikki might resent that."

"Oh, well, Nikki might, but Carla wouldn't. There's no sugar, spice, or anything nice about her. And she knows it. She's her own unique blend of stubbornness, sarcasm, and caffeine, but I adore her—thorns and all."

"Then we should probably go check on her. Colin said something about her growling at him over a mug of coffee."

"Ohhhh…it isn't safe to communicate with her until she's had at least one cup of coffee and decided whether to use the powers of caffeine for good or evil. We better make sure she didn't harm anyone."

She stood and he grabbed her hand. "Becca. Are we okay?"

A slow smile twisted her lips. "Yeah, I think we are." She opened the door and laughed. "Just don't go proposing again. I'm not even addressing that outburst."

When she disappeared down the hall, he grinned. "We'll see."

CHAPTER 11

Thanksgiving was the typical madhouse McCullough affair. All the aunts and cousins came to the big house, children were stampeding all over the lawn, and Italian Mary criticized the cooking. After dinner the men piled into the den to watch the game and the women clucked about everything under the sun in the kitchen. It was loud. It was obnoxious. It was home.

Braydon was beyond relieved Becca and her friends stayed for the duration of the weekend, but as the day progressed he found himself studying her in a different light. The haze of alcohol and sex had worn off, yet his query remained.

When she asked him to pass the green beans, he wanted to ask her to be his wife again, but he held back. Same when she asked if he'd like a cup of coffee after dinner. *Sure. Would you like to marry me after winter?* But he kept his mouth shut.

All of his life his family teased him about chasing perfection. Becca's life was far from perfect, yet he never wanted to run toward something as hard and fast as he wanted her. All of her. This was very different from everything else he'd known. This was deep and permanent. He just had to convince her his feelings were real and pray hers were the same.

Friday morning he took a ride with Kelly to pick up a shipment for the bar and get some perspective. It was nice to get out of the house for a while and spend some quality time with his brother. Especially since the longer Braydon was around Becca the more difficult it became to hold those inappropriate questions inside.

"Your lassie's cute," Kelly said as they headed back toward Center County.

"I know. And stop checking her out."

The corner of Kelly's mouth hitched up as he sent Braydon a sidelong glance. "You got it pretty bad for this one, huh?"

"I've never had it worse. I don't know how she does it, but I wanna be around her all the time, and I can't get her out of my head."

Kelly laughed. "Yup. Been there—am there."

Ashlynn was a remarkable woman and so good for Kelly. She had to be incredible to get his uninhibited brother to settle down.

"I can't handle it," Braydon confessed. "They all get away and I let them go. This one, I can't let go of. No one's ever felt this right or made me want things to this degree. I just want...her."

"For me," Kelly said, "a big part was imagining her with someone else. Couldn't do it. Every time I thought about her smiling at some douchebag the way she smiled at me I saw red. Those were *my* smiles. I wasn't sharin'."

Braydon hadn't thought about Becca being with someone else. Most of the time her life was so busy with Hunter and work, dating —period—was the issue. But when he tried to imagine her seeing other people—yeah, he threw that thought right out the window, because it was extremely unpleasant.

Without considering his words, he announced, "I wanna move home."

Kelly's brows darted up as he shot Bray a quick glance, then quickly returned his focus to the road. "Yeah? Mum would love that. Get Sheilagh to come back and she might have a conniption she'd be so happy. All her little chicks back in the nest."

"It probably won't happen."

"Why? You travel for work. How many of the buildings you design are actually in the city?"

"Maybe thirty percent. I'm on the road once a week."

"So get on the road from here."

"I can't do anything until I finish this deal I'm working on with Becca's company."

He chuckled. "Last time it was the boss, now the colleague. You really love dipping your pen in the company ink."

Then there was the greatest dilemma. "Becca would never move here."

Kelly turned again. "Wow, you really are serious about her. Why not?"

"Her home's in Pittsburgh. Her ex is there and they share joint custody."

"What's he like?"

"The ex? He's a dick."

"No, the kid. Sammy said he has some special needs."

"He's labeled autistic, but Hunter's a really sensitive subject with Becca."

"Well, yeah, just like Nate's a sensitive subject to me. He's her son."

"It's so different, observing her way of parenting compared to watching the rest of you."

"I bet."

"He looks just like every other kid I've met, except when he gets overwhelmed. When there's a lot going on he sort of drifts into his own world and self-stimulates. It's like you can see his curiosity, but our brains are too one dimensional to see what has him so intrigued. He's incredibly talented."

"So how's he special?" Kelly asked.

Braydon struggled to explain. Becca knew all the right words and proper, politically correct terms. "It's like he doesn't need socialization the way we do. People see that as a problem and want to teach him ways to socially interact, but I don't think he cares or wants to. There's this assumption that if a kid can't blend well with others and do the same thing every other kid that age is doing, he's wrong. But what if the world's wrong?

"Hunter's always thinking. It's in his eyes, the way he focuses so completely on some minuscule detail, something we've completely overlooked. Becca thinks it's best to nurture his personal interest. I mean, she wants him to have manners, but she isn't concerned that he doesn't want to play on sports teams or mimic what his peers are doing. He'd rather think independently," Braydon explained.

"You're pretty informed on this. Why should he have to do what everyone else is doing? Kids today are frightening. Look at the crap reality shows Kate's kids are obsessed with. If they're the trends being set, I'd say breaking away from the masses and doing your own thing's the safest bet."

"It's not that simple," Braydon explained. "He doesn't understand consequences. Sometimes he hits because he's frustrated. He mostly inflicts it on himself, but we can't allow that. Plus, when he has a meltdown, Becca usually walks away bruised. He's strong. Her house is like Fort Knox, because he runs and doesn't understand running into traffic could kill him."

"That's scary. I still remember freaking out when Nate learned to climb over the baby gate, and he never got farther than the kitchen."

"Yeah. And Hunter's fast."

"She does it on her own?"

"Mostly. The ex never showed much interest in "being a family" so she has no choice. It's her son. Would you draw a line with Nate? Bump him down in your priority list because you were exhausted or because you'd rather be doing something other than parenting?"

"No. My son and my wife are always first. No matter what."

They rode in silence for a while, but Braydon was enjoying their heart to heart. There was a lot on his mind. "You know what she told me one time?"

"What?"

"That she can never die, because no one will ever love her son or care for him the way she does and he'll likely need that kind of care his entire life."

Kelly let out a low whistle. "That's heartbreaking."

"Yeah."

Kelly cleared his throat. "Finn said he had an episode when they were there."

"Yeah, it was the first time I actually saw what she really went through. It was intense. The house could've caught fire and she wouldn't have stopped to put it out until she was sure Hunter was safe, and not going to hurt himself. It was devastating, because I had no idea how to help and I sort of just stood there. I've never felt so useless, and I don't ever want to feel like that again. I've really been researching, because I'm positive that won't be the last time. I can't imagine how many times she's been in situations like that or worse and handled them on her own."

"And you're up for this? Sounds like a big job for a guy that's not his father."

"His father never helped her. I see her and…she takes my breath away, Kel. I can't explain it. I want all of her and he's a part of her. He's a cool kid."

"Amen, brother. You got this. There isn't much I've seen you fail at."

"Lost Sammy."

Kelly snorted. "That's because we all look like shit when compared with Colin. He's a freaking saint. Only compete with yourself in life and you'll end up better than the man you were yesterday."

"Thanks."

"I speak the truth, Bray. You're a great guy."

His brother's words were comforting, but there were still concerns he needed to voice, even if there wasn't a ready solution. "Sometimes Hunter doesn't sleep for days."

"Why?"

"I think because his brain's always working, like he's always solving some theory in his head. He gets insomnia."

"What does Becca do when he doesn't sleep?"

"She stays up with him."

"Does he talk?"

"Yeah, but mostly when prompted or if he absolutely wants to communicate something. He doesn't seem bothered by silence like most people. He didn't talk until he was around five or six. And he can't be touched."

"Ever?"

"No, Becca does this thing with his shoulder and sometimes she holds his arm to keep him safe. But he doesn't hug or cuddle."

"That's gotta be difficult for her."

"Very." He sighed, thinking about how much she liked being held close. "I just wish I could somehow make life a little easier for her."

They pulled up to the pub and Braydon helped Kelly unload the truck. When they were finished stocking the supplies, they each had a beer. Kelly was eyeing him carefully.

"What?" Braydon asked.

Kelly leaned back and grinned. "Build her a house."

"What?"

"Build her a house, Bray. You have the land. You save every dime you make. You don't have to live in the city. She has no one there to help her. Our family's crawling with helpful, good-hearted maniacs. I know you always imagined building the perfect, architect's wet dream of a house, but maybe that's not what you're supposed to have. You could build the perfect house for her and Hunter."

"And would I be in that house?"

Kelly laughed. "That depends on how you play your cards. Whip out your *hammer* and nail her to the wall with some good ol' McCullough charm. It's what we do."

From the moment Kelly put the idea in his head, his brain went into overdrive. Visions of Becca's brightly colored house and all the functional rationale behind every touch flooded his mind, only his brain improved each design.

He'd create a multisensory room with balls, mats, and baluster swings. There would be a music room, not one with a hand me down upright from the church, but a great big grand piano and cathedral ceilings for the perfect acoustics. He'd design Hunter's bedroom with a bed that didn't have hard edges or sharp angles.

For Becca he'd create the perfect monochromatic space, a sanctuary for her to escape and find peace when she needed it. Every window would be custom fit with unbreakable security screens. There were some so strong even a blade, crowbar, or sledgehammer couldn't puncture them. That way she'd be able to let the fresh air in and watch her café curtains wave in the breeze without having to worry.

The more he considered the possibilities the more he wanted to build it. He was so motivated, he wanted to start mapping out the plans that very minute.

Rather than return to the big house, he took a walk to his acreage on the mountain. Unkempt grass waved like amber over the open space. Autumn's last buzzing insects hovered above the softened reeds of the meadow. It was a flat surface begging for purpose and offering countless possibilities. He smiled, thinking of how much Hunter would enjoy a safe yard to run in.

To the outside world, it would appear he was just standing in the open, staring at a patch of undeveloped earth. But in his mind, walls were erecting, calculations were formulating, angles were deriving from theorems, and colors were cataloguing every design decision. Perhaps his passion, architecture, was his own personal portion of the autism spectrum, because when he got lost in his ideas it truly did consume him.

The crunch of leaves distracted him from his thoughts. Turning, he found his father slowly approaching. "Hey."

"Hey." His dad came to stand beside him, taking in the view. "You thinking about finally doing something with this land?"

"Yeah. Been thinking about it all morning."

"This sudden initiative have anything to do with the lass?"

Braydon smiled, hoping he could convince her to be a part of his plans. "I hope."

"She's a sweet girl. Her friends are a little off, but your mother's enjoying them."

He chuckled, and his dad sighed.

"I remember staring at open land the same way you are now. I'd just married your mother without really thinking things through. Her father was trying to kill me every chance he got and I knew I screwed up. But there was something in my heart that told me I'd do it all over again, just to have your mother as my wife."

"Is that when you built the big house?"

Frank made a gruff sound. "A house is a huge undertaking. I've always been impressed with your ability to go out and build things from nothing, Braydon. Most people don't possess that sort of vision."

"You did."

His father shook his head and kicked a bit of dirt with his boot. "I cut down a tree."

"What?"

"I was pissed off at the world. I had no money, no way of buying a home. My dad gave me a plot, but what the hell good was that with nothin' to put there? When I started dating your mother, I carved our initials in a tree. After we eloped I did a lot of hiding. I was hiding from her father, maybe hiding from her a little too.

"I wound up standing right in front of that tree. As I stared at our weathered initials and the word 'forever' carved beneath them, I felt like the greatest failure. I was so furious with my shortsightedness, I went to my truck, grabbed my ax, and chopped down the tree."

"Why?"

"Because I promised her forever and I couldn't deliver. I was just a kid. That night, I went to face her father—and her. It had only been a few weeks. I thought if we acted fast, maybe the marriage could be annulled, and Maureen could marry a decent man that could provide for her the way she deserved."

Yet, here they were, nearly forty years later. Something had to have stopped his father from getting that annulment. "What happened?"

"Your grandfather tried to shoot me again." Frank chuckled then turned serious. "I couldn't see how our marriage was going to work. We were up against so many complications. When I sat her down to tell her just that, she surprised the hell out of me by confessing she was pregnant."

"With Kate?"

He shook his head, an expression of sadness weighing on his face like nothing Braydon had ever seen. "No. This one would have been named Mary, after Maureen's mother."

Braydon's lips parted with shock. His heart raced, as his eyes remained unblinking. His parents never spoke of suffering such a loss. "I didn't know."

"We don't mention her. Your mom lost her early on."

"You knew it was a girl?"

"We'll never know, but your mother swears it. Says she could tell."

He didn't know what to say.

"Once a year we go up to the far end of the north side. There's a copse of weeping cherry blossoms there. She was so early, there really wasn't anything to…you understand. So I planted trees and had a stone carved with Mary's name on it. I brought your mother there and wrote down all of our hopes and dreams, all of our promises, and we buried them there under Mary's stone for her to keep."

The hair covering his arms stood on end as the sentiment sent chills down his shoulders. "I'm sorry, Dad."

He nodded. "I promised your mother a home and a family so great she'd never feel that sort of hollow emptiness again." He cleared his throat. "The night she lost the baby I told Paulie and Colleen everything that happened. Paulie went with me to find the tree I cut down a few weeks before. Part of me felt like when I cut that tree I…" His father lost his composure for a moment and Braydon turned, pressing a comforting hand to his shoulder.

He gathered himself and continued. "For some reason I felt like that tree was connected to Mary, to us and our future. We brought it to the top of the mountain and now it sits in the wall beside our bed. I built your mother the house she deserved and I think we've done all right making it a home."

Braydon's lips tightened into a sad smile. "Yeah, you did, Dad. The big house is a masterpiece."

"You kids make it so. Your mother and I would love to see you come home and make a life here, Braydon. This is where you belong."

"It wouldn't be the life I predicted."

"Only fools and prophets try to envision God's plan, Braydon. Regardless of what your mother thinks, you're not Christ."

He laughed. No he certainly wasn't. "I have to get her to marry me first."

"Like every other man alive and in love, you give it your best and hope she takes pity on your soul and says yes. Show her what you're capable of. Build her a home that's more than just a house. Make her see the promise of your future together. Family thrives on this land and something tells me she's meant to be here."

"I think so too."

A stream of cackles and the loud tear of small engines ripping over the distance interrupted their conversation. He frowned. "Did they take out the quads?"

"Oh, the Devil took your guests for a ride. Alec's napping. Poor fool had no idea what he was marrying into. I can sympathize."

The quads drew nearer and Braydon turned. Sheilagh and Nikki shared one and Carla and Becca were on the other. Carla was driving and Becca's screams echoed through the trees. "At least they're wearing helmets."

"At least. Come on, let's go rummage through the leftovers."

～

It didn't take long for Braydon's mother to get wind of his plans. Normally, he'd be aggravated by her interference, but being that she was campaigning hard for everything he wanted, he didn't try to stop her.

Sheilagh and Alec left for Princeton Saturday morning. Nikki and Carla left Saturday afternoon, but before they left Carla demanded one last trip to O'Malley's to say goodbye to Kelly.

The house seemed quiet once everyone departed and he finally saw what Sheilagh warned him about with the flirtatious glances his father would send his mother. He had to remind them several times they still had guests in the house, but it was nice to see his parents still so in love.

"Ma!" he yelled, walking in on another game of grab ass.

"Sorry, love. You're father's a virile man."

He held up a palm. "Stop, before I need a cleaver to carve out my mind's eye."

Maureen winked at Becca. "What are you love birds up to this afternoon? You should show Becca around the mountain. Maybe take her for a tour of the town. It's nothing like the city. There's something magical about living in such a small town where everyone knows everyone. Wouldn't you agree, Frank?"

His father gave a silent nod of agreement.

They ended up driving around the mountain for most of the afternoon. Becca was thrilled to spot a few stags, but the bear were nowhere to be found this time of year. They drove into town and had dinner at a small diner, then strolled past the darkened storefronts as Braydon pointed out each shop and gave a brief description of each storeowner.

"You know everyone," she said with astonishment.

"Pretty much. This is one of those towns where the butcher's the mechanic's son, and the pharmacist's nephew. The pharmacist's wife is the preschool teacher and the director of the preschool is the taxidermist's daughter, who also happens to be the clerk at the farmers' market Ashlynn owns, thereby relating somehow or another to the McCulloughs. There're so many of us, we seem to have a connection to everyone."

They passed the mechanic's house located around the corner from Main Street. "Oh," Becca gasped. "Look at this place."

Braydon took in the old Victorian. "What is it you love about it?"

"It's so charming. You never see picket fences like that anymore. And look at those shutters. It's enchanting."

"They're handmade by the local carpenter." He made a mental note to give their home a Victorian exterior. He'd talk to the carpenter as soon as he had the dimensions and windows figured out. The picket fence would be a little tricky, being that it would have to be high enough to act as security. He could manage it.

When they returned to the big house, Becca was quiet. Braydon climbed into bed and pulled her close, sensing her melancholy. "What's wrong?"

She sighed. "I miss Hunter."

"We're leaving tomorrow. We can be home by ten if you'd like."

"Kevin doesn't drop him off until late afternoon." Her lips pursed. "But knowing him, he'll have no problem dropping him off early."

"Maybe you could call and tell him we'll be back earlier than expected."

"Thank you for understanding."

"Of course." He kissed her nose.

The weekend had run its course and while it turned out to be a wonderful visit, he, too, was anxious to return home and draw out some of his plans. That night Becca's mind was on her son and he sensed her homesickness. Rather than make love, he simply held her as they talked softly about their pasts.

The following morning, Becca was packed and dressed before Braydon even opened his eyes. Knowing she was longing for her son, he hurried to make his goodbyes and got them on the road by eight. His parents didn't make the usual stink about him leaving, because they knew he'd be back again soon.

When they returned to Becca's she pouted at the absence of her tree, still not used to seeing her yard so empty. "The house looks lonely."

He was about to suggest they plant a new tree closer to the house, but he kept silent, rather, deciding he'd plant an elm just like the one she lost in their new yard.

Kevin was scheduled to drop Hunter off that afternoon. Braydon wanted to get back to his home office to start working on the plans for the house, so he said goodbye to Becca shortly after carrying in her luggage. As he was starting his car another car pulled in behind him. Braydon frowned. Looked like Kevin decided to drop his son off a bit earlier than expected.

The car blocking his exit beeped, and he met the other man's stare in the rearview. He was curious to see what sort of man Becca's ex was.

Though Becca planned to call him, she hadn't yet. What would the man have done if they were still out of town? Braydon wondered if her ex still treated her home as his own at times. The thought made him uncomfortable.

Becca emerged from the house, her eyes a bit nervous, but her excitement to reunite with Hunter was evident in her pace. She pranced to the car and helped Hunter out. Kevin climbed out as well and Braydon frowned. Did he usually stick around?

Becca worked to guide Hunter toward the house. Kevin followed her, talking at a fast clip and glancing back at Braydon's car as Hunter twisted in her grip and laughed. He approached Braydon's car and bounced, his small hands pressing on the glass.

Bray couldn't leave without saying hello, especially since Hunter appeared excited about his presence, which was beyond flattering.

Turning off the car, he climbed out. "Hey, Hunter."

Hunter paced and laughed, but didn't say hello, only registering Braydon's greeting in short glances fixated on his proximity.

"Hi. I'm Kevin, Becca's husband."

Not anymore. Braydon held out his hand. "Braydon McCullough." This was awkward.

Becca tensed. Hunter was commenting on various things and seemed to be in a fairly pleasant mood. They stood in silence for a moment.

"What's your association with my wife?"

"Kevin," Becca said in an impatient tone.

There was no need to beat around the bush. The guy knew they'd just gone away together. "I'm dating her."

His face hardened at Braydon's bluntness. "Doesn't take long for you to move on, I see," he mumbled under his breath.

Becca didn't miss a beat. "I'm still light-years behind you. At least I waited for the sheets to cool, but they were never really that hot to begin with."

He wanted to give her a high five, but kept his expression blank. *That's it, angel, don't take any shit from this clown!*

"And whose fault was that?"

Whoa! Braydon's head jerked in the other man's direction, Hunter's presence the only thing holding him back from cleaning this asshole's clock.

Becca's face flushed deep red. "I'm not discussing this with you. Pop the trunk so I can get Hunter's bag. Braydon, will you keep an eye on Hunter?"

"Sure." But he'd also be keeping an eye on the other man.

Her ex followed as she moved to retrieve Hunter's belongings. The man continued to drill her with questions and accusations, but didn't open the trunk.

"Want to go inside and play piano, Hunter?" Braydon asked, his focus on the quarrelsome ex.

"Yeah."

Unsure how to guide Hunter without triggering a negative reaction, he carefully laid a hand on the boy's arm, which he immediately shouldered off. "Show me where the door is, bud."

Hunter took the steps slowly, his attention diverting to the numbers on the house and the plant sitting by the steps.

It was crucial that Braydon do this right. He took a moment to see what caught Hunter's interest. "Do you like plants?"

His head tipped to the side as his eyes squinted. His fingers released the waxy leaf and shook off the feeling as though the tactile sensation was revolting to him. "Slippery."

Braydon touched the plant. "Yeah. How about some piano now?"

Hunter stepped to the door, the distraction of the plant forgotten, and Braydon got him situated as quickly as possible. He immediately started playing a beautiful piece Braydon didn't recognize. So long as they could hear the piano through the walls, Braydon felt safe stepping away for a minute. He returned to the front porch where Kevin's posture had taken a hostile turn, crowding over Becca's smaller form in a way that had the hair on the back of Braydon's neck rising.

Becca's motions were jerky and obviously agitated. His teeth clamped tight as he marched down the porch steps.

"Open the trunk, Kevin," Becca repeated.

"How long? Was this going on before I left?"

"Kevin, pop the damn trunk or I'm going inside."

Knowing Becca didn't typically swear Braydon drew closer, his attention divided between her and the sound of the piano playing. Should the music stop, Braydon would need to rush back inside with Hunter, which he was prepared to do at a second's notice.

"I don't know if I'm comfortable with Hunter being around some guy I don't know. You're supposed to be taking care of our son."

And that, apparently, was the straw that broke the camel's back. Becca got right in his face, stabbing a finger into the man's chest. "I am taking care of him, just like I've done since the day he was born. Who I invite into my home and who I expose Hunter to while he's in my custody is none of your business and you have no right to question my judgment when I've been the one to make every difficult decision since day one. If you wanted the right to an opinion you should have taken your family a little more seriously."

"He's my son. I have every right to question you."

"Why, because you're suddenly taking some court ordered responsibility in his life?"

Intervening, Braydon swiftly opened the driver's side door, and pressed the trunk button. The tailgate popped open and Kevin scowled at him. "Get out of my car."

"Get away from my woman."

Becca notably tensed, her attention drawn to the house. Her

shoulders relaxed as she registered Hunter was playing the piano and therefore not in any trouble.

The man jerked back and laughed, not at all concerned about where his son had gotten off to the way Becca was. "Woman? Nice. Didn't know you had a thing for rednecks, Rebecca."

Rather than get into some pissing match with a guy who clearly never appreciated Becca, Braydon strolled to the rear of the vehicle and reached for Hunter's bag, so they could return to where they were needed.

"Who do you think you are?" Kevin snapped.

Bray took Becca's hand. "I'm the replacement. The last guy didn't do the job, so the higher ups brought someone in who could handle things better. Thanks for dropping Hunter off. We'll see you Wednesday."

Grasping Becca's clammy palm, he removed her from the hostile environment. They entered the house where Hunter still played and Braydon shut and locked the door. He stashed his bag on the table and turned to Becca, who was shaking with adrenaline.

"He gets me so angry!" she hissed.

"Yeah, he's a real prize." He looked out the window wondering what she ever saw in that rat. "He's gone now."

"How dare he question my judgment? The only reason he has *any* involvement in Hunter's life is because the courts insisted, and he doesn't want to pay the difference in child support. Half the time he picks him up late and drops him off early so he can play the bachelor, which he's been playing for most of his married life!"

Without giving him a chance to speak, she went on. "He never took an interest in this family or my needs. It was always *him* and *his* needs before ours. I would have given him everything if just once he applied himself to being the father Hunter deserves!"

Braydon rubbed his hands over her shoulders, not used to seeing her so distraught. "Well, he's gone now. Don't let him upset you. Look, Hunter's home."

Her rage gradually faded. Glancing at her son, she beamed and sighed. Braydon held back as she slowly walked to the piano. Becca got as close as she could without disturbing him. She kissed the tips of her fingers and gently placed them on Hunter's right shoulder. "Welcome home, bud. Did you have a nice Thanksgiving?"

Hunter's fingers played rapidly over the keys, but his head turned and bobbled for a split second. Then he tapped his chin to the top of his mother's fingers. It was the slightest acknowledgement, but it was still a response and contact, something Braydon never saw him do before.

It struck him that Becca also found the gesture unexpected as her shoulders lifted and she drew in a shaky breath. Her lashes flickered and her mouth tightened as her lips trembled. The impact of such a minor yet grand acknowledgement definitely hit her. Bray felt it too.

Stepping close to her, he slid his hand around hers and clasped her fingers tightly. Her grip was fierce, expressing how monumental what just happened was. "Did you see that?" she whispered, her eyes shimmering under a sheen of unshed tears.

He nodded slowly, his chest tightening with vicarious pleasure for the gift she was just given. "I saw."

He was prepared to leave so they could have time together, when Becca surprised him by asking, "Would you like to stay for dinner?"

It was as though a door to a secret passage had opened. The plans for the house could wait. He grinned. Yes, she was definitely *his* woman. "I'd love to."

Her face softened as she smiled at him, a heavy weight forming in his gut. She'd explained to him that these mild gestures, so often taken for granted, held a monumental impact. But to witness it, to actually feel the impact, was something entirely different. The significance of Hunter's gesture radiated in the air, as though the energy of the universe had shifted. So small, the mere touch of a chin to his mother's fingers, yet so meaningful, and for the first time, he truly understood what she meant by small victories.

CHAPTER 12

Miranda approached the tall bistro table and shut Braydon's laptop. "You seem busy."

He sighed. She was lucky his program saved automatically. "I was."

"Can I get you a drink?"

Tipping his chin toward his whiskey sour, he said, "No thanks. Already have one."

The pub was located on the same block as their office, so it wasn't out of the ordinary to run into other coworkers after five. "How about some dinner? My treat."

"Miranda, we've been through this."

She rolled her deep chocolate eyes. "Still? Come on, Braydon. If she was so incredible you'd be with her instead of sitting here at six o'clock on a Friday night."

"I had work to finish."

"What work? We have no new projects and the Apricot specs were sent out last Monday."

That was true, but he'd been engrossed in laying out the plans for the house, and it was risky doing that in front of Becca. Although Hunter was with Kevin this afternoon, she didn't sound into company at the moment. Braydon suspected she had her period, but didn't want to talk about it. It hurt, that she wouldn't communicate such things with him when there was a possibility she could be carrying his baby—a prospect that frightened her. It was a touchy subject so he figured he'd let it go.

"I'm working on something else."

Miranda's dark brow arched as she slid into the seat across from him. "Are you cheating on me, Braydon?"

He chuckled. "No, I'm only working for you. This is a family project."

Her hands folded on the sleek surface of the table, her fingers slowly fidgeting in a way that didn't fit her typical confident behavior. Although their intimate relationship had run its course, she was still someone he looked to as a friend of sorts. "Miranda, are you okay?"

Her eyes lowered as she forced her palms flat, ceasing all nervous gestures, but he sensed something was still off. "Is it because I'm too hard, Bray?"

He frowned. "What?"

"I'm the CEO and I'm a woman. Sometimes it's tough to draw the line after hours. I don't know if I have any softness left. And if I do, I'm afraid if I let it show I'll lose my edge and all those men salivating over my office would bully me out."

His posture softened as understanding dawned. "Miranda, don't discredit your strong attitude and don't change for other people. There's someone out there who will love you just the way you are."

"But not you."

He sighed. No, he didn't love Miranda, but he'd enjoyed their time together for what it was. "Miranda," he said slowly. "We knew what we had. It wasn't what either of us wanted long-term. You'd never give up the pace of the city for the life I'm after and we'd only be wasting each other's time pretending we suited for more than a few fun nights."

"I could change."

"No, you couldn't. You could pretend—for a while—but eventually you'd resent the life you were living, and me, because it isn't in your nature to be someone else." He watched her for a long moment. "Why are you suddenly doubting yourself?"

She sighed. "It's lonely out there, Bray. I miss your company."

But not him. "Anyone can give you company, Miranda. I need to be more than company to a woman."

Her vulnerable posture shifted, the impenetrable façade she usually displayed falling into place as her attention was drawn over his shoulder. He turned and found Nikki there, grinning. However, her smile didn't reach her eyes, which seemed to be zeroing in on Miranda.

"Miranda, right?" She held out her hand.

"Hello, Nicolette. It's nice to see you again."

Nikki turned to Braydon. "Mr. McCullough." Glancing back at his boss, she asked, "Am I interrupting?"

Shooting Miranda an apologetic glance, but knowing she wouldn't want any witnesses to her confessed vulnerability, he slid his laptop into the case and withdrew a twenty. "Actually, I was just leaving."

"I thought you'd be at Becca's." Nikki gave Miranda a pointed look.

Braydon stood and grabbed his jacket, not missing Miranda's slight wince as Nikki's comment hit its target. Miranda was his ex, but certainly not his enemy. "I'm heading there now, actually."

"Good. Tell her I said hi. It was nice seeing you again, Miranda."

"Likewise," his boss said with artificial professionalism.

"Goodnight, Miranda. Nikki." He turned and left the bar, irritated with Nikki's display. When he reached the sidewalk Nikki was right behind him.

"Yo! Braydon."

He pivoted, but she didn't give him a chance to respond.

"I know about you and your boss."

"It isn't a secret, Nikki."

"Some might advise discretion if that's the case, but I'm not some. If you still have feelings for her—"

"Stop right there, Nikki. Miranda and I are a thing of the past."

"Didn't look like it from where I was sitting."

"I wasn't concerned with the audience. Go ask her if you don't believe me. I have nothing to hide."

Her gaze narrowed. "As much of an asshole as Kevin was, when he cheated on Becca it killed her. Sometimes people have a hard time letting go of past relationships even when their hearts insist it's time to move on."

"Exactly why he's an asshole. But I'm not. I'd appreciate it if you didn't compare me to him." He'd let go of Miranda, so what she was suggesting didn't apply to him. Could she be referring to Becca? No, that wasn't right. He'd seen her and Kevin together. It wasn't pretty.

"Then maybe you shouldn't be sharing cocktails with your ex on a Friday night."

Now he was pissed. "First of all, I wasn't sharing cocktails. I was finishing up some work when she interrupted. Just because we once shared an intimate relationship, doesn't mean we can't continue as friends. We work together. She's an unavoidable part of my life. Second of all, while your concern is genuine, it's misplaced. I'd never do anything to hurt Becca. I love her. And third, this is the last time I'll be interrogated for someone else's behavior. Everyone needs to get it through their heads, I'm not Kevin."

"Good. I'm glad we're clear." She turned, but he wasn't finished.

"Wait a minute." He wasn't sure what he wanted to say, but something definitely had to be said. "I know you're only trying to protect your best friend, but I think it's time you realized I'm not the enemy. Why do I suddenly feel like I am?"

"People fall back into old habits, Braydon."

"Not me. When I walk away it's because I'm done."

"Are you sure?"

He scowled. "Yes, and putting any doubts in Becca's head will only make her more hesitant to move on with her life. I know she's your friend, so *be* hers. She doesn't need more paranoia. Everyone isn't out to betray her. I love her. I'd hurt myself before I'd let anything happen to her."

She sighed. "Okay." She nodded. "I'm sorry. I saw you two talking and it looked like a lot more than an employer and employee. I may have overreacted."

"Miranda is my friend. Our relationship didn't end our ties and I still care about her on a platonic level. I shouldn't have to explain myself when I haven't done anything wrong. And for future reference, I'll answer to Becca, but I don't answer to you."

Nikki stepped back and tilted her head. "Wow. It's nice to know you have a feisty side beneath all those designer duds. I'm sorry I misjudged the situation."

He supposed it was better she approached him rather than run back to Becca with a bunch of assumptions. "I don't mind your concern. But I won't be held accountable for someone else's misdeeds."

"You're right. She was upset today and wouldn't tell me why. I thought maybe…I didn't know if I had to kick your ass. You're a little tougher than I expected."

His focus diverted, zeroing in on the fact that something was wrong with Becca. "What do you mean she was upset?" He'd sensed she'd had a long week and maybe wasn't feeling her best, but he didn't know she was upset.

Nikki shrugged. "She wouldn't say."

Every passing second suddenly turned to a blatant waste of time. "I gotta go." As much as he wanted answers, it was a conversation to have with Becca, not her friend.

On the drive to Becca's his mind rolled over her friend's warnings. Miranda wasn't a threat. He knew where he stood and where he wanted to be. Becca however… She'd once commented on how deeply she struggled to accept her failed marriage. He'd never been married, so he had no personal experience to compare such bonds. She's also made a comment once about how she would have given Kevin anything if he only took more of an interest in their family. Could she really still be facing those demons still after he'd had an affair? It didn't make sense to him.

If she married Kevin, there were valid reasons. In that moment he realized how very different it was to date someone with a hodgepodge of exes compared to dating someone who was once married. Marriage was supposed to be forever. How did one reverse a commitment like that?

He was getting ahead of himself. This was all on the assumption that Nikki was implying something when she may not have even been referring to Becca. If he hadn't had so many issues with others being picked over him in the past, he probably wouldn't be having such a paranoid complex at the moment. He needed to chill.

When he arrived at Becca's and the house was dark. It was obvious she wasn't in any sort of outgoing mood, but her presence alone chased away much of his paranoia. Breathing a sigh of relief, he leaned in a brushed a kiss on her cheek. "Hi."

"Hi."

Yes, something was definitely bothering her. "You okay?"

She nodded and shut the door. "Just a long day."

He followed as she wandered to the couch where she'd seemed to be snuggling up with a soft blanket and pillow. Settling in beside her, he glanced at the evening news on the television. The volume was muted and she didn't seem to be watching it. "You sure you're okay, angel?"

"Yeah."

She wasn't being honest. Pulling her to his chest, he wrapped his arms around her. "Talk to me."

Sighing, she pressed her cheek into his shirt. "I got my period."

He expected she would. Though they'd slipped up, the chances of conception after one minor mistake weren't as great as people often assumed. Some of his siblings spent months trying to conceive.

"Okay," he said slowly. "Shouldn't you be relieved?" And really, he should be too, even if he was a bit disheartened, his disappointment was selfish. "I thought that's what you wanted."

Her lips parted, but her words were absent. Taking a deep breath, she said, "*Want* is a dangerous word, don't you think?"

Choosing his words carefully, he considered what she'd asked. Though Becca claimed to not want more children, at one time she had. Her fears were legitimate, but were they reason enough to disallow her dreams of family? This wasn't going to be an easy conversation and he didn't want things to turn volatile. "Sometimes our wants change with time, angel. It's okay to want something now and change your mind later."

"Please don't be all understanding right now. I can't handle it."

His chin lifted from where it rested on top of her head. "How would you have me be? Irrational?"

She shifted, pulling away to face him. When Becca insisted on physical distance, it was usually because part of her required emotional distance as well. "Human. Can you just be human for a minute?"

His head tipped to the side. Unsure if he should be insulted. "I am human." Her eyes closed and she remained quiet so he nudged her, trying to pull her back to him, but she shouldered him off. "Talk to me, Becca."

When her eyes opened, a sheen of tears built above her lashes. "I'm angry."

"With me?"

"No." She shook her head, running her palm over her hair. "With God, the universe, myself."

"Why?"

Pressing her face to her palms, she quickly dried her eyes in an attempt to shake off any show of emotion. "I don't want to cry. I've done that enough, but I'm sick and tired of every desire hurting."

What was hurting her? Was he? Their relationship? "Can you be a little more specific?"

"I'm talking about children, Braydon. You make me want things I convinced myself to stop wanting years ago."

It was a relief he was on the right track. "Who says you can't want children?"

"I do. I'm a coward."

He had fears too. Sometimes he chased "normal" so hard he lost sight of where he was running. "Do you think we're moving too fast?" Maybe they were.

"I don't know. I think it's way too soon to even be contemplating family. I mean, we're still getting to know each other and…"

Her words trailed off leaving him with a heavy, unpleasant feeling in his gut. "And?"

She glanced away, adding to his concern. "I'm still not over my past. I don't know if I can look to the future when something still seems to be anchoring me where I was."

"Over your past or over Kevin?" He had to ask. The idea of her reconciling with that jerk made no sense to him, but there had to be some good to the man that he wasn't seeing. However, he hoped she'd quell his worry with an emphatic no.

"I don't know."

His eyes closed at her regrettable omission. "I see."

"Do you? It's not Kevin—the man—but Kevin and my life before you, Braydon. Letting you in means letting that go and I don't know if I can. I'm scared and the last thing I want to do is hurt you."

His breathing turned erratic no matter how much he tried to quell his worry. Whether she realized it or not, her past had already let *her* go. Clinging to it was an illusion. But sometimes illusions made people do very foolish things. Quietly, he forced the words out. "Are you breaking up with me, Becca?"

"I don't want to."

"Then don't. Why are we even discussing this?"

Her eyes pleaded with him, her mouth tight. "Because it's important, Braydon. You're so different than me. You're courageous and I'm…not."

"You're only a coward if your fear stops you from trying. Being brave doesn't come without fear, Becca. This is new for me too. It's okay to be scared. Being a coward means not having the guts to face your fears. Don't give up on us without trying."

"I'm scared and I hate it."

He hated it too. When she expressed her fears like this—all valid —it amplified his own. Though he tried to bravely approach this relationship, there was a lot about Becca's life that intimidated him. He'd never dated someone with a child and the unspoken expectation that came with that sort of commitment challenged his faith in himself.

Taking her hand and rubbing his thumb over her knuckles, he asked, "What exactly are you afraid of?"

Tipping her head back, she blinked at the ceiling as a small tear escaped, racing past her lashes and losing itself in her hair. "Drowning."

It killed him to see her be so hard on herself. Taking control, he pulled her to him. Her head rested on his lap as he gently combed his fingers through her hair. "Me too."

She sniffled. "But you don't have to be here."

His hand stilled as he frowned at her. "I *want* to, Becca. This is where I want to be."

"But for how long? Eventually, everyone wants to leave."

A month ago, he'd have no answer for her. They'd started their relationship with a one-night stand. At no point during their first encounter, did he expect to feel so much for this woman. Now, however, all of that had changed. It was time to show a little of the hand his was hiding. "I don't see myself ever wanting to leave. You make me happy."

"You make me happy too."

"Isn't that enough, angel?" When she didn't answer, he whispered, "It's okay to try for happiness, Becca. Sometimes we miss and sometimes we hit, but no one's ever succeeded without experiencing some failure."

"My divorce was a big pill I'm still trying to swallow. The things I felt for Kevin were so one dimensional compared to the way you make me feel. If I can't quite get over losing that relationship, I'm not sure I'd survive losing ours."

"Becca..." Running out of words in the face of such jaded pessimism, he lost a bit of his calm. "Where am I going? You act as though I've given you reason to expect I'll leave. I'm right here. You need to stop doing this to yourself. I know you're scared, but I *promise*, you're worried over nothing."

"I just need to know that you understand that I'm still processing."

"I do understand, Becca. I can't imagine a marriage is an easy thing to let go of. You have to redefine your thinking. I know things would have been easier if we'd met a year later and you had a chance to find closure, but we met now. We can get through this together. You can talk to me about it. I never want you to think you can't share your honest feelings with me."

Her face pinched as a small puddle of tears gathered in the

corner of her eye. "You shouldn't have to listen to that stuff. Sometimes I don't even get the way I feel."

Brushing her hair away from her face, he said, "Should or shouldn't doesn't matter. I'm here because I love you. I didn't fall in love with an illusion and neither of us is perfect. Don't be afraid to lean on me. I promise I won't let you drown."

Shifting, she rose to her knees and looped her arms around his neck. Her lips pressed to his and she whispered, "Do you know how dangerous you are to my heart?"

"Maybe I'm not dangerous at all," he whispered, slanting his mouth to hers. Maybe, placing her heart in his care was the safest thing she could do. For as much as love seemed to frighten her, Braydon knew he'd never be able to hurt her the way her ex had. In time he hoped she realized that.

When she pulled away and cuddled into his side, he figured now was as good a time as any to address certain matters. "How do you feel about going on the pill, Becca?"

Her shoulders lifted and she sighed. "That's probably smart."

Figuring that would lay some of her preemptive concerns to rest, he said, "I think we both got ahead of ourselves. As much as I'd like to someday have a family, I don't want to make any decisions before we're ready."

He regretted his words the moment he saw her withdraw. "Braydon..."

Quickly holding out a hand, he assured, "We don't have to decide now. I understand all your concerns."

"Do you?"

"Becca, I understand, which is why I said we'll decide when we're ready. I'm in no rush. Kate lost a baby. So did my mum I recently found out. Sammy had a really scary labor with Liam, and Kelly and Ashlynn's son, Nate, was premature. Sheilagh can't get pregnant. And Luke is still waiting for approval so he can be a father. The only one out of all of us that didn't have some sort of complication was Finn. There's always fear where family's concerned and I wouldn't rush into starting one without fully thinking it through. However, accidents happen and if we found ourselves in an unexpected situation I'd do the right thing and adapt."

Her gaze fell to her lap. "I just have this feeling you expect my mind to change and you're holding out for that." Lifting her face, her stare locked with his. "It may never change, Braydon. If you *need* to have family, you need to find a woman who can give you guarantees."

He didn't want guarantees. He wanted her. If a future with Becca came at the expense of never having a family, he'd deal. She was that important to him, that different from every other woman he'd ever been with. Besides, she already had one great kid. "There are no guarantees in life, angel, but I know not having children isn't enough to make me walk away."

She blinked, her eyes again glassy with unshed tears. "I love you."

"I love you too. Now, stop putting unnecessary pressure on yourself. We've got plenty of time to decide our future."

"You're so different from Kevin."

His jaw twitched. He'd promised she could share her true feelings with him, but he was growing tired of hearing the other man's name. "Well, Kevin's gone now."

Her brow furrowed as though his words somehow pained her, but it was the truth, Kevin was gone. "He's Hunter's father, Braydon. He'll always be a part of our lives. He'll never be gone for good."

There was something off about the way she jumped to his defense. "I only meant you don't need to live by his edicts anymore. Don't measure your decisions against his opinions. You're apart for a reason and not because you shared the same opinion on most things."

She was quiet for a long time. "I think, if we ever had children, you'd make an incredible father."

"Thank you." She couldn't seem to let the topic go. The more she returned to the discussion of family, the more Braydon realized how greatly it was weighing on her. Perhaps she truly did want more children, but couldn't admit the truth to herself. His heart swelled as he silently admitted he wasn't ready to forgo the hope for family completely. "You're already an incredible mum."

She smiled, her eyes drifting. "If we had children, would they call me Mum?"

Now this, this was dangerous. He'd cauterized the topic, but she continued to pick. He didn't have the will to shut the topic down, not when hypothesizing about such an indulgent fantasy filled him with such pleasure.

He stretched and allowed his mind to venture, reminding himself they were only postulating. "I think they might. They'd have blonde hair and your lavender eyes and a wild McCullough streak. The youngest would probably curse like a sailor, having learned all the good words from his older cousins and his grandmother."

She giggled, surprising him with the ease at which she embraced the make-believe. "My children will not swear."

"Love, every McCullough swears." He grinned, having fun imagining such things. A sense of peace settled over him. His mind withdrew as he pictured his home on the mountain, his children romping over the same open land he and his siblings used to play. It wouldn't matter if their children were brilliant, in remedial classes, disfigured, shockingly beautiful, autistic or anything else. They'd all be special because they'd be theirs.

What did matter was the more he imagined his future, the more he admitted he hadn't been totally honest with Becca. Part of him was holding out hope that she'd someday change her mind. He didn't know how to shut off such expectation. If he confessed how much he someday wanted a family, she'd likely shut him out again, so for now, he kept these feelings to himself, hoping that with time, she'd find the confidence she lost and try for more.

OVER THE NEXT few weeks Becca welcomed Braydon's presence in their home, pushing herself to move forward and not dwell on the past. He often came to her house after work, bringing desserts they'd share after dinner. Hunter seemed to enjoy the occurrences he was there. Though her son never called him by name or spoke directly to him, he did acknowledge Braydon's presence in his own unique way.

Her son accepted Braydon into their private world. When they danced, Braydon danced with them. When they drummed, Braydon did an excellent guitar solo. When Hunter needed to be bathed, Braydon put on shorts and helped her get the job done.

Hunter's behavior was shifting slightly as he'd sometimes pause waiting for Braydon to follow as though expecting his attendance as a small piece of their whole. Children on the spectrum didn't typically mimic unnecessary adult behaviors like neurotypical children tended to. They copied only what their brains recognized as useful actions in order to accomplish tasks more efficiently. Yet, Hunter carefully evaluated Braydon's habits, picking up strange behaviors, such as adjusting the blinds the way Braydon tended to when the sun set each evening. This surprised Becca.

There was a precise rationalization behind everything Hunter did, whether outsiders recognized his reasoning or not. He had superior reasoning skills the rest of the world was still struggling to appreciate. When behaviors didn't waste time on superfluous social touches they typically weren't praised by society, but Becca understood her son's compulsions and it seemed Braydon was starting to as well.

Since Braydon's arrival, other excessive behaviors were also waning. Hunter didn't seem to flap as much or give into unnecessary impulses as frequently as he had before. Perhaps her son was maturing. Or perhaps it was the incredible man now sharing their lives.

Before Braydon, Hunter often stood several times throughout a meal in order to tap a specific spot on the wall three times between bites. These were slight differences, but they were occurring and Becca was trying to figure out why.

Some nights Braydon brought his laptop to finish up work from the office. He used programs Becca wasn't familiar with and had little interest in. Hunter, however, seemed curious. Her son had minimal social motivation regarding others. She knew he wasn't trying to get closer to Braydon as a person, but he appeared very intrigued by whatever was happening on the laptop.

One night she was cleaning up after dinner while Hunter listened to his iPod and Braydon worked from his laptop on the sofa. As she shut off the water she stilled.

Hearing her son's voice during music time caught her off guard. Drying her hands, she slowly approached the den only to find him hovering over Braydon's shoulder.

"And what about here?" Braydon asked. Hunter reached for the screen of the laptop and Braydon laughed, redirecting him. "You can't touch, bud."

Becca smiled at the gentle way he spoke to her son. Braydon looked around and reached into his portfolio. Withdrawing a large sketchpad, he slid it onto the table with a pencil. "Here. Show me on this."

Becca watched, confused, as to what they were doing. Stepping closer, she observed her son scribbling letters and numbers all over the paper Braydon placed on the floor. It was as if Hunter's hand couldn't write fast enough for his brain.

His head twisted as he solved some curious equation he was considering. Braydon grinned, clearly impressed with whatever all those numbers translated.

"What's he doing?" she quietly asked.

Braydon turned his smile on her. "He just solved the Golden ratio."

"What's that?"

"It's something used in architecture. If two quantities are in the Golden ratio, their ratio's the same as the ratio to the sum of the larger of the two quantities. It's a twentieth-century formula artists and architects used to create what they believed aesthetically pleasing. Basically, he unraveled the formula for phi."

"Pi?"

"No, *phi*. It's different."

"How did he know how to do that?" she asked, moved by her son's show of intelligence.

She truly believed people were only conscious of ten percent of the things they thought they knew, but people on the spectrum were much more aware. Their intelligence was sometimes impossible for the typical person to comprehend, which was why their thinking was so misunderstood.

"Do this one," Braydon said, flashing his computer screen to Hunter, which sent her son scribbling again.

The days that followed progressed with an energy she hadn't experienced in quite some time. Hunter demanded certain pieces of furniture be moved, which he'd done years before, but Becca never understood why. Braydon could somehow explain his reasoning now, telling her of equations, and finding numeric rationale behind each shift that would have otherwise been a mystery.

"See," Braydon pointed out one afternoon. "It's a mathematical equation that links to a sense of harmony. He's rationalizing the order of the universe, I think. It's soothing to him."

She watched her son work out the numbers and return to shift furniture around in the den. Hunter's mood had indeed been calmer. "Why is it soothing do you think?"

Braydon didn't seem to have all the answers, but he had some very good assumptions. "I think it's more along the lines of correcting an irritant. Some people never think about toilet paper or how it's placed on the roll, but my sister freaks out every time someone puts it on 'backwards'."

She frowned. "Which way is it supposed to go?"

He laughed. "I have no idea. Somehow Sheilagh always knows if it's wrong though. But maybe this is like that for Hunter. He isn't so much creating order, but rather correcting disorder by his interpretation. If he can rationalize the placement of the furniture with something as concrete as math, he's thereby removing the stress of chaos. At least that's my guess."

There didn't seem to be enough paper for Hunter to solve all the equations hidden in the shadows of their home, so one evening, after Hunter went to bed, Braydon produced a can of white board paint and they covered the entire wall of the hall. Hunter spent days filling the space with numbers and sums she couldn't decipher. Even Braydon had reached a point of cluelessness, but continued to encourage him all the same.

The days that Braydon had to travel were difficult. It was amazing how much she'd come to depend on his presence, not because he lent a helping hand—though that helped too—but because he made her existence happier.

She'd done a lot of thinking about moving on. Braydon made the future appear brighter than she'd ever expected. It wasn't until one afternoon when Kevin had Hunter and Braydon was away on business that she'd actually realized how profoundly he'd influenced her desire to let the past go. It was an ongoing battle, but she was making headway.

As she lifted the last two bags of groceries from her car, the neighbor's car pulled in to the adjacent driveway. Stomaching the same disquiet she always suffered at the sight of Loretta, the woman who'd ruined her marriage, she took a few moments to calm her nerves.

The only way she'd ever truly move on was if she accepted the state of reality and closed the past. With trembling hands, she lowered the bags back to the car and brushed her palms down her thighs. She could do this.

The alarm on Loretta's car beeped and Becca forced her feet to move. Cutting through the spaced out hedges dividing the yards, she cleared her throat. The other woman turned and tensed at the sight of her. "Rebecca."

"Hi." She needed to say more, but that was all she could manage at the moment. Maybe she should tuck tail and run. Maybe this wasn't a good idea after all.

Loretta paused, looking unsure. "Is there something you need?"

Her breath turned choppy as she truly looked at the other

woman. This was her neighbor, someone she saw nearly every day. There was no avoiding the past when it was shoved in her face like that. Becca licked her lips. "I wanted to tell you…" What had she meant to tell her? "I…forgive you."

Loretta's eyes widened. She wasn't a strikingly beautiful woman, but she also wasn't unattractive by any means. However, over time, Becca had come to realize that while Loretta's part in her divorce was not innocent, this woman wasn't the person that made vows to her. Betrayal could only be dealt by those she trusted not to hurt her and the ultimate betrayal had been done by Kevin, not Loretta.

"You do?"

She swallowed and nodded. "What you did was wrong, but I don't want to live the remainder of my life fearing I'll run into you. I'm finally starting over and I'm happy. My marriage wasn't happy before you came into the picture and it isn't right for me to hold you accountable for its end. While I don't excuse your actions, I do forgive them." She had to, not for Kevin, or the neighbor, but for herself.

"Wow," the woman said quietly. "I don't know what to say."

"You don't need to say anything. I just needed to hear myself say that. You're forgiven."

They waited in awkward silence for several moments. Finally, Becca nodded and stepped in the direction of her van.

"Would you like to come in for a cup of coffee?"

She stilled. While she could take this baby step in facing her neighbor, she wasn't sure she'd ever be big enough to embrace that sort of camaraderie. "I have groceries to put away."

Loretta nodded. "You know…he talked to me. I never meant to become what I was. At first, we were just neighbors, friends that would sometimes discuss life. The day you found us…it was the only time things went that far."

Curiosity was a dangerous thing. Cautiously, Becca asked, "It was?" She'd assumed Kevin and Loretta had a long-term affair.

"I'm sorry for what I did, if that means anything."

Breathing in, Becca exhaled slowly. "It means a lot. Thank you." It really did. Perhaps knowing such an inconsequential detail even restored a bit of her faith in Kevin's moral compass, no matter how cracked it was. Maybe it wasn't totally broken.

"He never spoke to me after that day. I'm not sure I would have talked to him anyway. What I did to you was horrible and while your forgiveness helps, I'm not sure I'll ever forgive myself. No woman wants to be a home wrecker."

But Becca wondered if their home wasn't already wrecked. Loretta might have just been the light shining on the subject they'd both refused to acknowledge. "We'd been having problems for a while."

"I know," Loretta said, shifting a step closer. "Which makes my actions all the more vile. He'd told me how burdened your relationship had been and while I sympathized, I never meant to put more pressure on an already weak thread."

Tilting her head, Becca measured the sincerity showing in the other woman's eyes. "He talked to you about us?"

"Sometimes. At first it was just small things, like with Hunter and the work you were doing to get him into new programs, but over time, our encounters turned into lingering conversations and he'd confessed you two were…strained."

She laughed sadly. "That we were."

"He loved you, Rebecca. He told me so many times."

The muscles in her arms tightened, as ice seemed to pass through her veins. "I loved him too, but some things are too broken to fix. Certain actions can't be undone."

Loretta nodded, her gaze falling to the ground. "I'm sorry to hear that. Many times Kevin expressed a desire to be a better husband and father. I think his intentions were somehow misplaced along the way. I didn't help matters."

"No," she agreed succinctly. It was getting chilly and she'd started to shiver more than what the climate demanded. "I just wanted to let you know I hold no ill will toward you."

"You really are a strong woman, Rebecca," she said in salutation. "I hope one day you find a man strong enough to be your match. Again, I'm sorry for what I did."

The words thank you wouldn't come, so Becca simply nodded and found her way back through the hedges. No matter how difficult it was to accomplish what she'd just done, her instinct told her it was the right thing to do, and once the morose haze faded she was certain she'd celebrate a new sense of pride in taking another big step toward letting go.

~

THE DAY they closed on the deal with Apricot, something peculiar happened. Braydon wasn't at the meeting, which was odd, since he was spearheading the development.

Still uncomfortable in Miranda's presence, Becca tried to be professional. After the meeting, she attempted to make small talk with his intimidating boss. "It's a shame Braydon couldn't be here today. He must be really busy with the other project he's working on."

Miranda frowned. "Other project?"

Unsure why the other woman was looking at her with clear confusion, she clarified, "Yeah, isn't he..." Thinking quick and not wanting to get Braydon in trouble with his boss, she played dumb. If Miranda didn't know about the project he was working on there was probably good reason. The question was, why didn't *she*? "I just assumed he had another project if he wasn't here. My mistake."

Miranda gathered her belongings from the table and smiled. "No, he had to go home to take care of some family business. He should be back tomorrow." Breezing out of the office, Becca stared dumbly, digesting the bomb her boyfriend's *very informed* ex just dropped.

He'd given Becca the impression he was occupied with something for work and that was what all the trips out of town were about. If something were going on with one of the McCullough's, why hadn't he told her? And why had he told Miranda?

She worried about his family, having come to care for each member. Was someone sick? Deciding not to assume anything until she had some answers, she texted him. This was likely one big misunderstanding.

WHERE ARE YOU?

HIS REPLY TOOK SEVERAL MINUTES. She didn't receive it until she was back at her desk.

AT WORK. What's up?

. . .

SHE FROWNED. Miranda was his boss. If he were "working" she would have said just that. Why would the other woman lie and say he was home dealing with family business? Why would *he* lie and say he was at work? Someone wasn't telling the truth. She just hoped the liar wasn't Braydon.

This wasn't a discussion to have via text and his short answer told her he was involved with something at the moment.

WILL YOU BE HOME TONIGHT? Kevin has Hunter. I thought I'd come to your place and we could talk.

FOR SOME REASON THE TERM "TALK" always put men in a panic and she regretted not choosing her words more carefully.

TALK? Is something wrong? I should be home around six.

SHE DIDN'T WANT to lie and say nothing was wrong, but she also didn't want to stress him out when he might have a long drive ahead of him. She, on the other hand was totally panicking over not knowing whom he was working for or what he was doing. And the fact that his ex seemed more informed than his actual girlfriend was putting her in a very distressing position. But most stressing of all was the fact that he possibly wasn't being honest with her. She hated secrets.

She kept her response short.

I'LL SEE you at six.

~

BRAYDON RACED HOME, knowing Becca was probably waiting for him. It was already seven and he'd told her he'd be home by six. When he walked into his apartment she was sitting on his couch watching the news. She shut off the television the second he stepped through the door. Nervous energy pulsed in the room.

"Where were you?"

"Sorry I'm late. There was traffic and I couldn't get out of there until after four."

"Out of where? Braydon, where've you been?"

The house was almost complete. Today a shipment of tile arrived and he was almost ready to unveil his surprise. He hadn't been sleeping very well, because now that it was getting close he feared Becca would freak at his high-handedness. She had a job to consider and her friends, a house, and of course, Hunter. Simply put, he was a restless mess.

"I was at work."

She scowled at him. "No, you weren't."

Why was she being so oppositional? "Becca," he said calmly. "I swear I was working."

"For who, because your boss said you were visiting family?"

Damn it, Miranda. "I was doing a project in Center County."

Her lips trembled and he pinched his temples as his good intentions rapidly turned into misinterpretations. The last thing he wanted her to feel was betrayed. All of this secretiveness was in hopes of surprising her. "I'm sorry I didn't tell you that's where I was going."

"Since when have you been working there and why is this the first I'm hearing about it? Your ex seems more informed of your whereabouts than I am."

"She's my boss, Becca. Please stop referring to her as my ex. I was doing something on family property."

Her brow lowered, as he seemed to dig himself deeper. "So you *weren't* working."

"I was. I just wasn't getting paid for my time."

"Miranda—"

"Enough with Miranda!" He snapped and her mouth snapped shut.

It was understandable that Becca had trust issues, but he'd never done anything untrustworthy. The inquisitions were getting old. Regretting his sharp tone, he quickly apologized. "Sorry." In a calmer voice, he explained, "She's my boss, Becca. Not my lover, not my mistress, and not anyone you need to worry about."

Her lips clamped tight. She was clearly upset.

Moving to the couch, he stared at her, but she wouldn't meet his gaze. "I'm sorry. I shouldn't have yelled, but it gets exhausting constantly having Kevin's misdeeds held against my record. I don't want to keep defending suspicions about a past I had no part in. I don't hold my past against you."

Her shoulders sagged. "You're right. I'm sorry. There's just something about that woman that makes me nervous."

"You have nothing to be nervous about." Sure, Miranda made a habit of propositioning him, but he'd made his position clear the last time they'd talked. Since then, she'd seemed to accept they would never be more than friends.

"Why didn't you tell me you were going to Center County?"

She seemed hurt and there was a quick solution to remedy that, but he wasn't ready to come clean. They'd had a great month and the holidays were quickly approaching. He didn't want to shock her and throw their groove out of whack. He'd hoped to present the idea of moving there slowly. "How about I take you up there at the end of the month and show you what I've been working on? I just need a little time."

She nodded, but he still sensed her tension. "I don't like secrets, Braydon. You missed the closing today."

"I'm aware. I signed off on the project last Monday. My part's done." He should have given her some sort of heads up he wouldn't be back in town in time to attend the meeting.

"Why didn't you tell me you wouldn't be there?"

He hadn't even taken off his coat. Taking her hands, he offered the honest to God truth. "It slipped my mind."

His phone rang, interrupting their discussion. The screen flashed Miranda's name and he quickly declined the call. Returning his gaze to Becca, he drew back as she glared at him.

"She's calling you? How often does she call you?"

"It doesn't matter, Becca. We're just friends."

She pulled her hands out of his. "It matters to me! And a second ago she was just your boss."

"You're being unfair."

"Braydon, you had *sex* with this woman. You had a relationship with her. It isn't ridiculous for me to feel uncomfortable about her calling you."

His phone beeped, announcing a message. Becca glanced at his phone. "She left you a message. Why don't you see what she wanted?"

He really didn't want to do that. Not because he had any indiscretions to hide, but because Miranda could easily say something that could be taken wildly out of context. "I'd rather not."

She stood. "I'm going home."

"Becca—"

Pivoting, she glared at him. "Don't treat me like an irrational person, Braydon. I'm a woman and I'm well aware of your appeal. I'm also extremely insecure, which I apologize for, but I can't seem to prevent. Don't be naïve and act like she might not want more than you. Be decent enough to be upfront with me. Is this something I have to worry about?"

He sighed. "No—"

"Then play the message."

If she was trying for intimidation, she failed. He knew her too well, saw through all her masks, saw her battle scars and recognized her fear. Her husband had cheated on her. Such a simple statement with such immeasurable significance. He'd never known such perfidy, but he understood how such a thing could shake a person's trust in all future relationships.

Deliberating for a few moments, he gave up. He didn't want to fight with her and her past made it imperative he be completely open. His thumb slid over the screen, playing the message on speakerphone. Hopefully disclosure would relieve her ungrounded assumptions.

"Hey, Bray. Just seeing if you're back in town. I thought maybe we could grab a drink. Call me."

Or not. Her expression was blank. He was an idiot.

"Becca, I swear I haven't done anything wrong." She remained silent. "Look, Miranda's made it clear that she's available, but I made it clear I'm not interested. She's lonely and just looking for a friend, which is *all* I offered."

"Did you tell her that?"

"Yes! Several times."

"Then why is she still calling you?"

"I don't know. I'm not in charge of her."

"That's right. She likes bossing people around, doesn't she?" She stood. "Remember when you told Kevin I was your woman?"

"Yes."

"Well...you're my man, Braydon. And I'll be damned if I let some bossy...whatever she is, sniff around my property. I'll talk to you tomorrow."

"You're leaving?"

"Yes. I need to go home and eat some ice cream. I'm mad at you so I'm afraid you can't come."

"Becca—"

"Goodnight, Braydon." And with that she left.

Five minutes later he received a text from her.

I'M ALSO JEALOUS. *I'm sorry. I love you.*

SHUTTING off his phone he sighed. It was nice having someone care enough to be territorial, but the insecurities had to heal. All he could do was be patient with her. Over time, he'd prove he was nothing like her ex and she'd eventually learn she could trust him.

~

BECCA'S HANDS were trembling as she knocked on Nikki's door. Her friend answered, a look of surprise on her face. "Becca? It's after eight." Nikki glanced at the bag in her hand, packed with chocolate, wine, and ice cream. "What's wrong?"

"Men suck!"

"This is news?"

She pushed her way inside and felt a wave of embarrassment when she spotted Todd, Nikki's husband. "Hi, Todd. You don't suck."

"Hey, Becca."

"Come on. Let's go to the kitchen," Nikki said then whispered, "They all suck sometimes, hon."

She dumped her bag on the counter and rummaged through the pints of ice cream. "I need a spoon."

"Okay. You wanna tell me what happened?" Nikki handed her a spoon and uncorked the wine. Becca didn't wait for a glass. Rather, she tipped the bottle back and took a long sip.

"I think Braydon's boss is after him."

Her friend sighed and settled into the seat across from her. "I sort of suspected, but now I'm not so sure."

"What?"

Over the next twenty minutes Nikki explained what she'd seen at the pub and Becca caught her up on the latest events.

"In all honesty, I don't think he's interested, Becs. He loves you."

"Then why is she still bothering him? Can't she take a hint?"

"Maybe it's weird because he works for her. Braydon seems like a people pleaser. Maybe it's just not in his nature to say no to an old acquaintance needing a friend."

She made a rude sound. "I do not like that woman. Who does she think she is with her fancy clothes and long legs?"

Nikki smiled. "You're jealous."

"Of course I'm jealous! Look at her, Nikki. The woman owns the company. She's tall and stunning and doesn't come with baggage."

"But Braydon broke up with her for a reason. He's with you now. If he wanted her back and she's opened the invitation, he'd be there, but he's not. Give yourself a little credit."

Rubbing her temples, she sighed. "But they have a *past*. People sometimes cling to what they know. I love Braydon, but I wasn't married to him for ten years. There's always going to be something Kevin holds over me *because* of our history." She stabbed her spoon into her melting ice cream and winced. "I hate that someone else could know Braydon as intimately as I do. It's like when Loretta told me how much Kevin was confiding in her. Why couldn't he talk to me about all those feelings of inadequacy?"

Her friend sighed. "Is this about Braydon or about Kevin?"

"Braydon. Both. God, I don't know. I'm a mess!"

Nikki chugged her wine. "Okay, I think you're overreacting. Marriage is different than an affair. It's hard to give up something you vowed your life to. I know your relationship with GQ came right on the tails of your divorce and you're still letting go of those broken promises, but what Braydon had with this woman wasn't marriage. They didn't have the history you and Kevin had. Stop projecting your issues on his situation. You'll make yourself and everyone else crazy."

"You're right. I know you're right."

"Honey, you have to mourn your marriage and move on. He's not coming back—luckily. Maybe it's too soon to accept your family isn't going to be what you thought, but you wouldn't want him after what he did anyway. I'm proud of you for confronting the neighbor, but don't reopen that can of worms too much. It's recycled garbage you don't need."

They both picked up a spoon as Nikki's advice sank in. "I think seeing my neighbor and knowing she isn't anything special really damaged me. Miranda's strikingly beautiful. I couldn't compete with Loretta. I certainly can't compete with Miranda."

"No one said you have to." Settling back in her chair, Nikki studied her for a long minute.

"What?"

"You're never going to get over your insecurities until you can look them in the eye, Becs. This woman's no better than you or anyone else. Let her know she's overstepping and she'll probably back off."

"I can't do that to Braydon. He has a right to his friends and he claims that's all she is."

"Do you believe him?"

Did she? She shrugged. "I don't know. He hasn't given me reason to believe otherwise, but I'm a head case. When she called tonight…it killed me."

"So tell him that. Maybe even tell her. The Apricot deal's done. I'm not suggesting you storm in their office and go batshit, but I see no harm in you claiming what's yours. If some woman was after Todd I wouldn't hesitate."

"You're different."

"Okay, then let her keep calling him. I'm sure *that* won't get old."

"Hey, don't be mean."

"Then don't be a tissue. You get your big girl panties on and tell this woman exactly who you are. She may sign his checks, but you're the one buttering his bread."

The idea of confronting Miranda sounded strong in theory, but the truth was it reeked of self-doubt—*her* self-doubt, not the other woman's. "I guess it'll just take time for me to get over my trust issues. I just hope it doesn't take too long. Braydon was right, he doesn't deserve to pay for Kevin's mistakes."

Nikki's hand rubbed over hers. "You'll get there. I have faith in you."

~

THE FOLLOWING morning Becca developed a few new nervous tics. Her palms were sweating profusely and her heart hadn't stopped racing. A little before lunch she took a cab over to Braydon's office. She made it as far as the reception area before her feet froze and she wasn't sure what to do next.

A crowd of executives in suits emerged from a room down the hall and she recognized Miranda's voice. One of the suits passing mentioned Braydon's name and she wondered if he'd been in that meeting.

Miranda's laugh trickled down the hall with enough force to galvanize Becca. She crept to the door and glanced inside. Her heart plummeted the moment she saw Miranda's hand touch Braydon's arm.

Braydon stepped back. "Miranda, stop."

At the sound of his protest, Becca stepped back. What was she doing there? Sure, she could say she was just visiting, but the transparent truth was she was spying. This was a mistake. He'd be hurt to know she needed to see proof in order to believe him and in that moment she wanted to turn back and run, disgusted with her insecure self.

Quickly pivoting, she rushed down the hall toward the elevator she'd arrived on.

"Becca?"

Crap. Shoulders tense, she slowly turned. "Hi, Miranda. I…uh… was looking for Braydon."

The woman smiled. "He's right in there." She turned. "Bray? You have a visitor." Surprisingly, her tone was polite, almost pleased. She turned back to her. "I bet you're relieved to be finishing up with Apricot. I think the entire deal went wonderfully for all parties involved."

Of all the things Becca expected, speaking to this woman as a peer hadn't been one of them. "Y—yes. I'm glad they chose your firm."

Braydon emerged from the office, his pace slowing as he spotted her speaking to Miranda. "Hey."

Miranda smiled. "I'll leave you two alone. Good job today, McCullough."

He nodded, but didn't take his eyes off of Becca. "What are you doing here, Becca?"

Scrunching her face, disappointed in herself on so many levels, she rushed out, "Being stupid."

"What?" He laughed.

Huffing out a deep breath, she confessed, "I was checking up on you. Or marking my territory. Or…I don't know." Glancing up at him with pleading eyes, she admitted, "I have issues. I'm sorry I blamed you for them."

His mouth curled into a half smile, gifting her with an

endearing shot of his dimple. "Did I ever tell you how adorable you are?"

Her neck extended. "Adorable? Did you hear anything I just said?"

Reaching out, he pinched her chin. "I heard everything, even the stuff you didn't say, angel." He shrugged. "It's sort of flattering to know you're territorial about me."

"But…you don't deserve my suspicions."

"No, but I don't mind. If coming here somehow helped you find a little peace of mind, then it's fine. I told you, I have nothing to hide. I'm an open book."

It did give her peace of mind and a little bit of a reality check. That he somehow realized that and didn't seem to mind that she was pretty much crazy—and a child—made her fall more in love with him. Swallowing her shame, she lifted her gaze to his. "I'm sorry."

He looked at her for a long moment, his gaze scrutinizing. Slowly, he took her hand. "Come with me."

Lacing her fingers with his, she followed him as they ducked into a conference room and he shut the door. He quickly spun her until her back met the wall and his lips crashed over hers. Drawing in a deep breath, he kissed her deeply, pressing his hips to hers. "Thank you."

He was thanking *her*? "For what?"

His face pressed to her neck as he sighed into her hair. "For coming here, for caring enough to look for the truth rather than gambling what we have on ungrounded suspicions. I'm not sure anyone's ever cared that much, Becca. It feels…good. Reassuring."

Impossible. Didn't he realize what a catch he was? Didn't the rest of the women out there see him? She wrapped her arms around his waist, hugging him. "I promise I won't always be this crazy."

"Mmm…" he hummed contently. "A little crazy can be fun."

But she knew she could be better. She had to conquer her trust issues. Otherwise, she might lose this incredible man and she was pretty sure there wasn't another man out there as wonderful as him.

~

THAT EVENING, after Hunter was in bed, Becca decided to address their future. Her life was subtly shifting in ways that led to dramatic change. Rather than continue to make harmful assumptions, she was learning honesty worked better for everyone.

The first person she needed to be honest with was herself. Braydon was immensely important to her and if she wanted all of him, she needed to get some answers. "Did you ever think of opening your own company?"

Shifting on the bed, he hesitated and then said, "I've been thinking about it a lot lately."

Though he'd hinted at the idea before, the way he tacked on the word *lately* gave her pause. "You have?"

He nodded. "I never wanted to work for a big company. I always assumed I'd eventually work from home, maybe have a small satellite office downtown for meetings."

She could imagine him doing that, but how soon did he expect to put these changes into effect? She should know these things, because if *home* was back in Center County, that would change a lot.

There was no doubt in her mind that Braydon would be successful no matter who he worked for, himself or a corporation. He definitely had a gift when it came to design. The Apricot deal had been an overwhelming success, thanks to his creativity. Combine that with his personality and his capability in matters, his endless abilities became almost intimidating.

"How about you?" he asked.

She turned, lost in her thoughts. "What about me?"

"Do you see yourself working for Nikki forever?"

She'd never given it much thought. It was a good job and she was comfortable in Pittsburgh. Nikki understood her homelife and understood family emergencies always took precedence over any work crisis. "Unless I have a reason to leave, I think I could stay there and be happy."

He was quiet for several minutes. "I built a house."

As though a ton of bricks landed on her chest, her heart stuttered. Her skin went cold with shock. "What?"

"I built a house." His expression gave nothing away. "In Center County."

Her throat constricted to a pinhole as she tried to swallow. He'd built a house? When? What did this mean? He was moving? "A *house?*"

He nodded, but didn't smile, which did nothing to slow her panic. "On the mountain."

Her lips parted as everything became clear. He was moving out of the city. "You built *your* house." How much time did they have left? How had he managed something so grand without uttering a word to her? This was so unexpected. She'd known he'd missed home, but she assumed they had more time. At no point did he lead her to believe his eminent departure would be this soon.

"*Our* house."

Snapping her head up, she frowned at him. "Our house?"

"Yeah. I wanted it to be finished before I took you to see it. It's almost done."

He built a *house*—in *Center County*—for *them*. Where was she when all this was decided? Shaking her head in confusion, she said, "But I live here." Her life was here. She couldn't just pick up and go!

"We don't have to. We could live together—there."

Sixty seconds ago she was lying on her bed pondering the future. No one told her the future was going to start a minute later. She wasn't prepared for this. "What are you talking about? Braydon, we haven't even discussed moving in with each other."

"I'm at your house nearly every night. The only time we're apart is when we're working or I'm traveling. Maybe it's time we had the discussion."

She blew out a puff of air. Her heart was pounding like a jackhammer. They were *dating*. Granted, she didn't have much experience with dating, but wasn't moving in together a big deal that should be discussed way before a place was selected? Didn't her opinion count for anything? She'd told him she liked when he decided *in bed*, but this was totally different! "This is a conversation we should've had before you invested in the first nail. I can't move, Braydon. Living together's one thing, but moving far away is totally different. Hunter's school's here."

Calmly, he took her hand and squeezed. "I want to live with you, Becca. You and Hunter." How was he so calm?

"This is a *big* deal, Braydon. You act like you're stating you want ice cream."

"I know what I want."

She shook her head. For as level headed as he was, she was that much more scattered and paranoid. "But I have a house."

"Do you love it? Tell me you love your home, and I'll back off."

He had an answer for everything. "Nobody loves their home

one hundred percent, but it's ours. It's Hunter's home. He's used to it. He's lived here his entire life. I can't just uproot him. He has school. I have a job. And I have to consider Kevin in all of this."

"Kevin could still see Hunter."

"How, Braydon? He lives in the city. Center County's hours away. It's an impossible commute."

"Nothing's impossible."

She shook her head, baffled by his optimism. He held such a positive outlook on everything. It seemed to amplify her pessimism, which made her cynical thinking all the more unflattering. "You aren't being realistic. People don't just stop everything and start over at this age."

Her mind was reeling. He built a house. A house. Not a fort or a shed. A *house!* As amazing as that was, it made her incredibly sad. He'd be moving there with or without her—the investment was made. She couldn't just leave her home and run off to Center County. She had Hunter to consider, bills to pay, a job to maintain. He hadn't even given her the chance to invite him to move in with them. That would be more realistic.

"Plenty of people start over, angel. You gotta be brave. Think about your life. How many memories of your home were fractured by your divorce? Your house is nice, but this bed we sleep in…you picked it out with your ex-husband. Every bit of furniture came before me. I'm trying to get you to take the next step. I want to take it with you, but I want you to—"

"Braydon. This isn't just about a house. Our home is in Pittsburgh."

"Why, though? It doesn't have to be. You can make a home anywhere you choose. I know you loved being at the mountain. I love it too. My family's there, but since falling in love with you I've been caught in a divide. I want it all, you, them, a home, I wanna make *our* home, *our* life, a place where we can grow together—you, me, and Hunter—as one. Family, Becca, isn't that what you want?"

She turned her face away as a tear escaped her lashes. "I can't."

"Why? I'm not asking for more than you can give, just a chance for the three of us to be whole. Give me every challenge and I'll conquer them."

"You're not considering the life we already have. Hunter's school—"

He stood and went to his bag. Returning to her with a sheaf of papers he said, "Sammy got this information for me."

"Sammy?" Everything was moving way too fast.

"Yeah, remember I told you she works for the school. It's information on the programs. There's a music enrichment program and a young engineers' club. Colin's working on a grant that would get the school a better resource room and he wants you to help him when it gets approved so that it's designed with every beneficial detail you can imagine. I've already given an estimate to do the work as an independent contractor. Our family's donating the lumber and Mallory's writing the grant proposal. Hunter would be in a smaller setting, but that may benefit him."

Scooting into a seated position, she took the papers with a trembling hand. She hadn't expected him to consider her circumstances so thoroughly. "You looked into all this?"

"Of course. I want you, but I want Hunter too. I want the whole package."

He painted quite the perfect picture. If only life were that easy. Shutting her eyes, she lowered the papers. "But my job..."

"You work to support you and Hunter, but if you didn't work you wouldn't have to pay after care. We'd have my income too."

"Braydon, I work because I need to. My mind needs those hours to focus on something that's solely mine."

He grinned. "I thought about that too. What if I told you that this spring there's a position opening up at the lumberyard? It's an office job, my dad's assistant's retiring and he needs someone smart and dedicated. You'd be right around the corner from the school and you'd only have to work until four each day."

"I don't know anything about that field."

"You know how to read schematics. You know how to answer phones. You'd handle payroll and all the other stuff the crew doesn't get involved in, like supplying equipment and ordering new materials. You'd also schedule shipments for the drivers. I know it's not the most glamorous job, but the pay's decent and you wouldn't have to stay as late as you do at the office now. If you're looking for something more intellectually challenging, there are other places to work, but at least you know you'd have options to start."

She laughed and sat back, flattered by his consideration yet somehow offended at the same time. "You've thought of everything."

"Not quite," he admitted. "There's the issue of Kevin."

This time when she laughed it was without humor. Kevin had been better since Thanksgiving. He seemed to be stepping up where Hunter was involved and actually honoring the custody schedule. Maybe he was finally coming to terms with their new family dynamic. However, changing their arrangement could destroy the slight progress she'd noticed.

Was she really ready to make a decision like this? Moving away from Kevin was monumental. Yes, her marriage was over, but moving out of the city and in with Braydon seemed like an extreme and blunt ending to her previous life. Every day she moved toward closure, but she wasn't sure if she was ready for that *yet*. Moving forward was supposed to be a process, and she was still processing.

Her lashes lowered and she sighed. "I can't make a decision like this in one night."

"I know. We have time. The house still needs some work."

She chuckled, attempting to hide some of her worry. "Who builds a house?"

"Me."

"That's a lot of pressure."

"That's why I held off telling you. Take the house out of the equation, Becca. I want this. I want us to live together, but I don't want it if it comes with regrets."

That's what she was afraid of too. Regret was a horrible thing to live with. She'd only be able to do this if her mind was one hundred percent made up. She didn't know how to rush certainty like that, especially when no situation came with guarantees. "You'd really leave your job?"

"Leaving the area doesn't necessarily mean leaving the company. Our firm does a lot of satellite work. Documents are emailed instead of shipped. I would only have to take a trip to the city once or twice a week and whenever we were trying to land a new client. A great deal of what I do can be done from home. Eventually, yes, I'd like to branch off on my own, but that doesn't have to be right away."

She sighed, her head was spinning. This was a lot. "I'll think about it."

"Okay." He leaned close and kissed her. "I love you, Becca. Take your time to consider everything I said. I know it's scary, but that doesn't make it impossible. It makes it exciting."

He seemed so enthusiastic, so certain. She didn't possess that sort of confidence toward life anymore. Her life was routine. Wake up, address the day, fight the battles as they presented, and pray for sleep so she could do it all over again. What he was asking of her was so far beyond her scope of imagination.

When Braydon fell asleep, she crept out of bed and wandered through the shadows of the house. Kevin still had crap cluttered in the corners, and boxes he refused to move. She stared through the window at her dark, empty yard, lacking a tree. It seemed the day that tree came down, so many illusions she'd been hiding behind fell. Maybe that was a good thing.

Stepping into the kitchen, she made a slow rotation, taking inventory of her home. Her kitchen table only had three of four matching chairs since the one broke several years ago. Her cabinets were dinged and scuffed. The tile behind the sink was cracked and her linoleum was peeling up by the stove.

As she moved through the house she noted every adjustment that was incorporated for Hunter. She no longer kept pictures around, because when the frames were knocked over, the glass was a dangerous mess she didn't always have the immediate time to clean up.

As she walked through the hall she tried to read Hunter's equations. It was a language she couldn't decipher, but one he'd started to use more than any other—another sign of change.

She found herself sitting at the piano bench, tapping a random key in the quiet house. Slowly, she dropped her head to the keys and started to cry.

Every room held a memory of her and Kevin screaming at each other. She'd polished every inch of floor with her own tears over the years. But if she allowed her mind to go back a bit farther, there were happy times shared in that home between her and her ex.

They'd painted the nursery together and planted rose bushes in the back. Those bushes were gone now, but at one time he had been devoted to the same dreams she once entertained. Giving up her home was the final farewell to all the hopes she'd failed to see through. It hurt, accepting that there would be no turning back, no second chances, and no do-overs.

But beneath all the pain came a soft comfort that was warm and thrilling. Braydon. Braydon was risky, but exhilarating. He made her dare to dream again. The only thing stopping her was her aversion to the possibility of more broken dreams.

Life would never change if she stayed where she was, but change came with risk. Staying was safe and the closest thing to a guarantee she'd ever get in this unpredictable world.

As she wept, she contemplated her fears. If she were to get sick, who would care for her son? No matter how much exposure Braydon had to autism, she still wasn't sure if he understood that autism was a lifelong journey. Deep down, she feared, like Kevin, Braydon might eventually reach his limit.

Autism defined the type of parent she was required to be. It taught her flexibility and sacrifice. It taught her that every day presented new beginnings and simple gifts that should be valued beyond all else.

She'd shown Hunter respect and kindness, and in turn, her son showed her a world she'd never expected, but this life had become all she now knew. He changed her more than any other human being or experience ever could. Did Braydon really understand that those changes would be expected of him as well if they all lived together? Could he commit to that?

Assuming Braydon knew what he was asking, the next question was, where would Hunter develop most? What was better for her son?

The city was fast-paced. When she thought of Center County, she thought of open spaces, room to run without the fear of traffic. She smiled as she recalled the echoes of the children's voices bouncing off the trees and the unbounded hospitality.

McCullough Mountain was a magical place with room to play. It was safe and thrumming with love, the love of one of the most incredible families she'd ever met. Deep down, she knew Hunter would love it there.

The transition would be a challenge, of course, but once he adjusted there would be no limit to how he could flourish in an environment overflowing with love and family. Hunter may not be able to tolerate touching or closeness, but her son knew how to love. He simply communicated affection in his own unique way.

But all of that came at a cost. Kevin's parenting might be in an upswing at the moment, but how long would that last if they moved away? Hunter deserved his father's presence in his life no matter how minimal Kevin's nurturing tended to be. She feared putting more distance between Kevin and Hunter would demolish the remaining connection their family shared.

She wanted to provide a life for Hunter that allowed him to reach his ultimate potential. Kevin should want to be a part of his son's life no matter what the circumstances—*should* being the troubling word.

CHAPTER 13

Friday morning Becca contacted the school to inform them that Hunter would not be in. She also informed Nikki she was taking a personal day with her son. They'd been on the road for over two hours and Hunter was listening to his iPod in the back while spinning with the wheels of a toy car. On most days Hunter was a good traveler, which boded well if she decided to do this. There could be a lot of commuting in his future.

As she took the exit she kept her eyes peeled for familiar land-marks. The town looked different now that they were in the midst of December. All the colorful leaves had fallen and there was snow on the ground, which she hadn't anticipated.

Braydon was working at the office and unaware that she'd decided to make the trip. Realizing she'd passed the turn off for the mountain, she spun around and took the road a bit slower.

When she pulled onto the private drive, her van labored to make it up the incline. The evergreens wore a dusting of white, and patches of brown grass showed through the snow covered ground. There were sled markings on the hill to her left. Hunter hadn't gone sledding in some time, likely since he was five. He'd probably enjoy that.

When she spotted the big house anxiety attacked her stomach. She should have called first. She merely wanted to walk around with her son, but now that she was here the idea of stopping by unannounced seemed a bit rude.

"We're here," she said, parking the car a distance from the house.

Everyone appeared to be gone for the day, but smoke rose from both chimneys and she wondered if Maureen was home. Climbing out, she helped Hunter from the van and tucked his iPod away. The moment his sneakers touched the ground he registered the snow. Sliding the door shut, she smiled as he marched around, admiring his footprints.

"That's snow. Remember snow?"

His head tilted as he paced to a slushy spot and jumped. She followed him as he explored. When he approached the edge of the forest a winged bird took flight and he laughed.

"I saw that," she said, smiling at his pleasure.

They approached the house and Hunter drifted over to the Jeep parked by the porch. His fingers ran through the dusting of snow collected on the glass and he shook it off.

"Cold?"

"Cold," he confirmed. "Wet."

A door opened and she rotated, keeping Hunter in her sight as he played with the snow.

"Becca, love, is that you?"

She smiled as Maureen stepped off the porch in a pair of goulashes and a bright orange hunting jacket. "Hi, Maureen."

"I wasn't expecting you."

"I'm sorry I didn't call. I wanted to get out of the city for the day and I just…I should have called."

The older woman waved away her apology. "Nonsense. Is Braydon with you?"

"No. He doesn't know I'm here."

Her expression turned nervous. "Oh." Replacing her surprise with a smile, she turned to Hunter. "And who is this lovely cherub?"

Becca tapped Hunter's shoulder. "This is my son, Hunter. Hunter, can you say hello to Mrs. McCullough?"

He shook his head and went back to playing with the snow. Maureen preened. "What a handsome fellow you are, Hunter. Do you like hot chocolate? I have some inside."

"Hunter, would you like some hot chocolate?"

"Chocolate."

Maureen's smile widened. "I'll take that as a yes. Come on then. Let's get warm before your little fingers freeze."

Maureen led the way and Becca directed Hunter toward the house.

"Cold," he repeated as he shifted his arms.

Becca continued at his side. "Yes, it's cold here. It'll be warm inside the house."

They made it into the kitchen and she guided Hunter to the table, but he chose to explore while Maureen heated up the chocolate on the stove. Hunter touched the walls and walked close to the deer head hanging in the hall only to laugh and walk away. This seemed to confuse him, but little by little he stepped closer to examine the oddity.

"So how are things with you and Braydon?" Maureen asked.

"Good. I heard he's been spending some time here lately."

"Has he?"

She laughed silently. "I know about the house, Maureen."

"Oh, well then, yes, he's been here quite a bit. Does he know you're visiting, love?"

Hunter yelled in the hall, his voice carrying up to the high ceilings, causing him to laugh and repeat the action. "No. I wanted to bring Hunter here to see how he liked it."

"The mountain's a wonderful place to raise children. I can say that because I know a thing or two about it. Raised five boys here and have no regrets. Boys need lots of room to run and play. They broke nearly every nice thing I've ever owned, but they're good boys and I've forgiven them."

Carrying the mugs to the table, Maureen opened the freezer and cracked a few ice cubes from a tray. "Let's give his a minute to cool, love. He seems to be enjoying himself anyway. Would you like some cake? I have some left over from dessert last night."

"Sure. Thank you."

When the cocoa cooled, Becca sipped hers carefully. It was creamy and unlike the powder kind she usually made. It filled her with a warm sense of comfort.

"Hunter, come have your hot chocolate." She stood, knowing he was involved in his exploration. Once she'd prompted him back to the table, he sat and Becca wrapped his hands around the mug. "Careful."

He took a big sip and smiled, his lip covered in a frothy, brown mustache.

"Do you like the hot chocolate, Hunter?" Maureen asked.

His lashes flickered as his head tipped to the side. "I like chocolate."

"I bet there are lots of things here for a boy your age. Do you like fishing?"

"I don't think he's ever been fishing," Becca admitted.

"Oh, well, Braydon loves the water. He has a boat I'm sure he'd like to show you. What else do you like to do?"

"Run."

"Oh, running. There's lots of room to run here. Maybe after our cake, I can find some hats and gloves and we can take a walk. You can show me how fast you run."

They finished their snack and Maureen disappeared as Becca wiped Hunter's face. When she returned she had a basket filled with mittens, gloves, scarves, and hats.

She poured the basket onto the table and sorted through the items. "Look at this, Hunter. Which hat do you like? This one's very soft."

Hunter came over and picked up a hat then dropped it. "Itchy."

"Oh, that one is itchy. Do you not like the itchy ones? Let's put all the itchy ones back in the basket." Becca was impressed how Maureen found a way to include her son. It was as if she'd known he might not accept just any hat.

She stood back and watched as Maureen and her son sorted through the pile, hiding away the scratchy fabrics, then sorting the water resistant materials Hunter claimed were slippery. In the end, they had all of the gloves paired up and organized by color. Hunter chose a blue pair and a soft wool hat. Watching Braydon's mother handle him with such patience made her love the woman even more.

As Hunter ran through the yard, Becca and Maureen took a much slower pace. There was nothing but open space for Hunter to explore. It was likely the most fresh air he'd had in ages.

They walked for over an hour, chatting and taking in the sights. Maureen asked lots of questions about her plans with Braydon, but Becca was honest when she told her she hadn't decided anything as of yet, and a lot depended on what would be the most beneficial for Hunter.

When she turned to head up the road, Maureen caught her arm. "Let's not go that way, love."

Thinking Maureen knew the land better than her she agreed then stilled. Looking back, she asked, "That's where the house is, isn't it?"

Maureen grinned. "You'll have to ask my son about that. It isn't my place to be leading you down certain paths. Those roads were built for you to take with him. If you choose to, that is."

Unsure if she was prepared to see what Braydon had created, she nodded and turned back in the opposite direction.

"Braydon's a good boy," Maureen announced, pride embedded in her voice. "He's always had an obsession with perfection. I warned him there was no such thing. I told him one day he'd fall in love with a woman that would turn his world upside down and have the ability to put him right on his arse. I like that you're different, Becca love. You're good for my boy."

"Well, I'm not perfect, that's for sure."

"No, but only one person was and they nailed that poor man to a cross. I'd say you and your son are perfectly human and that's all anyone's really expected to be in this life."

"Thank you, Maureen."

"For what? I'm just telling it like it is. Now, I won't go telling you about how much work my son's put into building you the perfect home, or how much research he's done to find you the perfect fixtures, or even how he attended the local PTA meeting with Colin last week in order to push that grant through. What I will tell you is that he loves you and he wants you and when a McCullough man sets his heart to something…well, there are wiser things a girl can do than turn him away."

She smirked. This was as subtle as Maureen McCullough could get. "I understand."

"Good. I knew you were a smart lass."

~

"WHAT DO you mean she was there?" Braydon's head was going to explode. "Did she see the house?"

"No, dear, I know better than to spoil your surprises. She came with Hunter and we had hot cocoa, went for a walk, ate lunch, and then she had to get him home because he was getting tired. Such a sweet little man, her son is."

"Ma, why didn't you call me when she got there?"

"Why would I do that? She came to see me, not you. She sees you all the time. Is it too much to ask that I have some company once in a while?"

"Jesus. Did she seem angry?"

"What the bloody hell would she be angry about, Braydon? I told you we had a nice afternoon."

He couldn't get over the idea of Becca driving there on her own and not telling him. She didn't do things spontaneously like that. "I don't understand why she wouldn't tell me she was going there. I would've taken her."

"Maybe she didn't want you to know. You men seem to think you can go on making every important decision without us. Well, you better learn now, Braydon, that isn't how a relationship works. You men give the green light when we women tell you you can. Just like your father, making big decisions without considering your love might want to form her own opinion. You're asking the lass to uproot herself from her home."

"I just thought the mountain would be a better home," he admitted with a ring of defeat.

"And it will be. There's no denying she loves it here. Hunter ran and played, and he's a lovely boy. He'll be happy here. But don't you go trying to decide for her. She'll agree to move when she realizes she's already made up her mind, but she needs to realize that at her own pace."

He was pulling into Becca's neighborhood and already sweating. It was hard to imagine his mother actually having a peaceful day with his angel and not doing anything to scare her off. "Nothing else happened?"

"Nothing else happened, you little shit. You've got yourself a good woman there. Have a little faith. And for God's sake, have a little faith in your family. We're not always a bunch of raging lunatics. We know how to be respectable when it counts."

He rolled his eyes. "All right. I've got to go. I love you, Mum."

"I love you too. Be patient with her, dearie. She'll come around."

He hung up the phone and parked the car. Taking a deep breath he tried to imagine what he'd be walking into. Gathering his courage, he went to knock on the door.

Becca unlocked the door and smiled when she saw him. "Hi."

"Hi."

"I ordered pizza. I thought you were the delivery man."

"I could have picked it up on my way."

"That's okay. We sort of had an odd day and Hunter's napping."

He took off his coat and hung it up. The house was quiet. He waited for her to tell him about her trip to his home, but she didn't. "I spoke to my mother."

She stilled. "Oh?"

"Becca, why didn't you tell me you were going there?"

"I don't know. I just sort of decided to go. I wanted to see the area again and it seemed like the perfect day to do something out of the usual. I needed to figure some things out."

"Did you?"

"I don't know." She wore an apologetic smile. "Hunter really liked it there."

He glanced in the den and saw Hunter sprawled out on a beanbag chair. He smiled, not used to seeing him out of motion. "He must have really exerted himself."

"Yeah. He's been out for almost an hour. I doubt he'll wake up until morning."

"Do you want me to carry him up?"

Her eyes widened. "He's heavy."

"Are you saying I'm weak?" he teased.

"Not at all. Have at it. I would've slept on the couch and just let him stay there."

He eyed the couch, deciding there was no way they'd both fit. Scooping Hunter into his arms he carried him to his bed. Becca followed and watched from the door, as Braydon removed his shoes and socks.

After sliding his little body under the covers and tucking him in, he quietly stood. Becca had a peculiar expression on her face. "Did I do okay?"

Her lips pressed tight and she placed a hand on her chest. "You did great."

Relieved, he nodded and silently stepped out of the room. She laid her hand on his wrist and whispered, "Braydon, I want—" The doorbell rang and she shut her eyes. "That's the pizza."

In the kitchen he set the table as she handled the delivery. As soon as he had their plates full, he got back to what she was saying. "So, upstairs, you were saying…"

"Oh, I was just thinking, if we live together in Center County, what would happen to my house?"

That wasn't what she'd started to say upstairs, but he decided to let her go at her own pace. "Well, you could rent it or sell it and take whatever equity you have."

"I don't know how much I'd get for it. Everything's pretty beat up around here."

He looked around and counted the bedrooms, running a quick list of amenities in his head. "Nikki would probably know better, but I bet you could sell it as is, for two hundred thousand. Deduct your closing costs and whatever you still owe the bank and the rest is yours. You could probably take some time off work when we—if you decided to—move." He laughed at her wide eyed expression. "Are you shocked by that?"

Her mouth hung open. "Well, yeah. How much would our mortgage be on the new house?"

"No mortgage."

She coughed and swallowed a bite of pizza. "What?"

"There's no mortgage. I've owned the land since I was eighteen. The lumber came from the yard and everything else came from a loan or my savings, but that doesn't concern you. I'm asking you to move in with me."

Her expression wilted. "Oh, so it would be your house and we'd be your roommates."

That was not at all what he meant. "No, Becca. You'd be my wife."

Her head lifted and her eyes widened again. "What?"

"You heard me."

"Braydon, are you asking me to marry you?"

"No. I already botched that once. I'm just warning you it's coming, so be prepared."

She stood, her chair making a slow glide over the linoleum. As she rounded the table he watched her carefully, unsure what she had planned. She took his pizza out of his hand and tossed it on the plate, sliding it away. Then she straddled his lap.

"Remember when we first met and you kept asking me what I wanted?"

"Yes."

"I want you to make love to me."

His body reacted to the soft way she gazed at him. They hadn't been intimate in over a week and he missed her touch, missed feeling his skin against hers. But more, he missed the assurance that they were okay. "Here?"

"Everywhere. I want you. Now."

Watching her blue eyes deepen to violet, he ran his fingers over her arms and up the back of her neck until they sifted through her hair. With one fast tug, he brought her mouth to his and kissed her passionately, possessively, loving the taste of her lips on his.

When he pulled away they were both breathless. Looking into the hall, he asked, "What about Hunter?"

"He's out cold."

"But what if he wakes up?"

"You're right. We better go upstairs."

He kissed her again, his head swimming with need. Standing, he lifted her with him and shuffled them to the hall. Her hands caressed the heated skin under the collar of his shirt as she kissed his neck. His body was so hard it was difficult to walk. He took a detour in the hall, pressing her to the wall and grinding himself into her hot core.

"Shit, we're smearing Hunter's work."

Pulling back from the wall where they'd smudged a bit of his formulas, Braydon pivoted and pushed her into the open coat closet. They laughed as he accidentally bumped her head on the shelf.

"Sorry."

"Shut up," she said as she pulled his lips back to hers.

Her hips twisted against his, the friction an incredibly delicious torture. He reached under her shirt and cupped her breast. She moaned, pressing her chest into his palm.

Glancing up, he noted the beam at the top of the closet. "Hold onto this."

She lifted her arms and gripped the bar. Braydon released her legs and yanked down her pants, past her bare feet, and tossed them aside. Looking back at the empty hall, still paranoid Hunter could wake up at any second, he quickly pulled the louver doors shut behind them.

His hands coasted up her thighs and lifted her knees over his shoulders. Using his thumbs to spread her folds, he dove forward and licked her sex. Becca cried out and tightened her legs, her heels digging deliciously into his back. He held her ass in the cradle of his palms as he feasted on her.

Sliding her feet back to the ground, he fed his fingers into her sex and pumped quickly. His mouth closed over her clit as she trembled in pleasure. When she came, her cries were only slightly muffled by the coats hanging to their left and right.

"Did your pill kick in?" It was a touchy subject he didn't want to get involved in right now, but if he had to stop and find a condom he'd probably die.

"Last week. We're good."

Best words he'd ever heard. "Turn around. Put your hands on the wall."

She giggled. "Yes, Officer McCullough."

He rose in the cramped space and shoved the coats out of his way. Something fell from the shelf, but he wasted no time seeing what it was. "I'm gonna fuck you, Becca. We'll make love later, but right now I need to be inside of you and I need it hard."

"God, yes," she breathed, shifting her feet to widen her stance.

He shucked his pants to his knees and grabbed hold of her ass, sliding his fingers around her hips and jerking her back. Her sex was swollen just the way he liked it. He gripped his cock and lined it up with her entrance. Placing a kiss on her shoulder, he thrust forward and filled her to the hilt.

She gasped and moaned as he withdrew only to pump his cock deep again and again. He fucked her against the wall until they were both slick with sweat and his knees had grown weak, but he couldn't stop. He loved having her like this, raw and needy, with such intensity there was no stopping them.

Suddenly her sex fluttered and clamped down on him, rhythmically pulsating with each thrust. She let out a stream of ludicrous words and gripped the overhead shelf as she came again, this time drawing his release with hers. His fingers clamped down on her breasts and squeezed as he held her to his front and filled her.

Spasms tore through him with each jet of cum and soon he was shivering with exertion. She wilted against the wall and he gentled his touch, turning her and brushing the hair from her face in order to see her eyes. When he found those baby blues, she smiled, her face flush with a soft pink glow.

"I love you, Becca."

Her hand cupped the side of his jaw and she kissed him softly. "I love you too, Braydon."

There was a long creak and then the overhead shelf collapsed on top of them, pummeling them with an avalanche of jackets, puzzles, and other random objects. Becca snorted and fell into a fit of laughter.

"The value just dropped to one ninety-nine," he teased and she laughed even harder, hugging him under the pile of crap they were buried in.

❧

LATER THAT NIGHT when they finally made it to bed, Becca couldn't sleep. She tossed and turned, trying her best not to disturb Braydon, but it was no use. "Braydon, are you awake?"

He shifted to face her, sheet prints already creasing his cheeks. "Yeah."

"Why do you love me?"

He chuckled. "Why do you love to ask the hard questions when I'm half-asleep?"

She shrugged and tried for her cutest expression. Hopefully he wasn't too upset she woke him. "It's the only time I really get to think about life."

His hand tunneled out from under the blankets and cupped the back of her head, drawing her close for a quick peck. "That's why I love you, Becca. You're strong, and sweet, and one of the most self-less people I've ever met. You're special."

She processed his words, letting them sink into her soul and fill her with warmth. "I used to loathe that word, special."

"But you don't anymore?"

Her mouth twisted to the side. "No. It's actually a compliment." She returned his kiss. "I think you're special too."

"Thank you. When you grow up in a house of nine, it's difficult to achieve special. Everyone's treated the same, or at least that's the goal, and it's not always easy to find your own unique place in the mix."

"Is that why you left?"

"I don't know." His eyes fixed on the ceiling for a moment. "I guess I left, at first, to go to college, but when I came home I couldn't find my place in everything. My brother married my girl-friend, Luke was off doing his thing, Finn was busy learning the business, and Sheilagh had left for school. Even Kelly was married. I didn't feel like I fit in the hole I left behind."

"Like a puzzle piece."

Turning to grin at her, he agreed, "Yeah, sort of like that."

"Do you think you'll be happy if you live there again?"

"It depends. If you're with me, yes. I don't think we're meant to refill the empty spaces we leave behind. I think they're like our fingerprints and we're meant to leave trails of them in our wake, not keep touching back to where we've been."

"I haven't left many fingerprints on the world," she admitted. She'd forever be competing with the impression left by his family. She didn't want to compete. She wanted him to be happy. Unfortu-nately, she doubted that would be possible this far from his home.

"Sure you have. Not every world's as big and fancy as the rest. But I think you've left a million imprints, and most of them are so gentle and so subtle it takes a special person to see them. I see them. So does Hunter."

That was it. She couldn't fight it any longer. Twisting, so that she could see his eyes, she whispered, "I want us to live together. If that means following you, I'd move to McCullough Mountain with you."

His eyes widened with his smile and he sat up, rumpling all the blankets. "Are you serious?"

She nodded, her heart fluttering faster than a hummingbird's wing. She could do this. There wasn't much holding her there, while all the McCulloughs seemed to be pulling him toward Center County. It was an amazing place. She'd even felt the pull when they visited, but mostly she was being drawn to this irresistible man. No one had ever tempted her to be so reckless.

"It's your home and you belong there. I get why you love it there. I love it too. It's so different from your apartment here. Your apartment's cold and lonely. I think that's why you stay here so much."

"I stay here because I want to be with you."

"But you also want to be with them and you should be. If you left, I'd be devastated and I think Hunter—in his own way—would miss you too. If you really think this is for the best and that we can make this work, I'll put in my notice and go with you. But I don't want to sell the house until we're absolutely sure."

"You'll love it. I know you will. And I'm already sure. I can't wait to show you what I've done."

She smiled, still a little too scared to entirely embrace the decision. It was surreal. "I'll have to talk to Kevin."

"Do you want me to be there when you do?"

"No. I think he'll be more understanding if I speak to him alone."

CHAPTER 14

*K*evin pulled into the driveway and Becca shut her eyes, steadying her nerves. As the garage door rolled open, she smiled and stepped out to greet them. Flies with honey.

"Hey, boys."

Kevin sent her a sidelong glance, his eyes constricted with suspicion. Okay, maybe she needed to tone it down. She could do this.

As he walked to the door, she said, "I was hoping we could talk. Do you have a few minutes?"

Hunter wandered inside and Kevin leaned against the van. "About what?"

"How about we go inside? This is more of a sit down conversation."

"Sounds important." He waved a hand, suggesting she lead the way.

Briefly checking on Hunter who was already lounging on a beanbag chair, toy in hand, she led Kevin to the sofa. Kevin sat a cushion away from her and waited expectantly.

Rubbing her moist palms over her knees, she met his stare. "I'm thinking about selling the house."

His head jerked in her direction. "Why?"

"I'd like to move."

"Where?"

She swallowed. "Center County."

His head rolled back and he settled into the couch a bit more. "With that guy, Brandon?"

"Braydon."

"You barely know him, Rebecca."

"I know him enough to know I want this."

"What about Hunter?"

"He'd come with me, of course."

He scoffed. "And what about what I want?"

This was where things could get touchy. "Kevin, you and I both know what a trial Hunter is for you—"

"And he's easy for you?"

"No, but I've always had a little more patience—"

"Don't give me that shit, Rebecca. This isn't about what's best for Hunter. This is about what you want."

"This is about what's best for our family."

"A family that doesn't include me." The vulnerability that flashed in his eyes gave her pause.

"You'll always be a part of Hunter's life—"

"As what? Some guy he sees on holidays? How long do you think that will last, Rebecca? How long until he hates being with me, because I'm so removed from his ordinary routine? This is bullshit."

"Center County's a wonderful place, Kevin. I wouldn't be considering it if I didn't think the environment would benefit him."

"Considering it? Sounds to me like your mind's made up."

It was, but she needed his consent in order to follow through with her plans. "Maybe if you saw him there you'd understand."

He laughed coldly. "Oh, yeah, I'll just call up my pal Brandon and set up a date."

"Braydon."

"Whatever. Don't I get a say in who you expose my son to?"

You didn't give me a say in who you exposed our marriage to. She clamped her lips shut.

"How would you feel if I told you I wanted full custody and planned to shack up with some broad you didn't know?" He laughed. "You'd never go for that. The answer's no, Rebecca. I'm sorry. My son's staying in Pittsburgh where he belongs. It's his home."

Cold dread knifed though her stomach. "You can't tell me no."

"Really? Okay, how's this? I think Hunter would flourish in a round the clock facility."

Her eyes blurred with immediate tears of fear. Blinking through her fuzzy vision, she cleared her throat and rasped, "How could you say that?"

"Maybe I think that's the best environment for him."

"You don't believe that." No matter how different Kevin's parenting was from her, they'd discussed such arrangements at length. He was only making a point, but the empty threat still frightened her. "You're just trying to keep him here without taking full responsibility."

He shrugged. "Why not? He'd only be a few miles away and I could see him whenever I want. You think it's fair for me to drive three hours to see him. Why isn't the same fair for you?"

"Because I'm his mother and he'd be with *me*, not in some dormitory with strangers!"

"He should be with both of us, God damn it. I'm his father."

"Lower your voice, please."

He stood and paced. "I would never put him in a facility, Rebecca. Certainly not when he has *two* capable caregivers fighting over him." A bit of his agitation visibly faded. "I can't, Becca. I can't let you take him away. He's mine too. Ours. This is *our* house. We chose it together, because it was a good place to have a family."

"Everything's different now, Kevin. He can't only be yours when it's convenient."

"That's not fair."

"That's the truth, Kevin."

"Because I can't do it like you do! Is that what you want to hear? Fine. You're a better parent than me. When we were a team..." He lowered himself to the couch and gripped her hands. "When it was the three of us it was so much easier."

Because she did all the work. "Kevin, we're divorced. This is all part of it. You had to know I'd move on eventually."

"Move on, yes, but Rebecca, I'm not ready to watch you move away." He glanced at the floor and quietly admitted. "I don't want this. I don't want my son and wife that far away."

He needed to stop thinking of her as his wife. "But I want this, Kevin. I'm in love with him."

He visibly winced. "What about us?"

She frowned. "Us? Kevin, what exactly did you think you were signing when we filed the divorce papers? Our relationship is an extension of Hunter. That's it. There is no us."

"What about us as a family? I never agreed to divorce my son."

"You were never married to fatherhood either."

His head lowered in defeat. "I screwed up, Rebecca."

"You screwed the neighbor, which is another reason I want to move."

"Everything was so messed up then. We were always fighting and Hunter wasn't sleeping. It had been so long since we'd slept together—even in the same bed. I was weak and I've paid for my mistakes."

"You've paid the consequence of your choices, Kevin. I didn't divorce you to punish you. I did it for my own self-respect. Our marriage ended because of your infidelities, not my need for revenge. But it was more than that. Be honest with yourself. Neither of us was happy."

"You're still mad. I get that."

Actually, she wasn't. She was happy and just wanted the guilt to go away so she could carry on with her life. "I'm not mad anymore."

"Then why are we fighting?"

"We're not. We're discussing our future."

He took her hands again. "Then let's talk about that and not some future with some guy meant to take you away from me. I've been seeing a counselor. He's helping me. I feel like I'm finally in a place to be the father Hunter deserves—the husband *you* deserve."

Standing, she pulled her fingers out of his grip. "Kevin, stop it. I'm not yours anymore. He didn't take me away from you. You lost me the first day you looked at another woman. You lost me after too many days of looking through me."

"I never looked through you, Rebecca. You were always there. I hate myself for straying. I was so bitter. I don't feel that way anymore. I've realized things since we've been apart." He slowly walked to her and only stopped when they stood a few inches apart. "I still love you, Rebecca. I know you still love me. I want to fix this. I want to fix us, make us the way we should have been all along. I know I can be a better father than I've been. Please, I'm begging you, give us another chance"

This wasn't happening. Her hands trembled as she took a step back. "Kevin, this isn't the discussion I wanted to have."

"I know, but could you just stop thinking about him for a second and consider us. I'm Hunter's father. I'm the man that should be raising him, not some guy I don't know that you just met. Me. This is my family—ours." Her breath hitched as he grabbed her hand, spreading her fingers over his heart and pressing her palm to his chest. "I love you. I loved you first. I made a mistake and I'm prepared to spend the rest of my life making it up to you, but you have to give me a chance."

It was taking everything she had not to let the tears fall. Blinking hard, she withdrew her hand and said, "You cheated. We can't be fixed, because you broke something irreplaceable when you broke our vows."

"But I love you. You may love him, but I know you still love me too. We have longevity where what you have with him is a gamble. He isn't Hunter's father. Don't expect him to accept our son as his own. Don't rush into something we'll both regret. Let me have a fighting chance, Rebecca. Please."

Shaking her head, she whispered, "You're scared. You don't love me anymore—"

"How could you say that? I'll always love you, Rebecca. You're my soul mate, my partner in this life. This isn't how things are supposed to end. We aren't finished yet. I know we're not. What about..." He drew in a slow breath, his pleading gaze drilling into hers. "We were supposed to have more."

"More what?"

"Children."

She took a stumbling step back, his words hitting her like a punch to the stomach. That was low, even for him. "Of all the underhanded things you could have said, I never expected that, Kevin."

"You're a wonderful mom—"

"I have to be!" she shouted, her arms flailing. "How dare you! I begged, I pleaded with you to have more children, and you refused. For eight years I carried around this emptiness until I finally accepted this was all God intended for me to have. We never had more children because *you* convinced me we shouldn't. It was always what *you* wanted. And now—after we're *divorced*—you're suddenly ready to try for more?"

"I was wrong. Give us another chance. Let me have a shot at giving you what you want. I'm ready. I should have helped more. I should have communicated more, been more affectionate, more patient. I'll read all the damn books you throw at me, Rebecca, just give me a chance. Together, we can do this."

Her entire body was quivering. "You need to leave now."

He crowded her, his palm cupping the side of her face. "I'm not just talking. I want you back, Rebecca. I want *us* back. But this time

I want more. I want to work together as a team. I want to date my wife, enjoy my son…try for a daughter. I want to make you happy. I know I've been a selfish jerk, but I've learned my lesson. Give me one more chance. Please."

Her shoulders trembled. There was nothing left to say. Eventually, he stepped away. "Think about what I'm offering. You're taking a gamble with this guy. You know me, Rebecca. We can rebuild what we've lost. We can build something better." His gaze met hers as he stood silently awaiting a response she didn't have. After a long moment, his mouth tightened and he nodded, quietly turning away to find their son.

She vaguely heard him say goodbye to Hunter. As the door closed her face pinched tight and she silently cried. Braydon would be calling soon and she had no idea what to tell him.

~

THE SECOND BRAYDON answered the phone he sensed something was wrong. "How'd it go?"

"Not the way I expected."

"Did you two fight?"

"No, not really." Her tone was quiet, bewildered in a way that worried him.

"You sound upset. What happened?"

"He doesn't want Hunter living that far away."

Understandable, but how much leverage did the man really have? "Does he have legal grounds to stop you from moving?"

"It isn't that simple. We'd have to go before a judge to work out the details if we can't civilly come to an agreement. I'm going to try talking to him again tomorrow."

"But tomorrow's Thursday." Where did that leave him?

"I know. I'm going to see about meeting him after I pick up Hunter."

Perhaps it was the sense of powerlessness regarding the situation with her ex, or perhaps it was jealousy. Either way, Bray didn't have a good feeling about the direction things were leading. Whatever was said upset Becca, and he didn't like the idea of this fool possibly bullying her. "I can come with you. Maybe if Kevin knew me a little better he'd be more comfortable with the situation."

"No, I don't think that would help. I mean, later on I'd like you two to get to know each other, but I don't think that time is now."

His mind went to the house and all the work he'd been doing there. "How long do you think it will take to convince him?" He didn't want to rush her, but he really wanted to start their life. Becca needed to conclude her business with Kevin in order for that to happen.

"I don't know. I need to talk to him again. I took him off guard and he got upset."

"Upset how?"

"Well, at first he was shocked, then he got a little spiteful, maybe even jealous. But then he did a one eighty and started talking about us as a family—"

"What?" This was a joke. The guy cheated on her and was a shitty father from what he understood. A man like that doesn't transform that easily.

"He said that he changed and that he wants a second chance as a family again."

He laughed, but when Becca was silent his amusement faded into something dark and disbelieving. "Becca, you know people can't change that fast. Tell me you know that."

"People change. What about everything you told me about Kelly and Luke and Colin?"

"They're different." Not really. They all changed for the people they loved. What if Kevin really did love Becca enough to change? "You're not actually considering this."

She was silent.

"Becca?"

"I don't want to talk about this right now. I love you, Braydon. Every decision I make revolves around my son and what's best for him. My interest in Kevin only has to do with the kind of father he is to Hunter."

It was a tedious topic, but they couldn't just sweep it under the rug. He wanted to know where they stood. Kevin was full of shit and she needed to realize that. Maybe things would go better if they were face to face. "Do you want me to come over?"

"Not tonight."

He got quiet as the severity of the conversation settled in. He didn't want to make things harder for her, but at the moment he wanted to shake her and bring her back to reality. Kevin was using Hunter as leverage. Maybe not, but his instinct told him this whole "us as a family" trip was bullshit.

Maybe Bray was pushing too hard for a decision. But she'd

already made up her mind—he thought—and now Kevin was screwing with her head.

She said she wanted to move to McCullough Mountain. He wanted that too. She was just getting cold feet. This wasn't about her wanting something else, it was about Kevin and his mind games, using her selfless nature to get what he wanted again with no regard to what would make Becca happy. It was extremely difficult to watch her get manipulated. He had to handle this delicately.

Sensing she was going to say goodnight, he pleaded his case in the most simplistic way he could think of. "I love you, angel. We'll figure it all out and I'll do whatever I can to help. You and I both know where you want to be. We'll get there. I promise. Get some sleep and call me in the morning."

"Thanks."

He frowned. No *I love you* back?

"Sweet dreams, Becca."

"Goodnight, Braydon."

The phone disconnected. Making a slow turn around his apartment, he eyed all of the boxes. Staggered by this new development, he wasn't sure if he should continue packing or hold off. He wandered to the sofa and sat down, his hands sweeping up a stack of documents he'd been going over for work.

He'd informed Miranda of his plans to relocate and, although she pouted, there wasn't much she could do to stop him. Becca would eventually see through Kevin's games. So long as they kept their eye on the prize, she'd get through this and once the ex realized he was offering too little too late, he'd back off.

Braydon decided to continue with his plans and file the request for relocation tomorrow. This was what Becca said she wanted and he wanted it too. His only wish was that he didn't have the tension that was now crawling up his spine and the fear of losing everything in the last leg of the race.

～

Two days later Becca sat at lunch with Carla and Nikki, filling them in on her life's latest drama.

"Noooooo," Carla breathed, clanking down her café latte. "Are you out of your mind? He *cheated* on you, Becca. The man is pond scum."

Becca had been expecting a reaction like this. "I know, but you should have heard him. He seemed so genuine and honestly sorry. He's *never* talked to me like that before. We actually had a rational conversation about Hunter and his upcoming IEP meeting. Kevin's never gotten involved with that stuff."

Carla's eyes were huge. "You're making a mistake. It's easy to talk about that stuff. Doing it's a whole other ball game. You're looking at this from Hunter's point of view. I assure you, Kevin's only thinking about himself." She turned to her sister. "Nikki, talk some sense into her."

Nikki seemed more reserved. Rather than her usual outgoing self, she wore an expression usually saved for boardrooms and negotiations. "He's her husband."

"He's an asshole," Carla snapped.

"True," Nikki agreed. "But if he's serious, maybe they could actually make this work. They have ten years and a child together. Who knows?"

"*I* know!" Carla pleaded. "Come on! We've heard this song before. It's played out. Kevin promises to get more involved and maybe shows up for a meeting. Becca does all the talking and he gets bored. He maybe washes a few dishes and tucks Hunter in a few times, but eventually she's doing everything by herself again. Becca, please don't fall for his crap. You're *happy*. He'll only make you miserable again. You love *Braydon*."

"Maybe it's possible to love two men."

"No. No, no, no, *no*. See who the good guy is here, Becca. It's not Kevin."

Her shoulders slumped. The way she loved Braydon was very different from the emotions she held for Kevin. His was an obligatory love, a shared concern for their child no one else in this world would ever compete with. But Braydon...he set her heart on fire. "He's Hunter's father."

"Yes, he donated sperm."

"Carla," Nikki warned.

"What? How could you condone this?"

Nikki's expression was blank, but her eyes appeared weary. "It's Becca's life. If this is something she needs to do then who are we to stop her? What goes on behind the closed doors of a marriage is between a husband and wife. None of us really know Kevin the way she does. Maybe there're some redeeming qualities in him after all."

"Thank you, Nikki." But Becca wasn't fully convinced. She was, however, one hundred percent confused.

Carla snatched up her latte. "I think it's a mistake."

Nikki's expression turned sharp, the same way it did when she seized a deal. "I'm sure Becca knows what she's risking. Braydon isn't the type of man to wait around after a woman leaves him for someone else. He's gorgeous and he'd have no trouble finding company. If Becca chooses to try again with Kevin she knows what the stakes are, don't you Becca?"

She couldn't breathe. Whatever she had for lunch now sat like a cannonball in her stomach. In a small voice she whispered, "I'm just trying to figure out what's best for Hunter. I have no intentions of rekindling a personal relationship with Kevin. I only want him to have a good relationship with Hunter and moving away might destroy that."

"A happy mom is best for Hunter," Carla said. "Braydon makes you happy. Kevin did nothing but make you sad. Fuck that toad. As your BFF it's my job to tell you when you're considering something very, *very* stupid. Nikki doesn't know what she's talking about. She's drunk."

"I'm not drunk. We're drinking coffee! I'm sober as a nun. You on the other hand…" Nikki turned to Becca. "If you and Kevin got back together, would you actually be able to…"

Her mind rejected the suggestion immediately. "Oh, no, it wouldn't be like that."

"Like what?" Carla asked, a look of aggravated confusion pinching her face. "Sex? Are we talking about sex? Sex with…" She silently gagged. "Kevin?"

"That's not even on my radar," Becca said. "Right now I'm just trying to figure out my address."

It was difficult to imagine mild gestures of affection with Kevin, let alone passionate ones. Her utmost concern was if they were compatible on a conversation level. Parenting required communication, which had been an issue for them in the past. The trust needed for intimacy might never be possible again for them and it wasn't something she was considering. No need to bog down an already complicated decision with more complications.

"It's like a death sentence," Carla mumbled into her latte. "Letting him come back would be like living on death row. I'd take the chair before the bed any day."

Placing her elbows on the table, Becca pressed her face into her palms and massaged her temples. "I don't know what to do."

"What's GQ say?"

"He hasn't said much. He's been sort of quiet, but I know he suspects something's up. I told him what Kevin asked for. He's just so damn understanding. But I feel him pulling back. Last night he didn't call me. He knew I was meeting Kevin again and I thought he would have called me afterward to see how everything went, but he didn't. I don't know if he's that confident I'll figure all this out or if —for once—he's actually scared."

"Awww." Carla pouted.

"Did you talk to him this morning?"

"Through text. Just a good morning. He didn't ask about last night."

"He's scared," Carla said, her brows peaking with sympathy. "You've gone and frightened the poor mountain boy. Not nice, Becca."

No, she didn't feel very nice at all. As a matter of fact she felt like a monster. Why was this happening when she thought she had her mind finally made up? She'd been so certain, and Kevin changed all that, making her second-guess everything. She loved Braydon. She loved Kevin too, but that had more to do with him being the father of her child than anything else, that and the fact that they had a decade of memories together.

She groaned. "I don't want to make difficult decisions."

"Then don't. Just hide in your house away from all the stressful people of the world like I do. Introvert is the new cool."

"Don't listen to her," Nikki said, patting Becca's arm. "She's an idiot."

Hunter loved Kevin. Maybe she *was* being selfish moving him away from his father. Did her son love Braydon as well? Hunter didn't express sentiments such as love, so there was no way of knowing for sure.

"Becs, you don't have to decide anything yet," Nikki said. "No one said you have to move *right now*. Take some time. Put some space between you and both men and see where your heart leads you."

"Go to the mountain," Carla hissed.

It had only been two days since Kevin announced his wishes of reconciling. Maybe Nikki was right. That wasn't a lot of time to make a life altering decision. And for all she knew Kevin might not feel so determined in a week or so.

The last thing she wanted to do was hurt anyone. She didn't

want to hurt Hunter, Kevin, or Braydon. She only wanted to do the right thing.

Wasn't the nuclear family the way things were *meant* to be? She and Braydon were still in the honeymoon stages. Who knew if their relationship had the longevity to make it? Who knew if Braydon really understood what he was asking for?

She glanced at her phone. No missed calls or texts. It was almost one o'clock. "Do you care if I take the rest of the day off, Nikki? I have a pounding headache."

"Sure, sweetie. Take whatever you need."

"This is why I hate leaving my house. It's depressing." Carla stood. "I love you, Becs. Don't be an idiot. That man loves you. And if you don't end up with him, how am I ever going to seduce his tattooed brother?"

"He's *married*." Nikki reprimanded her sister.

"What?" Carla shrugged innocently. "People get sick. Accidents happen."

"Carla!" They both snapped.

"Too soon?"

"Never appropriate," Becca said with a small laugh. Carla may not have helped her make a decision, but she always made her smile. Another thing she'd miss if she moved away.

She left the girls and drove straight home. When she pulled into the driveway her van slowed as she noticed Kevin's car already in the garage. What was he doing there?

Climbing out of the front seat she noted the boxes stacked along the wall. Maybe he finally came to get the rest of his crap.

Quickly entering through the garage, she called for him. "Kevin?"

"In the hall."

She followed his voice and a strange scraping sound coming from that direction. Her steps halted when she spotted the small bucket filled with plaster in his hand. "What are you doing?"

"Fixing some of these holes."

It was jarring, her husband dressed down and spackling dents in her home. Kevin didn't perform manual labor. Was he fixing the holes to help her sell the house or—no, she wasn't going there.

"You're home early." He smiled, throwing her off again. She couldn't recall the last time he grinned at her like that, without malice or narrowed eyes.

"How long have you been here?" He shouldn't be able to enter her home when she wasn't there. Sure, it used to be his home, but now the house belonged to her. He only had a key for emergencies with Hunter.

"About an hour. I also put a new trap in the kitchen sink."

She'd nagged him about that trap for close to a year. Funny, when he left she'd never got around to fixing it. She should have said thank you, but the words wouldn't come.

Dumping the putty blade into the bucket he stood and faced her. "You don't look so good, Rebecca. Are you okay?"

She rubbed her forehead. "I have a migraine."

"Oh." His expression turned concerned.

She used to get migraines all the time, but hadn't had one in a while. Kevin was never very sympathetic to how torturous these types of headaches could be.

His hand lightly touched her arm and she stilled. "Why don't you go upstairs and lie down. I'll get you some medicine and a cold cloth for your head."

Taken off guard, she nodded slowly. Her temples pounded, speaking was becoming difficult, and she'd seemed to be in some Twilight Zone where Kevin was considerate. The fact that Kevin was suddenly offering her some much-needed aid threw her for a major loop. "Okay."

When she reached her room, she slipped out of her work clothes and changed into soft cotton pants and a shirt. Removing the hairpins that felt like daggers, she sifted her fingers through the strands and loosened a bit of the tension gripping her scalp.

Kevin entered the room quietly. "Here you go, sweetheart."

Sweetheart? Sliding two white pills into her palm, he passed her a cool glass of water. She gratefully swallowed the pills. "Thanks."

"Lie down. I'll close the curtains."

She wondered if he noticed that she'd moved the furniture in the bedroom. Was he imagining her in their bed with someone else? She knew what that was like. Closing her eyes, she settled into the pillows as the room dimmed.

Her body flinched as he gently placed a damp cloth over her head. His palm slowly cupped the side of her face and she held her breath, silently freaking out at the unexpected contact. *He shouldn't be touching me like that.* She casually turned her face away from his touch.

"Get some sleep. I'll pick up Hunter, so don't worry about when you have to wake."

She remained silent as he exited the room, but her mind was reeling. This was not the Kevin she knew.

As she drifted in and out of sleep, she vaguely heard the soft vibration of her phone nearby, but couldn't recall where she dropped her purse. Sleep pulled her into a painless cocoon and she gladly let go of all other thoughts aside from resting and feeling better.

~

"HI. This is Becca Stevens. Leave a message."

"Hey, it's me. I popped over to your office to see how your day was going, but Nikki said you went home because you weren't feeling good. Maybe you're sleeping. Give me a call when you get this."

Hanging up the phone, Braydon left Becca's place of employment and headed back to his office. If she wasn't feeling good, he should go over there after work and help with Hunter. He'd never thought about how difficult being a single parent could be when the parent was sick and the child needed care, but he was glad to have the opportunity to help.

When he returned to his office he made a list of things he favored when he felt under the weather. It was a shame his mum was so far away, because her soup was like gold penicillin. He searched online for restaurants rumored to make good chicken noodle and placed an order.

After work he stopped at a drug store and stocked up on everything from tissues, to stomach medicine, to antihistamines. He also grabbed her and Hunter a pint of chocolate ice cream, just in case.

Becca's van wasn't parked inside the garage like it usually was, so he parked along the curb. Gathering his bag of remedies, he hefted them into one arm and rang the bell, smiling as the locks disengaged on the other side.

His smile fell the second Kevin opened the door. What the fuck was he doing there? "Uh, is Becca home?" Weird. This was weird.

The man shifted, blocking Braydon's view of the interior. "Rebecca's not feeling well."

"I know. That's why I'm here."

The other man frowned. "Did she call you?"

No, but he wasn't telling this goober that. "I brought her some things."

"She's resting."

Oh, hell no. Pressing his way inside, he said, "I'll just put this stuff in the kitchen and check on her then."

Kevin stepped aside, which was wise. Braydon placed the bag on the counter and put the ice cream in the freezer. He went to the den, but she wasn't there. He greeted Hunter and the boy smiled. "Hey, bud. Where's your mum?"

"Mom's sick." He went back to making some sort of origami bird. Several littered the floor.

Picking a small green bird off the carpet, Braydon said, "These are neat. Did you make them?"

"You can have it."

Braydon smiled. "Thanks, bud. I'll put it in my office at work."

Carefully tucking the bird in his pocket, he turned and came face to face with Kevin. Braydon's eyes narrowed as he spoke with constrained politeness. "I'm here now, so you can go."

"I have to make Hunter dinner."

"I brought soup. Dinner's covered."

The man's gaze drifted to Hunter then back to Bray. "I think I'll stay."

They appeared to share a mutual animosity. Braydon wasn't going to get into some pissing match with Becca's ex, no matter how much his interference pissed him off. Out of respect for Hunter he buttoned up and stepped around the man to search for Becca.

He found her curled on her side in bed, sound asleep. The room was dark, so he turned on the bathroom light, illuminating the space enough to make out her features. Gingerly, he sat on the edge of the bed. His fingers brushed a wave of blonde hair off of her face and he softly kissed her temple.

She drew in a slow, waking breath. "Hey." He loved the rasp of her voice when she woke.

"Hey. I heard you're sick."

Blinking sluggishly, she grumbled. "Word gets around fast."

"I stopped by your office. Nikki told me you took a half-day. I brought you soup."

She grinned. "You're sweet."

"Not that sweet. Kevin's here and I want him to go."

"He picked up Hunter for me."

"You could have asked me to do that."

"I didn't ask. He offered. He was here when I got home."

Braydon frowned. "Why?"

She shrugged. It seemed like that was all the explanation he was getting. He had a thousand questions running through his head, but held them back until she was feeling better.

Changing the subject he asked, "So what's the matter? I have a bag full of medicines and remedies downstairs. Tell me what ails the patient and I'll doctor you up. I can treat anything from a runny nose to explosive diarrhea."

She snorted. "Ew."

Chuckling, loving her laugh, he said in mock seriousness, "It's okay. I'm a professional."

"I had a migraine, but it's gone now. Kevin gave me some medicine."

"Ah. Well, thank God for Kevin." His tone dripped with sarcasm.

She tsked. "Don't be mad."

"I'm not," he lied and stood. "How about I bring you some soup?"

"I should get up."

"No, you rest. I'll go set Hunter up with dinner—I'll even give Kevin a bowl—and I'll be right back with yours."

She smiled and he left the room. When he returned downstairs the acidic sensation in his gut doubled. Kevin was sitting beside Hunter reading a book. Hunter didn't seem fazed that both he and Kevin were at the house at the same time, which he guessed was a good thing.

Braydon cleared his throat. "I'm gonna dish out some soup and take some up to Becca. Can you make sure Hunter eats?"

"I think I can handle it," Kevin said with a touch of derision.

He really had an aversion to this man. Heading to the kitchen, he located three bowls, deciding to feed himself last. He placed Hunter's on the table beside his Velcro board, a napkin, and a spoon. The soup had cooled, so there was no need to add a cube of ice.

He left Kevin's bowl by the container. Let him scoop his own.

When he carried Becca's bowl upstairs, she was in the bathroom. Braydon placed the soup on the nightstand and returned downstairs to refill her water. Shutting off the spigot, he turned and nearly crashed into Kevin. Stealthy creeper.

"I assume Becca's informed you of my intensions by now."

Braydon stilled. Out of his peripheral he assessed Hunter. He was busy eating and Kevin, apparently, thought this was the appropriate time to have an adult discussion. "She mentioned something about your regrets."

"I don't believe in regret. I believe in correcting mistakes and fixing things."

"That must be a new approach."

"Look, Brandon—"

"Braydon."

"Braydon," he amended. "I understand you care for my wife—"

"She's not your wife anymore."

"Regardless, I understand you care for Rebecca, but we have a history you can't compete with. Hunter belongs with us."

That was all he could stomach. He placed the glass on the counter and faced the other man. "That's where you're confused, *Keith*."

"Kevin."

"Right. That's where you're confused. There is no competition. What you have with Becca is history. I'm her future. So while we appreciate you helping out with Hunter, you're no longer necessary in her personal affairs. Stop filling her head with promises you and I both know you don't intend you keep."

The other man was silent for a moment, his eyes smoldering with resentment. "Who do you think you are? We're a family. Do you really want to be the man that destroys a family?"

"I'm afraid that man was you."

In a low and threatening tone, he growled, "Get out of my house."

"I'm not in your house. But you're welcome to leave at any time. Excuse me." He casually grabbed the water and stepped around Kevin to return to Becca.

Unfortunately, he followed Braydon to the hall. "Did she tell you she's considering it?"

He stilled, refusing to consider the other man's bluff and pivoted slowly, holding hard to his temper. "Excuse me?"

"I didn't think so. You may be new and fun and a vacation from reality, but I *am* her reality. Don't think for a second she wouldn't give up everything to have her family back together. I know my wife."

He ground his molars together. If this dickwad referred to Becca as his wife one more time... "You're not the reality. You're the ugly truth. She wants to move, but she's being patient because it would be best for everyone if you gave her your blessing instead of burdening her with more undeserved guilt. You wanna do something nice for Becca? Let her be happy. I'm telling you how, because it's clear you've never been able to figure it out on your own. Let her move on without the mind games and let her finally live the life she deserves. Unless something involves Hunter, stay out of it. You *owe* her that much."

With that he took the stairs and ended the discussion. It took a great deal of effort to remain calm when he entered Becca's room. She was pulling her hair up in a bun, so he placed the glass on the table and kissed her exposed neck. "Do you need anything else?"

"No. The soup was delicious. Thank you."

"You're welcome." He glanced at his watch. "It's almost Hunter's bedtime. How long do you expect your ex-husband to stick around?"

She sent him a sidelong glance. "Be nice."

"Oh, I am." She had no idea how close he was to freaking out and throwing that son of a bitch across the lawn. He deserved points for keeping his voice calm. Having Hunter present helped, but if Hunter went to bed and the man stuck around, Braydon wasn't sure what would happen.

"I know this is weird, Braydon, but he was here and I didn't feel good. It was nice that he offered to help with Hunter."

"Imagine that, Hunter's father helping."

"Hey."

"Sorry." He rubbed her shoulder. He shouldn't take a cheap shot at the man if he was genuinely there to spend time with his son—something Hunter was due—but the man's presence reeked of personal motive. Maybe he was over thinking. "He said you're considering his asinine proposal to reconcile." She was quiet. His skin immediately turned clammy. "Becca?"

Her sorrowful eyes pleaded with him and he stood. This had to be a joke. While he loved Becca for her patience, there had to be a limit where her ex was concerned. Even *he* had limits to how much he could tolerate. Extending his presence for Hunter was one thing. Schmoozing his ex-wife and tampering with their situation was something altogether different, especially if Becca was falling for his bullshit.

"You're kidding, right?"

She pinched her forehead. "I don't know what I'm supposed to do." Tossing down her hand, she whispered, "He's Hunter's father."

Yes, his *father,* not her partner. That ship had sailed. "And what the hell am I?"

"You're...my boyfriend."

The clear hierarchy of their statuses rankled. Stunned and uncomprehending he gaped at her. He hadn't believed she was actually considering letting this man back into her life more than what was necessary. He paced to the door and shut it quietly, offering a smidgen of privacy.

"Becca, you said you wanted to move in together. We have a plan. Kevin has a very different one. This isn't just about Hunter and you know it. You need to make it clear to him where you stand."

"Everything's moving really fast, Braydon."

His breath became labored. With every word it became apparent *she* wasn't sure where *she* stood. "Becca, you're divorced. *Divorced.* The man wants to reconcile—which is crazy considering he had an affair and ignored you. Don't mislead him into believing there's a possibility of—"

"I know my marriage is over, but my family..." she interrupted, baffling him with her refusal to tell this man to take a hike with all of his half cocked promises Braydon knew he wouldn't keep.

"Think of all the times he let you down."

Her expression turned pleading. "But our family—"

"*Him.* This is about him. Don't call it family when that was always his last priority. This is Kevin, doing for Kevin, like he's always done. What makes you think he's suddenly changed?"

"He's been seeing a therapist."

What the hell difference did that make? "And you've been seeing another man. Damn it, Becca, we have a plan here."

"But I had a plan with him too, a plan for our family, for Hunter."

His head was going to implode. Forking his fingers through his hair, he paced with agitation, trying to maintain his patience. "Right, and then Kevin proceeded to let that plan slip, habitually neglect you as his wife, argue with you about parenting, and *sleeping* with someone else." She winced, but they needed to be realistic. He loved her, and though she was hurting him, he didn't want to see her get hurt. "He'll do it again, Becca."

"You don't know that." Was she serious? How did this guy have such a hold on her?

Facing her, he gripped her hands and whispered, "I know he isn't right for you."

"I'm thinking about Hunter. What's right for him?" She pulled her fingers out of his grip. "I don't care about me."

"I care about you! I care about both of you!"

"What if moving isn't what Hunter wants? He's lived here his entire life, Braydon. He can't express his feelings on the matter and I can't prepare him for such a change. I don't know how he'll react if I take him away from everything he knows. It's my job to be his voice when he can't speak for himself and I'm scared!"

She was letting her pessimistic fear direct her. "He'll know new things. What if he's happier there?"

"What if he's not, Braydon?" There was no fight in her voice, only defeat.

He paced to the bed and sat, rubbing his temples. "Why are you so afraid to dream a little bigger, Becca? I want to give you more, but every step forward you run back to what you know. It won't harm him to try new things."

Her voice was low, a sort of mental depletion weighing on her features. "You think I don't know that, Braydon? I want my son to have new experiences. But you're missing the point. My job isn't to show him the whole world. It's to build a bridge from our world into his. If I make the wrong decision, he could regress. They said he wouldn't speak, and he did. His words are my salvation. I've met children who got upset and locked up their words for years. I'm not afraid of a temper tantrum. I can handle the minor episodes that eventually pass. But he could completely shut down if this is too much change for him. I couldn't survive that."

His heart pinched with speechless sorrow. Perhaps he was minimizing the actuality of everything she was risking. "I thought...I thought he liked it there."

"He did. But we were only there for a visit. The expectation to return home was always in his mind. Please understand how scary and stressful this is for me."

His head drooped low between his shoulders. "My goal was to make your life less hectic, angel. I never intended to make it worse. We'd have a huge family there to support us—"

"Your family. Not ours."

Her opposition was wearing him down. "I want them to be your family and Hunter's family too."

"But Kevin's his father, Braydon. Hunter deserves to have both his parents in his life. All the McCulloughs in the world can't replace his dad. As absent as he's been, losing Hunter would devastate Kevin."

His shoulders ached with tension, a thick, uncomfortable dread snaking slowly through his veins. They were going in circles. He could sympathize with everything she said, except Kevin being the victim of her moving on.

"No one said moving away removed Kevin from Hunter's life. He's a grown man. He has a car and the ability to visit whenever he wants. I'd never stop him from seeing Hunter." It was ridiculous that their plans might actually fail because of a man that only recently showed an interest in being an active parent.

He couldn't accept defeat, not when everything he wanted was right there, minutes ago, and now slipping through his fingers faster than he could handle. "Christ, I'll build a guesthouse for him to stay in if that's what it takes. Just tell me what it'll take and I'll do it."

"It's going to take time," she whispered, her eyes bleak behind a sheen of unshed tears. "Right now, I'm confused and I'm trying to figure out what the right decision is."

His chest constricted. "How much time?" The house was almost finished.

"I don't know."

They sat in silence for several minutes. "I told my job I'm relocating. My office is going to someone else at the end of the month."

Her head shot up, her lips parting in surprise. "I wish you hadn't done that."

"Why? That's what we talked about."

"I told you I needed to talk to Kevin first."

Yes, to tell him they were moving. At no point did he expect her to hang up their plans on his approval. His shoulders rocked with each breath. His heart ached. She asked for time, but where did that leave them? His lips pressed tight. He needed to know. "Do you still love him?"

"Braydon, don't."

"Do you?" Ice wrapped around his heart.

"He's the father of my child."

"Leave Hunter out of it. Do. You. Still. Love. Him?"

"I…I'll always love him."

A part of him he couldn't name—perhaps his soul—seemed to crack in two at her words. Face tense, he tried to hide how badly her confession wounded him, but his composure was quickly slipping. Forcing back every emotion threatening to take over his common sense, he stood. "Right."

"Braydon, wait."

He couldn't look at her. "For what, Becca? What the hell is this?" Though he spoke out of hurt and anger, his voice remained low. He'd lost the last of his fight. "You're supposed to move in with me to a house I've designed for us, and now you're telling me you still love your ex? Where does that leave us?"

"I don't know. It isn't like the love I have for you, but it also isn't something I can ignore, because I have to consider my son. We have a history."

He laughed coldly as he stared at the floor. "Now you two sound alike."

"What do you mean?"

"He just said the same thing to me in the kitchen."

"I don't think you can understand unless you've been married."

It wasn't fair for her to hold his inexperience against him. "I don't think you can understand unless you've had a good marriage."

"That's not fair."

"None of this is fair. And fair or not, it's the truth, Becca." He'd never been angry with her, but he was now.

"You knew I had a past—"

He couldn't listen anymore. Turning to her, he hissed, "You're divorced! Don't make it like I got involved with a woman only separated from her husband, standing on shaky ground. The night we met those papers were signed and sealed. He had his chance and *he* ruined it. You're giving him second chances before we've even had *one!*"

A tear tripped past her lashes. "It's not a second chance for me and Kevin. It's a second chance for Hunter. I love you, Braydon. But Hunter will always be my first priority. This isn't about restoring a relationship between Kevin and me. It's about him and Hunter. I wish you would understand that."

"A relationship that doesn't include me." He shook his head. "He wants you, Becca. Don't be naïve."

"I can't control that. I don't know what to tell you. Maybe this is all temporary, but taking Hunter away at the first sign of interest his father's shown in years doesn't feel right. I just…need some time."

He couldn't listen any more. He wanted to shake her until she saw sense. Self-preservation stepped in and he shut his eyes, knowing there would be no resolution in his favor—at least not on this day. "Well, let me make it easier on you. How about you call me when you've made up your mind and know for certain what it is *you* want? I've been second choice enough times in my life. It's about fucking time someone chose me first."

Taking two clipped strides to the door, he left, not having the courage to face Hunter and say goodnight, nor the restraint not to punch Kevin in his smug face.

He worked hard at not remembering the desolate look his ultimatum put on Becca's face. Part of him was so furious he wanted her to suffer, because he wasn't sure anyone had ever hurt him so deeply. He loved her, but love didn't excuse certain behaviors.

As much as he admired her day-to-day strength, playing the martyr was a tendency she needed to address. He was offering her a partnership. He had no interest in recreating her past. He wanted to give her a different future, but she had to let go. Until she grasped that, there'd be no progress.

Help he could do. Watching the woman he loved paint herself the victim he couldn't abide. He was the lifeline. Kevin was the old battered raft she'd nearly drowned by. They'd never stay afloat when so much was tied into her relationship with her ex.

Standing outside of Braydon's apartment, Becca drew in a slow, jagged breath and lifted her hand to knock. She wasn't sure if he was home, or if she was making yet another mistake, but she knew she needed to see him. It had been a week and every minute that passed without him abraded her heart.

The door opened and Braydon stilled. He didn't greet her or even offer a welcoming smile. She deserved his coldness.

"Hi."

His gaze ran over her features as though searching for answers she didn't have. The passing week had been an awakening, a taste of what may come. Kevin had been actively participating in their days and Hunter was thriving under the newfound consistency of both parents being present in his daily life. Yet Becca had never felt so hollow and alone.

Braydon must have discerned something in her, because he swallowed and his expression only turned more closed off. "What are you doing here, Becca?"

What was she doing there? If only she knew. On the floor behind him were boxes of belongings and stacks of old newspapers. He was moving ahead, with or without them.

Her face lowered. "I don't know."

She wasn't sure what she expected, but she couldn't blame him for leaving, not when she knew, deep down he wanted to be back home. She'd not given him much of a choice. And no matter how much this seemed like her own foolish doing, she hadn't felt like she'd had much choice either. No matter how much she wanted to go with him, Hunter came first.

Her chest shook as she breathed, fighting back the deluge of tears and pain that had been beating at her for days on end. She hadn't slept. She was unable to concentrate at work. She was starved for his affection, and the pain of having such an offering removed was simply too much.

"Have you changed your mind?" he asked.

No, she was as confused as ever. Her stagnant position of indecision left her in a state of inertia, the world moving on without her at a pace her life didn't allow. It was how it had always been and how it would likely always be. Perhaps letting him go was the most merciful thing she could do for him, but a selfish part of her wasn't ready to say goodbye.

"I still love you."

His face pinched, his eyes pleading for more. She couldn't give him more, but she could try to explain what he meant to her.

"No one will ever touch me the way you do, Braydon." She swallowed. "This hurts. It never hurt like this before. I never had such a hard time putting everyone else first, because I've never wanted anything as much as I want you. But I can't have you without taking something essential away from my son."

"Stop." He turned, his head shaking in a show of denial. When he faced her again his expression was blank.

No one would ever look at her the way Braydon did. No one would hold her and love her as thoroughly as he. The more time that passed, the more she sensed him coming to terms with their end, but she wasn't quite ready to accept such a fate.

"I'm sorry. I know I shouldn't have come here, but I needed to see you."

Her life ahead would be bleak and lonely. Though Kevin openly expressed a desire to rekindle parts of their past, parts not having to do with their son, it was out of the question. Becca would close off that part of herself, because she had no interest in a meager imitation of intimacy, not after she'd experienced true closeness with Braydon.

His eyes closed. "Have you changed your mind, Becca?"

"No," she whispered, her heart breaking. She wanted to ask him to wait, to be patient. If Kevin's presence faded, she'd be gone. That could still happen, but she had no right to ask Braydon to put his future on hold.

He sighed. "Do you want to come inside?"

Surprised, her face tipped up, her gaze fastening to his as her vision quivered and tears wet her cheeks. "Yes."

He stepped back and held the door. Crossing the threshold in a sort of trance, she stepped into his apartment, but made no move to remove her coat. Afraid to even whisper a word, she stayed silent. She didn't want to argue. She just…needed him.

Her fingers traced over the tape pressed to the seal of a box labeled books. He really was leaving. What would a life without Braydon be like? Her shoulders shook as she started to cry.

When the weight of his arms pressed around her, she shattered. From the beginning she'd warned him her life was complicated and tried to remind herself how dangerous it was to hope. Her foolish heart hadn't listened and now it was breaking. Yet she saw no way to remove the obstacles. Kevin was Hunter's father and she couldn't deny him a day-to-day life with his son because she wanted to run off and fall in love.

"Don't cry," he whispered, his lips pressing to the back of her neck.

Wracked with shame at involving him in her turmoil, she couldn't seem to stem the tears. She'd never meant to hurt him. Every touch was a cruel reminder of what she'd be giving up.

His chest pressed to her back as his hands slowly crept around her arms, his fingers unbuttoning her coat. He circled her, as she stood unmoving. His palms cupped her jaw, tilting her face until she met his gaze. She'd miss looking into those beautiful blue eyes.

"Don't cry," he repeated quietly, kissing away her tears.

Her body trembled as his lips pressed to her cheeks, her eyes. No one would ever touch her like that again. When his mouth ghosted over hers, pain unraveled in her chest and she shivered, allowing reality to cut her deep as her tears passed by like secret whispers of a love only they knew.

His kiss became firm, coaxing, and her head tilted, allowing him to take what he sought and surrendering to whatever he might offer. There was no punishment to his touch, only gentle acceptance. Perhaps he needed this as much as she did, even though it changed no part of their reality.

Her coat slid from her shoulders and whispered to the floor. They were only suspending actuality. Tonight would change nothing, and perhaps make the inevitable all the more unbearable, but she didn't possess the will to tell him no. Nor did she own a desire to stop him.

His face pressed to her throat and he breathed in her scent. Fingers skated beneath the hem of her shirt, searching. Her body leaned into his, stealing his warmth, his strength, balancing on shared sadness. They held each other. It was a strange sort of acknowledgement, as they both seemed to accept that this would be the last time.

He lifted her and her limbs wrapped around him as he carried her to his bed. Ironic that this was where it all began and this was where it would end. As the mattress pressed into her back, his weight blanketed her front. Her pants were removed, his mouth marking a trail up her legs.

Her belly quivered as he kissed her intimate places she couldn't imagine sharing with anyone else. Her voice was vacant, afraid if she spoke she'd beg him to stay. She arched as he pleasured her, fingers sifting through his curls as she memorized the silken weight of his hair in her hands.

His lips traveled over her belly and slowly teased her breasts. He didn't ask permission and there was no need. She belonged to him in a way she'd never belonged to another. When he entered her, the pain in her heart unraveled and seeped from her being in cold tears.

His face pressed to her shoulder as he slowly made love to her. Deep, deliberate thrusts rocked them as one. There was no purpose, no objective of pleasure, only a mutual need to be together one last time.

His body tensed and shivered. Her fingers traced over his strong back as she trembled, filling her.

"Stay," he whispered into her shoulder.

Chills coalesced over her skin as she spoke the truth. This was all they would ever have. "I can't."

His forehead pressed heavily into her shoulder as he sighed, defeated. She hated herself.

He slowly withdrew, stealing away parts of herself she didn't know she could live without. As he rolled to his side, facing away from her, she silently sobbed. It was as though he couldn't bear to watch her leave.

"Braydon…"

He didn't reply. His broad back was all she could see as his face remained turned away. Quietly, she forced herself off the bed and located her clothing. He remained turned away as she silently dressed. Staring back at him one last time, her fingers trembled to her lips. She'd hurt him enough and had to go. "You'll always be in my heart, Braydon. There's no amount of time or distance that can diminish my love for you. And letting you go is the hardest thing I've ever had to do. I'm sorry."

Lowering her head, she returned to the living room, picked her coat off the floor and quietly left. There had never been a more difficult journey than the steps she took away from him.

~

BRAYDON HAD NEVER SPENT a Christmas alone. Yet something kept him in the city, not ready to return home empty handed. As he wandered through the mall, most of the gates pulled shut over the storefronts, he aimlessly considered what he was doing.

He shouldn't have let her in when she came to his apartment the other night, but he lacked the will to tell her to go. Though it pained him to no end to see she'd not changed her mind and they were moving on, moving apart, he couldn't resist the opportunity to hold her one last time, feel her body around his, wear her scent on his skin.

Becca had called a few times after that, but eventually he'd stopped answering. Every conversation was a merry-go-round of unresolved regret, repeating her wavering words that had ripped out his heart. He loved her and thought she loved him, but with all of her indecision, it was clear he'd misjudged their relationship.

She was staying in the city and he was going home. Her last message proved she'd made no decision and his self-preservation insisted he force some space between them, no matter how much his heart objected.

To his understanding, Kevin was not living with her, but he was spending a lot of time at the house with her and Hunter. He was happy for Hunter, believing the boy deserved a chance to have an active father. But admitting this did nothing to curb the agony of loss he was suffering.

Deep down he knew Kevin had manipulated her, dangling his relationship with Hunter at her nose, and he knew damn well, she'd never put her needs before her son's. Hunter would *always* be her first priority. That was one of the reasons Braydon loved her. He never expected it to be the reason he lost her.

269

"A last minute trinket for your holiday sweetheart, sir?"

Braydon stilled, pulling out of his trance as a woman manning a kiosk full of winter baubles beckoned his attention. He glanced at her wares, seeing various snow globes, teddy bears, and candles.

Stepping closer, his attention snagged on a globe with only a park bench on a black path. The globe filled his palm, weighing heavy in his hand as he tipped it. A hundred white flakes spun in a small tornado exposing a red heart hidden amongst the flurries. "How much is this?"

"Ten dollars, but you can have it for eight."

He considered the other items. There was a small globe with a black locomotive inside. "I'll take both of these."

She carefully bagged up his purchase, wrapping each gift individually in a small red bag with green checked tissue. There were wiser things to do than see Becca one last time, but knowing he would be leaving soon, he couldn't seem to deny himself the chance. It was Christmas and she was all he'd hoped for. Perhaps he might find some magic after all.

Braydon managed the roads slowly as they had started to ice over. When he reached Becca's the windows glowed against the dark night. Taking a deep breath, he gathered his gifts and exited the car.

Approaching the door, his hand lifted to knock, but stilled. Through the glass he spotted Hunter. He was laughing. Braydon's gaze searched for what caused such a wonderful smile, and he spotted Becca and Kevin sitting beside him on the floor.

Putting aside all opinions he held for the other man, he watched the scene for what it was—a family sharing a Christmas. Though Becca and Kevin were not sitting close, the three of them formed a sort of whole. Who was Braydon to interfere with such rare harmony? It was then that he realized *this* was what she was holding on to.

Years ago, she'd married a man in hopes of having what she'd always wanted—family. Though Kevin had not been the perfect father or an honorable husband, Becca had been a good wife and deserved the life she was promised. Hunter had been a surprise in more ways than one, but she'd adapted, rising to every challenge and conquering every obstacle along the way.

He'd never loved anyone the way he loved her, and something about that love, perhaps the genuine truth of it, gave him pause. No matter what he wanted for himself, he always hoped she'd be happy. Perhaps loving her meant letting her go.

Stepping back, he tucked the two gift bags on her porch beside the hibernating plant and returned to his car. Glancing back one last time, he looked into the bow window at the front of the house. Becca smiled and laughed. It was a picture he'd never forget, one that would haunt him as much as comfort him as he moved forward with his life.

His only hope was that she found reason to smile like that every day. Maybe one day he'd smile again too.

BRAYDON TAPED the last box shut and sighed. All that was left in his apartment were a few empty bottles to take down to the recycling and his laptop. He'd been so enthusiastic about this decision three weeks ago, but since the holidays he'd been on auto-pilot, worrying he was making an enormous mistake.

His family had been so thrilled to have him home and see him start this chapter of his life. He finally had to break it to his mother that he'd be returning home alone. The hurt in her voice was comparable to what he was experiencing on the inside. If anyone was his champion in this world, it was his big-hearted mum.

A knock sounded from the door and he stilled. Every nerve in his body pulled taut as he sucked in a breath. Had she changed her mind? So many times he refused to accept the turn of things, insisting this had to be a dream. Maybe the nightmare was finally over.

Bracing himself for either the most painful goodbye of his life or the happiest kickoff to his future, he opened the door. Wrong on both counts. "Luke?"

"Hey."

Disappointment flooded him, but he hid his emotions well. "What are you doing here?"

"Mum told us about your lady. I'm sorry, Bray."

He sighed. "Are you alone?"

"Tristan and Kelly are parking the truck. We came to give you a hand and maybe get you drunk, if necessary."

Chuckling, he reached out and pulled his brother into a smacking hug. "Thanks."

"We missed you at Christmas." Luke pressed into the apartment after nearly dislocating his spine in a crushing, but very meaningful hug.

"I missed you guys too."

"This all of it?" Luke asked, eyeing the pile by the door.

"The rest is in my car. I sold most of the big furniture to other people in the building, since I planned to furnish the house with all new stuff."

"Well..." His brother didn't seem to know what to say. "We're still glad you're coming home. You belong there."

His smile was halfhearted. He'd been elated to finally return to the mountain. Only now his homecoming seemed bittersweet.

Hearing Tristan and Kelly's voices in the hall, he turned to greet them. "Welcome to my empty abode."

Hugs were exchanged and there was a moment so laden with unbearable pity, none of them seemed comfortable.

"This blows," Kelly finally said, breaking the silence.

"Yup."

"Sorry to hear about you and Becca," Tristan said.

He shrugged, hating the sense that he was depressing the hell out of everyone. "What are you gonna do? It seems my lot in life is constantly coming in second."

"Yeah, that's sort of why Colin didn't want to come."

Because Sammy chose my brother over me just like Becca's choosing Kevin.

"Shut up, Kelly," Luke snapped then quickly covered for Kelly's slip. "That's not true. He had something to do at Sammy's parents' this weekend."

"Sure." There probably was some truth to Kelly's statement. This entire situation reeked of past experiences and his older brother could possibly be reliving some outdated guilt. He couldn't waste time dwelling on that when his present was such a mess. "Well, you wanna help me load these last few boxes?"

Tristan nudged Luke toward the largest of the boxes and grabbed the next biggest. Kelly followed Bray into the kitchen where he surveyed the area once more to see if he'd overlooked anything. "I'm sorry I said that."

He shrugged. "Not your fault. It's true."

"No it's not, Bray. Colin would be here if he could."

"Where's Finn?" He didn't want to think about Colin. Funny how his new situation awakened past, familiar pains.

"He had to stay home with the kids because Mallory's in Princeton visiting Sheilagh. Some sort of crazy girls' night out."

He smiled. "Good. Sheilagh needs that. She's been a little down lately since the whole thing with Alec and no babies yet."

"Uh," Kelly shuffled closer and lowered his voice. "You should probably know, Luke and Tristan got turned down by the adoption people."

"What? Why?"

Kelly shrugged. "I think something about Tristan's past. He had some violence on his record that they wouldn't overlook."

"Not what happened last year? That wasn't their fault."

"No, before that. Some stuff from Texas."

"Can they appeal it?"

"Probably, but they're pretty devastated. I don't think they're ready to readdress the issue yet. Just don't bring it up. I think they were eager for the escape and the chance to focus on someone else's problems."

"Glad to be of service."

Luke came into the kitchen. "Everything's loaded up. You wanna grab dinner before we go?"

"I'd rather get on the road. If you guys want to stop somewhere that's fine, but I think I'm gonna head out. I wanna get there before dark."

"I'll ride back with Bray. You two go have yourself a nice dinner," Kelly said.

They split up, leaving Tristan and Luke with directions to one of the nicer restaurants in town. Kelly slid into the passenger seat and immediately started fiddling with the radio, which was fine since Braydon didn't much feel like talking and they had a long ride ahead of them.

The silence only lasted the first hour, however. Once they were out of the city and cruising along the interstate, his brother started with the tough questions. "You gonna go directly to the new house?"

Braydon was still trying to decide that. "I don't know. I may spend a few nights at the big house until I get everything set up. I need to get the cable company out and I still need to grab little shit like bed sheets and towels." His lips pursed. "I thought we'd be getting that stuff together."

"I don't understand. She got back with her ex? The one that cheated on her?"

"I don't know if they 'got back' so much as she's not making any decision right now. He wants her back and if they reconcile that means they can be a family again. I'm not comfortable messing with that."

"But the guy screwed around behind her back."

"Yup. He's a real prize."

"She'll be back."

He switched lanes. "Like Sammy came back."

"You didn't love Sammy that way."

"She was still mine."

Kelly twisted in his seat. "Are you really gonna go down that road, Bray? Colin and Sammy belong together. You've even said so. Don't let the hurt someone else caused affect your relationship with Colin."

"When'd you get so wise?"

His brother chuckled. "Ash has me on a fully organic diet. She says it's brain food."

The conversation rolled onto other easier topics and soon enough they were pulling onto the mountain. Braydon didn't have the heart to look down the road leading to his house. Rather, he chugged onto his parents' drive, feeling like a kid home from school with a big fat failure on his record instead of feeling like a man acclaiming the fruit of his success.

Kelly's truck was parked by Luke's barn and he didn't stick around, complaining Braydon had starved him near death and he needed to get home for sustenance. There wasn't much to unload, being that he wasn't sure where he'd be settling. For the time being, he grabbed the bag with his toiletries and a few shirts and jeans and headed in through the kitchen.

The house was quiet. "Mum? Dad?"

His mother came around the corner, a sad tilt to her head, her green eyes heavy with sympathy. Without a word she held out her arms and Braydon slowly walked into them. She kissed his head and hugged him tight.

"My poor wee angel. I'm glad you're finally home." Breathing in her familiar scent, he drew a measure of comfort from her nearness. She patted his back and gingerly stepped away. "I've made you're favorite. Go say hello to your father, and I'll set you up a nice big dish."

"Thanks, Mum."

He tucked his belongings on the stairs and headed to the den.

"Dad?"

"In here." His father stood and grinned with stilted happiness. He obviously knew. "How was the drive?"

"Fine. Kelly wouldn't shut the hell up the whole way here."

His father looked over his shoulder. "Did you leave him on the interstate?"

Chuckling, he said, "Nah, he went home to Ashlynn."

"Where are Tristan and Luke?"

"They stayed back to grab dinner."

"Guess you heard about their news, being that Kelly was feeling chatty."

"Yeah. That sucks."

"I don't think I've ever seen Luke cry, but boy did he want to when they found out. I wish there was something we could do for them. It's hard seeing your sons upset."

Perhaps talking about Luke was his father's way of recognizing his own heartache without drawing to much attention to Braydon's personal situation. "They'll figure it out."

He cleared his throat. "And how about you?"

He shrugged. "I'm here. Let's start with that. Who knows what comes next?"

Grinning with paternal tenderness, his father patted his shoulder. After a few minutes of small talk his dad went up to bed. Braydon returned to the kitchen where his mother waited at the table beside his dinner.

He settled in and enjoyed the home cooked roast and glazed carrots. When he was finished, she produced two mugs and a bottle of Tully from the cabinet below the sink.

"Do you want to talk about it, love?"

"Not really."

She waited a beat. "I know your heart's hurting, Braydon. I wish there was something I could say or do to ease some of your pain. It kills me seeing you like this when you were so happy a month ago."

"Being here helps."

She nodded. "Maybe you could call Jennifer and see what she's been up to."

Jenn was his ex from high school. Last he saw her she wasn't maturing very well. She still had a catty attitude that should have been left in grade school. "Nah. I don't think I want to date right now." Dating someone else wouldn't replace Becca anyway.

Her hand brushed over his arm. "I wish you would talk to me, love. Sometimes talkin' helps."

"I just don't understand. I'm so sick and tired of not being enough. It's like there's always someone better than me."

"Well, that's just a crock of horse shit, that's what that is, Braydon. You're as good as they get and if anyone disagrees I'll punt them right in the arse."

He chuckled.

"Sure, you've got quirks. You're a McCullough. That's what makes us charming. But you, my boy, are as perfect as a McCullough can come. I mean, you're neat and tidy and you know how to build things from nothin'. You're patient and kind. A wee bit selfish at times, but what man isn't? And with that Becca, oh, you were so wonderful with her and little Hunter. Makes no sense to me, love. Perhaps she's a bit soft in the head to be leavin' you for some jackass who never much treated her well to begin with."

"I think you're a little biased, Mum."

She scoffed. "I speak the God's honest truth! I know when my boys are actin' like bastards and when they're the victim of a situation. This lass made a mistake. As a matter of fact…she's going on my list."

"Your list?"

"Yes." She stood and bustled to the junk drawer. Producing a small scrap of paper, she jotted down something and slid the paper to Braydon. It said Becca just above the name Jasper.

"Jasper?"

"The butcher. He's on my list too. Tried to sell me lamb chops, claiming they were lean when I know he didn't trim a bit of fat off those chops." Her finger stabbed at the paper. "On my list!"

"How do you get off the list?"

"Oh, you don't. I usually just lose the paper in all the hullabaloo and forget someone's upset me."

His mother was insane, but he loved her. "Maybe I should start a list."

She slid him a pen. "Here, love, you can have mine."

Rolling the pen between his fingers, he wrote a K on the page, but couldn't bring himself to scribble the other man's name. It was a nice distraction, but that quickly reality came crashing back and his body seemed to hurt all over again. No breakup had ever affected him so deeply and he wondered when the pain in his chest would go away.

Dropping the pen to the table, he said, "I think I'm gonna go up to bed, Mum. I'm tired."

Her smile faded and in a very soft voice she quietly agreed. "Okay, love. Get yourself some sleep. Tomorrow's a new day."

He kissed her cheek and took the stairs to his old room.

AFTER BRAYDON LEFT THE KITCHEN, Maureen quietly cleaned up. As she washed the dishes her tears silently fell. Seeing her babies hurting always wounded her. And here there was nothing to do for it. Only time would mend her sweet boy's heart. She supposed she should be grateful he'd come home to lick his wounds. Of all her boys, Braydon was probably the most sensitive. And no matter how old and stubborn they became, sometimes a man just needed a mum's love. Well, she had plenty of that.

As she closed the cupboard, tucking the last dish away, she draped the worn dishtowel over the basin of the country sink. Her eyes combed the empty kitchen and a sense of warmth filled her. This was the heart of their home, a place that had seen many smiles and tears over the years. Laughter seemed tattooed into the grain of each log making up the high walls. She was being foolish, getting all sentimental at this late hour.

Yet, as she shut off the light she grinned. Pictures of her children scampering over the bare wood floors filled her memories. Scraped knees and nicked knuckles had been mended many times right there on the chair by the old phone. They were getting older —all her babies.

Shaking her head, she chased away the sentimental twitters tickling her heart and turned to take the stairs. She had grandbabies to love now and plenty of them—that being the Lord's reward for not strangling her own children when they rightfully deserved it—cheeky jackasses.

"What a family," she whispered, smiling in the dark as she stooped to pick up Braydon's shoes and tuck them by the wall. She tidied up his trail all the way to the bedrooms.

Changing into her nightgown, she paused and stared at her husband. The kitchen may be the heart of their home, but he was what kept her own heart beating when it broke in times like this. He had the love and foresight to see what their love could create and she leaned on him to share that hope and foresight with their children. He was one of a kind and he was—thankfully—hers.

Taking a moment, she basked in the memories that seemed to be flooding her. With every passing year, that love for her husband only grew. He was nothing like the young man he once was. Now his face was creased with laugh lines and his raven hair was turning dove white at the temples. But there was a time—it seemed only yesterday—that he was as young and wild as his sons. And she recalled her fair share of heartbreak, empathizing with exactly what her son was suffering now.

Maureen climbed into bed trying not to wake Frank, but as his snoring silenced, she realized he was up. She turned and faced him, not trying to disguise her tears that would not relent.

His large palm cupped her jaw, his thumb dragging under her eye. "What is it, Maureen?"

"He's just so heartbroken, Frank," she whispered. "This lass was different. He truly loved her."

"I know he did."

"I wish there was something we could do. These boys of yours have grown into such stubborn men. They won't show their hurt, but I know he's hurting somethin' fierce right now and all I can do is cry for him."

Leaning close, he kissed her nose. "You've got enough heart for all of us, love. Braydon'll recover from this."

"It seems the same thing happens to him over and over again. It wasn't supposed to happen with this one. And I know it's only a matter of time before him and Colin start brawling."

"What's Colin got to do with this?"

"He stole Sammy."

Frank laughed. "That was years ago."

"Ah, but Braydon never let it go, never stopped holdin' himself in his brother's shadow."

"They beat the shit out of each other, Maureen. That's how men let things go."

"But I know he's reliving all that old hurt. He's thinkin' this ex-husband of Becca's is better than him and he's always thought Colin was better."

"They're all equally rotten," he said affectionately. "Tomorrow they'll go to O'Malley's and get him good and drunk and by Sunday he'll be feeling better again."

"Oh, Frank, alcohol can't fix problems like this."

"Well, neither can milk, so I vote for getting him piss drunk and hoping for the best."

She rolled her eyes. *"Eejit."*

He pinched her under the covers. "Ya love me though, woman. *Eejit* or not."

"You're a pain in my arse." But she did love him. He was her rock. "And don't think you're getting' out of talkin' to him tomorrow. I don't mean small talk either. You talk to him, Frank, because he needs family right now and I don't want him getting lost in this heartache."

"I know, love. Life's full of bridges that need burnin' and bridges meant to be crossed. It's not always clear which is which. Braydon's going to have to make up his mind before he moves on and that's gonna take some time. But I'll talk to him, let him know he can stay here as long as he needs."

"Just promise you'll sit down with him."

"I will. Now get some sleep. I love you."

"I love you too."

THE HOLIDAYS HAD PASSED with stunted joy. Kevin joined them for a small Christmas dinner consisting of ham and traditional sides. He'd lingered as they decorated the tree before Santa came. But with every passing moment, Becca became more and more aware that this was not how it was supposed to be. Despite her son's joy as they opened presents, every show of happiness on her part was a sad imitation of cheer.

She smiled for her son, not wanting him to sense her true feelings. The truth was she'd never felt so hollow and alone. Though Kevin had been attentive, his presence grated. He was there for Hunter, she reminded herself regularly.

The day after Christmas she'd discovered the gifts on her porch. There was no card, but she knew the beautiful snow globes were from Braydon. He'd been there without her knowing and that was when the truth became unarguably clear. If Kevin was present, Braydon would be absent, plain and simple.

Kevin's attitude had been more patient than she thought possible, yet undertones of a personal reconciliation were an ongoing obstacle. Becca continuously rebuffed his attempts to get closer.

She'd allow him as much time as he desired with their son, but her heart was strictly off limits.

He'd pledged he was a changed man. However, comments about her unmatched, serviceable dishes and other lackluster parts of her world spoke of his lingering desire for a fancier life. Braydon would have never commented on such things. No matter how much Kevin attested to wanting a life with them, his grumbling told a different story. It seemed a sacrifice for *him* to be there and it shouldn't have been. Not when Becca sacrificed her own happiness in order to allow him the opportunity.

On New Year's Eve, Kevin showed up with champagne and high hopes, but Becca wasn't in the celebratory mood. The person she'd hoped to ring in the New Year with was gone. She sent Kevin home before midnight and welcomed the coming year alone. Everything inside of her begged for action, yet she was so depleted, so broken down by shame and fear, she couldn't seem to make herself move.

Her last conversation with Braydon replayed in her mind on an hourly basis. The last time they were together was the end. She could no longer dredge up the courage to face him, fearful she'd only disappoint him once more. Still, the words of their last phone call played in her mind like the echoes of a distant bell she'd never see in person.

"I can't do this anymore," he said quietly.

Her heart sank. "Braydon—"

"Tell me you changed your mind, Becca. This sitting in neutral is killing me."

Her eyes drifted to her son. He'd been building a train track with Kevin. Everything about the scene should have made her happy.

"Please, just give me a little more time."

He was silent for a long time. "I love you, Becca, but time isn't going to change anything. I think you've made up your mind." His voice sounded so depleted. "I don't want to keep doing this. We're getting nowhere. Please don't call me again unless you've changed your mind."

Several times she considered calling again, craving the sound of his voice, the closeness they once shared, but her compassion for him forbade it. Every selfish attempt to drag out their goodbye was hurting him. She didn't want to cause him any more pain, regretting that which she'd already inflicted.

After too many empty days and lonely nights, the silence finally broke her. She needed to see him, needed to hear his voice, look into his eyes and confess she'd screwed everything up. She didn't have the answers, but the turn her life had taken could not be the solution she'd hoped for. She loved her son, would do anything for him, but denying her own happiness was killing her.

She'd gone to his apartment after work to talk, but it was empty. Removing her key from the ring, she placed it on the counter and wept the entire way home. Becca waited until Hunter fell asleep that night to truly break down. Braydon was gone.

She was done making excuses borne of fear, and sadly, she'd hesitated too long, the realization that she *needed* to be with him coming too late. Despite all her efforts to do the right thing, provide the most organic environment for her son, she couldn't ignore her desire—no *need*—to have Braydon in her life. But she had vacillated and now, she wasn't sure she could fix any of this. She had no one to blame but herself.

Yes, Kevin had been more helpful and was doing more with Hunter, which was great, but he was still Kevin. There were parts of him she simply couldn't abide. And why should she have to? Their personal relationship was over. All that was left were echoes of lost hope in the shadows of her heart that now belonged to someone else.

Her love went to those that deserved it—Hunter and Braydon—which was where her loyalty belonged as well. It took her some time to process the finality of such an epiphany, but once she embraced her choice, all the weight that had been bogging her down seemed to ease. Clarity had been contaminated by past doubts—and her own stupidity. But she was done denying herself the happiness she deserved for obligations she'd met twice over.

It was time to put herself first, something a lot easier said than done. She just hoped it wasn't too late.

She considered calling him, but the sound of his voicemail when he didn't answer would be like having a layer of flesh ripped off, gutting her with the confirmation he was finished with her. Though she was ready to make a move, she wasn't sure how to proceed. She'd botched so much already. Everything was fragile.

Wandering through the dark house, she grabbed a box of tissues and collapsed onto the couch. So lost in her sobs, she didn't hear the door open.

"Rebecca?" With her name came the acute sense of distress.

"Kevin?" The man had impeccable timing. "What are you doing here? It's late."

"I wanted to see you."

Her body shuddered. It was becoming excruciatingly difficult to fake happiness at his presence, which was becoming more and more intrusive, treading on moments that had nothing to do with their son. Quickly collecting the crumpled tissues littered all over the sofa, she stood and swallowed back her erupting emotions. "You should call first."

"Call before I come to my house?" The sterile hatred she associated with his narcissism was magnified every time he laid claim to her house as though it still belonged to him. Her hand stilled over the trashcan, tissues soaked with tears for Braydon falling in with the rubbish. Pivoting slowly, she faced her *ex*-husband.

He sifted through the mail—*her mail*—sitting on the counter. Every gnawing thought overshadowed by the pressure of the last few weeks collided as her patience snapped with piercing clarity. "That's it."

"That's it?" He placed the mail back on the counter and frowned in confusion.

"Yes!" she snapped, at her wit's end. She collected her mail and stashed it in a drawer. "That. Is. It. This is *my* house. You can't just barge in here whenever you feel like it."

"Rebecca—"

"Ugh! Stop calling me that! No one calls me Rebecca. And you say that name in the most condescending tone!

He held up his palms defensively in surrender. "Why are you so angry?"

"Why?" She laughed, sounding a bit senseless. "Why am I angry? Okay, how's this? I *never* used to get angry. I'd let you do whatever you wanted, because I was too busy doing everything else, and that worked just fine for *you*. While I was busy holding this house together, raising our son, attending meetings, figuring out the bills, and aging myself twice as fast picking up all your slack, you were busy going to the gym, fucking God knows what, and having a mid-life crisis shopping spree we couldn't afford. I'm very sorry you were so discontent in our marriage, Kevin, but maybe if you'd helped out once in a while I could have been a better wife!"

Her head was spinning as her temper flared out of control. Had she really been disillusioned enough to consider cutting off her own personal needs for this man? He'd said it was for them, and she'd tried to do right by Hunter, but the truth was, no matter how much she would always care for the father of her child, she really disliked him for all of the terrible things he'd done and all the crucial things he'd never managed to do.

"I have needs, Kevin!" Maybe he didn't deserve to be attacked in that moment, but so many unresolved issues of their past had been excused without a word from her, she felt it was her due to—for once—lose a bit of her patience. "You hurt me more than anyone else ever has. You slept with another woman—*in our bed!* Do you have any idea how long it took me to get over that? And then you turned around and blamed it on me like I should have been blowing you in between IEP meetings and workshops and everything else I do around here."

"I've apologized, Rebecca. I don't know how else to fix things."

"You *can't* fix this! You broke us!" But deep down she knew they'd already been broken.

His face flushed a dark shade of red. "You're acting hysterical."

"*I am hysterical!* Because of you everything is messed up! I was happy. For once in my life I was happy. All you had to do was let me be, but you couldn't do that. You sat right there and pulled every trick in the book. My God, you even brought up having more children."

"I wasn't trying to trick you, Rebecca. I want things the way they were."

"Oh, I bet you do," she said coldly. "You had quite the life. The problem is, Kevin, I *don't* want things the way they were. I was miserable. *You* made me miserable. Catching you that day was probably the best thing that ever happened to me. It should've removed all my guilt and validated the ending to our relationship. But our marriage, our family, meant everything to me. I couldn't throw it away as fast as you and you took advantage of that. You took advantage of me!"

There was a noise in the hall and she froze. They both turned and found Hunter studying them, unspeakable questions in his eyes.

"Get back in bed, Hunter," Kevin barked.

Her blood boiled. "Don't you dare yell at him!" she snapped. Stepping to Hunter, she softened her voice and touched his shoulder. "Come on, bud. Let's go back to bed." As she passed Kevin she hissed, "I want you to leave. Now."

He caught her arm. "I want to talk about this."

"I don't. I said everything I needed to say to you months ago. I don't like the person I am when I'm around you. I want you to go and I want you to take your crap with you. For half a year I've nicely asked you to get the boxes out of the garage. If they aren't gone tonight I'm putting them on the curb tomorrow, because whether you like it or not, this is my house to do with as I please and you no longer belong here."

She'd allowed him too much leverage, too much of a say in her future. After ten years of marriage it was difficult to change her thinking, but finally doing so felt right. Her words, as cruel and overdue as they might be, vindicated the emotions she'd been hiding from.

Her hands trembled as she led Hunter upstairs. The lights from Kevin's car eventually reflected on the curtains, telling her he'd gone. As stoic as she attempted to be, there was no holding her tears inside.

Hunter's head rested on the pillows, his eyes studying her face. His small hand pressed to her eyes and she caught his fingers in hers so he didn't accidentally poke her.

"Sad."

His perception surprised her, wringing out more emotions. "It's okay, honey. Mommy's just upset. Try and shut your eyes and get some sleep. It's late."

He studied her for a long moment, not necessarily looking into her eyes, but observing her features. His small brow pinched as his head tilted. "Smile," he said.

Her lips trembled into a somber grin, but her eyes continued to weep. Her boy was so sweet. She hated the moments he saw her like this, moments she wasn't strong enough to hold it all inside. He shouldn't have to witness her tears.

"Braydon."

She stilled.

When Hunter was first diagnosed someone told her to expect moments of hope and moments of grief at the same time. Hearing Braydon's name cross her son's lips was exactly that. "What?"

"Braydon makes you smile."

Her lips parted, shocked by his insight. Hunter knew Braydon, not just in a superficial sense, but in a comprehensive way. Somehow, during all the spinning, stimming, racing, and rocking, her sweet son had interpreted one undeniable truth—Braydon made her happy.

Her shock lasted so long, Hunter's attention drifted to the stuffed monkey sitting on his bed. She swallowed and did what she should have done all along. She asked her son what he wanted. "Hunter, do you love Braydon?"

He made an affirmative sound.

"Did you like the place we visited with Mrs. McCullough, the lady with orange hair that gave you hot chocolate?"

He laughed. "She gave me blue gloves."

She chuckled, ever impressed by his memory. "Yes, she gave you blue gloves. Did you like that place?"

"Yeah." He bit his lip and rolled to his side, staring at the wall. He was getting tired.

"Would you like to go back there some time?"

"Yeah."

"Maybe we could stay there," she suggested gently, unsure if that was even an option at this point.

"And play in the snow?"

She smiled. "Yes, and play in the snow. And in the summers we could swim in the lakes. Would you like that?"

He laughed. "Yeah. But not to get my hair wet."

Drawing in a choppy breath, she smiled. "No, we don't have to go under water."

She pulled up the blankets, but rested by his side until he fell asleep. When he finally dozed, she carefully curled closer to his little body and slowly rested her hand over his, hugging him gently. "I love you, Hunter."

Sometimes autism was too complicated to explain, but other times it was so simplistic it showed her how uncomplicated love could be. She was done being afraid. It was time to welcome hope back into her life. She was certain of where she was meant to be, because the moment Hunter spoke Braydon's name her only regret was that Braydon wasn't there to hear him.

THE ROOM WOBBLED as Becca plopped on Nikki's couch. "I'm such a shmuck." Her plan to fix things with Braydon had fallen flat when he didn't answer any of her calls.

Nikki patted her leg lovingly. "You're not a shmuck."

"I'd hate to say I told you so—"

"Then don't," Nikki snapped, giving her sister a pointed look.

"It was only a matter of time before the real Kevin showed up."

"I freaked out," Becca slurred.

"The man is a cockroach," Carla argued. "There could be atomic warfare and he'd keep showing up. You did the right thing. Maybe freaking out got through to him."

Nikki refilled Becca's glass. "No one blames you for taking the time to consider your choices, Becca. You needed to realize this on your own. Now you can move on without the burden of self-doubt."

"I can't move on. Braydon hates me."

"He does *not* hate you. He's hurt. Men have pride. You took a little shit on his."

"You don't understand. He thinks I chose Kevin over him. It was never a matter of Kevin, only Hunter, but no matter how hard I tried to explain that he never understood. Now he'll think he's second choice."

"Not if you explain it to him. Show him your mind's made up and he's the one you want."

"He doesn't want to hear it. So long as he refuses to take my calls he'll never know my position changed."

"He didn't want to hear it while Kevin was still in the picture," Nikki said. "He's gone now. Eventually you'll get through to him."

"Correct me if I'm wrong," Carla interrupted. "But didn't he tell you not to contact him until you've made up your mind? Mind's made up. Nikki, get Becca's phone."

Nikki dug around in Becca's purse and produced her phone. "Here you go, my love."

"He won't answer."

Carla snatched the phone out of her hand. "Oh, just dial." They all waited in silence as the call connected. Carla frowned. "It went to voicemail."

Becca started to cry again. She'd been such a mess, she insisted Kevin take Hunter to *his place* for the remainder of the weekend. Perhaps the man was human after all, because he agreed with little protest.

"Give me that phone," Nikki demanded. She punched the contact information from Becca's phone into her own and hit send. They waited.

"Braydon, this is Nikki. You have thirty minutes to call me back on this number or I can't be held responsible for what happens. I've gone through too many tissues and too much vodka for one night to put up with this childish shit any longer. Call me back."

A minute later the phone rang. "Bingo." Nikki gave a cocky grin and brought the phone to her ear. "Good evening, Mr. McCullough."

"Good evening, but I'm afraid you have the wrong McCullough. This is Finn."

"It's his brother," Nikki hissed, tucking the phone away from her lips.

"We can hear him," Carla hissed back. "Tell him to put Kelly on the phone."

Becca smacked her in the arm. "Why does Finn have Braydon's phone?"

Nikki held up a finger. "Might I speak with Braydon?"

"'Fraid not. He isn't taking calls at the moment."

Her friendly demeanor vanished. "Why the hell not?"

"He's a little preoccupied with other things right now."

Becca's stomach flipped. Other things? What sort of other things?

Nikki's expression hardened. "What are you, his secretary?"

"Just a concerned relative."

"Well, why don't you tell your brother to grow a set and—"

"Nikki, don't." Defeated, she pleaded with her friend. "I knew he wouldn't want to talk. Don't yell at Finn."

"Is that Becca? How's she doing?"

Nikki frowned. "Becca's fine. Whose side are you on?"

"I'm neutral."

"Well, listen, Switzerland, Becca was figuring her life out and she wants to explain things to your brother, but the man's being stubborn and won't pick up the phone."

"I don't think he's capable of operating heavy machinery right now."

"Like a phone?"

"Yup," Finn agreed in a chipper tone. "He probably won't be calling her back until he pukes at least twice and sleeps for four to seven hours. We gave him a lot of liquor."

She cupped her hand over the phone. "He's wasted."

"Oh, like Becca!" Carla clapped. "You two are so meant to be."

Nikki held up her finger and stood. "Refill her glass, Carla. I'll be right back." Nikki disappeared into the kitchen for several minutes as Carla did as instructed.

"Drink up, pudding."

"I don't think I should have anymore." Her head was getting very heavy on her neck and the room kept spinning.

Carla waved her objection away. "Don't be silly. Now, which one's Finn? Is he the gay one?"

"No, that's Luke, his twin." Amazingly, she could still keep all the McCullough's names straight, even drunk.

"I don't know how Maureen did it, raising that many boys, but I'm sure glad she did."

Nikki reappeared a while later with empty hands. "Carla, go in the pantry and grab the last of the vodka. Becca, where are your shoes?"

"Why?" she slurred from where she slumped on the couch.

"We're going out for ice cream."

Oh ice cream! "'Kay. Carla, find my other shoe!"

"What am I, the lackey?" Carla shouted as she returned holding a bottle of vodka and a shoe.

"I'm gonna get a sundae," Becca garbled, though she wasn't sure how great ice cream would sit in her stomach at the moment. She really should stop drinking.

Nikki shoved on her shoe and patted her knee. "You can get whatever you want, sweetie. Just don't puke in my car."

"Okeydokey."

~

FINN GRINNED AT HIS BROTHER. "Thanks for driving us, Colin."

"Thanks for waking me up out of a dead sleep. Sammy's out for blood, by the way. You woke the kids."

"Nah, Sammy loves me. She'd never hurt good old Finnegan."

"How far's this diner?" Braydon asked from the backseat where he was wedged between Luke and Tristan. "I'm gonna get me some grits."

"We're almost there. Give him more from the flask, Luke."

"Feels like we've been drivin' for hours. I can't feel my legs."

"That's the whiskey," Luke commented, handing over the flask.

"No, he's feeling my leg." Tristan nudged him. "Hands to yourself, Drunkenstein."

"You guys are the best," Braydon called out, a stupid grin spread across his face. "Even you, Colin."

"How far's this place?" Colin asked, his hair still rumpled from bed.

Finn looked at the GPS on his phone. "About thirty more minutes," he whispered. "Nikki said it's right off Exit 40."

"Exit forty's far," Braydon slurred.

"Shut up," Finn called into the backseat as he turned up the radio.

"Then what? We're just dumping him there?" Colin asked. Colin had been asleep in his bed during the formation of their master plan.

"Yup. She's renting a room and sedating Becca with ice cream and vodka. Said she'll likely pass out by the time we get there with the package."

"The package being our brother?"

"Yup. He probably won't make it either." Peeking into the back, he noted Braydon's eyes looked about ready to close.

"And then what happens?"

"We leave them there without cars or money. They can live off room service for the next couple of days until they talk out their problems."

"What about clothes?"

Finn shrugged. "Worse comes to worst, they go naked."

When they reached Exit 40 Braydon was snoring like a buzz saw. Finn texted Nikki.

Is she asleep?

Out cold. They're in room 450. Honeymoon suite.

Colin parked the truck and they all filed out. "How we gonna do this?" Luke asked.

"You grab his shoulders. Tristan and I will take a leg and Colin can get the doors."

"We're gonna get stopped," Colin said.

"If we get caught you two are deaf and Luke and I don't speak English."

Colin rolled his eyes. "Brilliant."

"Sí." Finn smiled.

As they dragged Braydon out of the backseat his shoe came off. "Should I get that?" Tristan asked.

"Nah. He ain't walkin'."

He was heavier than they anticipated. Getting him into the

elevator wasn't an easy task. They may have bumped his head a few times, but Finn figured they'd blame any bruises on the booze.

"Is this the room?" Colin asked.

The door opened and Carla came out. "What? No Kelly? Now I'm disappointed."

Nikki entered the hall. "Holy crap. Is he alive?"

"Just a little tired," Finn laughed. "Where's sleeping beauty?"

Nikki grinned. "In bed. I took the liberty of hiding her clothes in the safe."

"Nice. I like your style," Finn said as they lugged Braydon's dead weight across the room.

Carla lifted the covers. "No peeking at my friend's derriere unless you show me yours."

They tucked Braydon in and removed his wallet. Nikki rummaged around under the covers. When she stood, she held Braydon's pants. "Fair is fair."

The men laughed. "Are we forgetting anything?" Luke asked.

"Don't think so. I've got her purse and Braydon's wallet. I only wish I could be a fly on the wall when these two wake up."

They quietly backed out of the room and shut the door, stifling their giggles.

"Now," Nikki said turning to face the men. "I just want to say, if this doesn't work out and he hurts my friend, someone's going to pay."

"Pshh," Luke waved away her threat. "You don't scare me. I was raised by an Irish mother."

Carla shoved Nikki aside and stood with the men. "Okay, have a safe trip back, Nik. I'll call you when we get there."

The men frowned. "Where's she think she's going?"

Grinning up at the men, Carla announced, "O'Malley's of course."

Finn laughed. This must be the one Kelly was afraid of. "Sorry, love, bar's closed."

"That's okay. I can hide in wait."

"Get in the car, Carla," Nikki snapped.

"You're no fun." She pouted as she left with her sister. "There's a perfectly good car full of Irishmen and an empty seat. You're such a kill joy."

CHAPTER 16

$\mathcal{S}$harp pain clamped down on Becca's skull the moment her sleeping mind roused. Carefully, she breathed through the throbbing in her head, weighing the agony and preparing to open her eyes. She needed a minute.

Everything was quiet. She must be in Nikki's house. Her mind scrambled to piece together the previous night's events, but distorted recollection left her memories a blur. Thank the heavens Kevin had Hunter, because today was going to be debilitation and one for the record books.

As her mind slowly assessed her body her eyes remained closed, not eager to face the intrusive brightness of morning. Taking a slow account of her state, she grimaced, which hurt like hell. Her fingers brushed her tender belly. Where were her clothes? She didn't sleep nude, certainly not at her friend's house. Her hand slid lower.

Where are my panties?

Palm gliding over her bare side, she grazed her exposed breasts. She wasn't wearing a stitch! Her hand flopped to her left and she froze. The sense of something—*someone*—beside her, giving off immense heat, set her heart into a panic.

Bracing for the sharp pain, she cracked her eyes. Everything was dark, so dark her ears clung to every identifiable sound. The slow hum of air vents nearby, the stillness of her surroundings, too quiet for a house, her hair scuffing over the starched fabric of the pillows —this echoless silence was not a part of her friend's house.

Oh my God, where am I?

The body next to her was wrapped in a puff of white sheets. She was having some Rip Van Winkle experience or a serious mental break, so she slithered her feet out of the bed, struggling with the tightly tucked linen.

Her toes made contact with stiff, muted carpet and she slunk like a snake out the bottom of the bed until her body dumped off the edge of the mattress and plopped on the floor with a muffled thud. Her landing reverberated through her skeleton. With no identifiable mark to her surroundings, she quickly sprang to her feet.

Fear and confusion palpitated through her. A thin beam of light sliced across a tiny pleat in the curtains. Tiptoeing to the window she cracked the panel and gasped.

I've been kidnapped!

With jagged breath fogging up the chilled glass, she searched for any recognizable landmark. The intruding brightness of morning galvanized her consciousness and panic drilled through her veins. This wasn't a dream. She was very far up from the ground in what looked like a hotel.

Pivoting slowly, her gaze searched through the shadows for any sort of weapon. The lamp was screwed into place so that wouldn't help. Carefully sliding open a drawer, she found a floppy bible. It would have to do.

Creeping around the bed, her hand slowly extended until her pinky hooked the edge of the sheet wrapped over her captor's head. The putrid scent of stale booze wafting from the body intensified the unpleasant sloshing sensation in her stomach. Wait, no, that smell was her. She sniffed and drew back. Maybe it was both of them.

Through the shadows she couldn't see much. A masculine arm pinned the pillow over his identifying features. With two delicate fingers, she slowly lifted his wrist.

The body jolted upwards. Eyes flashed open and her composure left with the subtly of a shotgun. The pillow tossed to the floor, she screamed, lost her balance, and then the bible came down with a defensive whack right across his face.

He groaned and dropped to his back, clamping his fingers to his nose. "Fuck!"

She stilled, recognizing that voice. *"Braydon?"*

"Becca?" His voice was muffled as his palms cushioned his face. He groaned. "Why did you hit me?"

"What are you doing here?" *Wherever here is.*

He stilled and she gave him a moment to rouse. Maybe he knew where they were or how they got there. "Turn on a light," he mumbled, still rubbing his face.

She quickly felt her way back to a lamp, cursing when she stubbed her toe on some anonymous piece of furniture. Distress had momentarily vanquished her hangover, but the second the lamp clicked on with the force of a thousand suns, the pain in her head came hurtling back and she gripped her temples.

Braydon sat up. "You're naked."

Her hand snatched a pillow off the bed as she scanned the room for her clothing. They were definitely in a hotel. "How did we get here?"

His gaze locked on her hips. Stomping her foot into the mauve carpet she snapped, "Braydon, eyes up here!"

"Sorry. I don't know. Last I remember I was on my way to breakfast."

"Breakfast?" She frowned. Who was he getting breakfast with? "Why aren't you naked?"

He glanced at his shirt and shrugged. Lifting the sheet, he peeked at his legs. "I'm in my underwear." His brow creased. "And I'm wearing one shoe."

"Braydon, what the heck happened last night?"

His head tilted as he glanced at the ceiling, likely trying to fill in the blank spots of his memory. Were they drugged? Could alcohol really make a person black out like that? How much had they drunk?

"Give me your shirt," she said, suddenly needing the bathroom —desperately.

"Then I'll be naked."

She glared at him and he relented, stripping off his T-shirt and handing it over. The material swallowed her. She tried not to weep at the return of his familiar scent when it surrounded her. Ditching the pillow, she rushed to the bathroom.

The restroom boasted a glamorous tub and his and hers sinks. Wherever they were it was nice. Her gaze scoured the room, only pausing when she spotted a folded piece of paper perched between the sinks.

Quickly finishing her business, she rushed to the vanity and snatched the note.

Good morning love birds.

We were sick of you two not communicating. You've probably noticed by now that Becca is as naked as a jaybird and Braydon is without pants. Your clothes are in the safe and no, we aren't telling you the code until you work out your issues. There is something for your hangovers next to the two toothbrushes we left. Feel free to abuse room service for all your other needs. Now, play nice.
Love,
Nikki, Carla, and all 300 McCulloughs

Becca brushed her teeth vigorously and washed her face. She really wanted to shower, being that her hair was having its own eighties revival, but they needed to get to the bottom of this first.

Exiting the bathroom, note pinched between her fingers, she announced, "You can thank your relatives and my friends for dumping us here. Do you have your phone?"

"I have a shoe and underwear. I can't find anything."

"Our clothes are in the safe."

He stood, and Becca shut her eyes, overwhelmed by the reminder of how good Braydon looked in his briefs. Disappearing in the closet, he asked, "What's the code?"

"They didn't say. We're trapped."

"Jesus, my head is killing me. I need a minute."

He disappeared in the bathroom and Becca heard him cursing as he fought with the pill bottle. Water ran and the toilet flushed. When he returned he handed her a glass and two capsules. "What time is it?"

Swallowing the pills, she glanced at the clock. "Ten." Her nerves were a jittery mess, so she tried to avoid looking directly at him.

"Did you find our phones?"

"I can't even find my purse."

"All my stuff's in my jeans."

"Then it's probably in the safe."

He sat on the settee and braced his arms over his knees as they contemplated their situation. "Do you know anyone's phone number?" he asked.

All her contacts were in her phone. It had been years since she needed to memorize a number. The only one she knew by heart was Kevin's cell. "No."

"Shit."

"There's no one you can call? I need to get home."

His eyes narrowed as he stared at her for a long moment. Expression hard, he said, "No doubt. I can call my mother."

He strutted to the room phone and dialed. They waited.

"Mum?"

Maureen's voice was loud enough for Becca to hear through the receiver. "Hello, dear! How are you feeling? Your brothers tell me you had a wee bit too much to drink last night."

There was a roaring, "Good morning, Bray!" in the background that had him wincing.

"Are they there?" he asked, bringing the phone back to his ear. "Let me talk to Finn."

"Finnegan, your brother wants a word. Oh. He says he's eatin' and he'll have to get back to you."

His jaw clenched. "Where are my pants?"

"Has anyone seen Braydon's pants? You really should keep better track of your personal belongings, love. Oh, okay. Kelly wants to know if you found the biscuit they left you."

He glanced at her and offered a frustrated smile. "Mum, Becca needs to get home and they stole all our stuff."

"Oh, dear. Stranded, are you? That's quite a pickle. Can someone go pick up Braydon and bring him some pants?" Laughter sounded. "Hmm. They're all busy, love. You'll just have to make the best of the situation until someone can come get you. Where are you?"

"I. Don't. Know," he growled.

"Well, there's no need to take a tone with me."

"Mum!" he snarled. "Put Dad on the phone."

"*Frank!* Telephone!" His head drew away from the receiver as his mother shrilled into the phone.

His father picked up the line with feigning cheer. "Good morning!"

"Dad, I need you to come get us and bring clothes. The guys dumped us in some hotel and stole all our shit."

"Did they now?"

"Dad," he growled again. In a more beseeching tone he begged, "Please."

"'Fraid my hands are tied, Bray. They won't tell me where you are."

He covered the phone. "Can you see any road signs from the window?"

She looked again. "There's a highway, but I can't see any signs from here."

"Dad, Becca needs to get to Hunter. We have to get out of here."

"Becca needs to get home to Hunter," his father informed the others. "They said they'll call you back in a few minutes. I gotta run, Bray. Have fun."

He stared, disbelieving, at the phone. "He hung up on me."

"I'm never drinking again," she muttered.

A moment later the phone rang. He snatched it up and barked, "Hello?"

"Well, good morning, GQ. I imagine you slept well."

"Damn it, Nikki. We need our stuff!"

She chuckled. "May I please speak to Becca?"

His arm shot out, passing her the phone. Becca wasted no time on a greeting. "You're a dead woman."

"Oh, pish. In a few hours you'll be thanking me. You kids have issues that need to be worked out."

"I'm not kidding, Nikki. I need to get home."

"No, you don't. I spoke to Kevin—see what a caring friend I am? He has Hunter until tomorrow and your boss just extended your weekend. You're free until after school tomorrow."

"How are we getting home?"

"Carla's picking you up when we feel you're ready."

"I'm ready now. This isn't funny, Nikki."

"Oh, it's a little funny, Becca. Did you take the headache medicine I left you?"

"Yes."

"See, everything I do is out of love. Now, go order breakfast and get to the make-up sex. Kevin knows to call me if he needs anything."

"Nikki!"

"Bye, Becca." The line went dead.

"I hate her."

They were quiet for several minutes. It wasn't a comfortable silence. Tension knotted her shoulders and with every passing breath the unbridgeable chasm between them seemed to grow. Braydon clearly didn't want to be trapped in a hotel room with her.

After their argument, his ultimatum, their last encounter, weeks had passed without them speaking. She wasn't sure how to break such silence. They'd never been awkward together, but now nothing felt natural.

Abruptly, he stood. "I'm taking a shower. Why don't you order something to eat? I assume the jackasses that dumped us here are paying, so be sure to order champagne and caviar."

With that, he disappeared into the bathroom shutting the door hard enough to make her flinch. She didn't know if she should cry or make a naked run for it. With no money or clothing she wouldn't get far.

When the water shut off she quickly picked up the phone and dialed the front desk. Her brain was moving in slow motion, still processing the fact that her friends had fed her enough booze to cause a New York City black out, that she'd accepted such amounts, and beyond all else, that she was in the same room as Braydon. She ordered pancakes, cereal, eggs, and a large quantity of coffee.

Braydon emerged in a puff of steam with nothing but a towel around his waist. Swallowing tightly, she said, "I ordered food. They're going to leave it outside the door."

He didn't make eye contact with her, which was probably for the best. Whatever her friends thought would happen here, they were wrong.

It was torture, seeing his beautiful body exposed and knowing he was angry with her and all of that which she desired was off limits. He might have been irritated with her, but nothing could come close to how furious she was with herself. It was clear he resented being trapped in her presence.

As she covertly watched him wander around the room, her body coiled and reacted to the enforced nearness until she couldn't take another minute of the deafening silence.

Springing off the bed, she announced she was going to take a shower. After ten long minutes under the cold spray her body started to calm. Her headache was subsiding and she'd feel better after getting some food in her belly.

Slipping back into Braydon's T-shirt—and taking a long breath of his nostalgic scent—she roughly combed her fingers through her hair. Great. He looked like a Roman sculpture and she looked like a wet rat. No makeup. No comb. No razor. Wonderful.

The food had arrived and Braydon appeared to have already eaten. Wandering to the small table in the corner, she picked at a dry pancake. For as starved as she was minutes ago, her appetite now vanished.

Out of the corner of her eye, she studied him. He scowled out the window as she considered their time apart. Did he miss her as much as she'd missed him? Had he been with other women? She desperately wanted to know exactly how he interpreted their break.

She cleared her throat. "There are probably robes in the closet."

He mutely glanced down at his exposed abdomen. The towel around his hips gaped between his knees, but he remained concealed. "I'm fine."

She sighed. "Braydon, I think we're here to talk."

"Do you have something new to say?" His tone was snide, something she wasn't used to from him. It smothered her courage and stifled all other comments.

Wandering to the window, she found herself blinking back tears. It wasn't supposed to be like this. She should have never let Kevin mess with her head. He had the ability to manipulate her more than any other person on this earth, because he had no shame in using their son as leverage. In that moment she wanted to strangle him, because the sad truth was, he never hesitated to take advantage of her forgiving nature, if it meant bettering his own situation.

It was her fault too, of course. She should have more of a backbone with him by this point. She was simply worn out from arguing. Their relationship had become a battleground years ago and any interaction with him left her in knots. Sometimes bending was easier than standing her ground.

She'd only wanted what was best for her son, but somehow, after so many years of putting everyone else's needs before hers, she'd forgotten the best thing for Hunter was having a balanced mother. While Braydon introduced an additional layer of spontaneity to her life, knocking her off kilter sometimes, he also brought her balance. He was the up to her down, the smile to her frown, and the endless reserve of confidence when hers was shaken.

"Are you crying?"

She flinched as Braydon's voice cut through the earsplitting silence. Wiping her nose, she lied, "No."

He let out a frustrated breath. "Women always cry while men have to hold it all in and deal with life."

He had so much resentment, and rightly so. Though his eyes remained dry and his emotions carefully concealed, she knew his pain was as real as hers—or she at least assumed. But she was sick and tired of everyone dumping all the blame on her shoulders. "Maybe women cry because men are jerks and they make us cry."

"Are you saying I'm a jerk?"

Her gaze remained fastened on the glass as the view blurred. "No. I guess that's why I'm crying." Wiping her eyes she whispered, "No one's ever been nicer to me than you have. If there's a jerk here, it's me."

"And where does nice get me, Becca?"

Her shoulders drooped as she slowly shook her head. "I never meant to hurt you."

"You failed."

Not the first time. His words sliced through her, cutting right to her heart. "I'm sorry."

"Yeah, well, that doesn't fix things."

But it was all she had. He clearly didn't want her anymore.

"Here." A box of tissues, so impersonal and cold, shoved into her view. She plucked two from the container and mumbled a thank you.

He noiselessly moved around the room, his steps agitated. The large hotel room seemed to shrink into a suffocating cage. Every emotion bled from his pores and ricocheted around the space until it crashed into her.

"I'm angry," he suddenly announced.

"I know," she quietly acknowledged.

"I think of you with him and I want to break something."

"It isn't like that."

He made a growl of frustration. "You don't belong to him."

A nervous laugh slipped past her lips. She didn't belong to anyone, but Hunter belonged to her and though her intentions were misguided, they were never anything but well intended, in hopes that she was doing right by her son.

"The thought of him touching you makes me sick," he went on, pacing. "He had nearly a decade to do right by you and fucked that up. Why does someone like that deserve more chances?"

He was right. Everything he said was true.

"How could you pick him over me? I never did anything but love and respect you. And you picked him."

"I didn't *pick* him. I just needed time to sort out my life."

"I don't want another woman in my life who can't appreciate that I value her. Christ, I never valued anyone the way I valued you. You should know how I feel by now. Damn it, you should know how *you* feel."

"I do," she cried. "Braydon, I'm deciding—not just for myself—but for two people. It *should* take twice as long to make such a monumental decision. I *love* you, but everything was moving so fast. We went from a one-night stand with no strings attached to an intense relationship. It kills me that you're moving away and I don't want to see you go! You've been planning to return home since you left the nest. The question of Hunter and I moving has only been on my radar for a minute in comparison to the time you've had to decide."

His expression sobered, a touch of vulnerability showing in his eyes. "You don't want to see me go?"

"That's why I've been trying to call you, but you won't speak to me and now you're so angry I don't know what to say."

He stilled. "I'm afraid to ask. If you say the wrong thing I may snap. I'm holding on by a thread here, as it is. Did you change your mind? I thought…" His words tapered off as his gaze lowered.

She'd never witnessed him so high strung, nor was she used to seeing such an optimistic man appear so downtrodden. Her pulse pounded steadily, the thrumming shaking her to the tips of her fingers.

Drawing in a deep breath, she confessed, "I never made up my mind. That's why I needed time—to decide." She swallowed. "I threw Kevin out two days ago. I, in no uncertain terms, told him our personal relationship was never going to reestablish itself and that I was in love with you. He was getting a little too comfortable in my home. The holidays were one thing, but it was never my intension to welcome him back. I only wanted him to be more present in his son's life. I also told him if he didn't get the remainder of his crap out of my house I was putting it on the curb."

When he wouldn't look at her, she turned away, her chest constricting with pain. Maybe it was too late.

Her back heated, drawing her shoulders up as he stepped close. His ragged breathing sent shivers up her spine. In a low growl, he asked, "Was he sleeping there?"

Slowly, she pivoted. "No, but he seemed to think your absence was an open invitation for him to barge in whenever he pleased. I never accepted his proposal. I only wanted time to consider the situation."

His blue eyes locked with hers as his chest lifted, his breathing labored. "Did he touch you? Kiss you?"

Her head slowly shook. "I'd never allow that, not when I feel so strongly for you."

"He's gone? You made it clear that your personal relationship is over?"

Slowly, she nodded.

A territorial growl ripped from his throat, as his mouth crashed down on hers, his tongue piercing between her lips. Strong hands gripped her behind, lifting her feet from the ground. The world spun as her back landed on the breakfast table, his arm sweeping out at the last second to clear the surface.

Platters crashed to the ground as his towel fell away. Hitching her thighs apart, the heat of his cock pressed at her wet sex. There was no foreplay, no softness. He sank into her to the hilt and gave a punishing thrust as he kissed her passionately.

"You belong with me, Becca. No one else. The thought of someone else kissing these lips, touching your body, I can't take it." He thrust hard again. "This is ours. Every touch your skin craves, I'll satisfy it. Every caress, my hand will provide. Every ache, every need, I'll be the one to take care of you. You ever question that again I'll seriously lose my mind."

"I'm not leaving," she gasped as he pounded into her. "This is where I want to be, with you. Only you, Braydon."

Shoving her shirt away, his hands cupped her breast, plucked and pinched at her nipples, then glided up her arms until her hands were pinned above her head. Staring down at her, his blue-eyed gaze devoured her features. He took her like his life depended on this connection they shared. She'd never felt so owned, so wanted. It was the most potent sexual experience of her life.

His fingers caressed down her sides until they closed around her ankles, spreading her legs wide. His attention pulled to the point their bodies connected. "Look at that, me inside of you. We're a perfect fit. Perfect together, but broken when we're apart."

Bracing her weight, her back bowed and saw what he was referring to. His cock slid slowly in and out of her sex, glistening with her arousal. It was erotic and intimate as hell and her body flooded with doubled need. As she studied him, his attention so drawn to their intimate connection, carnal desire took over. She became a woman untethered by fear and doubt, her desire wild and uncontainable.

Meeting his thrusts, she arched, her back off the table and took him deep. He released her ankles and the soles of her feet pressed into the surface of the table.

"I need to taste you." He abruptly withdrew, leaving her bereft for only a split second before his mouth closed over her clit and his fingers filled her, stabbing deeply into her sex.

She cried out as he relentlessly brought her to climax, stealing her breath as she shouted out words of love and passion. Her climax came, not from her body, but from her soul.

Wrung out, her muscles unlocked and she collapsed to the table, but he wasn't finished. Strong arms scooped her up and the room twirled as she was carried to the bed. He placed her on her tummy, parted her thighs and filled her once more.

His cock drove into her as his body covered her like a hot blanket. His arms stretched over hers, extending them far above her head. Flesh to flesh, they rocked into the bedding as his cock pulsed and heat flooded her folds. He held her so tight, her entire being pinned to this earth by his touch, and her body rejoiced.

There was no escaping and no desire to. He covered her so completely it was as though he were imprinting his soul onto hers.

"I love you, Becca." His lips pressed into her shoulder as her heart thundered within her chest.

"I love you more," she rasped, her voice raw from spent passion. "I can't live without you. When you're not a part of my day to day life I'm dead inside."

They stayed there for a long time and never once did she mind his weight. He wasn't crushing her, merely holding her, the way only he could. The pressure of his body over hers was the greatest comfort in the world. And then she started to cry.

At the first sniffle, he withdrew and rolled to his side, pulling her face to his. "Why are you crying, angel?"

"I hurt you. I'm so sorry, Braydon. I never meant to. I only wanted to make sure I was doing the right thing. I worry so much about messing things up for Hunter. I didn't want to be selfish, parts of me thought I was being selfless—letting you go. I'd gambled my future once before and lost. You own so much more of me than he ever did. If I lost you…it would break me in ways I'm not sure I could mend. But I was losing you anyway by trying to play it safe. I guess you've always had me. The moment I fell for you my heart was decided, but my mind still had fears to overcome. I'm yours, Braydon. I'm gambling on us with everything I've got, because without you I feel like I'm not really living. You bring me to life."

He pulled her close, hugging her tightly and sighed. "It's okay to be selfish every once in a while, Becca. You make me feel alive too. Without you, I have nothing."

"I just wanted to do right by my son without hurting anyone in the process. It took me a while to realize I'm a better parent when I'm happy. You make me happy."

"No one's getting hurt. Stop worrying and trust your gut, angel. I'm a safe bet, because I've never wanted anything more than to give us the life I know we deserve, the three of us, together. Let me take care of you. I think I'm good at it."

"I think you are too. No one's ever taken care of me the way you do. I'm speaking of an emotional level, Braydon. You see my inner self more than anyone else ever has."

He smiled. "You take care of me too. You fill something inside of me that's empty and hurts when you're gone. It's like you're the missing piece to my puzzle. I'll never take advantage of your kind nature or Hunter's. I swear. I know I'm not his birth father, but I think I'd make a pretty good stepdad someday."

Her heart swelled with such intense emotion she began to cry again. "He said your name."

He stilled, his lips parting in awe. "When?"

"The other night. I was crying and he said your name as though he knew the mere mention of you would make me happy." A tight smile pressed her lips. "He was right. No one makes me happier than you."

"Wow." He shook his head, clearly understanding the magnitude of such an occurrence. "I finally understand what you meant when you described his victories as yours. My man...I want to hug him right now." He shook his head again and quietly admitted, "I didn't expect that, but to know that he knows who I am and feels something so positive when he thinks of me...it's incredible, Becca. I don't have anything to compare a gift like that to."

"I know." She did know. "Braydon?"

"Yeah." He was still reeling.

"I've been thinking about family a lot lately."

His gaze drifted to hers. "Me too."

This was going to be difficult. For so many years she'd

submerged herself in other things to hide the pain of being denied more children. Somewhere along the line, fear had crowded her dreams, smothered her hope with doubt. The initial concerns coming more from Kevin than her, but he'd slowly convinced her she was not meant to have more children. Resurrecting that dream was frightening for a multitude of reasons, but it was a good frightening.

"When I was a little girl, I always dreamed of having a big family. I hated being an only child, and I never wanted my children to suffer the loneliness I did."

"But something changed your mind."

"Not something. A lot of things." She swallowed. "I had concerns after Hunter was born, but not enough to change my hopes of eventually giving him brothers and sisters, siblings that would love him as unconditionally as I do. Kevin felt differently. In his eyes, we'd failed. He believed it was selfish to overburden ourselves when Hunter's needs already overshadowed so much of our marriage. The meetings, the doctor appointments, the ongoing research, none of that ever bothered me, because it was all part of being a parent. The day Hunter was diagnosed Kevin decided we shouldn't have any more children. I was crushed."

"I think having Hunter has proven how suited you are for parenting, Becca. And his diagnosis doesn't define him. The issue isn't Hunter's inability to be the child Kevin expected. It's Kevin's inability to be the parent Hunter needed. No child's easy one hundred percent of the time. Any good parent realizes that."

Grinning at his comprehension, she considered what an incredible listener Braydon was. He had an immense capacity for empathy. That was probably one of his most attractive traits.

"As Hunter got older, my job as a mother became more challenging. It was extremely difficult not comparing my son to other kids his age. The year he learned to walk I was so happy, but at the same time so worried about how exhausted I had become. I was so rundown and Kevin started pulling away more and more. It occurred to me that maybe I didn't have the strength for more children, no matter how much I wanted them. Eventually, I stopped hoping for more babies and feared accidentally getting pregnant. I don't think my mind changed because of Hunter, but because my partner had somehow vanished. It's a process trusting in others when those you depended on most let you down."

"Are you still afraid?"

"Yes. There are always fears when it comes to parenthood. But I'm starting to realize a lot of my fear stemmed from Kevin's views and behaviors, not mine. I don't want fear to be the deciding factor in my life. I want the courage to hope and dream, because without hope there really isn't any point to living."

He smiled. "You want more?"

Pressing her lips tight, she gave a small nod. "You make me hopeful, Braydon. I know I freaked out when we forgot protection that time, but we were still in the beginning stages of our relationship. I had uncertainties to work through. I know now you're the person I'm meant to be with in this life and with you… Well, I think it would be lovely to have a family with you."

His hands cupped her face and he kissed her. "I think Hunter would enjoy having some younger siblings. How many should we give him? Three? Four? Six?"

Her face dropped. "Whoa. Let me take a breath. How about we try for one and see how that goes?"

"But Hunter's older. The little guy's gonna need a buddy. Let's shoot for two and if God blesses us with more we'll count ourselves lucky."

Her heart fluttered with rekindled enthusiasm. "Okay," she softly agreed.

"What about moving?"

"I told Kevin I'm selling the house. I don't want to live there anymore. It isn't a happy place for me. The memories aren't pleasant, aside from a few precious ones. I'd like to start over—with you."

"Lucky for you, I have the perfect place for new beginnings. All that's missing is the key to my future." He kissed her nose and whispered, "That's you, angel. You and Hunter."

"I do need to talk to Kevin again. I want to give him one more chance to be the bigger person and negotiate our situation in a civilized manner before I'm forced to take him to court."

"I'm coming with you. He pulls any shit and I'll deal with him."

"Braydon."

"What? I'm done playing games. You're a grown woman and I'm sick and tired of him getting in the way of your happiness. He either steps aside and lets you move on or I move him."

She smirked. "I like this aggressive side of you."

"Good, because I'm done passively waiting around for things to go my way. I know what I want and I'm taking it. Anyone gets in my way…they'll regret it."

She kissed his nose where a small mark showed from when she hit him with the bible. "My tough mountain man."

He growled and rolled on top of her. "And you're going to be my sexy mountain woman. I can't wait."

Neither could she.

CHAPTER 17

After convincing Nikki they'd talked out all their issues and then some, she finally gave up the code to the safe. Carla picked them up as planned and dropped them off at Becca's where Braydon decided to stay for a few weeks until they ironed out all the kinks and made arrangements for the move.

They faced Kevin the following weekend and Braydon proved to be a logical asset and diplomat. Kevin had immediately gone on the offensive when they asked him to sit down and talk.

"What's this about?" he asked, crossing his arms and ignoring the seat offered.

"We need to discuss our arrangement. The house is listed and I'd like to have a fair plan regarding Hunter's situation before we involve the courts," Becca explained.

Braydon cleared his throat. "We're giving you the chance to voice any realistic concerns so they can be addressed amicably, Kevin. It benefits no one to go into a situation like this as adversaries."

"I don't see how this concerns you," Kevin said snidely.

Becca spoke before Braydon had the chance. "It concerns him, because he *will* be a part of our son's day to day life. The moment you accept that the easier this will be for everyone, including Hunter."

Kevin drew in a slow breath and stared at the wall. When he exhaled, his body stiffly lowered into a kitchen chair. "Tell me how you see this working, though I'm doubtful there's a solution here that benefits *all* of us."

Braydon and Becca sat in the chairs across from him. "We aren't trying to start a war here, Kevin. The goal is for us to work as a team."

Her ex-husband shrugged indifferently. "I still want to see my son every other weekend."

Becca nodded. "Okay. I think that would make Hunter very happy."

He turned and frowned. "You do realize how far Center County is, Rebecca."

"I do. I also believe his time with his father is worth the drive. We can figure out a mid-point to meet on your weekends. There will be times Braydon and I will be returning to the city and we can plan visits in relation to Hunter's schedule whenever possible."

"You're also welcome to visit Center County," Braydon added.

Kevin appeared skeptical, but Becca went on. "You'll always be included in holidays and birthdays where Hunter's concerned. It was never my intension to deprive you of those celebrations. Hunter would expect you to be there."

At that, Kevin's opposition seemed to mildly fade. He quietly admitted, "It's going to be a difficult adjustment."

"For all of us," Braydon agreed. "But we want to make it as easy as possible for Hunter. I think the three of us are in agreement about that."

Kevin met his gaze. "You're taking away the two people I love most in this world."

Becca prepared to argue that Kevin had let them go long before Braydon even came into the picture, but Braydon responded first. "It may be cold comfort, but all I can tell you is that I love them too, and I plan to take very good care of them. I think, if you and I aren't enemies, we all have a better shot at success."

Her hand was shaking when she reached under the table and squeezed Braydon's. He was handling this awkward situation extremely well.

"It's a difficult pill to swallow," Kevin admitted. "But, oddly enough, I agree with you. I know you're not the enemy, Braydon. You're just the guy living the life I expected. I'm not your biggest fan, but I'm man enough to acknowledge you care for my son. I believe you genuinely do."

"I do."

Kevin let out a long breath. "Then there really isn't anything I can do. I already lost one person. I won't lose him too. Maybe—with some adjusting—we could actually make this work."

"We can," Becca promised. They had to.

Once Kevin had a more positive attitude, their transition took a smoother course. He was accommodating enough to take Hunter the following week. It seemed, now that the move was imminent, Kevin understood how valuable every second with their son was. Braydon handled a lot of the scheduling and miraculously, Kevin appeared more than willing to assist.

They had an appointment before the judge in a month to adapt their custody agreement, but in the end, Kevin seemed to accept the situation. He'd have Hunter two weekends a month, much like he did now, and during certain holidays. On the holidays he was without their son, he was welcome to join them on the Mountain. It would be a lot of commuting, but Becca knew she'd be back to visit Carla and Nikki often.

On moving day Becca was a mess. It was impossible to plan for a home she'd never seen. While her friends had pushed for her and Braydon to find their happy ending, they threw a tantrum when they realized there would be no more impromptu office visits or midweek lunches together. In the end, they cried over a box of Fritz's brownies—compliments of her man—and planned ahead for weekend visits.

She and Braydon spent the last night boxing up all of Hunter's toys, but Braydon kept suggesting she leave older items behind. "But what if he needs that?"

"We can come back if you decide you want it, but let's get there first, Becca."

Her house was listed, but they had some time before showings would be scheduled. Luckily her best friend was handling the sale. She supposed leaving a few items behind wouldn't hurt.

Becca had no doubt she'd be overwhelmed enough moving into a new home. She couldn't wait to see what Braydon designed. If anything, Braydon was good at his job. She'd seen his work from a commercial standpoint, but she couldn't imagine what sort of home he'd design for himself.

Secretly, she hoped it wasn't filled with the steely grays and cold metals he tended to lean toward in his apartment. She liked color and so did Hunter. There would definitely be some compromising ahead.

They rented a U-Haul and towed the van to Center County. It was convenient that Braydon's car was already at his parents'.

She was anxious from the minute they left, to the minute they pulled into town. At the base of the mountain, Braydon stopped the truck and faced her. "You ready?"

She snorted. "No."

The corner of his mouth kicked up. "Yeah, there's no preparing for this sort of thing." He held her hand. "Let's go."

As the large truck made a sluggish chug up the mountain she fidgeted. Her nerves jangled with such unrest she was surprised she didn't throw up. Everything looked different because there was so much more snow weighing down the trees and covering the ground. The roads were mostly plowed leaving large drifts on the shoulders.

The sweet scent of burning wood streaming from nearby chimneys comforted her in an odd nostalgic way. As they turned onto the road Maureen had stopped her from walking down, she held her breath. This was it. She was finally turning that corner, venturing down the path of her future—all the while holding Braydon's hand just as she was meant to be.

The truck made slow progress. Steep drifts buffeting the edge of the forest. It was so different from the city. Tread marked the path as they worked their way through the white slush.

A large Victorian mansion blocked her view. She leaned forward, trying to recall which relative lived there. "Are they our closest neighbors?"

He laughed and pulled the truck close to a snow bank and shut the engine. "Nope. That's your new home, angel."

Whipping her head around, she gaped. There was no way he built that.

"What do you think?" he asked, his own anxiousness showing.

"This can't be it."

His laughter turned nervous. "What do you mean? Of course it is. Do you like it?"

"Braydon…" There were no words.

Snow covered shingles followed neat peaks up to various angles of the roof. Paned windows, crisp and white, shined in the sun. There was a large wrap around porch and a copula with a copper soffit. The siding was cheery yellow with black shutters, much like the house she'd admired in town, but prettier. Moldings framed each crown with impeccable attention to detail. It was absolutely stunning and they were going to break it the second they stepped foot inside.

"Tell me you at least like the color."

She couldn't take her eyes off of it. It was so picturesque. "Braydon, it's *too* nice. How did you manage to build this in such short time?"

"I poured the foundation the week after Thanksgiving. Like anything else, I started from the ground up and looked to family and friends for the help I've always been able to count on."

She laughed. It was a short puff of breath she couldn't contain. Swallowing did nothing to bring moisture to her dry throat.

"Come on. I'll show you around."

When he came around the truck to her door she still hadn't moved or blinked or even breathed much. He took her hand and lifted her down. Though she didn't measure love by material things, this mammoth structure of beauty represented how committed he was to them. Like the foundation, he'd cemented himself in their life, offered strength and shelter and a safe place to belong. The meaning of such a grand gesture pierced her heart, opening up flutters of hope and spilling out all the hidden faith she held in this amazing man.

Guiding her through the snow to the gate at the fence, he held her shoulders and stood at her back. His voice was soft as he whispered. "When we first see something we enjoy, we experience lust. I remember the first time I saw you. You were so beautiful and innocent and nervous. I never expected to find everything I've found in you, but it was there all along. I just had to dig under the surface a bit and convince you to let me in. Everything about you seemed so perfect at first glance, angel, but as I got to know you, it was the wonderful imperfections that made me fall irrevocably in love with you.

"It's a pretty house. Go ahead and lust for a minute." His hand slid over her jacket and rested above her pounding heart. "But I intend to make you love it, not because it's pretty, but because of all the hidden treasures inside."

She turned and hugged him fiercely. The house was beyond lovely and pristine in a way that intimidated her. But that wasn't why she hugged him. No. She hugged him because no one had ever felt so strongly about her. Of course she loved him, but the way he loved her, it was euphoric and tangible, like a slow awakening from her hazy reality. Today was the beginning of the rest of her life. A happy life. And she couldn't wait to move forward with him.

Her gaze searched his blue eyes. "I love you, Braydon. Those words seem so small compared to what I'm feeling right now. Thank you."

"Love me, angel. That's all I need. Just love me."

Pressing up on her toes, she kissed him. This man, this incredible man, was perhaps the best thing that ever happened to her. So long as she had Hunter and Braydon by her side, it seemed all the worry and fear didn't quite matter, because they filled her with more hope than she'd ever thought possible.

Taking a deep breath, she turned and looked back at the masterpiece he'd created. There was no way it would always look as neat and perfect, not once they settled in. Poor Braydon probably had plans to decorate it with fancy, little, breakable knick-knacks that wouldn't survive the first burst of Hunter's energy. But she loved him for his efforts. Loved him so much it should probably be illegal.

"Do you want to see the inside?"

She did, but she didn't. He was so happy. She could read all the expectation in his eyes. It was a lot to live up to. "Please."

She pulled at the gate, but it didn't budge. "It's stuck."

"It's coded." He flipped open a hidden hatch and exposed a keypad. "The number's three seventeen."

Glancing at him curiously, she asked, "Three seventeen?"

"St. Paddy's Day. March seventeenth."

She laughed and punched in the code. A tiny red light flashed green and the locking mechanism released. "That's amazing. Where did you even find something like that?"

"You'd be surprised what you can find when you really want to keep those you love safe."

This was going to be a lot harder than she anticipated. If Braydon thought ahead enough to install safety locks, he probably thought of other things that were going to embed him further in her heart. She braced herself as they stepped onto the wraparound porch. There wasn't a keyhole on the door. Rather, another hidden keypad.

"All of the codes can be updated. There's an app I'll put on your phone. It lets you monitor the house and alerts you the second the security system's breached."

Yup. She was a speechless goner.

He typed in another code and the door opened a crack. "Ready?"
Nope. She nodded.

They entered into a large foyer painted a vibrant shade of coriander blue. The carpet was soft with a hypnotic pattern. It looked nothing like what she expected, mostly because she wasn't expecting more than sheet-rocked walls and unfinished floors.

"Oh my God."

His face split with a prize-winning grin. "Hunter likes to make tracks with his trains. I figured he should have a permanent one."

It was difficult to breathe. On the wall was a large, framed picture of her tree that had been cut down. She gasped. "Where did you get this?"

"I took it with my phone and had it blown up. The frame's bolted to the wall at each corner and the glass is plexi so it won't shatter if it gets bumped."

Her jaw nearly hit the floor. Brushing her fingers lightly over the photo, she blinked back tears, but her vision didn't clear. Wiping her eyes, she faced him. "I don't know how many more surprises I can handle. You've thought of so much and we've barely made it through the door."

He kissed her brow. "Let me show you the playroom. I think you'll like it."

They stepped into a dark room and the floor felt squishy beneath her feet. Braydon went to a wall and flipped a switch. Pink light traveled through a pillar in the corner. It was like a lava lamp filled with tiny racing bubbles.

He flipped another switch and a fish tank built into the far wall illuminated. "I thought Hunter would wanna help choose the fish."

The walls weren't painted one color, but several. Each bright shade swirled around objects and wheels that were bolted into place. There were soft beanbag chairs and pillows in all the primary colors. A school would be fortunate to have such a multisensory room.

"How did you do this?"

"I had some help, but once I knew what I was looking for I went a little crazy."

She went to the window and brushed her fingers lightly over the simple café curtains sewn in a bright red. "Café curtains."

"Watch this." He played with the security device on the wall and the mechanism beeped. As he slid open the window, cold winter air rushed in. "These curtains are made to dance in the breeze. Try to push your hand through the screen."

She pressed on the screen and it didn't budge. "What are they made of?"

"They're incredible, right? They can't be punctured. Every window in the house has them."

She turned and paced in a circle, then dropped into a plush chair with no hard edges. He frowned and kneeled beside her. "You okay?"

Lips pressed tight, she shook her head and sucked in a jagged breath. "No one's ever cared this much. I don't know how to process it."

"You have years to process. Right now just experience it."

She gripped his arm and squeezed. "Braydon…I'm the only person who ever loved my son enough to *try* to see the world through his eyes. You've somehow designed all of this from his perspective." She gave a watery laugh. "This is incredible. *You* are incredible."

"It's my job to know the people I'm designing for. Luckily, I know you guys by heart." He had the grace to blush. "And, in all fairness, I'm trying to convince you this is where you belong. I may have gone a little overboard, but I had a blast designing it. Don't cry. I want you to see the rest."

The kitchen was phenomenal. Child safety locks in all the right places and matching kitchen chairs. The bathrooms were enormous and already equipped with similar objects and water toys they had at their old house.

Becca was grateful to see Braydon had also incorporated parts of the house that catered specifically to him. It was after all *his* home. He'd designed a sleek and beautiful office as well as a man cave in the basement, which he said was for him and his brother's to drink, curse, and play cards without repercussions. It was clear he'd thought of everything.

"Go through that door," he said, gesturing to a nondescript entrance.

The room was painted completely white and Hunter's formulas were all there, scribbled on the walls. "How did you do this?"

"Sheilagh did this part. I emailed her pictures of Hunter's formulas and she copied them exactly. Everything's dry erase. He can even write on the floors."

Was it possible for someone's heart to burst from too much joy?

Too many wonderful emotions were bombarding her at the same time.

"I want to show you one more room, then I'll show you ours."

They returned downstairs and Braydon faced two pocket doors, grinning over his shoulder. "You'll love this." As he parted the doors she followed him into the room, her footsteps echoing.

No. It was simply too much.

A grand piano sat open in the center of the room. Cathedral ceilings reached to the highest point of the house. She stepped close and ran her palm over the pristine, white instrument. It was a piano suitable for the greatest musicians. "Where did you get this?"

"It was my sister's. There's some history to that piano. First, it was my Aunt Colleen's. She gave it to Kate when she was seven. We used it for Luke and Tristan's wedding, and now the family's passing it on to Hunter. It'll be nice to hear it played again."

Her face crumpled under the weight of so much gratitude. "Your family...I've never known such generosity. They all helped you with this?"

"That's what family does. My dad built the cabinets. Luke and Tristan did all the tile work. Mallory and Ashlynn filled the kitchen with groceries. Kelly supplied plenty of liquor and there's something else he gave us upstairs. Finn did all the moldings and Sammy was a godsend when it came to my unending questions."

"They're remarkable." How had she ever considered this to be the wrong choice?

Braydon showed her his home office and Hunter's bedroom. Once they visited every room, he took her upstairs to what seemed to be the final surprise, their bedroom.

His hand perched on the nickel knob and he faced her. "I'm so happy you're finally here."

Happy didn't begin to catalogue what she was feeling. "Me too."

The door opened and she gasped. A four-poster bed, adorned with gossamer white linen was the centerfold of the monochromatic room. Plush carpet, in the softest shade of ivory cushioned her steps as she moved forward, enchanted.

It was the room she'd described to him, her sophisticated space done all in white, complete with a snow colored fainting couch. She never wanted to leave.

"What do you think?"

"I think it's impossible for any man to pay that much attention to detail. Braydon, it's...I don't even have words to describe it. How did you do this? You took an image from my mind and made it real."

"Look over here. Remember I told you that Kelly gave us something else?" He turned her shoulders and she gasped at the portrait on the wall.

"Where did he get that?"

"He drew it. Isn't it amazing?"

"Yes, but when?"

Braydon shrugged. "After Thanksgiving. It's from the night at the bar, right after we said I love you for the first time."

It was an incredible drawing. The shading was so precise it could easily be mistaken for a black and white photograph. In the image, Braydon's forehead pressed to hers as they smiled into one another's eyes. "He *drew* that? It's breathtaking."

"Come sit with me. I wanna tell you a story."

She needed to sit. This was possibly the most overwhelming day of her life, and that was saying a lot. Settling beside him on the beautiful bed, she took a deep breath.

"When my parents were younger, my dad carved their initials into a tree. After they eloped, he cut down that tree. It's now a part of the big house. If you're ever in their bedroom, you can see their initials, right where he carved them over forty years ago."

Her chest softened at the romantic tale. "That's so sweet."

He squeezed her hand. "Come with me."

"Where are we going?"

"Outside."

Downstairs he helped her on with her coat. They went through the farm door in the kitchen to the backyard. The ground was covered with an untouched blanket of snow. In the center stood a baby elm.

"I planted you a new tree."

"Braydon." Emotion overwhelmed her.

"I carved something in it."

The snow crunched under their feet as he took her hand and walked her to the tree. There in the center, stood their initials. Her fingers brushed over the letters. "This is the most romantic thing I've ever seen."

"How about this?" He walked her around the tree and on the other side of the trunk was the words *Marry me.*

Yup. Hands down the most unbelievably romantic man to ever walk the face of the earth. Her lips pressed tight as she nodded through tears of happiness. Forcing her voice past the constriction in her throat, she whispered, "Yes."

His eyes creased as he kissed her. Whispering close to her lips, he asked, "You'll marry me? Really?"

She nodded, unable to get another word past the lump in her throat.

"That's a yes?" he asked again.

Sniffling, she bobbed her head and gave a soggy chuckle. "That's a yes."

He kissed her and she wept with joy, laughing at the puddle of emotion she'd become, her lips curved into an unbreakable smile. When he pulled away, he shouted, *"She said yes!"*

Becca jumped as a roar of applause and screams came from behind. Jumping she spotted what had to be nearly one hundred smiling people. Were they *all* McCulloughs? Her jaw dropped as they crowded in, shocking the crap out of her, and offering congratulations and hugs.

"Get out of my way, people! He's my bloody son!" Maureen bustled to the front of the mob and grinned, her green eyes shimmering with unshed tears. "There's my prince." Holding out her arms, Braydon went in for what looked like the greatest hug in the world. "Don't just stand there, Becca. Get your arse over here and hug me!"

She trudged through the snow until Maureen's arms gobbled her up. She kissed Becca's head and whispered, "I'm so happy for you two. All my babies have finally found the loves of their lives. I'll take you off my list now."

"Your list?"

Maureen waved her question away and squeezed.

Becca feared seeing the family again would be awkward after what she'd put Braydon through, but it seemed the McCulloughs were an endless well of understanding, taking great measures to welcome the good and forgive the bad.

Braydon's expression was elated. "Thanks, mum."

"Congratulations, son," Braydon's father said, a soft grin on his face.

Bray hugged his father and Becca heard Frank tenderly say, "I knew you could do it," just before he kissed his son's head.

The following minutes were spent twirling from one set of arms to the next. There were so many of them. When she recognized two high-pitched screams she turned and screamed as well. Nikki and

Carla came barreling at her, not stopping until they knocked her right into the snow. "You're getting married!"

"I can't believe it!" Nikki said.

"I can," Carla argued. "I knew you two were meant to be. Touched my cold romantic heart, not easily penetrated."

A shadow crossed over them. "Well, well, what do we have here? Nothing like three women rolling around in the snow."

Becca smiled at Kelly. "Hi Kelly. Hi Ashlynn."

Carla's attention jerked to Kelly's wife. "Ashlynn?"

Ashlynn smiled, her short, pixie like hair catching the sun and giving her an angelic appearance despite her flannel coat and hefty snow boots. "You must be Carla. Kelly's mentioned you."

Her friend's eyes went wide. "He did?"

Ashlynn nodded. "I thought it would be nice to introduce you to Kelly's cousin, Ryan. He's very handsome and happens to be single."

Becca's lips pursed into a tight smile. It was clear Ashlynn had a good sense of humor and a forgiving heart. It was also clear that Kelly had no secrets from his wife.

Carla shoved herself off the ground. "I like single. Is he a McCullough?"

"He's a Cloony," Kelly said. "But he's a hot blooded one, full of O'Leahy spirit from my mum's side of the family."

"Well, what are we waiting for?" Carla asked, grinning and brushing the snow off her clothes. She looped her arm through Ashlynn's as though they were old friends.

The horde moved into the house where Kelly cracked open some of the liquor he'd supplied. Everyone raved about the house and as the whiskey bottles emptied the laughter followed. Mallory and Ashlynn—once she'd successfully distracted Carla—offered plenty of warnings about McCullough weddings. "The aunts will make you insane, but the men make up for it, because they all wear kilts," Mallory warned with a wink.

The aunts, Colleen and Rosemarie, overheard their names and sidled into the conversation. "You'll not have to lift a finger, dearie. Like true clansmen, the groom and his kin come dressed in tartan with nothin' but a breeze and their *bagpipe* under their kilts. You'll be needed to save your strength for the honeymoon," Rosemarie teased.

"That's the truth!" Colleen laughed.

At some point, when the liquor had gone to everyone's head, it began to set in that she was actually getting married again. Becca sensed this time would be different. This time, she was madly in love with the groom and he happened to be one of the most honorable men she'd ever met.

Three things were for sure. One, the new Becca would have no regrets. Two, Becca McCullough sounded much better than Becca Stevens, especially when the word McCullough represented love and family, something she'd gone too long without. And three, she was definitely having smurf sex tonight.

A glass clanked, drawing everyone's attention. Luke stood, holding his beverage high and wearing a great smile on his face. "Eyes up here, maniacs."

When he had everyone's attention, he winked at her. "First, I'd like to congratulate Bray and Becca for finally getting their shit together." He tipped his glass toward his brother. "Bray, you built an incredible home. It's almost as beautiful as your future wife. I hope these walls hold many happy memories for you and our new family, Becca and Hunter."

Everyone cheered, and Luke remained standing. "I'm not finished. Since it's almost impossible to get all of us together at once, I figured I'd seize the opportunity and borrow a little of my brother's thunder. You don't mind, do you, Bray?"

Braydon raised his glass in good spirits. "Have at it." It was apparent how much he adored each of his siblings.

Luke nodded and returned his attention to his enormous family. "As most of you have already heard, Tristan and I were turned down for adoption." Everyone booed. "But when God shuts a door he opens another. Pennsylvania *finally* passed the vote and next week I'll be making an honest man out of him."

The room erupted in applause. Braydon beamed at Becca. There was so much joy within the house she felt as though her home was being christened.

"One more thing," Luke announced. "I'm sure it's no surprise that Sheilagh is plastered and it's not even dark yet."

"Whooooooo," Sheilagh cheered with a delayed, "Hoo!"

Alec hugged her close and signaled Luke to continue with a nod. Luke's smile turned contemplative. He actually looked on the verge of tears, which quickly silenced the room. When he spoke again, the room was still.

"We've all had an incredible past few years. I consider us beyond lucky, because through all of it, the good, the bad, and the ugly, we remained a family. Sammy, Mallory, Ashlynn, Alec, Becca...Tristan, you complete our family. It took me a long time to understand how deep the love of family goes, but I've looked and decided it's unending."

"Here! Here!" someone shouted.

"The last few weeks were trying for many of us. Everyone here has fought some sort of battle, and in those moments, when all seems lost, we somehow find each other and new solutions present themselves. That's what family is all about."

He turned to his sister. "Devil, will you come up here?"

Sheilagh stumbled to her feet, her face a radiant rosy pink. She smiled and skipped over to Luke who wrapped his arm around her shoulders and gave an affectionate squeeze. "Are you enjoying yourself, Devil?"

"When do I not enjoy myself, Luke?"

"Should you tell them or should I?"

"I think Tristan should do the honors."

Everyone looked to Tristan, who wiped under his eyes before standing and joining the others. "Family," he greeted in a thick Texan draw. "Alec, you wanna get up here?"

Becca leaned over and whispered to Braydon. "What's going on?"

"I have no idea."

Alec joined the others and together they faced the room anxiously waiting to find out what this was about.

"Well," Tristan began. "As it turns out, we had two goals today. One, to wrangle Becca into saying yes to Braydon, and, two, getting She-Devil nice and drunk. You see, after next week she won't be able to drink for some time."

Becca frowned. What were they talking about?

"After much discussion and careful consideration," Alec took over. "My wife has consented to be a surrogate. We know it's not the traditional way of doing things, but that's how things seem to work in this family. Next week Sheilagh and Tristan will be seeing a specialist and if everything goes accordingly, this time next year we may be welcoming another McCullough to the clan."

Becca gasped and everyone started talking at once. Sheilagh stepped forward.

"Quiet!" she shouted, demanding everyone's attention once more. "The embryo will be part of me and part of Tristan, but the child will be all of ours. He or she will have a hyphenated name and, of course…" Her teeth flashed with a grin of pure elation. *"We're moving to the mountain!"*

Everyone jumped to their feet and cheered. Ashlynn, Sammy, and Mallory raced to Sheilagh and squealed as they swallowed her in a group hug. Becca's heart pinched at such a show of love.

Braydon took her hand and squeezed. She slowly appraised the people filling the room. Frank smiled into Maureen's eyes as he wiped away her tears and she laughed with unveiled joy.

Tristan brushed a hand lovingly down Luke's face and smiled. They turned to Sheilagh and hugged her, then Alec. The two couple's approached them.

Luke smiled. "Bray, we know you spent a fortune on this house to get it perfect, which, of course, you nailed."

"He is the golden son," Sheilagh teased and Braydon blushed.

"Well," Luke continued, "we have an offer for you."

His brows perked up. "I'm listening."

Alec grinned. "Sheilagh and I would like you to build us a house—"

"Right next to ours," Tristan added.

"With an adjoining nursery," Luke explained. "Sort of an en suite set up. We know it's different, but we all agree you're the guy to make it flow and think of all the details we might overlook."

Becca thought it was a brilliant idea. Braydon's smile widened. "I'm honored. I'd love to build something like that for you guys. But what about Alec's job in Princeton?"

Alec kissed Sheilagh's cheek. "I'll still be a professor at the college, but I'll be running the online philosophy courses now, only traveling to New Jersey on an as needed basis."

They seemed to have everything planned. Braydon affectionately whacked his brother on the shoulder and pulled him and Sheilagh into a hug. "I'm really happy for you guys."

Luke met Becca's gaze and said, "We're happy for you too."

She nodded, overwhelmed by the family's welcome. As they continued to discuss future plans for the next house Braydon would be building on the mountain, her attention snagged on Finn. He approached Mallory, arms weighed down with laughing children, pure worship in his eyes. Pressing a kiss to his wife's lips, Finn laughed and pulled his family into a group hug as the little ones squirmed and giggled.

Tallulah chased baby Liam as he ran for shelter between Sammy's legs, interrupting Colin as he attempted to kiss his wife.

They laughed and scooped up the children, tousling their hair lovingly.

Kate's kids dashed around the house as Anthony smiled at his preoccupied wife and slowly walked to her, surprising her with a slow kiss. She melted in his arms and the evident affection they shared took Becca's breath away.

Kelly passed Nate to Sheilagh who blew raspberries into the baby's tummy. He then snatched his wife's hand, a mischievous gleam in his blue eyes, and raced out of the crowded room with Ashlynn skipping behind him.

In the corner Italian Mary spoke softly to Braydon's grandmother as she helped her into a chair. The gentle assistance spoke of timeless friendship and priceless tenderness.

The aunts cackled and teased the uncles as the cousins congratulated the soon to be parents. There wasn't a single face in the room without a smile.

This was family. This was love. This was McCullough Mountain.

"You okay?" Braydon whispered, stealing her attention from the unforgettable display unfolding around her.

She nodded, her eyes weepy with more joy than she'd ever experienced. "I love this."

"I love you. Only one thing's missing."

Yes. Hunter should have been there.

Braydon checked his phone and grinned. "He'll be here in a little bit."

Her heart jumped in surprise. "What?"

Braydon smiled. "It's his home too. I wanted him here, but I also wanted to show you the house first. I arranged everything with Kevin and he'll be dropping him off in about an hour. We'll get everyone cleared out by then so things are peaceful, and then we'll welcome him to his new home."

She wasn't sure if a heart could break from happiness, but hers was so tight in that moment she feared it might burst like a star turning into a supernova, more brilliant than a thousand suns and powerful enough to outshine an entire universe. That's what he did to her.

For years, time passed with tears, but with Braydon, moments went by in brilliant flashes of joy. The tears had gone by and now the sun was finally shining as if to say there would be no more rain.

She took Braydon's face in her hands and smiled up into his incredible eyes, so full of vitality and ideals. "Thank you. Somewhere along the line I forgot heroes existed in real life, but you reminded me. You saved me from myself, Braydon. I can't imagine my life without you. I just wish there were words for how much you make me feel."

His forehead pressed to hers as he whispered, "You don't need to explain it, angel. I feel it too. It's messy, unconditional love." And with that, he leaned close and kissed her deeply.

EPILOGUE

"Fourteen chocolate chips!" Hunter shouted, his smiling face smeared with melted chocolate.

"I thought there were sixteen," Braydon said, flipping the pancake on the griddle.

Hunter rocked and gave a hardy laugh. "I ate two."

Braydon smiled at him, head over heels for the delightful ray of light Hunter was in their world. "Okay, we're ready for the next one."

Braydon's hand curved over Hunter's as he lifted the ladle full of batter and carefully poured the next pancake onto the griddle.

"Careful hot," Hunter warned.

"Right. It's hot so let's be careful," Braydon agreed.

They were still settling into the house, but Hunter had made the transition beautifully. He came home every day, energized and full of different experiences from his new school. The family had welcomed Hunter and Becca with open arms, each relative taking the time to get to know them.

At first, he and Becca feared the McCulloughs would overwhelm Hunter, but as it turned out, he was more than capable of adapting to their presence. He even seemed to thrive under all the energy they supplied to his daily life.

Braydon's mum had reintroduced herself to Hunter, as Nanna, and he adored the woman who had once given him blue gloves. With innate affection, his mum managed to slowly breach Hunter's physical limits and they were all amazed at how quickly his tolerance for physical contact began to change. Though Hunter still couldn't be held or hugged, he was learning to tolerate touch, slowly grasping that contact was a show of affection. This moved Becca in immeasurable ways.

"Okay, drop the chocolate chips in. We're about ready to flip this one."

"Only ten, Braydon," Hunter said as he fisted the morsels.

He sent him a sidelong glance and smirked. "You get your sweet tooth from your mother."

"These are my teeth," Hunter said, giving him a cheeky grin.

Once the chocolate chip pancakes were complete, Braydon shut off the griddle and pushed it back on the counter to cool. He carried the plate to the tray waiting on the table, already set with chocolate milk, flowers, and silver wear. "Where's your card, bud?"

Hunter ran into the playroom, his footfalls heavy with excitement. When he returned he held a handmade card. The front showed an origami pinwheel incorporating every color of the spectrum. "Can I see?"

Hunter handed it to him. Pulling the card open, Braydon found a picture inside with three people and a yellow house. "Is this us?"

"Yeah."

He smiled, noting that each person had a heart drawn on their chest. A family. "She'll love this, Hunter. You did great."

"Hearts for Valentine's Day."

Braydon nodded. Hearts for Valentine's Day.

As he carefully carried the tray upstairs, Hunter already bouncing by the bedroom door, he took a moment to let his gratitude sink in.

It seemed like yesterday that he'd come home from college for summer vacation with expectation of his future falling into place like a perfect puzzle. As the years passed, he'd lost a bit of faith in himself and the happy future he'd hoped for. But meeting Becca and Hunter had changed that.

They redefined his purpose, brought him more joy than he ever assumed possible. Though Hunter seemed to embrace their new home, there were still curious moments of silence. Those moments would always be there, but underneath it all would be the foundation of their love and family. Of all the things Braydon could build, *this* was where he defined his pride. Not in a house, but in a home.

And through all the spins and twirls and laughter and tears, he'd come to understand that, sometimes, love spoke without words, and if one listened to the silence they could catch glimpses of all the colors that painted the world as an exceptionally beautiful place.

Giving Hunter a nod, he whispered, "Let's wake her up."

The End

If you enjoyed CONTROLLED CHAOS, you will love HARD FIX, the next story in the McCullough Mountain Series.
Skip ahead for a sneak peek inside

Never miss another book release!
Click here to sign up for Lydia Michaels' Newsletter.

Follow Lydia Michaels on Instagram and Facebook!

What to Read Next?
Click here to claim your FREE Book from Lydia Michaels!

Billionaire Romance
Falling In | Sacrifice of the Pawn | Calamity Rayne

Small Town Romance
Wake My Heart | The Best Man | Love Me Nots | Pining For You |
Almost Priest

Emotional Favorites
La Vie en Rose | Simple Man | Wake My Heart | Sacrifice of the
Pawn | Forfeit

Romantic Comedy
Calamity Rayne

Erotic Romance
Breaking Perfect | Protégé | Falling In | Sugar

First Books in Binge Worthy Trilogies and Series
Almost Priest | Falling In | Wake My Heart | Forfeit | Original Sin

Paranormal Vampire Romance
Original Sin | Dark Exodus | Prodigal Son

LGBTQ+ & Menage Romance
Broken Man (MM) | Breaking Perfect (MMF) | Forfeit (MMF) |
Hurt (Non-Consensual) | Protege

Sexy Nerds & Second Chances
Blind | Untied

Teacher Student, Workplace, and Age-Gap Love Affairs... Oh my!

<u>British Professor</u> | <u>Pining For You</u> | <u>Breaking Perfect</u> | <u>Falling In</u> | <u>Sacrifice of the Pawn</u>

Single Dads & Single Moms
<u>Simple Man</u> | <u>Pining For You</u> | <u>First Comes Love</u> | <u>Controlled Chaos</u> | <u>Intentional Risk</u>

Dark Psychological Thriller & Tortured Hero Romance
(TRIGGER WARNING)
<u>Hurt</u>

Non-Fiction Books for Writers
<u>Write 10K in a Day: Avoid Burnout</u>

About the Author

Lydia Michaels is the award winning and bestselling author of more than forty titles. She is the consecutive winner of the 2018 & 2019 *Author of the Year Award* from *Happenings Media,* as well as the recipient of the 2014 *Best Author Award* from the *Courier Times*. She has been featured in *USA Today, Romantic Times Magazine, Love & Lace,* and more. As the host and founder of the *East Coast Author Convention,* the *Behind the Keys Author Retreat,* and *Read Between the Wines,* she continues to celebrate her growing love for readers and romance novels around the world.

In 2021, Michaels released the groundbreaking, non-fiction series, ***Write 10K in a Day,*** to commemorate her career in the publishing industry. She looks forward to many more years of exploring both fiction and non-fiction writing, teaching about the craft, and learning from the others in the author community.

Lydia is happily married to her childhood sweetheart. Some of her favorite things include the scent of paperback books, listening to her husband play piano, escaping to her coastal home at the Jersey Shore, cheap wine, *Game of Thrones,* coffee, and kilts. She hopes to meet you soon at one of her many upcoming events.

You can follow Lydia at <u>www.Facebook.com/LydiaMichaels</u> or on Instagram <u>@lydia_michaels_books</u>

SAMPLE HARD FIX

hen...

"MOVE YOUR ARSE, Maureen, or we're gonna miss it!" Colleen's voice pitched from the school parking lot, her rump balanced on the window of their father's hand-me-down Ford Falcon as her skirts bunched over the mint green door, her other sister, Rosemarie, thumping the horn repetitively as she waited behind the wheel.

"Late for what?" Maureen called, her books weighing down her right arm as she bustled to the car.

"They're takin' O'Malley's!"

Maureen's steps staggered at the fender of the old Ford. "What on earth are you talkin' about? Who's taking it? And where?"

Colleen's beanpole body slithered through the window and the door popped open as she scooted to the other side of the white leather seat. "Liam Cloony, that's who! Now get in!"

As soon as the door shut, Rosemarie gunned the boat of a car into drive. Pedestrians on an unhurried journey scowled and dodged the rambling vehicle in favor of life over death.

"Move your bloody arses, people!" Rosemarie growled from behind the wheel.

"I don't understand," Maureen repeated. "How does someone

take a bar? There isn't far you can take a place cemented to the earth."

"Don't be daft, Maureen," Colleen said, balancing her elbows on the back of the front seat so she could stare out the wide windshield. Whoever gave her sister a driver's license should have been driven to the middle of Center County and shot. Maureen remained safely in the back, her white knuckled grip glued to the handle on the door.

"They aren't takin' it anywhere. They're claimin' it. Liam won it fair and square in a game of poker and it's too good of a price to let go."

"You think Caleb O'Malley is going to just hand him the keys?" They were nuts and Maureen wasn't much in the mood for an Irish brawl.

Colleen's grin was pure evil, her eyes set with dumb love. "That's why Paulie's going."

Maureen rolled her eyes until she saw brain. "You think every Italian has a mob connection. The only thing Paulie Mosconi's good at is pronouncing pasta and doing whatever his mean old mum wants."

"His mum wants him makin' a living for himself," Colleen argued defensively. Chances were she'd end up marrying the poor sot. There wasn't much Colleen wanted that she didn't get.

"Workin' as what, a bar back for Liam?"

"They're going to be partners, isn't that right Rosemarie?"

"I don't know why you're bitchin', Maureen. They get this bar, you'll get served."

That was true, but not something Maureen found remarkably persuasive. True, her sisters were adults, while she was still a seventeen-year-old senior in high school, but there wasn't much they did apart. While some girls went off to finishing school, her father was old fashioned and of the mindset a woman didn't need much more knowledge than how to change a diaper and read a recipe.

It wasn't always fair, but it was all she'd known and after seventeen years, she'd grown used to his dated philosophies. Maureen didn't think herself overly qualified for things outside of the home anyway—nor was she overly motivated to seek higher education.

She wanted one thing and it wasn't part of any curriculum. She wanted to fall in love.

The tires squealed as her sister took the bend and yanked the wheel. Hand over hand, she directed the Falcon into O'Malley's parking lot.

"There's Paulie," Colleen sighed and fluffed the curls of her fiery red hair.

Rosemarie slid the car into a slot and quickly adjusted her breasts in her blouse. They sure did get ridiculous around boys— well, men. Paulie and Liam were close to twenty-five years old, which wasn't too much of a difference considering her sisters were both in their twenties now. As far as age differences went, Maureen sometimes wondered if she were an afterthought or an accident where her parents were concerned.

"Who's that tall guy?" Maureen asked as they climbed out of the car.

Colleen blew a large bubble, the gum sweetening the dry May air. "That's Frank McCullough. He and Paulie are old friends. Good thing he brought him. Frank's built like an ox. Works for his dad up at the lumberyard. Quiet. Sort of dull, but he'll definitely be the muscle we need if Caleb O'Malley tries to pull any shite." She blew another bubble and proceeded to chew like a cow as they approached the trio of men.

Maureen's voice shriveled to something irretrievable and deli- cate, lodged in her chest as she stared at the dark haired man. The dark denim of his Levis almost matched the pressed black cotton of his shirt. The sleeves were bunched and rolled casually up his thickly muscled arms, already tanned in a way that told Maureen he spent a lot of time outdoors.

His collar was open and his neck wore a layer of dark stubble, something unarguably sloppy, but she liked it for reasons she didn't understand. Her classmates didn't have facial hair like that. *This* was a man.

His hair was beyond windblown, a mess of strands flipped and quaffed like a collection of broken blackbird wings. It was atro- cious and unkempt, yet, she couldn't stop covertly admiring it. Her head remained tilted down as she studied him from under her lashes, her body facing Paulie so her attention wasn't too obvious.

He grinned at something Paulie said, but made no comment. While the other's prattled on about the events that brought them there, this man remained silent.

She found herself waiting for the slightest show of emotion. When he finally laughed, her heart seemed to leap into her mouth as her palms suddenly moistened with dewy sweat. His teeth were perfect, his lips full and tanned with the rest of his face. She never saw such rugged beauty. He was like a bear in the wild, gorgeous in his own right, but intense and deserving of space.

Slowly, he turned and Maureen froze as two of the bluest eyes she'd ever seen rested on her. Breath turned hot and heavy in her lungs. With each slow pull she became aware of her breasts pressing against her cheaply made dress. His lips closed over his teeth, hiding his smile as he stared at her. Her mind demanded she look away, but her body was frozen, literally held in place by that intense stare.

The others continued to discuss their plan of overtaking the bar, but this man just stared. His inspection, so unyielding and concentrated, became too much and she snapped her gaze away, severing the connection.

But she still sensed his eyes on her. So many men had come home from the war amputated and her father said some men claimed to still feel what was no longer connected. She felt him, felt the weight of his stare and the strength of his regard. Nothing had ever felt so vacant and so extreme at the same time.

"Let's move," Liam said, his words finally penetrating her bewildered mind.

She turned and frowned as her sisters fell into step after the men. Reaching out, she grabbed Rosemarie's sleeve. "You can't go in there with them. What if there's a fight?"

"Exactly," her sister said grinning. "I don't plan on missin' it. Wait here by the car and beep if you see the constable." She turned and followed the others inside. They disappeared behind a green door and the parking lot was suddenly silent.

Maureen frowned. They were a bunch of imbecilic morons. People didn't win bars in card games. This sort of nonsense was exactly why her father grumbled every time Rosemarie mentioned going out with Liam Cloony. The man was a child who had somehow evaded the war and accomplished absolutely nothing while the others did their time. Yet, Rosemarie adored him.

She'd once told Maureen, *"When I'm good and ready I'll decide it's time for Liam to step up and be a man, and when I do, you can bet your arse his shenanigans will be over. Two things you should understand about life, Maureen. There's divine intervention and then there's the guarantee of really good sex. I'm not God, but I'm certainly no slouch in bed. Liam will do fine."*

Apparently, sex was why men got married, according to her

sisters. Maureen wasn't so sure. Her father had always said a man was incomplete without a wife but once married, he was finished. Her mother was an easy woman, nurturing and always busy. Deep down she believed her father loved her mother very much, but they hardly showed affection. Maureen didn't want that sort of love. She craved a love that was fierce and far too passionate to keep inside. She wanted a love that held fast with bonds too strong to weaken over time.

The doors of the pub burst open and she jumped back a step as two drunkards stumbled out, one wearing a torn shirt, the other walking with a bit of a limp. A ruckus of clattering dishes and shouts sounded and silenced as the doors again closed. Dear lord, they were truly fighting in there.

Glancing at the two men hobbling to their car, she debated. It was illegal for her to enter the bar, but her sisters were in there. "For the love of Christ," she muttered, tossing the keys onto the front seat of the Falcon.

She pressed through the green door. Having never entered a pub before, she wasn't sure what to expect, but certain this was not the norm. As though everything were moving in slow motion or under water, Van Morrison's *Into the Mystic* played deafeningly from a large jukebox in the corner as bodies slammed into tables, knocking over chairs and glasses shattered. The stench of spilt lager tickled her nose.

Something hurled through the air and the shrill echo of her sister's scream caught her attention. Whipping around just in time to duck an oncoming bottle, she gasped and squatted low behind a fallen table.

Her sisters were perched on a pool table, Rosemarie cheering Liam on as he rolled across the floor with Caleb O'Malley. Colleen was shooting off her mouth at some poor bastard that made a grab for her leg and got a good taste of her shoe—the penny of her loafer likely lodged in his throat by now.

"Cops!" someone yelled and the shouting got louder as everyone scramble for the doors.

It was absolute mayhem. Maureen couldn't do more than stare as bloodied men punched with one hand and helped their opponent up with the other as the law came to take them all away. Perhaps it was the lingering taste of war that left them with such a thirst for violence. Perhaps it was simply men being boys.

Van Morrison continued to croon as the pub bore ransacked

markings of a true brawl. Though everyone was angry, they were smiling—bunch of drunken, sodden lots. Didn't they know their bar was being commandeered?

A firm hand closed over her arm and she gasped, prepared to defend herself, but unsure how.

Dark blue eyes held her as his grip tightened. "Come along, lassie, before the constable hauls you away for drinkin' underage."

Breathless, she whispered, "But my sisters—"

"They'll be fine. Liam and Paulie will see to them."

She shouldn't have gone with him, but those eyes of his seemed to cast a spell on her. Over the slap of flesh and the splintering wood, she somehow made out Van Morrison's poetic words of running into the mystic and rocking a gypsy soul and suddenly she was standing, racing through the riffraff and out of O'Malley's—holding none other than Frank McCullough's strong hand.

His fingers swallowed hers as he pulled her close. The heat of his broad chest burned into her shoulders as he guided her out the door. His large palm rested heavily on her lower back and for those few seconds she had no fear of any danger.

Sirens whined in the distance. "My truck's this way," he called as he hauled her toward the back of the lot.

It was an old black Chevy, desperate for a good washing. He beat her to the passenger handle and popped it open. Not giving her a chance to climb inside, her feet left the ground as he quickly deposited her inside the truck and shut the door.

As he opened his door the sirens seemed closer. "We have to move."

The truck roared to life and she breathed in the sweet scent of his clothing, memorizing it, before the fumes of diesel stole the fresh air. There was no chance for talk during the bumpy ride through town. She was too stunned to speak anyway. Soon he was hauling her down an unpaved road she never visited before.

Her mind returned to her sisters, assuming the police were now at the scene asking questions. "Do you think anyone will be arrested?"

"You're not to worry about Rose and Colleen. The police will assume they're innocent on the fact that they're ladies."

She chuckled. "I don't know that Colleen fits that title."

He grinned and disarmed her with a quick glance, those fiery blue eyes burning into her soul. "I believe you're right, but the constable doesn't know her the way we do."

"You know my sister?" It struck her as odd that Colleen would know this man and never mention him. He was far more handsome than Liam or Paulie. Perhaps that was the issue, his attractiveness put him out of reach and therefore not a suitable conquest.

"Aye. I'd be remiss not to know the lassie my best friend plans to wed."

"Paulie's going to marry Colleen?" she nearly barked.

He chuckled, the sound deep and throaty. "If she'll have his sorry arse."

Although her father would be disappointed, there was no doubt in her mind that Colleen would eagerly agree to be Paulie's wife. "When?"

Frank tsked. "Now, what kind of friend would I be if I told you that? If you're anything like your sisters, I'm certain you can't keep a secret for shit."

Her belly tightened and rolled as they took another road she didn't recognize. Something about him was undoing all sorts of neatly kept knots inside of her and making her feel loose and giddy as though she were a feather blowing in the wind.

The question in her mind became too significant to discard. "Do you have a girl—a lassie?"

"No."

His simple answer warned her it was a subject he didn't care to delve into, so she let it drop, sparing only a small wish that she were a bit older. He was perhaps the most handsome man she'd set eyes on, not counting the lads in catalogues and such.

She rarely considered boys. They were childish and unappealing. However, she was only seventeen and far too young to set her sights on a man. Perhaps it was a result of having older sisters and hanging with their older friends that left her with a taste for maturity.

Either way, she'd figured—since Elvis had gotten fat and no longer appealed to her—that she'd worry about meeting a husband once she came of age. Her eighteenth birthday was soon and now that she met Frank McCullough that made her anxious to age faster, as if she could somehow catch up to him.

Straightening her shoulders, she sucked in her tummy and lifted her chest. Casually, she used the fingers of her left hand to wriggle her skirt a bit above the knee and waited for him to take notice.

He pulled into an empty, unpaved lot marked only by a chain

link fence. "We'll wait here for a while until things settle. Then I'll take you back to your sisters."

She looked around seeing nothing but trees and the long run of fence. "Is this private property?" No point in running from the cops only to be arrested for trespassing.

"Yes, but not to worry. It's McCullough property."

"You own this?"

He nodded.

"What is it?"

He studied her for a moment. "How old are you, Maureen?"

It seemed imperative that she form her answer in a mature manner. No seventeen and eleven months type response would do. "I'll be eighteen in July."

He grunted and nodded. "This is my family's lumberyard."

"You work here?" she asked, recalling what her sister knew of him.

"Have since I've been a boy. My dad hasn't been well since the war. With so many men drafted he came back to a mess of issues and needed someone to help him run things." He glanced at her. "You don't want to hear about this."

On the contrary, she was enthralled by the fact that he was speaking to her at all. "No, go on."

He shifted, dragging his thick forearm over the wheel and facing her. It made her feel very important. "My dad enrolled in the military when I was ten, thinking we'd win in no time and he'd return a hero—*if* he ever made it to combat at all. I grew up in the yard, delivering thermoses to my dad and uncles and running their lunches out to them when my mum had it ready. Soon enough they had me climbing trees and marking acres, because there was such a shortage of able men. When my dad deployed for Vietnam my uncles still let me work and as I got older the work got a little more demanding."

"Do you like it?"

"Aye. I love being outside and I like doing something for my family. My mother looked to me as the man of the house since I was merely a boy. I liked that too."

There was pride in his tone, something she respected and filed away as another appealing quality. If anything, Frank McCullough was a capable fellow—no, *man.* He'd been a man far before the law would label him as such, and that was beyond attractive.

"When my father returned he was sick."

"Was he hurt in the war?" So many soldiers had returned home missing limbs and wearing scars.

Frank tapped his head. "Aye. The war hurt his mind. It isn't right for a man to spend so many years staging battles and watching death. As resilient as the human soul is, some scars are permanent. At first I thought he just needed time to acclimate himself to society again." His head shook slowly. "But he'll never be the same. There's a rage inside of him too great to burn out in this lifetime."

"I'm sorry." Once again she suffered her immaturity. Her inability to come up with comforting words left her with a sense of great inadequacy.

His head tilted, setting a dark strand of hair just to the side of his sharp eyebrow. His lashes were so thick she had the urge to run her fingers over them. "You don't have any brother's, do you?"

It was becoming difficult to concentrate on his words, but she desperately wanted to keep their dialogue going. "No. The O'Leahey's are cursed with girls." She laughed. "My poor father was bald before I was even born."

His smile was tight, his eyes creasing affectionately as if something she'd said pleased him. "You're a bonny lass, Maureen O'Leahey. I think I'm rather grateful your dad had nothing but girls."

Her breath caught as she stared at him, unsure if she'd imagined his words or if he'd actually said them. "How old are you, Frank?"

"Twenty-five."

And there it was. Lowering her gaze, she casually shifted her skirt back over her knee and folded her hands on her lap.

Though his was clearly American, his slang reminded her so much of her mother. Words like lass and bonny were familiar and soothing, having heard them since she was a child.

"Things have probably settled by now," he said, turning to face the wheel again.

Disappointment weighed heavy in her chest as the truck started and they silently drove back to town. It was foolish to think a man like Frank McCullough would take interest in a young girl like her. She'd be wise to not think of him in terms of attraction anymore.

When they reached the pub, Colleen grinned and met them at the truck. "I was wondering where you two got off to."

"I didn't want your little sister getting hassled by the police."

Maureen grimaced at the use of the word "little". "Where's Rosemarie?"

"Inside. Cleaning up."

"What the bloody hell is she cleaning up for? Did the constable tell her she had to?"

Colleen grinned. "Now, what kind of woman would she be to not help Liam straighten up their new bar?"

"What? Caleb actually gave it to him?"

"What choice did he have? The man was indebted to Liam for nearly fifteen grand."

"But the bar has to be worth far more than that," she argued and Colleen shrugged, clearly tapped out of her knowledge on the subject.

"There's likely a mortgage to be paid. I'm sure Caleb's debts are to more than just Liam Cloony."

Unbelievable.

"It's closed now if you want to go in," Colleen said. "I'm waitin' on Paulie. Tell him to move his arse, will ya?"

She and Frank entered the bar, but he no longer held her hand or pressed his palm to the small of her back. He held the door for her, which she now found irritating and misleading. Their shoes crunched over broken glass.

"Watch your step, love." His words provoked a sigh, but she stifled the moon-eyed response she also sensed coming. This one was too charming for his own good and she was a damn fool to think it had anything to do with her.

The place was in shambles. "I'm not sure it's worth a cent now," she mumbled.

"They'll have it clean in no time," Frank answered.

Paulie stood in the center of the rubble. "Did you see the way I took out that one bastard with the arms the size of tree trunks and the big barrel chest? Ah, he was no match for me—"

"Paulie," Frank called. "Your woman's in the back growing impatient with waitin' on your arse."

That fast, Paulie's regaling tales of the brawl ceased and he was out the door like a well-trained pup. She shook her head at the control Colleen had over that poor man.

Rosemarie yelled from the back. "We'll be replacin' those pool tables too. And this bar will be needin' a fresh coat of lacquer. Are you listening, Liam? I won't be moving in until this pub is right and proper, you remember that. Oh, there you are, Maureen," she smiled. "Grab a broom in the back and start sweepin'. We've got lot's to do and the mortgage is due by the fifteenth. No time to spare and every minute those doors are closed we're losing money."

She stared, dumbfounded. Frank returned with two brooms and handed her one. She swept, in awe of what they were doing and what it signified. It was a lot to process.

"Are you really going to move in with Liam, Rosemarie?" she asked quietly as she swept alongside her sister.

She grinned. "I'm ready. I want to have babies, Maureen. Could you imagine, us having our own sweet babies someday?"

"But you're not married." Their father would never allow it.

Rosemarie's smile was the sort that spoke of many secrets and warm affections shared between her and the man that held her heart. "Liam asked Father for his permission last month and he said we'd have his blessing if Liam could provide a home for us and find a way to make a decent living."

She wasn't sure about the bar being decent, as it was won in a poker match, nor was she clear on how this amounted to a home. "Will you live with his family?"

"No, silly. We'll live here. There's an apartment upstairs. It's nothing special, but we can stay there and save for a house. Down the line, maybe you or Colleen could live there if you need to. Since we own the deed there's no rent."

Part of her was jealous and thrilled for the sudden turn her sister's life was taking, but a greater part felt left behind. It was only a matter of time before Colleen moved out of the house as well. She wanted to be happy for her sisters, but it was tricky embracing such emotions when she was terrified for herself. Her parents were not the greatest company to those that didn't get a kick out of the nightly news *Gunsmoke.*

By the time the damage was cleaned up it was dark. There was much to still be repaired, but for the most part the bar seemed a heap nicer than when she'd first seen it. Frank had disappeared sometime while she was cleaning and it hurt that he hadn't said goodbye. Her disappointment was again inappropriate, for obvious reasons.

It was getting late and Rosemarie seemed reluctant to leave when Liam was so devotedly inspecting his new enterprise. Begging for the keys, Maureen took the Falcon home alone, something she imagined doing a lot in the future.

When she got home the house was dark, her parents each sleeping on their chairs in the den. She quietly locked the door and went to her room at the corner of the first floor. Three twin beds. What would she do with all that empty space when the time came?

She didn't want to think about it, but her mind wouldn't let her focus on much else.

She considered the friends she'd be graduating with in two weeks and measured their appeal in matters of amusement, suitability as a spouse, and even potential company for summer gallivanting. Did teenagers gallivant after they graduated or did summer become just another season?

Several of her classmates were scheduled for June weddings. While they'd been planning prom, others had been picking bridesmaids and bouquets. The future was indeed daunting. The only skill beyond homemaking that Maureen possessed was an ability to type forty words per minute. She'd likely spend the next year wasting away in some dingy office with a sad excuse for a window.

Before she fell asleep, she thought about the bluest sky her memory could conjure, comparing it in all its many facets and tones to the depths of Frank McCullough's eyes. Though the sky could blush vibrant shades of pink and darken deeper than sapphires, she decided his eyes were the victors when it came to exquisiteness, and she wondered when she'd be able to see them again.